CHAINS OF THE SKY

J.Y. FOREST

PROLOGUE

A sizable flock of birds soared through the sky as they focused on finding shelter, eager to end their long migration. Keen as they were, however, not one failed to notice the enormous gathering of clouds swallowing the horizon before them. Such a thing would have been impossible to miss; the contrast between their clear surroundings and the approaching white sea was as pronounced as night and day.

Nervous squawks echoed through the flock as the upcoming obstacle drew near. They hadn't survived as long as they had by remaining ignorant of the sky's dangers. Low visibility, high humidity, frigid temperatures—the clouds ahead threatened all that and more. No creature with a working sense of self-preservation would seek to fly under such conditions.

The sky, however, clearly cared very little for what they wanted. If anything, the mass of clouds picked up speed as it drew closer, advancing like a predator that had spotted its prey.

They needed to make a choice. Turning back and flying around the clouds would certainly be the safest decision, but that would mean taking a significant detour, one that the desperate animals could ill afford. Food and rest had been scarce for them lately. They needed to find shelter as soon as possible.

So they pressed onward.

As expected, a frigid humidity assaulted their senses as they plunged into the barrier of clouds. What they did not predict, however, was that the surrounding climate would clear and grow milder as they flew deeper inside.

Confusion spread among the flock. Such cloudy skies often blinded those who flew through them while disorienting all sense of direction with their chaotic wind patterns. Anything that entered such a climate often fell prey to its turbulent, merciless whims. The jarring difference between expectations and reality informed those bracing themselves that the ocean of clouds was mostly hollow inside.

Surprised but not unhappy with the discovery, the curious birds examined their new surroundings. The task was, again, easier than expected, as the gaps within the clouds were in just the right places to allow outside light sources to properly illuminate the interior. At first glance, their whereabouts seemed no different from the sky outside. After a while, however, it became clear to the flock that the oxygen was growing thicker the farther they flew.

Then they saw them—countless landmasses floating in the sky, each one bound to the next by metallic chains holding them in place. From a distance, the sight resembled a giant cage, as a staggering number of chains were all entwined around the islands like a massive spiderweb.

Instinct drove the birds to continue. Had they been human, they might have realized that the view couldn't have formed naturally and that those responsible for its existence might not take too kindly to intruders such as themselves. But all the desperate flock could consider was their need to roost.

As the birds flew close enough to survey the islands, they saw that their surfaces resembled the earth below. The forests, rivers, and most importantly, other living creatures indicated life was sustainable there. Focused on their original goals of food and shelter, the flock flew onto the closest suitable habitat they could find: an island covered in greenery and dirt placed at the edge of the interwoven threads of chains.

They landed in a meadow, attracted by the buzz of flying insects. The fresh air, beautiful trees, and calming shades of yellow and light green felt gentle and welcoming to the weary flock. Upon finding a pool of water surrounded by trees in the center of the meadow, they happily jumped in and made themselves comfortable. Soon, their cries echoed across the pond, the peculiarity of their current location soon forgotten amid the meadow's natural ambience.

A peaceful mood settled around the area, lulling the flock, weary from continuous flight, to sleep. Had they been more attentive, they might have noticed the careful, predatory footsteps closing in on the pond. But the animals, both exhausted from their travels and relieved at their success in finding shelter, could not bring themselves to care about such things.

That was, until a few found their heads flying off their necks without warning.

Startled by the sudden death of their companions, the rest of the flock shrieked at their unseen attacker, trying to intimidate them out of their new territory. A pack of humans, looking not at all frightened, emerged from the trees in response, dashing toward them at speeds far beyond what should be possible for their kind.

The birds, not expecting more than one assailant, flew off in a panic, quickly escaping their attackers' reach. Or at least, they thought they had. Despite a lack of physical contact between them and the humans, several members of the flock dropped dead mid-flight, their bodies torn to pieces like their brethren at the lake. The rest of the flock flew higher, hoping to gain some distance, only for a couple of their pursuers to jump hundreds of feet to pluck them from the air.

The survivors fled the island, believing the humans incapable of giving chase once they no longer had ground to traverse. Much to the flock's surprise, the humans leapt after them. Instead of plummeting to a certain gruesome demise, however, they landed on some nearby clouds and proceeded as if they were on solid terrain. Jumping from one cloud to another, the humans continued their pursuit of the tired animals, steadily closing the distance.

The fleeing flock was in complete disarray. The floating islands, the unseen methods of killing, humans that could run on clouds—it all defied what they understood to be common sense. Even the sky appeared to have turned against them, as the clouds surrounding the birds rearranged themselves to give the pursuing humans a path to tread no matter where they went, while gusts of wind blew the creatures back toward their pursuers.

The birds that kept their wits about them dove straight down, desperate to exit the perilous airspace. That, too, proved to be in vain, as the clouds they had so easily entered now physically repelled them, preventing them from leaving.

In the end, the flock was at the mercy of what lay within the mass of clouds, though not in the way they had first imagined. Not once did it cross their minds that the realm's inhabitants had lured them in, as desperate as the creatures themselves for ways to sustain their kind.

CHAPTER 1: ATRAVEL

It has been twelve days since my wife's passing. Much to my regret, I find that the only person remaining who I feel any genuine sense of connection with is my son, my only child. As I look at him now, he reminds me considerably of my younger self. I am proud of him, so very proud. I just pray he does not beat his father to the grave as his mother did.

As I reflect on how fleeting life is, I feel the need to write my thoughts to both aid future generations and leave a record of my existence. May those reading this find wisdom in what I transcribe here.

Azel swore silently as he knelt with the other youths before the pond. Their leader, a woman with a lithe build and braided hair, stared down at them with an inscrutable expression.

The other hunters, seeming indifferent to their plight, dutifully gathered the carcasses of the creatures they had just slain. One, taking an interest in the dark patterns marking the backs of their quarries' severed heads, asked his colleagues whether they knew of any similar species.

Azel wished he could switch places with them. Why had things turned out this way? How had everyone else screwed up so badly?

"Talk," their leader commanded. "What happened here?"

A moment of silence passed as the kneeling youths nudged one another, trying to get someone to speak. Azel, at the rear of the roughly thirty-person group, went unnoticed by his peers. He ducked his head and crawled, praying that the others would conceal his presence as he tried to get away.

Their leader, unfortunately, did not fail to notice him. "You there, answer me. What happened here?"

Azel stiffened as everyone directed their attention toward him.

"I-It would appear as though a flock of birds made their way inside Atravel's borders, Head Huntress Islea," he stammered, addressing her by her title and surname in an awkward attempt to be as respectful as possible.

"I'm aware," the woman responded. "I'm asking why there was an attack on the flock before my signal. We were preparing to capture the birds alive before they could leave the pond. A pile of corpses and a chase across the edges of our nation were not part of my orders."

Azel, perplexed, looked up at the head huntress. While her words were objectively critical, no hint of judgment colored her voice. Rather, her tone was completely emotionless, no different from when she had given the orders to hunt down the flock.

The young hunter fell silent, his mind racing. The head huntress probably already knew what had happened, seeing as how she had singled out the culprits and gathered them in front of her. A flat denial over their actions would be refuted immediately by the no-nonsense woman in front of him.

Hoping to portray himself in a more innocent light, he answered with a melodramatic sigh. "We made a move before your command. Some of the rasher members in this group were competing to showcase their power and precision, you see, and dragged the rest of us into it. We ended up unleashing air slashes toward the birds' necks, scaring away the rest of the flock."

"I see. And who are these rasher members?" Head Huntress Islea asked, her eyes unblinking.

Azel clicked his tongue; he'd hoped she wouldn't call him out on that. He quickly searched the group for members that were generally disliked, praying everyone else would play along. "Him. And her. Also him."

The accused immediately started protesting, only for their voices to die down when their leader silenced them.

"Quiet." The woman approached Azel, her eyes unblinking as she stared at his face, as if committing it to memory. "Your name?"

"Az-Azel, ma'am," the young hunter stuttered, fear evident in his eyes.

"And what purpose do you serve within this group?"

"An unspecified one, ma'am," he admitted. "I'm as much of a nobody as you can get."

"Azel, you will carry the corpses and accompany me until we report what happened to the higher-ups," the woman ordered, pointing to the baskets of slain birds the older hunters had finished gathering. "The rest of you may join the others in cleaning up this mess."

She then turned and walked away from the group, leaving them muttering in confusion.

Azel was the most confused of the bunch. Was this supposed to be a punishment? She had spoken in such a calm, even voice, the same one might use to describe their day—no outburst of anger, no bitter tone of disappointment, nothing. It was impossible to tell what she was thinking.

Following the head huntress's commands, the rest of the hunters cleaned up the dead bodies and forced the animals they had captured alive into cages. Once they had finished, everyone gathered around the edges of the island and jumped off, only to be caught by floating clouds that carried them away.

***

Azel fidgeted on the rapidly ascending cloud where he sat. Some of the other hunters were taking a moment to relax and enjoy the view, looking down on the nation of islands its inhabitants referred to as Atravel. He, however, had no such luxury. Head Huntress Islea stood next to him, and he still had no idea whether he was in trouble or not, as she remained as stone-faced as ever.

Azel thought back to his memories of their leader, trying to recall how she had behaved toward those she had punished in the past to better understand his predicament, only to realize she had *never* shown any form of discernable emotion in the short time he had known her. In a way, the head huntress was far more intimidating than someone with a short temper. One would at least know what to expect from such a person.

Unspoken fears cycled through Azel's mind until the clouds eventually reached their destination, an island that dwarfed the others, located at the peak of the webbed chains. Known as Ivory Island, the landmass was covered with tall, imposing white towers, every single one far more grandiose than anything built on the islands below.

Led by Head Huntress Islea, the hunters headed to one of the towers and stood in front of a heavily adorned stone door. Azel, dressed in cheap clothes and still carrying the basket of dead birds, couldn't help but feel shabby in comparison.

A voice echoed from inside the building. "Enter."

The head huntress then turned around.

"The rest of you stay here. Except you, Azel. You will follow me inside."

Azel, uncertain of what was to come, could do nothing but obey, his eyes taking in the full view of the interior as he walked behind her.

Staircases covered the tower's walls, each of them leading into a section of the building reserved for unknown purposes. Between the staircases, a floating figure looked down at them. Both Azel and the head huntress immediately knelt and waited for the hovering being to acknowledge their presence. The person above was an emissary, said to be able to understand and act on the will of the Great Arbiter, the almighty creator of the skies and heavens. They were not to be spoken to unless one initiated conversation.

After a moment of silence, the figure descended and landed before them. He was a weary-looking old man adorned with fine clothes and a mane of graying hair. That, combined with his tall stature and hawklike gaze, gave him a very dignified aura despite his apparent frailty.

"I received your message," he said authoritatively. "Your report, Head Huntress Islea?"

The woman stood.

"We hunted down a flock of birds loitering around the Radiant Meadows, Emissary Striaen," she said, formally addressing the man by his title and family name, as was expected of her. Addressing a huntress such as her by her title was generally considered proper etiquette. Addressing an emissary in such a manner was an unspoken requirement for every single person living in Atravel. "They seem to have come from the world underneath. Judging from their plumage and their unusually high vitality and intelligence, I believe we are quickly approaching the site of our beginnings."

The old man nodded. "Very good. This confirms the reports the outer forewarners sent me."

"Regrettably, we failed to capture them all alive, as you can see." The head huntress gestured to the carcasses. Azel shifted uncomfortably behind her, trying to look as inconspicuous as possible while still holding the basket of dead animals.

The old man didn't even bother looking at him. "Pay no heed to the deceased. This is all clearly a gift from the Great Arbiter to bless the upcoming Grand Sabbath."

The woman remained silent, neither affirming nor denying his statement. Looking at her with a complex expression, Emissary Striaen walked toward the head huntress and spoke quietly. "I'm sure the Great Arbiter knows what's best and acts accordingly, Head Huntress Islea."

A strange pressure emitted from the woman's figure. Azel stared at her, taken aback. Her face was as indecipherable as ever, but it was the closest thing resembling emotion that he had ever felt from her.

What that emotion was, however, remained a mystery to him.

Emissary Striaen, in contrast, seemed uninterested in the change in her demeanor. "Now, if you would please take the flock to the appropriate island to be properly examined, we might be able to introduce a new species to sustain our people."

"And the remains?" Head Huntress Islea asked, her voice normal, as if nothing had happened.

"Dispose of them in whatever manner you'd like."

The head huntress stared at the old man in silent contemplation before continuing.

"Then consider them a gift from me." She then turned around. "Azel."

"Yes, ma'am?"

"You have a new job. As of now, you are under Emissary Striaen's employ. Your first task will be to prepare and distribute the meat you are holding as he desires."

"Excuse me?" Azel asked, bewildered by his abrupt appointment.

Emissary Striaen glanced at him before facing the head huntress again. "A... gift, is it? Have you already ascertained that these animals are clean and suitable for consumption?"

"I believe you have the connections necessary to confirm such things faster than I," Head Huntress Islea said. "Taking that into account, no one is more suitable to gift these to."

The old man sighed. "Then I suppose I'll accept your offer. Now then, I believe you were about to relocate these new animals?"

Recognizing her dismissal, the head huntress headed out of the building, leaving a stunned Azel behind.

"Well, you better get to it, then," Emissary Striaen said, snapping the young hunter out of his daze. "I want these animals properly skinned and preserved before the evening lights set in."

"Yes, of course," Azel replied, still not understanding what had just happened.

***

Emissary Striaen escorted Azel to a staircase leading to a kitchen within the tower. Time passed as the young hunter struggled with the process of skinning, butchering, and vacuum sealing the dead creatures. The old man remained silent throughout it all, presumably preoccupied with his thoughts.

It wasn't until Azel had finished his work and was on his way to the exit that the emissary bothered to address him. "Why did the head huntress choose you for this task? I can tell you don't have experience preparing meat."

Azel responded truthfully. "No clue, sir."

The old man looked at him skeptically. "You don't know? She picked you out specifically from everyone else. Are you truly nothing more than her subordinate?"

Azel couldn't answer. What was he supposed to say?

Emissary Striaen narrowed his eyes and walked closer. "*I suggest you make this easier for yourself and tell me everything you know.*"

Feeling a strong compulsion to obey, Azel retold the events of the day to the authoritative figure before him, going into detail about how the head huntress had singled him out after the incident with the flock.

Emissary Striaen paced the room, paying little heed to Azel's presence as he murmured to himself. "Hmm, curious. It's almost as if—"

The old man's words came to a halt as he abruptly stopped walking and stared at the building's entrance.

Azel glanced at the pristine white door. There was nothing unusual about it, save for how pointlessly ornate it was. He turned back to the emissary.

"Is something wrong, sir?" he asked.

As soon as those words left his lips, the doors to the building burst open to let in an unruly crowd of people.

Emissary Striaen quickly flew out of the way to avoid being run over. Azel was not so fortunate; the furious mob roughly shoved him aside, pressing him against a wall.

The emissary looked scandalized.

No surprise there, Azel thought as he struggled against the crowd. Barging into a building made for an emissary in such a way could be considered a criminal offense.

Despite how single-mindedly the crowd had entered the building, the people it comprised couldn't have been less united in their goals. They were all in fierce arguments with one another; some even looked like they were ready to exchange blows.

Azel's attention was drawn to an argument at the center of the crowd that seemed to be the source of the chaos.

"Why are you bringing this up now? Do you know how long it has been since then?" a tall and imposing man shouted.

"And there it is. You're dodging the subject again. If you had just done a better job, there wouldn't be anything to complain about, now would there?" the woman next to him retorted. Despite her relatively modest stature, she had just as much presence as the man towering over her, if not more.

The man looked offended. "Are you implying I did my job poorly? Your son was inherently unworthy. Those who suffer do so because of their wrongdoing before the Great Arbiter. You can't blame *me* for that. Children take after their parents, after all. I say we should have you tested again to make sure there wasn't a mistake!"

A stunned silence filled the air. The man had clearly crossed a line.

"And there you have it!" The woman gestured melodramatically at the man. "Look! Look at how he insults us. Look at how he shames those he's wronged to keep them silent. Is this man truly fit to look over other people when he can't even watch over his tongue?"

Many in the crowd cheered in approval. Azel found himself captivated by the woman's words. She had delivered them with such intensity that he couldn't help but pay attention to her.

Another woman from the crowd stepped in, trying to mediate between the two. "Soleil," she said, facing the unusually compelling woman. "Please calm down. I understand how you feel, but Head Caretaker Desen has a right to defend himself against your accusations." She then faced the angry man. "Head Caretaker Desen, I don't think what you said just now was wise. The Great Arbiter does not make mistakes. You can't go around questioning his decisions."

"Exactly!" the man spat in contempt. "The Great Arbiter decides. It is unreasonable to blame me for any of this!"

Azel raised his eyebrows. That man was a head caretaker?

The caretakers were those stationed at the Nesting Islands, a group of islands placed at the very bottom of Atravel. These islands housed fledglings, the children of Atravel, until they were old enough to find their roles in society.

It was the caretakers' duty to ensure the fledglings under their care were raised properly. The head caretakers were given the responsibility of managing the caretakers under them so that the Nesting Islands worked as intended.

Azel, who had left the Nesting Islands not too long ago, couldn't help but think the short-tempered man in front of him seemed wholly unsuited to look after children, much less lead others in doing so.

A booming voice from above interrupted his line of thought.

"Enough!"

Azel looked up toward Emissary Striaen, who had done something to his voice to make it echo throughout the entire building. He then sent a downward spiral of wind that forced the entire crowd to their knees. Any resistance they might have given was quickly snuffed out when he started pulling the air out of their lungs, forcing them to focus on holding their breath. "This is absolutely unacceptable! I demand to know the ones responsible!"

Releasing his hold on them, Emissary Striaen flew to the center of the crowd. "I hope you have an adequate explanation for this disturbance, you two. As for the rest of you, *calm down.*"

The crowd quickly settled at the emissary's terrifying display of power. They seemed to have just realized exactly where they were and had grown timid at the thought of retribution.

Azel took the chance to disentangle himself from the crowd. He made his way to a nearby corner, listening in to the conversation taking place.

Looking unnerved at the old man's deadly glare, the head caretaker spoke frantically. "Orator Mistral here is blaming me for her son's failure in the last Ascension Ceremony. She believes the caretakers under my command did a poor job in preparing her son for it and is calling the entire Nesting Islands system flawed."

Emissary Striaen gave out a weary sigh. Azel imagined that it was not the old man's first time mediating an argument on the subject. The Ascension Ceremony, a ritual all fledglings had to go through to be considered full-fledged citizens of Atravel, was subject to many a heated debate throughout the islands.

The emissary turned to face the accused. "Orator Mistral, when you hold Atravel's traditions in contempt, you insult those who uphold them, including the emissaries. Do not think I take this insult lightly."

The woman gave Head Caretaker Desen a spiteful glare as the brunt of Emissary Striaen's hostility shifted to her. She recovered quickly, however, as her next words were as eloquent as the ones that came before. "I apologize if I overstepped my bounds in any way, sir. That was not my intention. Would you allow me to explain myself?"

"Speak."

"Thank you. As you are all undoubtedly aware, the Ascension Ceremony is the most important part of a fledgling's life. A caretaker should be doing everything in their power to prepare them for it. Despite this, I have reason to believe that this man has been shirking his duties and simply abuses his position to gain favor with those in power."

"Baseless accusations," the head caretaker growled.

"Do you have any way to substantiate these claims?" the emissary asked.

"The upcoming Advent Trials should be an excellent opportunity," the woman answered. "I want us to observe the fledglings during this time and judge the caretakers based on how they perform. If those under tutelage fail to meet expectations, I'd like for us to question how the Nesting Islands are run and make changes if necessary."

"There's no—" Head Caretaker Desen started before the emissary motioned for him to stop.

"What would you be looking for, exactly?" the old man questioned. "What standards would the fledglings have to meet to satisfy you?"

"It is the caretakers' duty to raise the fledglings into functioning members of Atravel. So we would check to see that every single one of them was, at the very least, given a fair chance to learn our society's principles. From there, we can observe how their natural talents were nurtured and developed. For that purpose, I would like you to attend, Emissary Striaen. Talent expresses itself in many ways, after all. And who better to judge that than an emissary himself? After all, no one understands the nature of the sky better than the emissaries, right?"

The head caretaker scoffed, along with many others in the crowd. The expected response. Telling an emissary to go out of their way and descend to the Nesting Islands to settle a personal dispute was simply ridiculous.

"Why do you all mock the idea?" Orator Mistral questioned as she turned to face the crowd. "The emissaries embody the will of the Great Arbiter. I find it hard to believe that the Great Arbiter, our provider, would overlook our struggles, regardless of who we are. As those who carry out the will of the Great Arbiter, the emissaries should do all they can for the benefit of Atravel!"

Azel, despite his skepticism, found himself nodding along. Something in the way she delivered her points made him want to listen to her.

Emissary Striaen, however, seemed displeased with her last statement. "You presume much. Do not insinuate the emissaries are free to do whatever they wish. They have much to be concerned with."

Orator Mistral looked unfazed. "Oh, of course. I beg your forgiveness. I didn't mean to imply otherwise. But surely, at least one of the emissaries can attend, considering how important this is?"

She then continued in a pained voice. "I do not wish to question the emissaries' judgment, but when I see the problems we all face, I cannot help but wonder what we could be doing differently."

The raw emotion the woman put into her words moved Azel, who would normally roll his eyes at such melodrama. He had enough experience in persuading other people to understand that the person before him was a natural. The way she had so easily whipped the surrounding crowd into a frenzy was a testament to her charisma. But the emissary seemed to either not notice or not care, as he looked as apathetic as when she first started.

He sighed. "Oh, very well. I will attend. There is something I wish to observe down there myself. Will this be enough to satisfy you?"

Orator Mistral looked surprised. "Wait, you'll go? I mean, yes. That will be more than enough."

"If that is everything, then you are all dismissed," Emissary Striaen said. "And I mean *all of you*," he emphasized, addressing everyone who had rushed into the building.

Relieved that the emissary did not seek to punish them further, the crowd hurried to leave. Head Caretaker Desen looked disgruntled, while Orator Mistral looked like she had more to say, but abiding by the emissary's orders, they both left with everyone else.

Azel, left alone with the old man, was at a loss for words for the second time that day. A crowd barging into an emissary's home? An evaluation of the caretakers of the Nesting Islands? When was the last time such a thing had happened?

Strangely enough, Emissary Striaen did not look worried at all over what he had just agreed to.

Well, why would he be? Azel realized as he thought about it some more. He was an emissary, after all. His existence was the highest form of authority in Atravel, supposedly blessed by the Great Arbiter himself. No earthly force could affect him.

Chapter 2: The Nesting Islands

The story of the Great War and Atravel's creation is present in the earliest written records we possess. While the tale itself is intriguing, it is crucial to recognize the true reason for its existence, why we continue to recite it throughout the generations. For the sake of our nation's survival, it must never be forgotten.

Aer groaned. It was way too early in the morning for this.

In front of him was the same sight he saw every day, a forest with white trees and towering stone pillars scattered throughout the area. The forest was one of the most prevalent landmarks of the Nesting Island he had lived on his whole life.

The people he passed on his way from the woods all looked in his direction with a mixture of amusement and annoyance. Many of them pointed fingers and whispered among themselves.

Not hard to guess why. Aer looked to his right.

Next to him, an adolescent boy gasped for air as he sprinted forward with all his might. His scrawny frame, ill-fitting clothes, unkempt black hair, and intensely focused gray eyes gave a haunting impression to those who saw him.

Aer couldn't help but wince at how worn down he looked. It bothered Aer that the person next to him could appear so haggard, as his face was identical to Aer's own.

I don't look like that right now, right? Aer self-consciously wondered before addressing his twin brother.

"Relax, Alius. There's no need to rush. I'm sure *nobody* will care if we're late," Aer said as he effortlessly matched his brother's pace by propelling himself forward with gusts of wind.

"That's. Not. The. Point. Aer," Alius panted between gasps. He then stopped running for a moment to catch his breath. "The caretakers made a big deal about today's message and told us that every fledgling should attend. Something important is happening, and I'm not going to miss it. We're behind enough as it is."

Before Aer could respond, Alius broke into another sprint, moving even faster than before. Aer sighed, putting a bit more power into his propulsion to keep up with his twin. It was bad enough Alius had woken him up for this. Why did he have to draw so much attention to them too?

***

It took some time for them to reach their destination, a stone pillar hundreds of feet tall. Engraved on top of the doorway placed at the pillar's base were the words Public Lecture Hall.

Aer dusted himself off as Alius gasped for air in front of him.

"You all right?" Aer asked dryly. "You look like you could use a break. Want to head back home and take a nap?"

Alius glared at him before entering the building. Aer bit back a grin and followed him inside.

A podium surrounded by tiered balconies housing over a thousand seats on each level came into view. The first floor was almost completely occupied by other fledglings and their supervising caretakers. Many of them glared at the twins as they entered, looking disdainfully at their dirty, ill-fitting clothes.

Aer shrank under their gazes as he closed the door.

I know, I know. He averted his eyes. *You don't want us around.*

Aer tried to find his way to the upper levels of the building, far away from everyone else's line of sight, but Alius dragged him straight toward the center of the first floor.

Ignoring the voices that came their way, the brothers gazed up at the podium. There, a woman who looked only slightly older than them stood, anxiously waiting for everyone's attention.

"G-Good morning, everyone," she started with a stutter. "My name is Ciel. I'm here as an instructor today. Is everybody settled d-down?" Her eyes flitted around the audience, searching for positive reactions. When none came her way, she timidly continued. "Th-That's good. The head caretaker asked me this morning to talk to you about Atravel's formation and the traditions that it fostered. Many of you may already know of the tale, but considering the upcoming celebrations, it might be helpful to remind everyone of its significance."

"She doesn't seem very used to this, huh?" Aer whispered to Alius.

His brother didn't answer. Alius's focus was entirely on the center platform.

The speaker, Ciel, took a deep breath to compose herself.

"Th-Then, I'll begin. Long ago, we lived not in the skies but on the earth's surface. These were not peaceful times. Battles engulfed the land with no end in sight. Pride, resources, loved ones, ideology—any and every reason was given to justify destroying one another."

Aer sensed a subtle shift in the air at those words. He couldn't explain why, but he soon found himself unable to look away from the podium.

"And so the scope of the battles grew," Ciel continued. "Eventually, a war vast enough to encompass all civilizations throughout the nations came to be. So pervasive was this war, in fact, that there existed not a single being uninvolved in the conflict. None could claim innocence."

The audience stirred as the person in front of them transformed. She now spoke with passion, her previous anxiousness forgotten. Aer wasn't sure if she was still even conscious of the gazes directed her way.

"The outcome was catastrophic, with humanity itself on the verge of being wiped out entirely," Ciel said, utterly engrossed in her tale. "Yet the war did not end. Even at their lowest point, humankind found themselves unable to let go of their reasons for fighting. The violence that had continued for so long had become ingrained into their very beings. Chaos reigned as civilizations collapsed and people became indistinguishable from feral beasts."

A hush swept over the crowd as they were taken to the times described. If any voices remained, Aer didn't notice. He was too absorbed by the scenes that Ciel was detailing in his head.

"That is when the Great Arbiter, the champion of the heavens, the ruler of the celestial realm, intervened. Disgusted by man's folly while also sympathetic toward the countless cries of pain, he gathered the few who no longer desired to take part in the bloodshed and moved the land underneath them to the skies, leaving the others to destroy themselves. He then gave his chosen ones two gifts so they could properly take care of themselves within this new environment. One was the ability to command the skies, allowing them to shape the atmosphere surrounding them to suit their needs. The other was landmasses containing different environments and animals, allowing them to produce what they needed to sustain themselves. And so our great nation, Atravel, was born. Now we traverse through the beautiful skies to show appreciation to the Great Arbiter for his miraculous deliverance. In a process we call the Sky Cycle, we use our power over the heavens to carry Atravel across all landscapes, displaying the great strength of his blessing. At the end of our pilgrimage, we return to the original site of our salvation. There, we hold the ceremony known as the Grand Sabbath, a three-day period where we take the time to rest and celebrate our good fortune, after which we begin the Sky Cycle anew."

After a moment, Ciel released a sigh of relief. Several of the caretakers in the audience clapped. She bowed nervously, looking considerably more aware of her surroundings than she had just a few moments ago.

Aer sank back into his seat. It wasn't the first time he had heard the tale; it was an often-repeated account of Atravel's origins. The way this woman told it had an unusual impact, however. He, like the rest of the audience, had been in a trance throughout the whole thing.

"N-Now then, the reason I told you this story is because, during the upcoming Grand Sabbath, every fledgling on this Nesting Island will go through something known as the Ascension Ceremony," Ciel stammered, much more withdrawn now that she was no longer immersed in her story.

Someone from the audience asked the obvious question. "What's it about?"

Ciel looked unsure of how to respond. "It will be a ritual where the skies attest to the Great Arbiter's continued favor over our people. Beyond that, I'm not allowed to say. It will happen soon, though, which is why the caretakers felt the need for me to give you all forewarning— so you can prepare yourselves for what's coming."

Another voice rose from the audience as someone pointed out the obvious contradiction. "But you're not telling us any details about it, so what's the point? We can't prepare in any way."

"I-It's not my place to tell you that. You'll understand why when you're older," she replied, trying her best to avoid eye contact.

Aer and Alius exchanged confused looks. Why the secrecy?

The other fledglings seemed to be thinking the same thing, as they continued bombarding the flustered woman with questions, trying to glean whatever information they could.

"Have you gone through it?"

"Y-Yes, I have. All adults have."

"What was it like?"

"As I said, I can't say anything!"

"Is there a reason you can't tell us?"

"I-It's better that you don't know until then. It'll make it easier for the caretakers to—"

An authoritative voice echoed throughout the room. "That's enough."

Everyone looked around to see who had spoken. Without anyone noticing, Head Caretaker Desen, the Nesting Island's overseer, had entered the scene.

Confused, Aer inspected the building. Where had the man come from? He hadn't been there when the brothers had first entered the room, and the only entrance Aer could see was the stone doorway at the front of the building. Opening it should have alerted everyone inside.

Aer frowned. If the building had a more subtle way to enter, he would have appreciated knowing about it before he and his brother burst in and drew everyone's ire.

The crowd fell silent. The head caretaker held authority over the other caretakers on their Nesting Island. It was unusual for him to attend a lecture like this in person instead of ordering someone to send a message for him. Everyone watched attentively as he made his way toward the center stage and raised his voice to address everyone in the room.

"Good morning, everyone. We have called you up here to go over some very important upcoming events. Now, all of you have lived on this Nesting Island for as long as you can remember. I am here to tell you that will soon no longer be the case."

A lot of excited murmuring passed through the young audience. Head Caretaker Desen cleared his throat as a signal to quiet down before he glared at Ciel.

"I would like to remind those who have experienced the Ascension Ceremony that they are *prohibited* from passing around detailed information," he said forcefully as she shrank under his gaze. "Now then, as you have all just heard, the next Grand Sabbath is quickly approaching. During that time, every fledgling residing on this Nesting Island will be required to go through the Ascension Ceremony. Once this process is over, you will be released from the Nesting Islands and be free to move about as you please."

"Until then, we will carry out a process known as the Advent Trials to determine your potential roles in our society. During this time, people from all over Atravel will come down to the Nesting Islands and inform you of what they do for a living. Fledglings interested in the occupations discussed have the option to go through the different trials designed to test for traits suited for each line of work. If the visitors are sufficiently impressed, they may choose to recruit promising fledglings afterward."

"Normally, I would tell you all to participate in the Advent Trials at your leisure. While the Ascension Ceremony has always been mandatory for every fledgling, the Advent Trials have always been a voluntary way for talented and willing fledglings to show off what they can do."

The head caretaker then paused and frowned.

"Due to certain recent events, however, all fledglings must now take part in the Advent Trials as well." He scanned the room. "Unfortunately, I can see that not all fledglings are currently present. We'll have to fix that. Show up at the Eastern Borders ten days from now. Tell everyone you know about this, especially those who did not attend today. The caretakers *will* make sure that every fledgling on this island attends, so I prefer you save us the trouble of searching for you all."

The fledglings' surprise was plain to see. A gathering of every fledgling on the Nesting Island would be a difficult task to oversee. Why were they going through such an effort?

Preemptively shushing the crowd, the head caretaker voiced the question on every fledgling's mind. "Now then, you may ask why we would go to such lengths to make you all attend." A trace of bitterness crept into his voice. "Recently, there has been some debate about the caretakers' competence. As a result, authorities from above have deemed it necessary for you fledglings to be properly tested to judge how well we have raised you. Any other questions?"

Aer said nothing, like the rest of the audience. The head caretaker was clearly unhappy about what he had just mentioned. Trying to avoid the attention of an angry authority figure was only natural.

Natural for everyone except his brother, of course.

"How exactly are we being tested and evaluated?" Alius asked without a shred of hesitation.

"Those visiting the island will hold examinations requiring you to complete certain tasks," Head Caretaker Desen answered. "What those tasks are may vary. Some might test an individual's theoretical knowledge, while others may require group participation in overcoming practical challenges. Based on how well you perform, you could secure a future career path right away."

"What happens if we don't impress them?"

"Then you'll have to find some other way to make a living."

"And how would we do that?"

"That's not for me to decide." The head caretaker shook his head. "Once this is all over, you will assume full responsibility for yourselves and leave this island. Maybe you could ask a friend or family member to introduce you to their field of work."

The brothers shared a frown. They didn't know *anyone* outside the island, much less someone who would be willing to vouch for them.

"So the people who have no one to turn to," Alius continued. "How do they feed themselves? Where do they live? Or is that none of your business?"

Aer turned to his brother, alarmed. Alius was clearly insinuating something with that statement.

Fortunately, the head caretaker didn't seem to have noticed. "Assuming you properly apply what you've learned from the caretakers, you should be fine."

"What if the caretakers *haven't* taught us anything?" Alius's voice grew increasingly accusatory.

Head Caretaker Desen shrugged dismissively. "If you haven't learned anything despite all the opportunities we provide, the higher authorities should be reevaluating your competence, not ours."

Those listening to the conversation snickered. Aer tried to shrink from their view as much as possible. He just wanted to go home.

Alius, of course, looked completely unfazed. "Are the Advent Trials just part of the Ascension Ceremony? Or are they two different things?"

The head caretaker paused, as if pondering how to answer the questions without giving too much information. "The latter. As I have stated, the Advent Trials are a way for us to determine what jobs you fledglings are suited for once you leave the Nesting Islands. The Ascension Ceremony, on the other hand, is more of a coming-of-age ritual. Atravel at large considers you an adult once you reach your sixth Grand Sabbath. Every fledgling on this Nesting Island has gone through five, so the upcoming Ascension Ceremony will be a farewell of sorts."

"Then why is there so much secrecy around it?" Alius asked, voicing the question the rest of the crowd had dared not put into words. "Are you hiding something from us? If so, why?"

"I thought I said that passing around detailed information about the Ascension Ceremony was prohibited," the head caretaker muttered, a dangerous edge to his voice.

He wasn't the only one who didn't like Alius's questions. The gazes of the caretakers surrounding the brothers had turned cold and disapproving.

Alius looked like he still had more to say, but Aer was fed up with the attention they were gathering. He quickly altered the air in front of Alius before he could ask another question, willing it to block out all sounds coming from his brother.

Alius opened his mouth to speak, only to be met with dead silence. He cocked his head in confusion and looked around. The bewildered expression on his face quickly morphed into comprehension as he met Aer's eyes.

"*What gives?*" Alius mouthed, giving Aer an outraged glare.

Most of the people watching looked confused as to what was happening. Some of those who knew that air could be altered to dampen noise began laughing, thinking one of the adults must have shut Alius up before he could ask another question. The more observant people, who realized it was Aer silencing him, looked reluctantly impressed.

Acting as if nothing was amiss, the head caretaker clapped his hands to gather the crowd's attention.

"No more questions?" he asked, looking eager to end the assembly.

Nobody answered. They knew a rhetorical question when they heard one. The caretakers were projecting a menacing aura.

"Then this discussion is over," the Head Caretaker declared, shooing the fledglings out of the building.

The room quickly emptied, the echoes of hushed but excited whispers reverberating throughout the walls. Aer quietly exited the room, eager to escape the judgmental gazes of everyone around him.

"Well, that happened," he muttered as soon as he stepped outside. He yelped when Alius suddenly grabbed his collar and pulled him back.

"You didn't need to do that," Alius whispered.

"Learn to take a hint, Alius. Couldn't you tell that they weren't going to talk about it?" Aer replied, shaking off his brother's hand.

Alius wasn't convinced. "We were talking about some important things back there. I think we can afford a few questions!"

A voice that didn't belong to either twin interrupted them. "Or, you know, you could just make do with the information they gave out like everyone else. But of course, you two idiots had to make an embarrassing show of things."

Both Aer and Alius spun around. A tall boy with a disdainful expression looked down at them.

Aer groaned in exasperation. Gail was the last person he wanted to see that morning. The overbearing fledgling constantly harassed the brothers whenever they dared to show themselves.

Incidentally, he also happened to be Head Caretaker Desen's son.

Alius was the first to respond. "What do you want, Gail?"

"Nothing much. Just curious what the fuss was all about. Rather sad, really."

"What are you talking about?" Aer asked warily.

Gail shook his head in disapproval, smirking. "I'm saying it's pathetic that you got your brother to speak up so you could silence him in front of everyone. Were you proud of yourself when you showed off in front of all those caretakers?"

Alius looked incredulous. "What kind of delusional nonsense are you spouting? Does Aer look like he wants to stand out? Why would I even go along with something that stupid?"

"Oh, I don't know what goes on in the minds of the less capable. Though I imagine the fact that neither of you are good enough to be part of the Blessed must eat away at you and might cause you to act irrationally for the sake of attention."

Aer rolled his eyes. The Blessed was a select group of fledglings who had been chosen by the caretakers to be taught the finer details of Sky Control, the skill of shaping the atmosphere surrounding oneself. Those with natural talent at Sky Control were considered to be gifted by the Great Arbiter with a powerful command over the heavens, commonly referred to as Sky Authority. By giving said fledglings advanced lessons, the caretakers hoped to develop their abilities to their highest potential.

At least, that was how it went in theory. Fledglings were placed in the program based on recommendations from the caretakers watching over them. While those who were admitted were often talented, it was far easier to be noticed by a caretaker if one had the support of the right people, as the caretakers had a vested interest in catering to those higher in command.

Gail's father was the head caretaker of their island. As a result, the caretakers under his command often focused much of their attention on his son. Those who weren't linked to someone important, like Aer and Alius, were often overlooked for someone with more influence.

Trying to call out the unfairness inherent in the system, however, rarely went well for anybody. As the Blessed received tutelage that allowed them to outperform everyone else, the caretakers could simply claim they were innately superior and that naysayers were just bitter at their own lack of ability.

Alius scoffed. "What, that stupid meeting circle where you guys pat yourselves on the back for having the right connections? We don't need people making us out to be more than we are. I bet Aer's better than you anyway."

Gail's face flushed red. He blew an air current at Aer's and Alius's feet, knocking them off balance.

Alius quickly picked himself up, furious.

Aer looked around anxiously. A crowd was gathering, curious over the commotion the three of them were raising. He turned back toward Alius, whose face signaled to Aer that he was seconds away from charging at Gail.

Aer pulled at Alius's clothes before his brother could make a move they would both regret.

"Come on, Alius," Aer whispered. "Let's go."

"But—"

"It's not worth it."

Ignoring his brother's objections, Aer grabbed Alius and leapt, blowing wind through his oversized clothing to gain momentum, propelling them high up in the air and out of everyone else's sight.

Aer willed the wind to blow as hard as it could, trying to steer and parachute them safely to the ground. Easier said than done, as Alius was struggling in Aer's grip the entire time.

"Would you calm down?" Aer shouted to no avail as they swerved into a nearby pine tree. Upon impact, he felt sharp pricks all over his body. "Ow!"

Aer then quickly scrambled around, trying to move away from the pine needles poking his face, only to realize that he was no longer holding Alius. His brother had instead landed headfirst into the tree's trunk.

"Oops. Hey, Alius. You okay?"

But Alius wasn't listening.

"What a moron," Alius grumbled as he shook off chips of wood that had lodged themselves in his hair. "He even heard us arguing about what happened in there. So why would we suddenly be working together to make you look good? How does that make sense?"

Aer wearily agreed. "Yeah. I think Gail was just picking a fight."

"And I would have given him one! Why'd you stop me?"

Aer removed the pine needles that had gotten stuck in his clothes. "We were getting a lot of attention back there."

A pause.

"*And?*" Alius asked.

"What do you think would happen if you started a fight with the head caretaker's son? What if a caretaker showed up? Who do you think they would side with?"

"But Gail started it!"

"So? You think they'll care? You already got on their bad side when you asked all those questions earlier. You think they'll stick up for you against their boss's son? When said person happens to be in the building we just left?"

Alius fell into sullen silence. "That's just stupid. We're as much a part of this Nesting Island as anyone else. So why does he get to come up to us, start a fight, and make it out to be our fault?"

"I know, I know. Come on. Let's get out of here before anyone catches up. I don't want to get involved with them any more than I have to," Aer said as he untangled himself from the tree's branches and made his way down.

Alius grumpily followed his lead.

Going back down the path they came from, the twins walked in silence until they reached a fork in the road. The path on their left led to a stone cliff known as the Perch. Built on the side of the cliff were clusters of buildings reserved for fledglings that the caretakers approved of. At the very top of the cliff stood several well-kept buildings reserved for well-regarded caretakers. The buildings' higher elevations let the caretakers easily watch over the fledglings under their care.

The path on their right, on the other hand, led to the Spiral Forest, a woodland reserved for the fledglings who the caretakers didn't want to waste their time with.

Alius stopped walking and stared at the Perch. "You think there's any way for us to make a name for ourselves and change how we're treated?"

Aer quietly proceeded toward the right, choosing not to answer him. It wasn't the first time Alius had asked that question, and it probably wouldn't be the last.

Chapter 3: The Charity Tree

I must admit that while the Great Arbiter may be perfect, we humans certainly are not. It is quite easy to misconstrue what the Great Arbiter may be communicating to us, especially when we all have biases that shape how we interpret events. But unless the Great Arbiter himself decides to converse with us face-to-face, we must work with the knowledge we have.

Leaves softly crunched under the brothers' feet as they drew near a familiar clearing. The pale trees encompassing the path ahead signaled to them they were reentering the Spiral Forest, the sector of the island they called home.

The Spiral Forest was named for the shape of the trees growing in its lands. The trunk of every tree grew in an arc around the center of the woods, with each tree growing at a sharper angle upward the farther one went inside. At the very center was a countless number of trees, all twisted together in the form of one giant tree.

While this enormous coalition of trees, referred to as the Charity Tree, was an impressive sight, the structures built over it were decidedly less so. On the branches of the "tree" were wooden platforms that held small, worn-down treehouses that had likely been built long before Aer and Alius were born.

The Charity Tree was a great convenience for the caretakers. As the plants it comprised were all of different types, it offered a vast array of fruits, nuts, and seeds among its edible leaves. That, along with the sheer amount of housing space on its branches, meant the only thing the caretakers had to do to "take care" of the fledglings most of the time was to hand out basic commodities like cheap toiletries, small containers, and used clothing while bringing in some laborers to maintain and sanitize the structures when they saw the need. This allowed the caretakers to keep up appearances of being good supervisors, despite leaving most of the children to fend for themselves.

Of course, there were differing levels of involvement depending on how badly a fledgling needed outside help. Back when Aer and Alius were still infants, the caretakers stationed at the Charity Tree begrudgingly gave them the bare minimum attention required to keep them alive. Once the brothers reached the point where they could physically take care of themselves, however, the adults assigned to watch over them promptly exited their lives.

Nowadays, the only times Aer and Alius interacted with the caretakers was when they acted out, as was the tendency for many a fledgling once they grew more aware of how poorly they were treated compared to those who lived at the Perch.

Balancing themselves on one of the outer root trees growing at a low incline, the twins walked until they reached a ladder that led to a wooden platform stretching across some of the lower branches. They then crossed a wooden bridge built on the edge that connected to a higher platform, which itself was attached to other bridges leading to even higher platforms. They continued their ascent around the network of platforms and bridges encircling every level of the Charity Tree, passing the homes of the other fledglings along the way.

Aer relaxed as they walked by some fledglings dressed in worn clothing. Unlike everywhere else, he and Alius didn't get any judgmental glares. The fledglings here kept to themselves, minding their own business.

That suited him fine. He just wanted to go back home and forget the day's events.

Though one thing did nag at him. The fledglings they passed were much more jittery than usual.

What's going on with them? Aer wondered before Alius shook him out of his thoughts.

"Aer, slow down already," he wheezed. "We ran enough this morning."

"Really? I still have plenty of energy left, though," Aer nonchalantly replied, earning a glare from his brother.

"Must be nice, being able to propel yourself forward like that. I'd get a lot more done if I could move like you do."

"I could just push you along with me," Aer suggested, only for Alius to immediately reject the idea.

"*No.* Last time we tried that, I ended up tripping and landing right on my face because we couldn't match the timing of my movements with the strength of your gusts. Honestly, I thought my face would peel off."

"Then there's nothing for you to do but get better at Sky Control."

"If it were that easy, I would have done it already." Alius sighed. "It seems to come naturally to you, but I can't get it to work for me no matter how hard I try. You know, this trip would be a lot easier if we lived near—"

Aer cut him off before he could finish his sentence, knowing exactly where he was trying to lead the conversation. "We wouldn't have had to make this trip at all if you hadn't dragged us out to the announcement in the first place."

Alius constantly argued that they should be living near the bottom of the tree. That way, any trip away from their home and back would be as short and convenient as possible. Aer, in contrast, wanted to live near the top specifically because it was more difficult to get to. That way, fewer people would crowd their living space. It would also limit the number of people coming out to harass them, both in and out of the Spiral Forest.

Their current treehouse was a compromise neither of the two was satisfied with, placed halfway along the height of the Charity Tree.

"Give me a break already," Alius grumbled.

Aer shrugged. At times, he couldn't help but think that things would be so much simpler if the two had just lived separately. They would both be free to do whatever they wished with no arguments over what to do next; their contrasting preferences wouldn't matter if they didn't have to interact with each other.

But in the end, Aer wasn't willing to seriously discuss the idea. As annoying as he found Alius time and time again, he knew his situation would be far worse if his brother weren't there. The fledglings who lived there had to take care of themselves since they were young with little support from the rest of the world. As a result, they all tended to be wary of others, as the adults raising them didn't exactly inspire trust and confidence. The twins were no exception. As someone Aer had grown up with since birth, Alius was the only person Aer could talk to without having to second-guess his intentions.

When the two of them finally reached their platform of residence, they were met with a crowd of fledglings gathered in conversation.

Alius gave Aer a puzzled look before calling out to the group. "Hey! What are you guys doing here? Did something happen?"

The person physically closest to them, a girl in a wheelchair, turned to face them.

"Nira," Alius greeted. She was a neighbor to the brothers, living in a nearby treehouse placed on the same platform.

"Oh, it's the twins," she replied, acknowledging their presence. "You guys hear about how we might have to leave this place soon?"

Alius lit up. "The Ascension Ceremony, right? Aer and I were just talking about it."

"You guys went to the meeting?" she asked.

"Yeah! Couldn't ignore something that important."

"Okay, good. Someone from the Perch just dropped by to say that we were all supposed to be at the meeting and how we should have *run* toward the public lecture hall this morning." Nira then took a moment to deliberately glance back at her wheelchair. "He then said something about how it's our fault that we're not going to be prepared to leave the Nesting Island and left without explaining anything, the annoying twerp. We were hoping someone could fill us in."

Alius gave Aer a smug smile. "See, Aer? Aren't you glad we decided to go? It would be terrible for all of us if, for some silly reason, we'd slept in instead of attending."

Before Aer could deliver a scathing reply about how stupid Alius had looked running around that morning, the group crowded toward them, bombarding them with questions.

Aer groaned. He just wanted to be done with it all already.

Alius seemed to have no such thoughts, however, as he immediately stepped forward to answer what he could.

"Calm down, calm down. I'll tell you everything I heard," Alius responded. "But I don't have all the answers. The caretakers were quite secretive about the whole thing."

"Why?"

"I had the same question, but Aer stopped me before I could ask."

Aer rolled his eyes. Of course Alius was still holding that against him.

***

Alius spent the next portion of the day relaying what he heard from the meeting to a noisy audience, ignoring several annoyed caretakers who passed by just to tell them to quiet down.

Aer, who would rather just head home, tried to tell Alius to finish as quickly as possible. But he had a much softer and quieter voice than his brother, one that was easy to talk over, so the growing crowd simply drowned out his opinions. It was a testament to how big the news was that fledglings from all over the Charity Tree, many of whom the twins had never even spoken with, came to listen to Alius.

Eventually, however, the excitement died down.

"So, people from outside the Nesting Islands will be judging us in these Advent Trials, which test us to see how well we would do in certain jobs. Once that's over, we go through the Ascension Ceremony, and then we're made to leave?" Nira summarized once Alius had finished. "And this is all mandatory?"

"Yep!" Alius nodded. "Apparently, someone higher up thought the caretakers weren't doing their jobs properly. So we all have to show off what we can do in the Advent Trials."

Despite Alius's enthusiasm, most of the other fledglings seemed more anxious than thrilled by the news.

"Come on, guys. This is a great opportunity. If we do well, we can show up those stuck-up idiots at the Perch in front of everyone," he said, desperately trying to rile the others.

Is this about what happened this morning? Aer wondered. *It feels like he's trying to drive as many people as he can to prove Gail wrong. If a bunch of no-names from the Charity Tree outperform those from the Blessed, it would support Alius's point that the caretakers pick its members through connections over talent.*

"But we can't beat them," a member of the crowd said pessimistically. "The caretakers said we just have to show up to these trials, right? Then that's all we need to do. We're just going to embarrass ourselves in front of everyone else if we challenge the Perch and prove how much better they are than us."

Alius looked frustrated. "You don't know that. Even if they are better taught, we should still try our best. We'll be leaving this Nesting Island soon, right? We won't have a Charity Tree to rely on out there, so if we don't figure out something for ourselves before then, we'll be forced to take whatever jobs they pick for us or starve. And I don't think people like us will have a lot of great options. Wouldn't it be nice if we could impress those on the other islands while we have the chance? They might decide we're important, despite what everyone here says. This could be our only shot to be something other than some no-names who don't matter."

Aer sensed a bit of desperation in Alius's last statement.

No, there's more to this than just embarrassing Gail, he realized. *He might have been planning this ever since he heard of the Advent Trials. Still, it'll take more than this to convince the others.*

Aer examined the other fledglings. As he thought, most of them looked skeptical. Only a handful looked like they were even considering the idea.

Alius seemed to sense the same.

"Just think about it," he said, pushing his appeal. "What if we do well? We could leave this life behind. People wouldn't look down on us for existing. It's bad enough that the caretakers and Perch fledglings think we're worthless. We don't get taught anything we need to know, get passed up from being chosen for anything important, and have to live in cramped, dirty spaces—all because we weren't born with the right connections. Are you really okay with being treated that way by everyone in Atravel for the rest of your lives?"

He sighed in frustration when the other fledglings didn't respond. "Don't you guys have any ambition? What about you, Nira? You could make up with your parents if you—"

Aer moved to silence the air around his brother for the second time that day. He was quite sensitive to hostile emotions, having endured many an interaction with caretakers and Perch fledglings alike. Consequently, he had also learned how to flee and hide his presence from other people. They were valuable skills to have as a Charity Tree fledgling—which was why he could recognize Alius's mistake and hurried to cut his oblivious brother off.

But the damage was already done.

"And exactly why would I want to do that?" Nira snapped.

An uncomfortable silence settled among the fledglings. Parents, or family in general, were not a popular topic around those parts. If a fledgling lived on the Charity Tree, it usually meant their family didn't get the caretakers' permission to let them live on the Perch.

Some had family members who tried but failed to convince the caretakers to place them on the Perch. The caretakers were quite discriminating in terms of social status. They didn't want those who came from questionable backgrounds interacting with the more important children they were raising. Quite a few fledglings lived here because the caretakers deemed their relatives unacceptable in society.

But most fledglings who lived on the Charity Tree had been outright abandoned by their families. That was why people referred to it as the Charity Tree. The giant tree provided charity to those who had nowhere else to go.

Aer and Alius, like many other Charity Tree fledglings, had never even seen their parents. Whether that meant they had died, were struggling to take care of themselves, or didn't consider the twins worth their time, Aer didn't know.

As most fledglings here fell into the above two categories, there was little mystery over why family was seldom discussed on the Charity Tree.

Occasionally, however, a fledgling with perfectly respectable family members lived here anyway. Nira was unusual among the youths here in that she knew her parents and could talk with them whenever she wanted, as they were both caretakers on their Nesting Island. She just hated them too much to do so.

From what Aer knew, Nira used to be both a resident of the Perch and a member of the Blessed. He and Alius had occasionally seen her around during that time but had never actually talked to her. Back then, she'd avoided interacting with the Charity Tree fledglings, like everyone else at the Perch. It wasn't until recently that she had moved in, intending to live off the tree like them.

When the fledglings had first heard the news, they were all confused. *Why would anyone choose to move from the Perch to here?* Aer and Alius questioned, as did many of their neighbors. It wasn't until they saw her in person that they began to understand why.

The brothers didn't know when or how it had happened, but she had become paralyzed from the waist down. To get to her new home, she'd had to be wheeled around by two caretakers who'd looked like they would rather be anywhere else. There had been a tense silence between the three as they'd climbed the Charity Tree. When they had finally dropped her off in front of her treehouse, close enough for Aer and Alius to overhear, they'd told her to avoid mentioning them and that she shouldn't show her face around the Perch again.

The heated argument that had followed ended when Nira started shouting at the top of her voice about what exemplary role models they were, abandoning their daughter at a whim. They'd given her one last glare in response before leaving her under the care of those stationed here, quickly fleeing the area while hiding their faces from any curious onlookers.

Word spread quickly. By the end of the week, the entire tree had learned of those caretakers' identities.

It wasn't hard for everyone to fill in the gaps from there. The caretakers took pride in the fact that they housed and taught the most gifted fledglings in the Perch, citing any fledgling's accomplishments as a result of their great guidance. If a caretaker had children of their own, they made sure to talk their accomplishments up and compared them positively to other fledglings, as it reflected well on them. Therefore, a daughter who couldn't walk and keep up with others would be considered a shame to any caretaker.

The fledglings who lived around Nira had sensibly chosen not to push her for more details at that time.

Alius looked troubled. He seemed to have realized his mistake in bringing up the subject.

"Right. Sorry. Forget I said that," he mumbled sheepishly. "But still, you're all looking at this the wrong way!"

Try as he might, the awkwardness of the situation had ruined the momentum of Alius's speech. The fledglings were more preoccupied with avoiding Nira's ire than listening to what he said.

The novelty of the news that Alius brought having worn off, the fledglings left for their own matters, most of them trying to escape Nira's gaze. Nira silently wheeled herself away from the scene, trying hard to avoid eye contact with Alius.

Aer went to his now-silent brother to nudge him home.

***

Aer hurriedly dusted off the familiar wooden walls of the treehouse while searching for some food. The old buildings had no lighting, and the use of fire was completely prohibited in the Spiral Forest. They would be left stumbling in the dark if they didn't take care of their needs before night fell.

Seemingly oblivious to this, Alius sat in the corner, grumbling to himself.

"Alius, if you're going to sulk, do it after you've gotten some food and cleaned up," Aer criticized.

"Not now. I'm thinking of how to convince everyone to give it their all in the Advent Trials."

"You still haven't given up on that?" Aer asked, knowing full well what the answer was.

Alius looked put off. "Of course not! These trials might be our only hope of overcoming the Perch and the conditions they put us in. Shouldn't it be normal for us to make the most out of this?"

Aer smiled wryly. "No. I think most of us here would rather avoid picking a fight with them. You're just weird."

Alius scoffed but chose not to argue, instead joining Aer in getting some food. Aer passed him an oily fruit as he set a pot full of nuts and beans between them.

Once they had finished their meal, Aer plopped onto the floor and leaned against the wall on the opposite end of the room from his brother, staring up at the ceiling. Thinking back on the day's events and knowing the near future would likely be even more hectic, he tried to sleep. At least for the moment, he wanted to avoid thinking about the troubles that would inevitably come his way.

Chapter 4: Preparations

Discrepancies in power and status often lead to curious interactions. One can glean much about another's true character by how they respond to higher authority. Many resent a perceived gap in power, but what actions they take in response should determine how they are to be handled. Those who yield are often the simplest to deal with, but one must be prudent in perceiving another's true intentions; many flatter as they subvert authority in ways unseen. Possibly the most dangerous, however, are those who openly rebel. They need to be stamped out and made an example of before they can influence others to follow in their footsteps.

Soleil gazed down as the cloud beneath her feet carried her closer to her destination: an isle placed above the center of the Nesting Islands. The buildings on its surface were far more radiant than she remembered them being. Clearly, the caretakers had been busy polishing up the place for the guests to come.

She smiled. This was proof of her efforts. It had been difficult to convince as many people as she did to listen to her. There had been fierce opposition every step of the way, especially from the caretakers. Not everyone who professed to be her ally was on her side either. There were people genuinely full of the same resentment as she was, but just as many people were seeking to sensationalize the matter for their benefit. Many simply wanted to see those in power fall so they could seize the positions that would become available for themselves.

But in the end, Emissary Striaen, whom many considered to have the greatest degree of favor from the Great Arbiter, had agreed to hear her out. This was as ideal a situation as she could have hoped for. He had given her voice legitimacy by acknowledging her plea.

She inspected the islands she had called home during her youth. There were hundreds of different Nesting Islands positioned in five circular rows at the bottom of Atravel, each connected to one another through the steel chains present everywhere. One could tell which fledglings were due for the next Ascension Ceremony by the ring of isles their Nesting Island was on.

To ensure there were no mix-ups, the fledglings were prohibited from leaving the Nesting Island they were placed on until they came of age. In contrast, the caretakers frequently moved around the islands as they saw fit, making sure everything proceeded as planned.

If a complicated issue regarding the Nesting Islands came up, the buildings on the isle placed above the center were used to discuss what to do next. They doubled as lodging for guests from other islands who wished to observe the Advent Trials.

Normally, this location would be deserted until the Advent Trials took place. However, it appeared as if her words had reached more people than she had expected, as thousands had gathered down here days earlier than the norm.

As soon as she had landed in the general area, she was immediately swarmed by caretakers eager to leave a good impression. They guided her to the entrance of the main building, where she saw the head caretakers greeting the guests from the other islands. Among them, Head Caretaker Desen seemed to be particularly fixated on surrounding himself with the distinguished.

"Conductor Sen, Forewarner Aviense, welcome! I intend to give you an insightful look at how we caretakers educate our impressionable youth down at the Nesting Islands. Through our efforts, we hope to raise young fledglings into respectable members of Atravel such as yourselves."

Soleil repressed the urge to gag as she walked toward him. She had been hard at work to convince people in positions of power to gather here for this day. Of course that snake would take advantage of her efforts to climb the social ladder.

Upon noticing her, the head caretaker dropped his sycophantic facade.

"So you came after all, Orator Mistral," the man sneered, not even trying to hide his disdain. "I don't expect you to comprehend how much effort we put into this, but know that your arguments will sound quite foolish once we're done."

"It's an honor to be here, Head Caretaker Desen. I hope I didn't upset you too badly during our last meeting," Soleil said in a pleasant manner. She knew better than to meet his provocations in front of everyone. Her words would be more convincing if she could make her opponent look unnecessarily petty while proving herself as fair-minded and generous.

Upon entering the main building, Soleil moved around, observing everyone inside. Keeping a head count of those in positions of power, she confirmed that everyone she needed present was there. The only one missing was Emissary Striaen.

She took a deep breath, apprehensive. If the emissary failed to make an appearance, she could simply use that fact to strengthen the arguments she had made throughout the past Sky Cycle, but far more could be gained if he showed up.

After the caretakers had ushered all the guests in to sit down, a sense of restlessness permeated the area. Soleil strained her ears to hear the whispers going around.

"Is this everyone?"

"Everyone important, I think."

"You're forgetting about Emissary Striaen."

"Please. You really think that an *emissary* would make the trip down to these dinky little islands?"

"I wouldn't rule out the possibility. There are a lot of important people in this room who I normally wouldn't expect to see down here. And some emissaries have come to the Nesting Islands in the past."

"That only ever happened when it was time for their relatives to go through the Ascension Ceremony. I doubt it'll happen for some civil debate like this."

Soleil frowned. She had come to a similar conclusion and was still perplexed over why the emissary had gone along with her proposal. He really should have no reason to descend to Atravel's lowest levels.

"Should we get started without him, then?" someone asked.

A voice then echoed throughout the building. "Have some faith in my words. I said that I would attend."

Everyone fell silent. The emissary had been floating over the caretakers the whole time without them noticing.

Everyone in the vicinity immediately knelt, as custom dictated. While doing so, Soleil looked for a chance to seize the crowd's attention without seeming too disrespectful.

Unfortunately, Head Caretaker Desen was the first to speak. "It is our great honor to host you in our lowly abode, Emissary Striaen."

The emissary quickly descended to the caretaker's location. "Have you made the preparations for the upcoming trials?"

"Yes. Please follow us."

The caretakers led the emissary outside to a cliff that provided a bird's-eye view of the Nesting Islands, taking special care to avoid accidentally bumping into him along the way. Soleil, along with everyone in the building, followed suit, wanting to hear the emissary's thoughts.

"As you can see here, we caretakers spare no effort in maintaining the Nesting Islands," Head Caretaker Desen boasted, gesturing below them. "I'm managing this one for the upcoming Ascension Ceremony. I suggest you observe the fledglings who come from here for a proper evaluation of my efforts."

Emissary Striaen scrutinized the island below him for a moment before nodding. "Everything seems to be in order. Are you certain you can properly address all the grievances that others may have with you?"

"But of course." The head caretaker looked around, his head turning until he found Soleil. He then gestured for the surrounding caretakers to escort her to their location.

"Well? I trust this will be satisfactory, yes? Or would you like to complain about something else?"

"Nothing seems wrong from a surface glance," Soleil admitted. "But only at a surface glance. I don't suppose you would mind if I went and stayed down there personally?"

"Stayed down there?" the head caretaker repeated blankly.

"Yes, I think I'll make myself at home on this island you oversee. Monitoring your everyday actions would be the easiest way to confirm things are as you say."

"And where would you lodge?" the head caretaker asked.

"At the Perch, of course." Soleil smiled. "Or is it too much trouble for the caretakers to be hospitable to a guest who's curious about their affairs?"

The head caretaker forced a smile, likely due to the emissary listening in. "Of course not. We welcome you with open arms."

***

Bang. Bang. Bang.

Aer awoke with a start. His eyes darted around to identify the source of the noise, only to find that it was his brother kicking a wall in frustration. Sighing loudly enough for Alius to hear, Aer covered his ears and tried to go back to sleep.

News of the Advent Trials and the Ascension Ceremony had not taken long to spread across the entire Charity Tree. Since then, Alius had been busy trying to improve his Sky Control—key word being *trying*. The only thing Aer was sure Alius could do reliably at this point was complain about his lack of results. In truth, Aer suspected his brother wasn't as committed to the task as he made himself seem. His complaints felt oddly attention seeking.

When the noise continued, Aer blew a gust in his brother's direction, knocking him against the wall he was kicking.

"Would you quiet down?" Aer yelled. "There aren't any other rooms in this treehouse! I can hear everything you do from here!"

"Then help me! How do you move the air around you like that?" Alius shouted back, looking as irritated as Aer felt.

Aer sighed. "I just... will it to move the way I want it to."

Alius rolled his eyes. "That helps. What, are you going to tell me to *feel* my way around the air next?"

"I don't know how to explain it in more detail!" Aer snapped. "It's like explaining how to breathe. It just happens."

Alius sat in front of him. "Fine. How about that silencing trick, then? Most fledglings can't pull it off, so it can't be that simple, right?"

"I just force the air around a certain area to stop moving entirely."

"How does that work?"

"I don't completely get it myself, but sound goes through and alters the air in its own way. Even now, there are changes in the air as we're speaking. So if you freeze the air between us and stop it from making those changes, then sound won't go through."

Alius pondered this for a moment before staring intensely at the air in front of him.

"Did it work?" He looked at Aer with hope in his eyes, his voice not at all muted.

Despite his exasperation at Alius's antics, Aer couldn't help but chuckle.

"Yeah. Can't hear you at all."

"Very funny," Alius replied sullenly.

Having told Alius what he wanted to hear, Aer stood and stumbled around the treehouse in search of something to eat. Finding nothing, he looked for some water to wash his face. When he couldn't find that either, he turned to Alius.

"Did you eat and drink *everything* we stored up?" he asked incredulously.

Alius let out a nervous laugh. "I *may* have taken a few late-night snacks while practicing."

Aer gave him a dirty look.

"We'll just get some more!" Alius reassured him. "There's someone I need to talk to on the way, so this timing's actually pretty convenient for us."

"For you, you mean," Aer corrected him.

A few minutes later, Aer had tied some of their clothes together to use as makeshift bags before stepping outside. Alius grabbed as many empty containers as he could and followed. After making sure they had everything they needed, they descended the Charity Tree and walked until they reached one of the rivers nourishing its roots.

Aer hummed lazily as they used the river to wash their faces and clothes while filling up the clay pots they had brought with water. It was earlier than he was used to, but it was a familiar routine.

Alius, however, had not drawn any water. Instead, he vigilantly inspected the area. "It should be somewhere around here," he muttered.

Before Aer could ask him what he was looking for, Alius dashed away.

"Found it!" Alius exclaimed.

Aer looked toward where Alius was heading. On the other end of the river was a treehouse built on an unusually low-level platform, one barely above the ground. Alius ran up to it and knocked on the front door. The door opened to reveal a very tall teenager, one unusually well built for someone who lived on the Charity Tree.

Aer recognized him as one of the older fledglings on the Nesting Island. If he recalled correctly, his name was—

"Kiel," Alius greeted him. "I'd like to talk to you."

The bigger fledgling gave him a questioning look. "Alius, right? Most people don't come out here this early."

"Oh yeah. My brother was complaining about not having any food or water. You think he could learn to be more patient and wait until—"

Aer crossed the river as quickly as he could to smack the back of his brother's head.

"You're the one who woke me up this early after devouring everything we had! Don't go and act like this is somehow my fault!" he exclaimed, staring daggers at Alius.

"So how are things going for you, Kiel?" Alius asked, acting as if nothing had happened.

Kiel snorted, looking amused at Aer's outburst. "Just about to take my morning jog. I was considering not doing it, though. The past few days have been exhausting. We're supposed to be meeting at the Eastern Borders today, right? I've been having trouble contro—I mean, calming the others down."

"Actually, I wanted to talk to you about that," Alius said.

Aer realized why Alius had come here. Kiel had a strong influence over the other Charity Tree fledglings. The older boy was quite crafty and charismatic despite his physically imposing appearance. By living on the bottom platform near the river, he had made it so fledglings had to pass by his home to get water. He took full advantage of this and went outside often to communicate with others. His home's low elevation also allowed him to take the initiative in greeting outsiders to the Spiral Forest who reluctantly came by to deliver news. Since most Charity Tree fledglings hated interacting with those from the Perch and vice versa, he had accumulated some goodwill from everyone involved by relaying messages for both sides.

In the end, he had become an unofficial spokesperson for the Charity Tree fledglings. His familiarity with everyone on the Charity Tree, the feelings of gratitude and debt he had gathered over time, and a towering figure that put him physically a head and shoulders above everyone else all gave him an authority within the Charity Tree on par with those of the caretakers.

It then made perfect sense why Alius had sought him out. If Alius wanted the other fledglings' help, Kiel would be the first person to approach. Aer was even beginning to suspect that Alius had purposefully eaten all their supplies so they would have an excuse to go meet with him.

***

Kiel stood at the doorway, listening quietly as Alius talked about his plans to get those in the Charity Tree to outperform the Perch at the Advent Trials.

"I see." Kiel nodded. "So that's why you were looking for me. Because you thought I might be able to sway the others."

"For the record, this wasn't my idea," Aer interjected, trying to emphasize that he didn't want to get involved. "I doubt people from the other islands will pay us much attention to begin with."

"It's because they won't pay attention that we need to leave a lasting impression," Alius argued.

Kiel's gaze shifted between the brothers before eventually focusing solely on Alius. "How were you planning to go about this exactly?"

"I was going to work it out along the way," Alius answered. "I'm sure more options will open up if I can get more people to join us."

Kiel nodded. "And? What's in it for me?"

Aer shot Alius a warning look. He doubted Kiel's self-appointed role as their representative was for wholly altruistic reasons. He was likely gauging how useful Alius would be to him in the future.

Don't promise him anything you can't give him, Aer repeated in his mind, hoping Alius would get the message.

He was unsure if Alius understood anything, however, as his brother spoke rather brazenly.

"You spent a lot of time making yourself someone important here, but do you really think it'll stick once we're off this Nesting Island?" Alius asked. "The people you're well liked by won't be any help to you once we leave, since none of us have any significance on the other islands. You'll have to start from the beginning if you want to get well connected."

Kiel gave a wry smile. "You're right. That's been bothering me quite a bit the past few days. So? What does that matter to you?"

"If the fledglings from the Charity Tree impress those from the outside and gain some recognition for themselves, you'll have more influence right out of the gate, right?" Alius reasoned.

A pause. "True."

"Then I think what I'm aiming for helps you too. If we do well in the trials and it ends up helping all our futures, you just gained some powerful friends."

Kiel appraised Alius for a moment before breaking into a grin. "All right, I admit I'm interested. Let's talk more about the details inside." He gestured into his house.

Aer grew uneasy. He couldn't read Kiel the same way he could read his brother. While Alius might be fine with taking the risk, Aer didn't want to make any promises to someone he barely knew.

"I think it's time we started gathering some food," Aer murmured, trying to give Alius a reason to leave.

Alius gave no sign he had heard Aer, however. Instead, he headed inside, ignoring his brother completely. Annoyed, Aer started walking away, hoping Alius would follow. When nothing of the sort happened, he excused himself and went back on his own.

Aer grumbled as he made his way back to the Charity Tree, jumping from branch to branch to grab whatever fruit he could reach along the way. Alius was *aggravating* at times. He had always been the more headstrong one between them, sure, but it wouldn't have killed him to talk things over before charging forward. Not that he would have listened to Aer's objections in the first place, but he could have at least given some sort of warning about what he planned to do.

By the time Aer had finished gathering food, Atravel's morning lights had reached the Charity Tree. He leaned against the trunk of a conjoined tree as rain washed over him. This was a daily occurrence; the clouds hanging over the Nesting Island rained showers every morning to replenish the rivers nourishing the Charity Tree while minimizing the chances of something catching fire. It also gave the people living there an easy way to clean themselves, which was good, considering their limited options.

From the corner of his eye, Aer saw a few early risers among the fledglings leaving their treehouses to start their day. He sighed. Most of the other fledglings were still probably asleep. *They* didn't have a brother who would devour all their supplies then leave them to gather food by themse—

Oh, there he is, Aer thought as he saw Alius walking toward him triumphantly. *Things must have gone well for him. Or at least, he thinks they did.*

Aer let out a bit of his frustration by sealing a few bags of fruit and firing them in Alius's direction. Looking surprised when the bags suddenly shot toward his face, Alius nevertheless managed to catch them midair before they hit him.

"Really, Aer. You could be a little more careful."

Aer ignored his brother's complaint. "Nice reflexes. Now help me carry this, you slacker."

The two walked back home while helping themselves to Aer's spoils.

After he filled his stomach, Aer's displeasure had died down enough for him to calmly ask Alius what had happened. "So, what did you guys talk about after I left?"

"We talked about what the trials might be about and how we should prepare for them," Alius answered.

"Is that all?"

"No. I also told him about how I tried to talk everyone into putting some effort into the Advent Trials and failed," Alius said. "He told me to try convincing my neighbors properly this time."

"Well, you did mess up pretty badly there," Aer remarked dryly. "Though I don't know why he would ask you to try again, knowing that. Aren't you more likely to drive everyone away at this point?"

"It's not like I *can't* convince them," Alius objected. "I probably would have gotten a few people to compete if I hadn't mentioned Nira's parents."

"So what will you do now?"

"I'm going to start by getting Nira to reconsider. If she joins us, the others who were worried about upsetting her might come too."

"Or they could start wondering what kind of backdoor deal you made to make her join despite her clearly not wanting to," Aer pointed out.

"Right, then," Alius said, pretending not to have heard him. "I'll go ahead and apologize for bringing up her parents. Just in case, I should probably take a few of these as gifts."

Aer elbowed Alius as he reached for an unopened bag of fruit.

Alius winced in pain. "What?"

"If you want to give her some food to win her over, get it yourself. What I gathered stays with me."

"Fine."

While Alius took the time to gather the fruits on some nearby branches into an empty cloth bag, Aer dropped the rest of their supplies back home. Afterward, they both walked to Nira's treehouse.

Alius took a deep breath as he stood in front of Nira's door and knocked. Aer stepped back, ready to intervene should Alius say something offensive again.

"What is it?" Nira asked as the door opened.

An awkward silence settled between Nira and Alius. The two had not spoken since their argument. Despite his earlier bravado, Alius seemed to be at a complete loss for words, standing there quietly.

Aer nudged his brother impatiently.

You're the one who wanted to do this, Aer thought as he glanced between the still pair. *Don't get cold feet now.*

To Aer's mild surprise, Nira also wore a guilty expression. If anything, she appeared more nervous than angry.

Moments passed as the two just stared at one another, prompting Aer to elbow Alius in the back.

"I'm sorry," Alius managed to blurt out. "I shouldn't have brought up your parents. But I still meant what I said earlier about the Advent Trials."

Despite how stiff Alius's words were, he seemed to have succeeded in easing the tension. Aer had to admit that had he been in his brother's position, he might not have worked up the nerve to say anything.

Nira relaxed a little. "Don't worry about it. I think I was a bit too touchy. To be honest, I've been worried about what to do in the coming days. I don't care about my parents' opinions, but I don't like the idea of everyone from the Perch looking down on me. What if they need me to walk or run in the trials?"

"Ah, I could help you move around," Alius said, looking encouraged by her positive response.

"Not sure I'll be allowed help. The only thing I can really do is keep up my strength until then."

Alius responded by handing Nira the bag of fruit he had gathered.

"Not quite what I meant, but thanks anyway." Nira laughed. "The caretaker assigned to take care of me tends to be lazy about things like food, so this helps."

Well, that was easier than I thought it would be, Aer thought as Alius and Nira both gave an awkward smile. *She might have come to us eventually if Alius hadn't beaten her to it.*

The ground beneath them swayed, interrupting their conversation. Aer, trying not to stumble, searched for the source of the disturbance.

"I presume you've all heard the news by now," a voice echoed throughout the woods.

Aer looked straight down to see a group of caretakers standing by the base of the Charity Tree.

"All fledglings must show up at the Eastern Borders this afternoon. We're here to make sure no stragglers remain. You will all march toward the designated area as quickly as possible. Anyone found loitering here by noon will be dragged there and given a penalty in the Advent Trials for wasting the caretakers' time. No exceptions."

"And there you go. Looks like I'm going to be penalized before the trials even start," Nira muttered. "Wait. What are you—"

Aer looked back at his brother and Nira. Alius had tossed the bag of fruit into Nira's house and was grabbing the back of her wheelchair.

"I said I would help you move, right?" he said cheerfully.

Any response she could have given was cut off when Alius started running down the bridges, holding onto her wheelchair.

"Aer, come on!" Alius shouted.

As Aer followed his brother down the Charity Tree, he couldn't help but wonder how the caretakers planned to force every fledgling to attend. He looked back to see the caretakers blocking all but one of the exits to the Charity Tree. They then escorted all the fledglings they could find down to the exit. Their actions were precise and methodical, almost as if they had done it before.

As they trekked forward, Aer saw the caretakers searching for any stragglers in the woods. He was surprised at how seriously they were searching the area, listening for any signs of noise from disobedient fledglings and turning over every possible hiding spot. Aer had lived there his entire life and hadn't known half those locations even existed.

He put his surprise over the caretakers' unexpected diligence to the back of his mind once he caught sight of fledglings from the Perch joining them at the Eastern Borders.

The Eastern Borders were, as the name implied, the easternmost parts of the Nesting Island. It was there where one could catch a glimpse of the other floating islands of Atravel. Unfortunately for any curious onlookers, tall steel gates fenced off the island's edges. Any fledgling found to have somehow crossed those gates was severely punished.

Today, a row of caretakers vigilantly stood in front of the gate, glaring down at any fledgling who dared approach. Unsurprising, as more people had gathered there than Aer had seen in his lifetime. He had no trouble believing that everyone on the Nesting Island was present then and there. It would be easy to lose track of a few people in all the chaos.

Alius, who was still wheeling a rather disoriented Nira around, signaled Aer to follow him. Probably the only way for them to communicate, as Aer couldn't make out an individual voice among the sea of people.

Aer stuck close to his brother's side and scanned his surroundings, trying to get a feel for the situation. Despite how busy the crowd was, he could see a clear divide between those from the Charity Tree and those from the Perch. The caretakers were arranging the Perch fledglings to make the Charity Tree fledglings behind them less visible.

When the last of the fledglings had settled in, the head caretaker's voice echoed throughout the area. "I see that everyone has arrived. Good. It's nice to know my instructions didn't fall on deaf ears. Now, if you would direct your attention over there, we can get started."

They all looked to where he pointed. Adults they had never seen before were walking toward the Perch. Some took the time to stare back, the Perch fledglings taking most of their attention.

"These people are visitors from the other islands. They will be occupying this Nesting Island until the Advent Trials are over," the head caretaker said. "During this time, they will explain and demonstrate what they do for a living. If you find yourselves interested in their career, attend the corresponding trial. You will have your chance to impress them there."

The head caretaker then cleared his throat to redirect the fledglings' attention toward himself. "You all will be required to participate in at least three trials. Of course, if you feel confident in your abilities and want to give yourselves more opportunities in the future, go ahead and sign up for more. Just don't do anything to embarrass yourselves. The visitors will hold continuous lectures on different parts of the island for the foreseeable future. They will be staying at the Perch in the meantime to assess how well the fledglings here have been raised."

The caretakers started distributing paper forms to everyone in the area.

"A list of each lecture is being passed around right now, along with where and when they'll be held," the head caretaker explained. "You can apply for the associated trials once these lectures are over. Now then, I need to welcome our guests. You are all dismissed."

Aer, Alius, and Nira struggled to get their forms, hampered by the sheer number of people in front of them scrambling to grab one. By the time they received their papers, escaped the crowd, and started the journey back home, they were left thoroughly exhausted.

"The visitors are going to be visiting the Perch to get an idea about *our* lives, huh?" Alius grumbled. "Figures."

"Those people from the other islands will focus on fledglings who they think have the most potential," Aer said. "The caretakers will make sure that the visitors look at those whom they prioritized more than anyone else. They probably won't pay much attention to anyone at the Charity Tree."

"That sounds about right." Alius sighed. "We need some way to close the gap in knowledge. We can attend all the lectures we want, but the guys from the Blessed all receive special lessons from the caretakers. We don't get that."

Nira, who had remained quiet ever since they left the Spiral Forest, looked between Aer and Alius before speaking. "If that's the problem, I could share what I learned during my time as one of the Blessed before I came here."

When they both stared at her, she started stammering.

"O-Of course, a more qualified teacher would be better for you guys, but like you said, the caretakers won't pay attention to you. So just keep the idea in mind—"

"You can do that? Forget the caretakers! When do we start?" Alius shouted, unable to contain his excitement.

Nira looked confused. "Wait, really? We can start as soon as you want, but you're fine with learning from me?"

"Of course I am," Alius replied. "Ah, why didn't I think of that? We need to figure out what to learn for each trial quickly. Hey, how far do you think we can get before the trials start?"

Aer remained silent as Alius planned out the upcoming days with a grin. His brother seemed certain that they could make a future for themselves if they were evaluated with complete objectivity. But Aer considered that too optimistic. Rather, he was discouraged by what he'd just seen. That gathering had contained more fledglings than Aer could keep track of. What could he or Alius do to make them stand out in a positive way? Furthermore, the caretakers had dismissed them their entire lives—how could Alius be so sure the visitors wouldn't do the same?

Chapter 5:
The Value of One's Role

As we are limited to the resources that the Great Arbiter has provided for us up here, we must both preserve what we have and seek more renewable means of sustenance. For that reason, all those who lighten the burden we place on our surroundings and on ourselves have their place in Atravel, so long as their contributions remain significant.

Azel glared at the dish in front of him in frustration, on the verge of tossing it aside. He thought he had seasoned it well enough until giving it a taste.

Where did I go wrong? he wondered before asking himself a more important question. *How did I even get myself into this situation?*

Ever since the head huntress had placed him in Emissary Striaen's service, Azel had been stuck on food preparation duty—which was a problem, since he had no talent in cooking. The emissary knew it too. After sampling Azel's food, the old man had handed him over to a chef visiting the Nesting Islands, eager to be rid of him.

This is ridiculous, Azel fumed. *I don't know the first thing about fine dining. I could never meet an emissary's standards.*

Of course, such complaints earned him zero sympathy from his new boss, who wasn't keen on taking someone so unskilled as an apprentice and yet couldn't refuse an emissary's direct appointment. Azel was sure the chef would dismiss him as soon as it was safe to do so. Which wouldn't be a problem if the head huntress would stop rejecting his attempts to return to his old role. He had nowhere else to go to make a living.

Why had the head huntress appointed him as a chef, of all things? Maybe she did it to get rid of him. Had he failed to meet her standards for a good subordinate somehow? Did everyone else just want him gone?

That must have been it. The other hunters were probably having a good laugh at his expense while he struggled alone. They would regret that. Someone would eventually notice how unfair the whole situation was and fix it. They would surely…

Who was he kidding? He wasn't important. Nobody cared about him. Certainly not enough to stand up for him. And he didn't care about anyone either.

He didn't belong anywhere.

***

Chaos ensued the day following Head Caretaker Desen's announcement as fledglings all over the Nesting Island tripped over themselves to get an audience with the visitors. The caretakers, trying to both accommodate the visitors and keep the fledglings under control, were in even more of a rush, further escalating the sense of disarray that pervaded the Charity Tree and the Perch alike.

As for Aer and Alius, the two were making their way to a field just outside the Spiral Forest. As they approached their destination, they found themselves blocked off by yet another unruly crowd of fledglings.

Aer winced at the sight of the mass. There must have been hundreds of people there, all moving in different directions. Would all the lectures be so hectic?

He quickly sidestepped the incoming swarm of people, only to lose sight of Alius in the confusion. He sighed. Nira had been right to sit the lectures out, asking Alius to summarize them for her instead. Had she attended in person, she likely would have been trampled by the disorderly mob. If only he had done the same.

No. Alius would have smacked him for even suggesting the idea.

The only consolation was that the Perch fledglings seemed content to ignore the brothers this time around. Aer had mentally prepared himself for the same condescending gazes they received last time, but unlike last time, he and Alius weren't the only members of the Charity Tree here, so they stood out a lot less in comparison.

Once the crowd had settled, Aer spotted his brother waving from a distance and made his way across.

"There you are!" Alius exclaimed. "You know, you make things hard on me when you just move on your own and disappear like that."

"Right back at you," Aer shot back. "If I kept count of every time you acted on your own—"

"Good morning to you all."

The twins faced forward as the voice of an old woman echoed throughout the vicinity.

"Now that I have your attention, we can get started," she said, addressing the crowd of fledglings before her. "I am here because I was requested to deliver a lecture explaining the duties of a forewarner to you fledglings."

The lecturer paused for a moment, waiting for the noise of the crowd to die down before continuing. "A forewarner is someone who senses potential difficulties through the air and informs the proper authorities. There are two different types of forewarners. The first type, the outer forewarners, spend their time at the very edges of Atravel. They have a duty to detect any incoming obstacles in Atravel's path. As we fly through the skies, we must keep a vigilant watch to make sure we don't run into anything problematic, such as high-reaching mountains from the outside world."

Aer briefly wondered if Atravel had ever been in a collision before for there to be an entire occupation to prevent such incidents from happening.

"The second type, the inner forewarners, have the responsibility of discerning any changes within Atravel's atmosphere. Those who control the skies have the responsibility of routinely changing the air around them to be inhabitable. That is how we breathe up here, where the air would otherwise be too thin. The inner forewarners' job is to confirm that the overall air quality and pressure remains fit for life."

That last statement stuck out in Aer's mind. It brought up the question of what would happen if Atravel didn't have enough people to create breathable air.

"Both occupations require you sense the winds around you and properly identify what it means. The outer forewarners, however, require more range, while the inner forewarners require more focus and attention to detail." The old woman straightened her back and faced the other way. "And now, for a demonstration. I'd like some volunteers to display a form of Sky Control right now. Do it subtly. I will, without looking, discern how the winds move."

Aer and Alius watched quietly as four fledglings raised their hands and did as the old woman instructed as she sat perfectly still. Once they were done, she nodded before turning back around.

"You will all be happy to know that the air on this island has no abnormalities," she stated. "Now then, from what I sensed, two of you blew wind eastward while someone else jumped and used the air to slow their descent. Lastly, one of you used Sky Control to lift and twirl a tree branch in that direction."

The fledglings looked impressed. To pick that out in a sizable crowd was beyond them all.

"This is the most basic ability that all forewarners must have," the lecturer explained. "One must learn how to *feel* the air around them."

Feel the air around us, huh? Aer chuckled to himself as he recalled the argument he'd had with Alius the day before. He then gave his brother a knowing look, to which Alius scowled.

Aer listened attentively to the forewarner as her lecture continued. He wasn't particularly interested in the occupation, but mastering such a skill would help him avoid other people before they could approach him.

He tried practicing throughout the lecture, taking in the old woman's descriptions of how a forewarner sensed through the air as he tried to connect to the atmosphere around him.

After focusing for a while, Aer felt his skin tingling as he grew hypersensitive to the surrounding breezes. Next, he had to decipher what all the sensations meant.

Aer's eyes wandered over the crowd. Alius stared at him quizzically.

So this is what it feels like when people breathe normally, Aer noted as he observed and matched his sight with his sensations. He then expanded his senses. Up ahead, the wind twisted in patterns too unusual to be natural. *Seems like someone's practicing their Sky Control over there,* Aer guessed as he continued to pore over everything around him.

After some time had passed, he nodded in satisfaction.

I think I've got it.

Having spent time memorizing how everything had felt to him as it happened, Aer was certain he could accurately tell what was going on by what he felt, at least within a short distance. The only sensation he couldn't properly identify was a small but consistent vibration occurring behind the lower body of a fledgling standing at the very back.

Aer's focus snapped back to the lecturer as she clapped her hands.

"Let's end this here. And to the young man passing wind in the back, it's unhealthy to hold it in for too long. Do your business somewhere before joining another lecture."

Giggles filled the crowd as the old woman turned to leave.

***

"Well, that was interesting," Alius commented as they walked away from the lecture. "Think you might be interested in learning how to 'sense the world around you'?"

"I think it's too early to decide anything," Aer replied, staying silent about his own activities throughout the lecture. Alius would almost certainly push him into participating in that trial if he was aware.

"Right. Let's head to our next lecture, then."

"Now?"

"Yes!" Alius insisted, pulling Aer along. "We should look around as much as we can while they're still there. Come on. We're hitting all the lectures we can today."

Aer frowned once he realized where Alius was leading him. "Wait. We're heading right to the Perch. They're holding lectures there?"

"Yep." Alius smiled. "This is great. I've always wanted to check out the place. And now, we'll have a reason to be there. They won't be able to say a thing about it."

"Aren't you worried at all?"

"Nope. Let's go."

Straying from the path they would have taken to get home, the brothers followed an unfamiliar road until they came to tall stone ledges at the base of the Perch's cliff.

"So this is where they stay," Alius muttered.

Aer felt more hostility here than at the previous lecture. The people from the Perch were clearly less receptive of those from the Charity Tree coming near their home. A clear divide separated the crowd of fledglings based on where they lived.

A man brushed past them as he made his way to the front.

"Quiet. I know that the audience today is more *unrefined* than usual." He gave a pointed stare at the group of fledglings from the Charity Tree, easily identifiable by their shabbier clothing. "But that's no excuse for this behavior. Now, I'm sure you all know what a caretaker is. The expectations of the job, however, are somewhat less well known. Teaching younger generations requires you to know quite a bit of our history, our infrastructure, and the tenets of Sky Authority. Now, who can tell me the first law the Great Arbiter gave us? When did we receive it? How do we apply it in our everyday lives?"

A raised hand came from the crowd of Perch fledglings.

"The first law passed down by the Great Arbiter states we must detach ourselves from the mundane matters of this material world. We received it when Atravel was first formed, when the Great Arbiter separated us from the secular societies that surrounded us. We apply it in our everyday lives by avoiding worldly conflicts and concerns. By doing so, we free ourselves from things beneath our notice."

"Very good. Knowledge is the most important aspect of being a caretaker. The corresponding trial will have a written portion testing everything you know."

The rest of the lecture continued like this, with the caretaker asking question after question and the Perch fledglings answering each one perfectly. The Charity Tree fledglings who had bothered to attend the lecture were predictably clueless throughout the whole thing.

To Aer's complete lack of surprise, Alius was not in a good mood by the end of it.

"What a load of garbage," he muttered.

"I take it you don't want to be a caretaker," Aer said. It wasn't a question.

"Of course not. They treat us like we're not even there on a good day. Why would I want to join them?" Alius asked. "Then there's that nonsense about the 'mundane matters of the material world.' They're just using it as an excuse to ignore all the problems right in front of them."

"Like us?" Aer asked.

"Right. Like us. Like everyone at the Charity Tree. They don't want to bother with us, so they teach that our problems are things they shouldn't care about. Then they pat themselves on the back for following what they teach. How *noble* of them. They care about the fledglings related to them. They care about appeasing the higher-ups by taking care of their children. Shouldn't those things also be 'mundane' matters?"

"Well, think about it this way," Aer said reassuringly. "If you somehow become a caretaker, you might get a bit of revenge by taking out your anger on any particularly obnoxious Perch fledglings."

Alius paused.

"That *would* be an upside." A crooked smile formed on his lips.

Their next lecture was short and direct. The lecturer appeared uninterested in talking any more than he had to.

"The duty of a carrier is to move Atravel through the skies," the lecturer stated matter-of-factly. "This job requires a good amount of power and control over the air as well as the ability to follow commands and coordinate well with others."

The lecturer then pointed to a nearby boulder, which began to float and circle the group. "As you can see, I am moving this boulder around using the air surrounding it. If you become a carrier, you will use your power with others on a much larger scale in different ways. It may sound simple, but many who apply for the job are surprised to find how grueling the work can be. You will do this day and night, following the commands of those above. Those unconfident about the strength of their Sky Authority should not apply for the Carrier's Trial."

"Well, that sounds straightforward," Alius noted once the lecturer left. "Too bad it's not an option for me. You interested?"

Aer shrugged. There was little to complain or be excited about. All it involved was carrying rocks.

"What's next?" he asked Alius.

"Let's see…" Alius stared at his schedule incredulously. *"Bird rearing?"*

"The proper term for it is 'falconry,' according to this form," Aer corrected as he peered at the parchment in Alius's hands.

Aer and Alius went to where the lecture was to be held and waited with the other fledglings. Eventually, a woman equipped with a leather hood and gloves strutted in front of them. More interesting than her attire, however, was the black-and-white falcon placed on her arm.

"As I'm sure you are all aware, the Great Arbiter gave us control of all aspects of the sky when he moved us up here," the lecturer said while staring at the bird in front of her.

Everyone in the crowd nodded. They were all familiar with the story.

"Now, when I say all aspects, I mean *all* aspects. We possess dominion over its natural inhabitants. Communicating with creatures tailored for the sky and making them follow our orders is a key part of Sky Authority."

She then raised her arm and spoke to the bird. "*Fly and sing.*"

The falcon flew off her arm and began squawking around the crowd. After a while, the lecturer stretched out her arm and spoke. "*Come back.*"

As soon as the words left her lips, the falcon returned to her extended arm. Several members of the audience clapped.

"Quite the positive reaction," the lecturer commented. "Now, how is this useful? You see, aside from scouting out locations for you, these animals are the most common way of contacting people from other islands. Communicating with multitudes of them and getting them to deliver your messages is very convenient if you don't wish to travel from island to island. For that purpose, the hardiest, the quickest, and the most intelligent birds are reared on an island above. It is a falconer's job to bring up these animals to be responsive toward human commands."

The lecturer then petted her falcon. "For our trial, we will match you all with various birds. Your job will be to communicate with these animals and command them into completing a series of tasks we have set up. Prospective falconers will be taught how to raise these animals at a later date."

The lecture continued with the woman explaining the varying mindsets different animals could possess and how to adjust commands as needed.

"Okay, that was cool," Alius admitted once it was over.

"Yeah, that was definitely one of the more interesting lectures," Aer agreed.

"Well, Aer? You want to try being a falconer?" Alius asked.

"It'd be nice to get birds to obey my every whim," Aer replied dryly. "I could leave everything to them and never have to leave home."

"So, you want to go for it?" Alius asked eagerly.

Aer thought about it a bit more. "I don't know. I admit it'd be kind of interesting if I could do such a thing, but I'm not sure I want to make a living off it."

The brothers hurried to their next lecture, only to find that the lecturer was nowhere to be found. Confused, they waited with the rest of the group until one of the Perch fledglings spotted a wiry-looking man standing far away from the group. When the fledglings tried to get closer, a light rain descended upon them, courtesy of a small cloud hovering just above their reach.

"A rain provider has the duty of watering the crops and the trees of Atravel," the wiry man explained, chuckling at the wet and irritated crowd. "They are also expected to put out any fires that may erupt throughout our nation as quickly as possible. To do this, one must be used to quick travel and be able to arrive at the designated location at a moment's notice. A familiarity with the landscape and its landmarks is required of all rain providers."

When a fledgling raised their hand to ask a question, the lecturer ignored them, choosing to focus on the cloud above them instead.

"Unfortunately, the ability to move clouds and make them rain is a bit beyond the level of Sky Control we expect from you fledglings," the lecturer stated condescendingly. "Instead, our trial will measure how quickly you can traverse through this island's landmarks to water the correct plants and soil. Those who have made themselves familiar with the terrain and are confident in their speed and response time should give it a try."

"Well, that was annoying," Aer said upon the arrogant man's departure, wringing out his clothes before summoning a breeze to blow them dry. "He could have told us all that without giving a practical demonstration."

"I think you could do well as a rain provider," Alius said, appearing unbothered by the state of his clothes.

"What makes you think so?" Aer asked.

"Well, you already seem to be good at everything that the trial requires. You can move way faster than I can, and I'm sure you can respond quickly enough to whatever they throw at you. Plus, you've already proven how well you can alter the air."

Aer shook his head. "I can silence noise, and that's about it. I don't know where to begin on moving clouds."

Alius shrugged. "How different could it be? I'm sure you'll figure it out just fine."

Their next lecture took them to the edges of the Spiral Forest.

The only lecture so far to be held in this area, Aer noted. The number of people attending was also a lot lower than the other lectures.

A portly man walked in front of them and began speaking. "A mechanic creates and maintains the technology present in Atravel. Instead of using any applications of Sky Control, this job focuses more on technical knowledge and building equipment to best benefit Atravel as a whole. It's also our responsibility to make sure everything keeping Atravel together, such as the chains attached to this island, continues to hold."

He then pulled out a small device containing a rotor inside for everyone to see. "I have here a model of a windmill. You may have seen larger versions of these around this Nesting Island. The ones attached to the top of the stone towers here generate the energy needed to keep various equipment going. As Atravel is always moving through the sky, there is never a shortage of wind currents. The Perch also has several watermills to grind food and pump water by using the power from the rivers surrounding it. These mills are an excellent example of something we built to sustain ourselves. As Sky Control allows us to direct both wind and rain, we can actively influence how much power these generate."

The lecturer looked to the crowd for a reaction, only to be met with dead silence. He then impatiently pulled out another device, a piece of metal placed in the middle of a disc with a smooth top surface. "You fledglings may not be aware, having lived on this island your entire lives, but there are much larger versions of this device attached to the exterior of almost every island in Atravel. By converting the air directed toward its sides into a lifting force to raise the islands, these devices can aid the carriers in their effort to keep Atravel in the air as we travel through the skies. They can even serve as an emergency option to keep the islands afloat in the event those responsible for moving Atravel happen to be incapacitated."

The lecturer paused and faced the fledglings. "Well? Has this caught any of your interests?"

Aer stood silent and observed those listening. Alius, at the very least, looked somewhat interested in the mechanic's demonstration, but the general reception was unenthusiastic. From what Aer could tell, most of the Charity Tree fledglings simply didn't understand what the man was talking about, while the Perch fledglings seemed to have low regard for him and his counsel.

The lecturer, looking like he wanted more of a response, reached for another device. "It's a different field of technology than the windmills, but things like this have also been designed by mechanics in the past."

He then took out a clear vial. "These small bottles contain pockets of air. They're meant to be used in emergencies. Should we experience a sudden loss of atmosphere and suffer from oxygen deprivation, we can attach these to specific masks, which can tide us over until we find a way to fix the situation."

When the crowd remained unimpressed, the lecturer's shoulders sank. "The trial for being a mechanic will require you to take some devices of your choosing and explain their design and utility to the proctors as well as finding alternative uses for them," he said sullenly. "You can find me in this area if you have any questions."

"I suppose it's something to consider if we have no better options. Not that I want to be caught dead in such an undignified job," Aer heard a member of the audience not so quietly utter as the lecturer began to leave.

The lecturer stayed silent, but Aer could tell from his face that he had heard the provocation just fine. Even if he hadn't, it was clear from the audience's attitude that most of the Perch fledglings were belittling the portly man and his profession. The disapproval on all their faces was impossible to ignore.

"I never knew some of those things existed," Alius said in wonder as they walked away from the forest. "I don't know why people look down on being a mechanic so much. It's useful. The wages aren't bad either."

"There's something we're not getting here," Aer agreed. "Anyway, where to next?"

Their next lecture took place inside one of the stone pillars. As soon as those attending were seated, the lecturer blew a melodic tune with a strange instrument.

"We conductors are artists who alter the sound we send to our audiences," she said as her song echoed throughout the room. "The gift of Sky Control allows us to change how vibrations travel through the air."

How is she doing this? Aer wondered. All different kinds of songs were entering his ear simultaneously, and yet it didn't feel jarring at all. Furthermore, the lecturer wasn't even opening her mouth as she gave her speech. The notes from the instrument were speaking for her.

"Knowing how to create certain vibrations that the ear can receive and understand harmoniously is the mark of a conductor. The Conductor's Trial will have you put on a performance for us. You may use whatever instrument or method you like. We will judge your performance accordingly."

Once the lecture had ended, the conductor shooed the fledglings from the stone pillar to make room for the next group.

"How did she do that?" Alius looked mystified. "You think the instrument has anything to do with it?"

"I don't know," Aer replied. "More importantly, it's getting late, and I'm getting tired. You still want to keep going?"

"Just one more," Alius insisted, looking somewhat exhausted himself.

Their last lecture of the day took place near the Charity Tree. Their lecturer was a strict-looking man who stood on top of an outer tree of the Spiral Forest.

"An enforcer is someone who ensures that peace is kept throughout the islands. You're all probably familiar with what we do to a certain extent, seeing as many caretakers here have a double job as an enforcer. Depending on how skilled you are and where you're placed, however, you may have to deal with more threatening things than a disobedient fledgling. The Enforcer's Trial will pit you against one another. You will need to show that you can subdue others in an appropriate manner."

Aer held back his urge to yawn as the lecture continued. The lecturer gave guidelines on how to act and explained their policy on handling certain situations. In particular, the way different types of people were handled was given a lot of focus. But Aer wasn't really interested in an occupation where he had to confront other people for a living.

Once they returned home, Aer and Alius both slumped onto the floor, their brains still processing everything they had learned today.

"Let's get some rest for now," Alius said. "We'll be doing this again tomorrow."

"Mph," Aer grunted in reply. He didn't have the energy to muster an argument.

***

The next few days went by rather similarly. The lectures were long but informative. They all followed the same pattern, with each lecturer speaking about their profession and giving a demonstration. Just from the lectures, the brothers were starting to get a picture of life outside the Nesting Island.

What was just as informative as the lectures, however, were the opinions of the Perch fledglings and the caretakers in the audience and how they reacted to certain subjects. Aer and Alius initially had no idea as to why everyone seemed to look down on being a mechanic. After a while, though, it became apparent that people generally looked down on professions that required no usage of Sky Control. The lecturers of such subjects had wavering confidence and often shrank in front of others. The crowds gathering at these lectures were often much smaller as well. If anything, mechanics were among the more respected fields that fell into this category.

Conversely, occupations that required higher levels of Sky Authority seemed to be considered more distinguished, as they displayed greater favor from the Great Arbiter. The lecturers for these subjects spoke in high-handed tones and generally had much more confidence.

The more recreational subjects like conducting seemed to be considered more high risk, high reward. If a person could make themselves known in said occupations through their works, they could live luxuriously. Otherwise, it seemed difficult to earn a living through such a field. It did, however, sound as if those who explicitly used Sky Control in their work had an easier time getting by.

***

The brothers ran toward the center of the Spiral Forest as the sky dimmed.

Aer tried not to let his impatience show as he ran alongside his physically slower brother. It was the last subject they could cover. After that, there would be no more lectures to attend, and he could finally get a break from running all over the island.

A stone-faced woman stared at the twins as they reached the lecture site. As soon as Aer met her gaze, however, the woman turned away and began addressing everyone in the area.

"A hunter is someone who manages the wildlife species of Atravel. As we are separated from the rest of the world, the natural resources we have right now are all that we can expect. Therefore, we hunters must make sure that animal populations within Atravel remain stable."

Aer frowned. Something seemed very strange in the way she spoke, but he couldn't quite put his finger on it. Unlike the other lecturers, he couldn't sense any sort of pride or self-deprecation from her. In fact, he couldn't sense any emotion from her words at all.

"To do this, we watch over several caged islands above us that are reserved for wildlife. We make sure those animals stay in the territory they're allocated to and keep them in order. On occasion, when life from the outside finds its way here, it is our duty to hunt them down and, if possible, integrate them into Atravel's greater ecosystem."

And if you can't? Aer wondered.

Likely having come across his question before, the head huntress answered, unprompted.

"Every now and then, we have to put some animals down. Usually, it's for the sake of food, but on some occasions, an animal's presence endangers the greater good. You may believe that to be successful at this job, all one needs is to be able to run and catch a fleeing animal. Unfortunately, chasing down an animal and facing it head-on is often quite inefficient. Knowledge of poison, traps, and how to best conceal your presence as well as understanding habits and how to strike your target when they're at their most vulnerable are more valuable traits in these situations."

Aer had a feeling that he *really* didn't want to cross this woman.

"An understanding of population growth and how it affects the relationship between prey, predator, and environment, along with the ability to weed out undesirable elements for their survival, is expected of a hunter. Our trial will ask you to recognize and incapacitate the more problematic animals we bring before you."

After that lecture, Alius dragged Aer to sign up for the trials. Much to Aer's displeasure, the caretakers directed them toward the Perch when Alius had asked where to go.

"Aer, over there." Alius pointed to the lakeside at the bottom of the Perch's cliff, where the caretakers were handing out paper forms for the upcoming trials. As they approached, however, a voice stopped them.

"What are you two doing here?"

Alius, recognizing the voice as Gail's, spun around and gave a defiant glare. "We're here to participate in the trials. What's it to you?"

Gail pushed him aside. "Don't bother. They're not here for you."

Aer signaled for his brother to calm down.

Predictably, Alius ignored him. "Yeah? Then why is our participation required? Maybe some guys outside the Nesting Islands figured out that you guys from the Perch weren't all that special."

Gail grabbed Alius by the collar. Alius did the same.

"And what's this?" a deep voice rumbled behind them.

They all turned around. Head Caretaker Desen was standing right next to them.

"Nothing, Father," Gail said, letting Alius go.

"I would certainly hope so. It would be a disgrace for my son to embarrass me in front of everyone by getting into a fistfight in broad daylight."

The head caretaker then turned his attention to Aer and Alius.

"Charity Tree fledglings," he said disinterestedly. "I recommend you take what you need and leave."

Aer swallowed nervously. That wasn't a recommendation. It was a warning.

Alius angrily gathered a stack of participation forms by grabbing whatever he could from the nearby caretakers.

"Excuse us," Alius muttered, storming off.

Aer quietly followed before looking back, expecting Gail to gloat over how they had been chased away, but nothing of the sort came. Instead, Gail gave them a look of utter loathing, as if the brothers had wronged him somehow and managed to walk away scot-free.

Chapter 6: The First Trial

Aer yawned loudly, not even attempting to hide his drowsiness.

"Not much of a morning person, are you?" Nira asked.

"If possible, I'd like for the morning lights to be more considerate of me as a person and show up later in the day," Aer grumbled.

The two of them were out on the southeast edge of the Spiral Forest, practicing their Sky Control. Aer had been hoping for a break once the lectures had ended, but his brother, driven by his grudge against Gail and the head caretaker, had asked Nira to follow through on her offer of teaching them as soon as she was free.

She had agreed, but after a few days of practice, it became clear her lessons simply weren't helping Alius, a fact made only more apparent by Aer's rapid progress within the same time frame.

At the end of the week, Alius had asked Nira a question. "How well do you think we'll do in the trials if we continue like this?"

"Aer has some serious talent," Nira responded. "I'm certain most of the fledglings at the Perch took a lot longer to learn what we just went over. I think he could learn enough to not embarrass himself if we keep going at this rate, assuming he schedules some of the more competitive trials for later. As for you—"

"Stop. You don't need to say it." Alius sighed. "I think it would be more efficient if we played to our strengths. Aer clearly gets Sky Control better than I do. So he should try to get to the level where he can blow away the judges while I focus on what I can do: making sure the other fledglings here follow our lead."

From that day onward, Alius left home by himself early in the morning, leaving Aer alone to cram all the information Nira had been taught back at the Perch before the trials.

"Wonder what Alius is doing right now," Aer said to no one in particular.

"Aer, focus," Nira admonished, snapping his mind back to the present. "Do you remember what I said about breathing?"

"That there are certain types of air that we can and can't take into our body, right?"

"Right. The caretakers teach the Perch how to clean the air around them so they can breathe anywhere. Now, see if you can do the same and clean up the air around us."

"Is something wrong with it?"

"Why don't you check and see?"

Aer used his senses and felt tiny substances permeating the air surrounding him. He had gotten much better at perceiving things using his Sky Control since the forewarner's lecture. Nira had him consistently practicing the skill once she found out he could do it.

"What are these things?"

"Flower seeds. I think the trees around here are beginning to pollinate. Bad for anyone with allergies."

As if on cue, Aer started sneezing violently.

"Normally, I would let you learn it bit by bit, but we don't have much time before the trials," Nira said pitilessly. "We're staying here until you figure out how to clean the air yourself."

"You're terrible," Aer groaned. His nose was clogging up. He focused on the air around him once more then blew winds that combed over every seed in the vicinity. He then gathered them all in front of him and blew the mass as far from him as he could.

Nira looked surprised. "That was quick. I thought we would have to stay here the whole day before you managed something like that."

Aer blew his nose into a nearby leaf as a response.

A few minutes later, they moved on to their next lesson.

"Next, we're going to go over how to block winds from reaching certain places," Nira explained. "The caretakers consider this an exercise in control."

She then pointed to a branch above them. "See those leaves hanging off the branches there?"

Aer nodded.

"I want you to blow air on those leaves with everything you've got except the one hanging in the center. Make sure that one doesn't move an inch."

Aer stilled the air around the center leaf. He then blew forceful winds at the cluster of leaves. All but one of the leaves were blown off the branch. The one that remained, however, stayed completely motionless.

"Again, you got that a lot quicker than I expected," Nira noted, looking a little envious.

"That wasn't too different from changing the air to silence noise, honestly," Aer replied.

"Wait, you know how to do that?" Nira asked incredulously.

"Sound travels through the air. If you stop the air from moving, sound can't travel through it either," Aer explained.

"Sure, I know that," Nira stated. "But I didn't expect you to. Most fledglings I know don't. How did you learn this? You sure the caretakers didn't teach you anything?"

"I figured it out on my own," Aer answered. "Alius attracts a lot of unwanted attention, so I had to figure out some way to keep him quiet."

Alius's voice interrupted them. "I really hope that isn't the only reason you learned that trick."

Aer turned to face his brother, only to be greeted by Kiel's towering figure. Alius waved from behind him.

"What are you guys doing here?" Aer asked. "I thought you were on the Charity Tree, trying to rally everyone you could find."

"We were just about to do a head count of all the fledglings we convinced," Kiel replied.

"You want to join us?" Alius asked.

Aer personally didn't care all that much, but he could tell Alius wanted to show him their progress. "Sure, let's go."

"You guys go ahead. I'm heading back home. I don't feel like wheeling myself everywhere just to say hi to everyone," Nira said.

Aer walked around the Charity Tree with Alius and Kiel as they conferred with those they met on what they planned to do during the trials. Aer counted around three dozen fledglings who agreed to join them in appealing to the visitors, likely due to Kiel's influence.

"Not as much as I'd expected, to be honest," Kiel commented. "Think this many fledglings could make enough of an impact?"

"We might convince more if we ace the early trials," Alius murmured.

Aer silently agreed. Based on the reactions of the people they met, Aer could tell they shared a grudge against the Perch's fledglings but believed being overlooked in favor of them was a foregone conclusion. Surpassing them in the initial evaluations could certainly change a lot of minds.

Aer stopped. Why was he even humoring the idea? He didn't care how things turned out. The only reason he was doing all this was because Alius had been adamant in dragging him along.

He then felt it—breathing from three different sources trailing their movement. He darted behind one of the outer trees curving toward the center of the forest, where he spotted some fledglings spying on them. They were dressed far too nicely to be from the Charity Tree.

"Doesn't look like we're alone," Aer said.

Alius and Kiel looked to where Aer was staring. Once the eavesdroppers realized they were no longer hidden, they ran off.

Aer and Alius shared a look. Perch fledglings rarely ventured so far into the Spiral Forest.

"What are they doing here?" Kiel asked. "This is my territory. They should know to communicate with me if they have business here."

"Should we chase them?" Alius asked.

"You guys head back," Kiel replied. "I'll ask around and find out what's going on."

On their way home, Aer and Alius stopped by Nira's front door to fill her in on what had happened.

"You think they felt threatened by us?" Alius asked her, looking rather smug.

She immediately dismissed the idea. "Honestly? I doubt it. The Perch fledglings only care about jobs that require high levels of Sky Authority. The people here just aren't competitive enough in that area to worry them."

"As far as they know." Alius grinned at Aer. "Speaking of which, how's Aer doing?"

"He's a natural," Nira replied. "To a frightening degree. He intuitively understands how to manipulate the air around him. He has a surprising amount of raw power too. There are still some gaps in his technical skills, but he's learning quickly. He's also figured out a few tricks that aren't commonly taught back at the Perch. We should have started tutoring sooner. If we had more time, I think he could compete with the very best."

Aer felt a bit embarrassed by Nira's glowing assessment of him.

Alius, however, held his chest high, almost as if they were talking about him instead of Aer.

"I'm sure he'll be able to do that anyway," he declared proudly.

The brothers returned to their treehouse once they finished their conversation. Before Aer could sit down and relax, however, Alius dropped a stack of papers in front of him.

"What's this?" Aer asked.

"Entry forms. I plan on signing us up for every trial in this pile," Alius replied.

"You can't be serious."

"I am. What Gail said annoyed me, so I feel like we need to show the Perch up at everything."

Aer skimmed through the forms Alius handed him.

"You could have been a little pickier. Why do we even have the Caretaker's Trial application? I thought you hated the caretakers."

"I was just thinking that the caretakers stationed here at the Charity Tree do absolutely nothing. You do absolutely nothing unless I drag you out. It's the perfect job for you," Alius teased, snickering.

"Haha," Aer said dryly.

"Don't be like that. Look, if you don't like the idea of being a caretaker, you can be a performer instead. They apparently make a living by entertaining audiences in whatever way possible. Just imagine it, all those eyes staring at you, judging you if you screw up. Doesn't that sound like fun?"

Aer gave Alius a flat stare. They both knew he would sooner give up on human interactions altogether.

Alius laughed. "I'm joking. We're not really going to attend all these trials. They were just among the forms I grabbed. Besides, you still need time to practice so you can prove to the visitors that the caretakers made a mistake writing us off."

Aer sighed. "I still don't feel like that's possible."

"Well then, do your best to catch up for now."

"Easy for you to say. You're not the one competing."

Alius's face darkened. "I would if I could, Aer. Unfortunately, I don't seem to have the ability to do so. Believe me, if I could switch places with you, I'd do it in an instant."

Seeing Alius's mood drop, Aer tried to change the subject. "So? What trial did you want to sign us up for first?"

"The one for being a rain provider," Alius responded.

"And when does it happen?"

"Tomorrow."

"Alius!"

"It's fine! You'll do great."

"What's fine? The Perch fledglings will be entering with proper tutoring from the caretakers. I don't know the first thing about being a rain provider. How do you expect me to overcome that gap by tomorrow?"

"I said it's fine!" Alius insisted. "All we're supposed to do for this trial is run around the island. You know the terrain as well as anyone. You already know how to boost your movements with wind. You do it all the time. And Nira said it herself—the raw power of your Sky Authority isn't any worse than those at the Perch. You shouldn't have a handicap on this one."

"And you're sure that's all? We're just running around the island?"

"Positive!" Alius exclaimed. "The lecturer said it himself, didn't he? He doesn't expect us to move clouds yet. Instead, he's testing our speed and response time by seeing how quickly we can water the right places."

Aer stopped to contemplate his brother's words. Alius seemed to have given this some thought.

"All right, fine," Aer conceded. "Just give me some warning next time."

***

A knock on their door woke them the next morning. Opening it revealed Kiel standing in front of the doorway.

"Hey."

Aer took a step back as Alius shot forward to greet him. "You figure anything out?"

"I don't have any names, but it looks like someone tipped them off that we were gathering people to do well in the trials and discredit the selection process for the Blessed."

"So they came here to scout the competition?" Alius asked.

"That's what I'm guessing," Kiel replied. "I need to dig up some information to be sure, which is why I need you to handle recruiting by yourself. Feel free to mention my name if you need to be more persuasive."

"We were going to participate in the Rain Provider's Trial today," Aer interrupted. He was not risking being the only Charity Tree fledgling there.

"Ah, right. Never mind, then. I'll send some guys your way," Kiel said.

"Thank you," Alius replied. "See, Aer? Told you there's no handicap for you here."

"Not sure how having more people will help me do better in a jog across the island," Aer pointed out. "At least with this, I won't be the worst one participating."

"You need to stop thinking so negatively. I'm telling you, everything will work out." Alius grinned.

Alius's good mood was short-lived, however, with not a trace of his smile remaining by the time they reached the trial site.

"How fast do you think the people here are?" he asked anxiously. "You think I can outpace them just by running normally?"

"Why are you getting nervous now?" Aer asked, exasperated. "Where did all that confidence go?"

"I didn't think we'd have this many people watching us!" Alius exclaimed, pointing to the dozens of visitors who had come to observe the trial. "I'm used to the caretakers looking at us like dirt, but I don't want to embarrass myself in front of so many strangers, especially when they're the ones deciding our future."

While Aer understood how his brother felt, he also wanted to point out that it was Alius who had dragged them there while completely disregarding any apprehensions Aer may have had. Not wanting to get into an argument with Alius then and there, however, he stayed silent, instead focusing on what the adults observing them were saying.

"And I suppose those fledglings are from the Charity Tree?" he heard one ask.

"We get some stragglers who take part in the trials every Sky Cycle," another answered. "It can't be helped, especially since attendance in the trials is mandatory this time around."

"Still, having too many of them here can make it difficult to keep track of the ones who matter," a third voice echoed in his ears. "I wish they'd be more mindful of how much they get in the way."

Aer averted his gaze. He always hated drawing attention to himself because of moments like these.

It relieved both brothers when more Charity Tree fledglings arrived at the scene, drowning out their presence. It was easier to act normally when they weren't singled out by those watching. Soon enough, they were completely invisible, as hundreds of people had gathered in attendance.

Once all the participants were present, the lecturer who had explained the rain providers' duties stepped forward to give instructions.

"There are certainly more fledglings here than I expected," he commented, giving those from the Charity Tree a look of haughty disdain. "Do all of you have your forms for this trial?"

The lecturer then nodded as all the fledglings took out their forms.

"I will explain the rules, then," the wiry man stated, handing out a stack of papers as well as some torso-sized water containers with numbers boldly emblazoned on them and straps attached to the sides. "Everyone take a map and a container."

Aer took one of the water containers and staggered slightly under its weight.

"You are to carry those on your back," the lecturer instructed. "If you will all look at your maps, you can see that we have laid down multiple posts on the landmarks of this island. We will measure your ability to make quick judgments and pass by all these posts and water them in the shortest time possible. You may take whatever path you'd like to reach your destination and use any method you find suitable so long as all the points on your map have been watered. It is, however, crucial that you are certain of the direction you are heading before proceeding. Depending on what path you take, you may find yourself at a dead end."

Aer examined his map. Markers were placed on numerous stone pillars as well as the Perch's cliff, the Charity Tree, the Western and Eastern Borders, along with the edges of the lakes to the north and south.

"I, along with other rain providers, will proctor this trial, keeping track of your progress by the numbers put on your water containers," the lecturer explained. "At some points in the trial, we proctors will shout, 'Fire!' to which those nearby will be expected to drop everything and head straight toward said proctors to water the areas they are standing over. The 'flames' that you put out will be marked and deducted from your overall time. Once you're finished, you are to turn in your map, your water container, and your trial form to the rain provider stationed there."

The lecturer then looked over the fledglings from the Charity Tree and sighed. "I don't exactly expect an amazing performance from all who showed up today, but try not to embarrass yourselves in front of the visitors. Once you are ready, we'll begin."

Tensions among the fledglings rose as everyone moved to the starting point for the trial. Aer looked over his map one last time, plotting out a route in his head.

As soon as the proctor gave the signal to start, a large gust of wind blew through the area. Both Aer and Alius as well as a good number of Charity Tree fledglings were blown off their feet. By the time they had gotten back up and reoriented themselves, the fledglings from the Perch had left them behind.

"You can't be serious!" Alius exclaimed. "There has to be some sort of rule against this!"

Aer looked up at the lecturer, who, despite looking surprised by the attack, dismissed Alius's complaints and did nothing to reprimand the offending fledglings.

"Apparently not," Aer said.

"Of course not," Alius muttered. "Fair. Impartial. No bias whatsoever."

"Do you remember where to go to get to the lake?" Aer looked at the map in his hands. The details of the route he had planned to follow had been knocked out of his head.

"It was to the north of the Spiral Forest, wasn't it? We're currently at the Western Borders, and the Charity Tree is over there, so probably that way?" Alius pointed.

"All right, then, we should hit the two stone pillars on our way to the Perch," Aer replied, looking at the map. "After that, we should head south and water all the landmarks there and circle around the Southern Lake to the Eastern Borders before heading toward the Charity Tree, then the Northern Lake. Or we could go up to the Northern Lake right after the Perch and follow the river down to reach the Southern Lake, making stops at all the landmarks along the way. After that, we would head straight for the Eastern Borders."

"Better go with the latter," Alius suggested. "We need to run through all these places. We can stay hydrated if we follow the river. We would also know where we're going the entire time."

"Right." Aer rushed forward. He then looked back at his brother and the other Charity Tree fledglings as they struggled to keep up.

"Don't worry about me!" Alius reassured him. "Keep going!"

Aer nodded before running ahead.

***

"Fire!"

A stampede of fledglings rushed to the source of the voice. A good number of those from the Perch stared at Aer in both annoyance and bewilderment as he overtook them to reach the proctor first.

Aer took a deep breath as he watered the ground underneath the proctor. He then quickly resumed his sprint to avoid retaliation from the fledglings behind him.

As his brother had assured him, he didn't seem to be at a disadvantage in terms of speed. In fact, judging from the others' pace, he was probably one of the faster fledglings there.

However, that was only true when he remained unimpeded. Some of the more belligerent fledglings had taken to blowing air currents to knock him off his feet whenever he passed them, disorienting him again and again. In the time it took him to get back up, they had already completed their tasks and left.

He sighed. The fledglings from the Perch didn't seem to take kindly to someone from the Charity Tree outpacing them. If he didn't want to keep getting blown away, he would have to move stealthily and avoid facing large groups. Fortunately, he knew the area like the back of his hand. Alius had dragged him around the stone pillars for lectures long before this trial.

Aer took a detour from the straight dirt road, avoiding the group of fledglings that had run past him. Once he saw the stone pillar he was supposed to reach, he blew himself straight toward it.

A proctor for the trial observed him with some sort of viewing lens as he passed, writing something down as Aer watered the stone pillar.

Aer continued the trial like that for a while. Whenever he sensed a large group ahead, he would diverge from the straight path to circle around them. While this would mean a longer path to travel, it was better than the alternative of being blown away yet again.

Reaching the lake, he washed his sweaty face. Unexpectedly, he was in better physical condition than most of the fledglings he came across. Whether it was because Alius was always dragging him around or some other reason, he wasn't sure. Whatever it was, he wasn't complaining.

Taking another look at his map, Aer compared the distance he had crossed with the distance he had left. With the late start he had gotten and the detours he had taken, he doubted he could catch up to the Perch's faster fledglings.

Well, that's to be expected. Next, I should follow the river from here through the Spiral Forest to the Southern Lake. There are a lot of landmarks down there… Wait a minute.

Aer was quite familiar with that part of the island, having frequently used the rivers as a water source. He knew the way the river flowed and at which point of the river he would have to stop. He was also aware of what type of trees existed in the area. Aer looked at the map again as an idea took root in his mind.

There's no way this will work, the rational side of Aer's brain criticized as he looked for a large enough tree near the lake, one made up of a relatively light wood. Once he found one, he wrenched it out of the wet soil with the most powerful air currents he could muster, tearing apart many of its branches as he did so. He then blew the whole thing onto the river.

Confirming the tree could float, Aer emptied his water container and leapt onto the tree. He then tied his map and the baggiest part of his clothing onto the branches that were sturdy enough to still be on the tree. Making sure he had a firm grip, he blew the tree forward using his clothing as a sail. He used any spare focus he had to blow air currents to tilt himself and the tree in the proper direction so he didn't tip over.

Despite his initial doubts, the makeshift raft carried him down the rapid flow of the river, saving him a lot of energy and time to his next destination while letting him avoid coming face-to-face with other fledglings. Pleasantly surprised by his success, he sped the tree along the river's path until he got close to his next stop. He then used his Sky Control to blow the river's water onto the nearby landmarks, spraying them down with gusts of water and mist. After confirming that the bewildered proctor watching over the location had spotted him holding up his water container, Aer continued down the river until he had gotten close to the next landmark on his map, where he repeated the process.

Good thing Alius said to head to the lake first, Aer thought once he reached the end of the river. He took one last drink as he refilled his water container.

***

As Atravel's morning lights dimmed, Aer left the Southern Lake and reentered the Spiral Forest on his way to the Eastern Borders, his last stop. He was certain he was the first fledgling from the Charity Tree to do so.

He sensed another group in front of him. Looking forward, he spotted Gail near the front of the group, looking very winded. With a burst of air, he closed the distance between himself and the others. Alius would be elated if he could pass Gail here.

They hadn't noticed him yet. He needed some way to pass the others without being spotted; there were too many fledglings to fight against, and getting blown back so late in the race would stop him from overtaking anybody.

Aer observed his surroundings, seeking alternative paths before pausing. He was familiar with that location as well. It was the part of the forest where Nira had brought him to learn how to clean the air around him.

Aer stopped for a moment as another idea struck him. He quickly scanned the air for pollen and gathered all he could find to his location. Condensing as much as he could into a giant ball, Aer then fired his creation at the group.

The ball of pollen burst on impact, its contents spreading throughout the group of fledglings.

Unfortunately, Gail didn't seem to be allergic, as his pace remained unchanged.

Most of the people running alongside him, however, weren't so lucky. Many started sneezing violently, while others dropped to their knees, clutching at their throats and noses as they tried to cough out what they'd breathed in. Aer had gathered enough seeds to make the surrounding air a visible mix of brown and yellow.

Aer hurriedly filtered out the air in front of him and ran past them before they had the chance to understand what was going on.

Aer exited the forest right behind the few fledglings that had managed to ignore the pollen. He had nowhere left to hide past that point, but there also wasn't much distance left to reach the Eastern Borders.

The fledglings before him fired air currents at him as soon as they were aware of his presence. Not many people were left to do so, however, and Aer managed to blow some wind to shield himself.

I might just be able to do this.

The distance between him and the other fledglings had disappeared. Aer was met with expressions of exhaustion and annoyance as he passed them one by one. It didn't take long for him to be neck and neck with Gail, who led the pack.

Unable to resist, Aer turned to face the tall boy. What kind of face would he make when he was overtaken?

Gail roared in response.

Aer flinched. Whatever he had expected, it wasn't that. Unfortunately, that moment of shock was all the others needed. One of the fledglings quickly fired an air current at Aer's feet, causing him to be thrown into the air and land face-first in the dirt.

Aer groaned. It was a dirty trick, but it had stopped him right in his tracks.

By the time he recovered, Gail and the others had already reached the rain provider. Gail then dropped to his knees, panting heavily. Clearly, this was also his last stop.

Aer wiped off the dirt on his clothes and staggered toward the goal, trying his best to ignore the ringing in his head as he unloaded the full contents of his water container on it.

"Well done," the proctor standing over the landmark complimented him as he took Aer's map and water container. He then gave Aer a sheet of paper in exchange.

"A recommendation," the proctor said as Aer stared at him quizzically. "If you feel as if this is your calling, then hand this form to the head rain provider once you leave the Nesting Islands. He'll take care of things from there."

***

It wasn't until long after the evening lights came that Aer spotted Alius leading the Charity Tree's fledglings toward his location.

"Aer! How did you do?"

"I did all right, I think. Was one of the first to finish."

"Oh, good. You managed to finish. The rest of us didn't reach all the landmarks. Who got here before you?"

Aer pointed toward the mentioned people.

Alius's face twisted in displeasure. "Gail too?"

"I *just* lost out to him."

"None of the adults called them out for attacking us during the trial?" Alius asked incredulously.

Aer shook his head.

Alius raised his voice for everybody to hear.

"Guess sabotaging people you don't like is also part of being a provider!" he yelled as some of the Charity Tree fledglings around them cheered. "You guys hear that! I'm not taking it back! You all can go—"

Alius stopped as Gail came up to him and shoved both him and Aer to the ground.

"What are you doing?" Alius shouted indignantly.

"What did you guys do?" Gail shouted back. "You knew you couldn't take us on in a fair competition, so you sabotaged us instead?"

Aer blinked. Gail looked outright furious.

Alius was just as angry. "What? You guys were the ones who kept blowing us off course!"

"Who cares! I can't believe how badly you humiliated us in front of everybody!"

"What are you talking about?" Aer asked.

"None of us from the Perch felt right this morning. You guys did something to make sure we weren't moving the way we were supposed to."

Alius looked skeptical. "You have proof we did anything?"

"Like I need that. Who else would benefit from this? I should have expected something like this from you ingrates at the Charity Tree. You're all worthless wastes of resources who can't appreciate our generosity in providing for you when we shouldn't even tolerate such filth living next to—"

Before Aer could register what had happened, Alius had risen to his feet and punched Gail in the jaw. Shock flashed across Gail's face before he charged at Alius. It didn't take long for things to devolve into an all-out brawl between the two.

Aer grabbed at Gail's clothing and tried to drag him away from his brother as nearby enforcers ran up to them and pulled Alius back.

"What do you think you are doing, fledgling?" one of them asked. "Why are you attacking the head caretaker's son?"

"I just felt like rearranging that ugly mess he calls a face, sir," Alius said defiantly.

Aer groaned. This wasn't going to end well.

The enforcer blinked. "Would you care to repeat that? I *must* have misheard you."

Aer shook his head frantically, trying to signal his brother to stop, but Alius refused to back down.

"You know what I said. I meant every word."

"The head caretaker will be informed of this incident. He is undoubtedly more capable than I of issuing a proper punishment for your behavior. You are to obey his words and accept whatever punishment he gives you. And if you two fail to comply… well, I'm sure he can think of what to do from there."

"Wait. *You two?*" Aer asked incredulously.

"Yes. *You two.* You also laid your hands on the head caretaker's son." The enforcer pointed to Aer's hands pulling at Gail's clothes. "I didn't see you do anything to stop your brother either. Do your best to beg the caretakers for a light punishment."

The enforcers left before Aer could protest.

Gail sneered.

"Serves you right," he spat before yanking his clothes from Aer's grip and walking away.

"*Good job*, Alius," Aer grumbled.

Alius rolled his eyes. "Oh, give me a break. He deserved way worse than anything I could have done."

Chapter 7: The Perch

My son asked me a curious question the other day. He wanted me to explain what differentiated us from other people. This was something I had never even thought to question previously, it being so self-evident. Our behavior, our understanding, and our respect toward the Great Arbiter clearly set us apart from the rest of the world. When I answered him as such, he then suggested that perhaps things would be different had others been raised under the same conditions as we were.

What a pointless thing to brood over. I surmise the argument he had earlier with those Charity Tree fledglings is still on his mind. Nevertheless, I explained to him that since Sky Authority was a gift from the Great Arbiter, those most loved by him have the greatest Sky Authority and the highest positions in Atravel. I told him not to feel sorry for the less fortunate, reasoning that there must be something fundamentally wrong with them if the Great Arbiter put them in that situation, alluding to the stories of how Atravel was first formed and how the Great Arbiter only saved those who no longer desired conflict to prove my point.

Regrettably, he didn't seem entirely convinced. I may have to discuss this with him in more detail during our next conversation.

Soleil willed the beating in her chest to settle as she took her place between Atravel's representatives for the Advent Trials. They had gathered on the isle held above the center of the Nesting Islands to discuss the fledglings' results so far. Listening to their discussion were the many guests she had convinced to come down to Atravel's lowest islands for her cause—which, of course, included Emissary Striaen.

An old woman, who Soleil knew to be an accomplished forewarner, started the meeting. "Now then, I believe our first order of business should be to discuss Orator Mistral's issue with the management of the Nesting Islands. I believe she criticized the caretakers and called them negligent in their duties?"

"Yes. Not the first time we've heard this complaint in Atravel's history, but it rarely gains this much support," a sharply dressed man Soleil didn't recognize answered. "May I ask how the fledglings under your supervision did?"

"The attendance rate was higher than in the trials of previous Sky Cycles, likely due to the trials being made mandatory this time around. The results observed in my trial are also somewhat lower than expected. Putting those two facts together, I'd say that the higher turnout of fledglings only participating to meet their requirements brought down the average. But if we adjust for that, the overall level of the fledglings I tested is comparable to those of past participants. Nothing too out of the ordinary here, really."

"Similar results on my end." The man nodded. "What about you, Rain Provider Lien?"

The proctor being questioned cleared his throat. "Ignoring the much higher participation levels from those less qualified and the slower average times that would naturally result, participant performance was all around weaker compared to their predecessors. Comically enough, one of the best times was even given to us by a Charity Tree fledgling. There have also been cries of foul play by nearly all participants, but most proctors overseeing the examination agree no observable rule violation took place."

"Ah, I saw that trial," the sharply dressed man commented. "A fight broke out in the end, didn't it?"

The old woman then turned to Head Caretaker Desen. "What are your thoughts on this? Perhaps you could shed some light onto the behavior of the fledglings under your care?"

"I say we take the fledglings from the Perch at their word about being sabotaged while ignoring the complaints of those from the Charity Tree," the head caretaker responded dismissively. "The Charity Tree fledglings have proven to be a bunch of savages. Attacking the victors the way they did was disgraceful. Their word is hardly reliable."

Murmurs of assent passed throughout the room.

Soleil took a deep breath as she prepared her argument. She couldn't let that snake lead everyone else's opinions unchallenged.

"*One* of the Charity Tree fledglings exhibited that type of behavior," she pointed out. "Just one. Hardly fair to group them all under the actions of an individual. Furthermore, I don't think the Perch fledglings were particularly well behaved either. They interfered with the Charity Tree fledglings at every opportunity they had in the trial."

"The proctors judged their actions to be within the rules, isn't that right?" the head caretaker asked Rain Provider Lien, to which the man reluctantly nodded.

"Rain providers need to properly communicate with other people in emergency situations," the proctor stated nervously, looking as if he was trying to convince himself. "Which is why all participants are expected to deal with unexpected obstacles within the trial. That includes other competitors."

"While that may be true, I still think the Perch's fledglings went against the spirit of the trial by specifically targeting those from the Charity Tree," Soleil said sharply. "Furthermore, this wasn't an Enforcer's Trial. The primary purpose was to evaluate an individual's ability to cross distances, not their ability to subdue others."

"And those from the Charity Tree weren't doing the same?" the head caretaker shot back. "If anything, I think it showed that the participants from the Perch had the foresight to predict danger and prepare beforehand."

Emissary Striaen cleared his throat. Everyone else immediately fell silent.

"So, you hold that the fledglings from the Charity Tree were at fault and that the Perch did well to preemptively act against them?" the old man inquired, to which Head Caretaker Desen nodded. "Either way, it doesn't reflect well on your tutelage. Aren't you supposed to be making sure that both sides are properly raised to avoid situations like this? Perhaps Orator Mistral has a point."

The head caretaker paled. Soleil smiled at the sight.

"With all due respect, Emissary Striaen, it's hardly fair to hold us accountable for the actions of those predisposed to be incompetent and unwise," the head caretaker said pleadingly. "I said it before—those who suffer, suffer because of their wrongdoing before the Great Arbiter."

Emissary Striaen frowned.

While Soleil was delighted over how the emissary seemed to dislike how the head caretaker put down those at the Charity Tree, she couldn't fathom why. Out of all the people in Atravel, none were as privileged as he. Unlike everyone else here, who had all clawed their way to reach as high as they did, Emissary Striaen had been born into success. It was rumored that the Great Arbiter had personally blessed those of his lineage all the way back to Atravel's beginnings, as many of his ancestors had possessed unmatched Sky Authorities and had become emissaries before him. If anything, Soleil had expected the old man to hold disdain for those less able and wholeheartedly agree with the head caretaker's unempathetic views.

"Perhaps. We shall see," Emissary Striaen said after a long pause.

A moment passed as everyone made sure the emissary had finished talking. He clearly had more he wanted to say, but nothing else came.

"While the Rain Provider's Trial results are rather strange, I feel as if it is too early to make any conclusions at this point," the sharply dressed man said after the tense silence.

"Quite right!" the head caretaker hastily agreed. "Moving on to a more important subject, I have been getting complaints that these buildings are getting too crowded. For that, I apologize. More people showed up to observe the Advent Trials than we caretakers could have anticipated. Therefore, I would like to offer our esteemed visitors a chance to stay with us at the Nesting Islands."

The head caretaker then shot a quick glare at Soleil. "I know some of you have already taken advantage of our hospitality, but I would like more of our visitors to feel welcome. Surely, spending more time with our caretakers will quell any doubts you may have of them."

***

"Well, here we are," Aer whispered to his brother. Alius gave a barely audible grunt in response.

They stood on a marble terrace placed on top of the Perch's cliff. One very annoyed-looking caretaker assigned to the Charity Tree had knocked on their treehouse door that morning and led them all the way there to carry out their punishment.

The brothers looked around. All the Nesting Island's landmarks were visible from that height and angle. They just needed to turn toward the Spiral Forest to look down on the Charity Tree and spot the platform on which they resided.

The caretaker who had led them there knocked on the door of the building attached to the terrace. Eventually it opened, and out came Head Caretaker Desen.

"So, you're here," he said to the twins while dismissing the caretaker who had escorted them with a wave. "I heard from the enforcers that you two attacked my son after he completed the Rain Provider's Trial before you. How petty."

"He attacked us fir—" Alius started before Aer elbowed him.

The head caretaker didn't seem to notice. "Normally, a very painful punishment would be in order. Fortunately for you two, visitors from the other islands will be lodging at the Perch soon, and we caretakers are short a few hands, which is why your punishment will be to clean the Perch's cliffside buildings to make sure everything is as it should be. My son will be there to make sure you properly maintain the area."

Not bothering to close the door, the head caretaker walked away from them and spoke into a gray tube connected to the wall of his building. His voice then echoed throughout the cliff. "Gail Desen. Come out to the top of the Perch. I repeat, Gail Desen, come out to the top of the Perch."

Some time passed before Gail entered the scene, eyeing the twins as he came close. "Yes, Father?"

"Get some mops and cleaning rags. You are to manage these two as they help the caretakers sanitize the Perch. Head down to the bottom of the cliff and work your way up from there. The visitors will be staying on the top floor of the Perch, so the caretakers will be focusing most of their cleaning efforts here. But it is possible some of them will want to check out the lower structures, so I want all the areas you cover to shine once you're done."

"Yes, sir," Gail answered, sneering at the brothers as he did so.

***

"You missed a spot! Are those eyes for show, you moron? I said to *clean* this wall!" Gail shouted hoarsely as he threw a wet rag at them.

Aer could feel Alius fuming next to him. They were cleaning the exterior of one of the Perch's buildings while Gail sat in some shade, barking orders at them. He was clearly relishing the control he had over them, as he happily hurled abusive language at them every chance he could.

The few times Alius had tried to insult Gail back, Aer quickly silenced the air surrounding him. Alius glared at Aer in frustration whenever he did so but sighed in grudging acceptance once the moment passed. Starting another fight with Gail would not end well for them.

Aer's blood also boiled at Gail's insults, but he kept himself under control by distracting himself with his surroundings. The space held a lot of curious sights that he couldn't see in the Charity Tree. For one thing, the buildings all jutted out of the cliffside. How did the buildings placed higher on the Perch not fall off the cliff?

Alius also looked curious about their surroundings. Even if he wasn't willing to admit it, Aer knew Alius was dying to see how the accommodations compared to the Charity Tree's treehouses.

They would have their chance to inspect things more closely soon enough, as Gail ordered them to head inside once they were finished cleaning the exterior.

Aer got a better idea of how the buildings were held up once they went inside. As they stepped into a hallway connected to a bunch of smaller compartments, it was apparent that the interior stretched deeply into the cliff. The portions visible from the outside only made up a fraction of the living space. Assuming the buildings above were built the same way, the jutting parts were likely held in place by the sheer volume of space lodged inside the cliff.

Aer began wondering how someone would go about building all that. Were the caves already a part of the cliffside before the buildings were built? Or were they all man-made? Was that a common way to build structures outside the Charity Tree?

He was shaken out of his thoughts when Gail ordered him and Alius to mop up the hallway. As they cleaned their way inside, they passed by several learning facilities, shops, and lodging spaces. The brothers noticed with no little envy that even the shabbiest lodging space had its own bathroom, bookshelves, kitchen, and bed.

"This place is huge," Alius whispered to Aer, voicing their thoughts. "Does every fledgling here get their own room? That's too much, even for the Perch."

Gail, who had been listening in from behind, interrupted them.

"Get to work," he said, looking smug at their awed faces. "You're here to clean, not gawk at things you'll never have."

As Aer and Alius continued cleaning, some of the fledglings they passed decided to entertain themselves by throwing garbage over the places they had just scoured.

Fortunately, the caretakers in the area didn't seem to find that amusing—not out of any sympathy toward the brothers but because they themselves were quite busy making sure everything was presentable for the visitors.

"That's ten marks for each of you," one of them admonished while jotting something down. "We need this place spotless as quickly as possible, and you're all throwing *trash* onto the floor?"

"Hold on!" one fledgling protested. "That'll decrease my rank! I need next week's allowance to buy—"

"Looks like you won't be able to buy it, then," the caretaker said dismissively. "Next time, think before you act."

Aer stopped cleaning for a moment to listen. He and Alius had picked up quite a bit on how the Perch was run in their brief time there. The conversation cleared up the last details in his mind.

From what they had gathered, the fledglings there were all scored relative to one another on their behavior and academic performance. Those of a higher rank were given more currency to spend and were assigned to better rooms, with those of the highest ranks accepted into the Blessed, which gave them a level of authority over the other fledglings. In contrast, those barely hanging on to the lowest ranks were threatened with being evicted to the Charity Tree.

A ruthlessly methodical system, all in all.

Upon noticing Aer listening in, the penalized group of fledglings drew near, presumably to take out their frustrations.

"Why are *they* here in the first place?" one asked, just loud enough for the twins to hear.

"I heard the caretakers needed more people to clean this place for the visitors."

"Aren't they just making it dirtier by being here? I know I wouldn't want to touch anything that someone from the Charity Tree put their hands on."

Alius gave them a rude gesture before Gail kicked him in the back.

"What's wrong with everyone here?" Alius muttered angrily.

Aer frowned. He knew that interacting with the residents wouldn't be pleasant, but things could get tiring quickly if every encounter was going to turn out like this.

Fortunately, the fledglings they caught sight of next were too busy to spare them any attention. Rather, they were too focused on some sort of competition among themselves.

Scattered throughout the room were pillars of varying heights. The competing fledglings jumped from one pillar to another, trying to gain as much altitude as possible while the opposing team tried to knock them down with gusts of wind. All the participants carried a wooden bar, and a goalpost stood at each end of the room. The goalposts had notches, and the primary aim seemed to be for those running to land their bar at the highest notch they could reach while the goal's defender moved to intercept them. The points were then tallied based on the height of the notch where each attacker landed their bar.

The fledglings gave an impressive display of acrobatics while playing, dashing around the room while doing somersaults and flips in the air to avoid the others. They were clearly using Sky Control, as the speed and heights they reached were far too great to be purely physical.

What surprised Aer the most, however, was how active the caretakers were. Compared to the ones stationed at the Charity Tree, they were far more involved with the fledglings' activities.

"Your footwork was sloppier than usual," Aer overheard a caretaker say to one of the fledglings. "Remember to take breaths between steps when you're not directly in the action. Focus on lighter landings so you can recover immediately. Pay attention to your opponent's movements."

"Yes, sir," the fledgling panted.

"They're pretty good," Aer muttered.

The fledglings there were faster than the ones he'd competed against in the Rain Provider's Trial. Comparing their speed to his own, Aer wasn't sure he could outpace them in a footrace as easily as he had the day before.

Alius seemed to be thinking along the same lines, as he bit his lip in worry while observing the competing fledglings.

Looking at them, Gail smiled smugly. "Of course they're good. The only reason someone like you could even hope to compete in the Rain Provider's Trial is because of your sabotage."

Aer felt a flash of panic as Alius whirled to face Gail.

Just let it go! Aer screamed in his head. *Don't get us into more trouble!*

"You were blabbering about this nonsense yesterday too," Alius said mockingly. "Again, what are you talking about?"

"Don't act innocent." Gail glared at them. "We were tipped off that fledglings at the Charity Tree were planning to outdo us in the Advent Trials using whatever means possible. You guys spoke to that invalid, Kiel, so you could outperform us in front of the visitors."

"And?"

"The morning before the Rain Provider's Trial, we received anonymous packages of food. We all assumed they were gifts from the visitors who wanted to support us. We learned during the trial that everyone who had eaten from the packages couldn't move properly. The only ones who have anything to gain from sabotaging us are you guys. It's not hard to add everything up and figure out what happened."

"You sure about that?" Alius asked. "You really think a bunch of Charity Tree fledglings could walk around the Perch unnoticed? Where would we even get this food? The only stuff we get to eat is whatever we can grab off the Charity Tree."

Gail paused. "Maybe you didn't do it directly. You could have bribed someone here to do it for you."

"What could we possibly offer someone who lives here? In case you didn't notice, you guys already have *everything*," Alius countered, gesturing at their surroundings.

"Kiel might have been able to negotiate. Isn't his influence the reason you sought him out?"

"Yeah. We wanted more people to join us, and he has a lot of sway with everyone at the Charity Tree. We didn't team up with him so he could sabotage you."

Gail turned away, scoffing. "Right. I'm sure."

The rest of the day dragged on as the two continued cleaning the Perch under Gail's orders. By the time they finished for the day, the sky had grown dark.

The brothers couldn't help but pay attention to the little fires that had been lit to brighten the insides of the Perch. As those living in the Charity Tree were prohibited from creating flames, sights like this were a rare occurrence for them.

Aer stretched his limbs. His muscles ached. Alius looked similarly worn out.

"Slow," Gail criticized. "We haven't even finished the lowest floor, and you guys did such a sloppy job. But it's late, and I want to sleep. Go home. I'll have one of your caretakers bring you back here tomorrow."

After Gail dismissed them and threw them out of the Perch, Alius tapped Aer's shoulder.

Aer sighed. He wasn't in the best mood. "What is it?"

"I need to talk to Kiel. Let's head to his house before heading home."

***

Kiel was not happy when Alius knocked on his door.

"Where were you two? You were supposed to talk to me after the Rain Provider's Trial ended so we could discuss our next move. Instead, you completely disappeared on me for the entire day? What time do you think it is?"

Aer, feeling overwhelmed, stayed silent as Alius relayed the day's events to him.

Kiel grimaced. "What a disaster. I was hoping you two would help me on my trials, but that's impossible if you're stuck there. How much longer do you think this punishment will take?"

"As long as Gail wants. Considering how mad he is about how the trial went, it might take quite a while."

"*Wonderful,*" Kiel fumed. "A punishment that goes on as long as that spoiled brat feels like it should. Just great."

Alius stared at Kiel. "That reminds me, I wanted to ask you something."

"What is it?"

"How familiar are you and Gail with each other? He seemed to know you personally, called you an invalid. Judging from the way you're talking, you seem to have a grudge against him too."

Kiel paused. "He's my younger brother."

"Wait, what?" Aer and Alius both exclaimed.

"Well, half brother to be precise," Kiel explained. "Gail was born from an affair."

"How have we never heard about this?" Alius asked as Aer stared in shock.

"Because my father would much rather pretend I don't exist. I've never really lived up to my father's standards. Once he learned how Gail was gifted in Sky Control, he divorced my mother, married Gail's, and pretended things have always been that way."

Alius looked abashed. "I'm sorry."

"Forget it. I got over it a long time ago," Kiel said dismissively. "So, Mr. Perfect Son called me an invalid, did he? Did he say anything else about me?"

"He thinks you sabotaged them by somehow poisoning their food before it started," Alius answered. "Thinks you pulled a few strings to make it happen."

"Ridiculous," Kiel immediately replied. "I didn't go anywhere near the Perch the past few days, nor did I talk to any of the fledglings living there, so how could I poison their food?"

"Right? Of course you didn't," Alius said. "You were with me the whole time we were recruiting other fledglings. You wouldn't have had the time to pull off something like that. Gail just wants to find some way to blame us for not doing as well as he wanted."

Kiel nodded. "Right. You can vouch for my innocence. Not that the Perch will consider you a reliable witness."

"Right." Alius sighed. "If they did, we wouldn't be stuck in this mess."

Kiel stared at Alius for a moment before smiling. "Not to make light of your punishment, but this is a good opportunity. You guys now have a reason to be at the Perch. Think you can do a little scouting for me?"

"Scouting?" Aer asked.

"What you said about Gail bothers me. He said that someone tipped them off about what we were doing? It would explain why Perch fledglings were scouting us out, but I'm curious who told them."

"It's not like we were keeping it a secret," Aer said. "You guys were recruiting other people pretty openly."

"Yes, but the Perch normally wouldn't pay attention to the Charity Tree's activities. I'm just wondering who went out of their way to tell them."

"The caretakers?" Alius offered. "The ones stationed here could have caught wind of it and passed it on to the Perch."

Kiel shook his head. "I don't think so. I speak with the caretakers here often to get an idea of what's going on around the island. You guys might not know this, but the caretakers also have a hierarchy among themselves. The ones stationed here are ones that couldn't get a position at the Perch. I expect them to be mostly apathetic toward the whole thing. If anything, they're probably rooting for those in the Perch to fail. New positions might open up if the Perch caretakers do badly."

Alius looked at Kiel doubtfully. "You sure about that? I never got the feeling that they were on our side."

"Because they aren't," Kiel said flatly. "I'm sure they don't care about *us* one bit. But most of the caretakers' influence comes from the fact that they watch over and teach those who grow up to be important people. Without that, they're nothing. If they're here at the Charity Tree, it means that they're pretty much at a dead end career-wise. My point is that the caretakers I know don't have the motivation to rat us out, and I know everyone here."

"Everyone?" Aer asked skeptically.

"Look, I'm not all that good at Sky Control either," Kiel said. "And my relatives couldn't care less about me. If dear old Dad has taught me anything, it's how important the right connections are. I need to do what I can to get by."

***

The twins walked back home while reflecting on what they had learned.

"I had no idea," Alius told Aer as he shut their front door. "I had no idea Kiel was Gail's brother. I had no idea that the caretakers stationed here have no future and are treated as less than those at the Perch."

"That last bit does explain a lot about how little they care about us," Aer noted. "They have no reason to."

Alius's shoulders slumped. "I don't like it. That could be us in the future. We need to work harder on the trials. I was so sure that the only reason you didn't crush everyone in the Rain Provider's Trial was because they kept blowing you off course. But after seeing some of them move in the Perch today, I don't feel as confident."

"That been on your mind this whole time?" Aer asked.

"Yeah." Alius sighed. "We shouldn't be wasting our time in the Perch. We need Nira to teach you more about Sky Control. But—"

"But we can't do that while we're still being punished for *your* attack on Gail, right?" Aer irritably finished for him. He still found it grossly unfair that he was being punished for Alius's bad temper.

Alius looked regretful. "Yeah, that's my mistake. I shouldn't have punched him. I still think he deserved it, but doing it in front of all those caretakers might not have been the smartest move. I'll find us a way out of this. In the meantime, let's keep observing the people there to see if we can figure out who gave us away. Maybe we'll learn something."

Aer said nothing as he lay on the floor in a huff. He doubted they would find anything.

CHAPTER 8: PITCH AND NOISE

My son is quickly coming of age. I am praying for his future, for him to excel at everything he puts his mind to. May he not stray from the path I and many of our ancestors have laid out for him.

As Aer predicted, their attempts to gather information from the Perch bore little fruit despite their best efforts. None of the fledglings there wanted to be within the same room as them, much less share useful information. When they did interact with the brothers, it was solely to demean them. Gail watching over them further complicated things, as he happily jumped at the opportunity to punish them whenever they dared focus on anything other than cleaning.

Once the day ended, both Aer and Alius fell to the floor in exhaustion. Gail had not gone easy on them today, either, despite them still being sore from yesterday's efforts.

"Don't come back here for the next three days," Gail said as they struggled to get back to their feet.

The brothers stared up at Gail in surprise. Was he giving them a break?

"I need to participate in some trials. I can't be bothered to look over you two during that time. We'll continue this once I'm done."

"Of course that's why. When will we be free to go for good?" Alius asked.

"Once you're done," Gail answered unhelpfully.

"But if we keep going like this, Aer and I won't have time to practice for our trials."

"Well, that's too bad, isn't it?" Gail sneered. "This is a punishment for a reason. Figure something out."

Aer watched over Alius warily as he gave Gail a hateful glare.

"What about you?" Alius asked Gail, not even trying to hide the spite in his voice. "Shouldn't you be practicing more for your own trials? Do you really have enough free time to be watching over us day after day?"

"Father told me to keep a close eye on you."

"So you're getting punished with us?" Alius taunted. "Good. At least there's some form of justice here."

Gail sneered. "What are you talking about? The likes of you two clearly can't be let loose on the Perch without supervision, and the caretakers are busy preparing the fledglings for the trials and cleaning the upper buildings of the Perch. If anything, it's a sign of Father's trust in me that I'm the only one watching you."

"Keep telling yourself that. You're stuck with us until we finish. The time you spend doing this is time you could have spent preparing for your own trials. Doesn't look like your father thinks much of your time or effort if he thinks it's best spent watching us."

That shut Gail up. A moment of tense silence passed before he angrily chased them out of the Perch. The brothers, needing no encouragement to leave, fled the scene.

"What are you doing, provoking him?" Aer berated Alius once they were out of earshot. "Why do you think we're here in the first place?"

"I was hoping that this punishment might get cut short if I pointed out how he's being held down here as much as we are," Alius said. "Guess it didn't work. At the very least, I wanted him to quit and have someone else oversee us."

"I wish." Aer sighed. "Next time, tell me before you act on your *brilliant* ideas."

"Nothing bad happened, right?" Alius said defensively. "Anyway, we're free for the next three days. Let's not waste time. You focus on studying with Nira. I'll tell you if there's any trial we can participate in and do well in during that time."

Aer frowned, silently comparing the day's work with the amount of time he would likely have to spend practicing. His workload didn't seem any lighter outside the Perch.

***

"You two got yourselves into a real mess, huh?" Nira commented the next morning, once Alius had finished explaining where they had been for the past two days.

"Tell me about it," the brothers answered simultaneously.

"I'm a bit surprised by your punishment, though," Nira remarked. "I expected something like a beating or a public humiliation, maybe both at the same time. Cleaning the Perch is usually a punishment reserved for Perch fledglings."

"They said they needed to make the place presentable for the visitors," Aer explained.

"Still, they must be seriously undermanned if they're letting fledglings from the Charity Tree inside the place," Nira replied. "It makes sense, though. Most of the Perch's fledglings are focusing on the trials. Their performance reflects how well the caretakers have been doing, so it's no wonder they don't want to interrupt them. You guys, on the other hand, they couldn't care less about. You two are pretty much free labor."

"Which is why we need to make the most out of this break. Who knows how long we're going to be there for?" Alius said. "So please. I need you to teach Aer as much as you can as quickly as possible."

"Seeing how much I'm doing to help you guys out, can I ask for a favor in exchange?" Nira asked.

"Name it," Alius replied immediately.

"I need to participate in some trials myself. Obviously, the more physical ones are out of my reach, but if it's solely based on Sky Control, I should be able to do all right."

"So go ahead and sign up for them," Alius replied. "We have plenty of forms back home. I'll grab them right now."

True to his word, Alius left and returned with the entire stack of participation forms he had grabbed from the caretakers. "Here. Help yourself."

"There's just one more thing." Nira's voice shrank. "The thing is, I don't want to face the Perch again by myself. So I was wondering if you guys could sign up for the ones I wanted to attend."

Alius's face brightened. "Sure, we can do that." He handed Nira the stack of papers. "Tell me which ones you want to go for. Aer and I will back you up." Alius then faced Aer. "You're okay with that, right?"

Aer nodded wearily. It was more work, but Nira was helping them too much for him to refuse in good conscience.

Nira looked over the stack and handed Alius back one of the forms.

"The Conductor's Trial?" Alius asked as he grabbed the sheet of paper.

"Yeah. I used to play music quite a bit back when I was in the Perch. Might as well take advantage of that experience."

"That's fine, but we don't know the first thing about music," Aer interjected. "We can't really back you up there."

"I can teach you," Nira stated. "We still have plenty of time before the Conductor's Trial, and you already have some idea of how sound travels through the air. I'm sure you can at least master the basics before then."

"Still, wouldn't we just drag down your performance?" Aer asked.

"The thing is, there's only so many sounds I can make by myself at one time. It would be a more solid performance if I could have some people backing me up."

"All right." Alius nodded. "What else?"

Nira looked over the forms for a moment before handing Alius another sheet of paper.

Alius raised an eyebrow. "The Falconry Trial?"

"Yeah. With my legs being the way they are, I thought it would be useful to get a bird to follow my instructions and reach things I can't grab."

"Ah. That makes sense," Alius replied. "It's a practical choice."

Nira then handed him back the applications.

"Wait, is that all?" Alius asked. "You know you need to participate in at least three, right?"

"I'll think about the last one later. For now, I want to focus on these two."

Alius nodded. "All right. I'm going to talk to Kiel about what we should do from now on. You teach Aer what he needs to know for those two trials."

***

"Well then, Aer, what do you know about sound?" Nira asked once he wheeled her down the Charity Tree to a nearby stream.

They had moved here at Nira's suggestion; the caretakers stationed near their homes would likely not appreciate the excessive noise they were about to make.

"Things make noise. It travels to our ears. Our ears try to make sense of it all," Aer said plainly.

"That's simplifying a lot of details, but yes. Do you know how to adjust that noise?"

"No."

"Then we'll go over that first. Go to the other end of the river and try to hold a conversation with me from there."

Following her instructions, Aer jumped to the other side.

"Can you hear me?" he asked.

"Stop, stop. You're just shouting," Nira replied. "Don't put your lungs into it. Use Sky Control to change the air so your voice carries over. You know how to silence noise, right? Instead of stopping the sounds completely, try to sustain those vibrations through the air as far as you can."

"Like this?" Aer let the air transmit his voice to her.

"Better. Next, try to change the pitch of the sound by altering the air."

"How?"

"Try changing how it moves through the air. The higher the frequency, the higher pitched the noise becomes."

Aer stared at her blankly. "Sorry, could you repeat that?"

"Right, they don't really teach things like this here. Maybe visualizing it will help. Look at that pond over there."

Aer looked to where Nira was pointing at a pool of water formed by a split in the river.

Nira then picked up a small rock and tossed it in. "See those ripples on the surface? Just imagine sound traveling through the air in the same way. The bigger the waves are, the louder the noise. The closer the waves are to each other, the higher pitched the noise."

"Oh, is that how it works?" Aer asked. He then visualized the ripples on the air around him and imagined moving the waves closer together.

"How's this?" he asked before closing his mouth in surprise. His voice had become childishly high-pitched.

Nira laughed. "Good job. Now, try to control it better."

Aer spent the next few hours getting the hang of modifying the noises he made. By the end of the day, he could perfectly control the volume and pitch of the words coming out of his mouth.

Nira gave a sign of approval. "As expected, you mastered that quickly. We might actually do well in the Conductor's Trial."

"I don't think Alius and I will be making decent music by that time, even if I can control the noise and pitch."

"I'll try to keep your melodies simple. I'll take center stage; you two just need to harmonize with me."

***

"We're taking the Mechanic's Trial," Alius announced once Aer returned home.

Aer gave him an exasperated glare. The evening lights, signaling nighttime, had fully seeped through the clouds. It was too late in the day for Alius to spring the information on him with no warning.

"It happens the day after tomorrow. Kiel and I agreed it was the best one we could take on short notice," Alius explained. "Being a mechanic doesn't require *any* Sky Control, so there's nothing you have to learn beforehand. Plus, I want some options for my own future."

"Fine." Aer sighed. "Is that all? I kind of expected you to sign us up for everything you could during this time."

"While I'd like to take as many trials as we can, I'm not sure we can properly compete against the Perch fledglings in all of them," Alius replied, looking bitter. "Based on what we saw in the Perch, we're missing years of basic training and instruction in a lot of subjects. Instead, we'll pick our trials carefully and focus our time and attention on standing out in those. So for now, we'll go with just this one."

"How restrained of you," Aer remarked sarcastically. "Anyway, the day after that trial, we'll be back at the Perch to clean up their messes. I'm guessing you just want me to keep practicing with Nira until then?"

"Yeah. I'll go with you tomorrow too. I should know what we're going to play in the Conductor's Trial."

The next day, Aer continued practicing altering sounds with Nira while Alius stood back and listened.

"You've gotten quite good," Nira commented. "Let's try one last thing. I'm going to shout over you while covering my ears. Try speaking to me using Sky Control to silence my voice while making yours impossible to ignore."

Aer did so perfectly while Alius watched in fascination.

"Very nice. I'm convinced that you can control noise perfectly." Nira nodded approvingly. "Let's move on to the music portion. Here, try singing with me. I want you to replicate what I do in a lower tone."

Nira then began to sing. Aer tried to follow along, using Sky Control to lower his pitch, but both Alius and Nira winced.

"We might have a problem here. You can change the sounds well enough. It's just that you're completely tone deaf," Nira said.

"Well, I'm sorry! I never learned how to sing, okay?"

"Still, Aer. That was terrible," Alius remarked. "Even I could do better than that."

"You want to try?" Nira asked him.

Alius nodded and replicated Nira's melody. It wasn't as elegant as hers, but there was a world of difference between his and Aer's performance.

"How?" Aer asked his brother. He had never heard Alius sing in his life.

"It wasn't that hard. I just copied what Nira did."

Aer tried again, attempting to repeat what he had just heard. He stopped when both Nira and Alius grimaced.

"Your voice doesn't carry over well." Nira buried her face in her palms. "It trails off at the most important parts. The timing of your intonations is off. There's no melody to it either."

"That might be because I'm used to speaking for the two of us," Alius theorized. "He might not be able to project his voice properly because he's not used to talking."

"If that's the case… Aer, can you play an instrument?"

"I've never even touched one."

Nira pulled something from a bag attached to the back of her wheelchair. "Try this, then."

"What is it?"

"A flute. I brought a bunch of musical instruments for you two to practice with for the Conductor's Trial. Now, pay attention to my fingers."

She then blew into the flute and played a simple tune.

Nira handed Aer another flute. "Try to repeat what I just did."

Aer blew into it while clumsily imitating her fingers' movements. "How'd I do?"

"Horrible. Same problem as your singing. You can control your volume and pitch just fine, but you don't have a good grasp on what the notes you're making are supposed to sound like. Plus, your rhythm is all over the place," Nira said. "Alius. You try."

Alius blew into the instrument. The notes were squeaky, but they were still recognizable as the same ones Nira had played, unlike Aer's.

Alius looked delighted as they continued their music session. Nira taught the brothers the basics of pitch, intonation, and flow while showing them how to read musical notes on paper. But in the end, only Alius gave a passable imitation with all the instruments Nira had brought. Aer, to his dismay, proved hopeless with every single one.

"Okay, I clearly have no musical talent whatsoever." Aer sighed, throwing his hands up in frustration. "Let's call it a day. Alius can focus on the musical portion for us instead. I don't think I can play anything like this."

Nira nodded wearily. "That… might be for the best. Alius seems to be much better at this. I was hoping all of us would play something, seeing how few people we have, but it'll take too much time to get you to a passable level with, well, *any instrument*. I don't think my ears can take any more of this either."

Alius started laughing before badly disguising it as a coughing fit when Aer glared at him. Aer then rolled his eyes. His brother was enjoying this reversal of their usual situation a bit too much.

After seeing Nira off and returning home, the brothers began discussing their plans for the upcoming Mechanic's Trial.

"They want us to explain the inner workings of the devices that the lecturer showed everyone, right?" Aer asked. "But we've never even seen those things aside from his presentation and don't know anything about how they function. So how are we supposed to get ready?"

"You worry too much," Alius replied dismissively. "The fact that they didn't mention anything in particular probably means there isn't anything specific we have to know before then."

Aer couldn't help but feel that this was wishful thinking on Alius's part and had a hard time falling asleep as all the worst-case scenarios played out in his head.

***

Once morning arrived, the brothers headed toward the site of the Mechanic's Trial, located rather close to the Charity Tree.

Aer observed the participants as they entered the scene. Not many people from the Perch were taking part in the trial, and only a handful of caretakers were supervising them as well. The Charity Tree fledglings far outnumbered everyone else there.

Kiel, who was participating himself, nodded to them from a distance.

Aer breathed a sigh of relief. The atmosphere didn't feel nearly as oppressive as it had in the Rain Provider's Trial.

"Gather around!" an adult nearby called out.

The fledglings turned toward the adult's voice. The middle-aged man, who Aer assumed to be the proctor, stood between several other adults in front of a wide table.

Aer took a better look at the table behind them. There, various objects that he didn't recognize were haphazardly laid in a pile.

"Some of you may not understand what you see here," the proctor stated. "Allow me to explain. These are all well-established, mass-produced devices used by the rest of Atravel for their convenience. Now, the reason I'm showing you this is because few fledglings have any prior knowledge about this subject. The caretakers prefer to put their focus on fields that more clearly show how blessed we've been by the Great Arbiter."

The proctor then gave a bitter smile. "That doesn't mean this line of work is any less important, just less noticed. It does, however, mean we can't expect much from you children at this point. All we can test for is your diligence."

The proctor then gestured toward the table. "Those wishing to participate in this trial will pick a device laid out on this table. You will have a week to study what you chose and explain what it does and how it performs its function. To make sure you have a firm understanding of what you're studying and how useful they can be in your everyday life, you will be asked to find a nonstandard way of using the device you choose. We will give them to you in bulk and hand you each a textbook explaining their functions, after which you can experiment with them."

The proctor then gestured toward the table. "Gather around and pick out the objects you're interested in."

At those words, the crowd immediately rushed toward him.

Aer patiently waited for the crowd of fledglings to clear, but Alius grabbed him and pushed his way through to get to the table as quickly as possible. By the time it was their turn, however, the table had practically been wiped clean.

"Not much left, is there?" Alius asked the proctor.

The proctor lowered his gaze. "I apologize. I honestly didn't expect this many fledglings to participate. Usually, this trial is a lot less popular."

Aer fought the urge to blame Alius, but his brother's efforts to get more people from the Charity Tree invested in the trials had clearly backfired.

Alius, oblivious to Aer's annoyance, stared down at the table. All that was left were a dozen finger-sized cylindrical silver objects that seemed to have been ignored by the other fledglings for appearing too plain and simple.

"These are recorders," the proctor explained. "They preserve whatever noise is placed into them for future use by engraving sound vibrations as marks within their interior. Blowing a set amount of air into one afterward triggers certain vibrations within the mechanism, which are directed by the previously made marks to recreate the noises stored into it. This allows one to hear messages left behind by others even if they aren't physically present. Many influential figures use these to send urgent instructions, warnings, or secrets to those they can't meet in person."

Aer looked around. No other fledglings seemed to be going for the devices. Perhaps they couldn't think of an alternative use for them and were waiting for the proctors to restock with more complex equipment.

Aer considered doing the same. It would be easier to do well in that portion of the trial with a multipurpose tool. There would be much more to explain as well, giving additional opportunities to impress the proctor.

None of that mattered, however, as his brother grabbed all the silver devices with no hesitation whatsoever.

The proctor laughed. "I appreciate you taking those off my hands," he said, handing them both a textbook. "I look forward to seeing how you use them for the trial."

The proctor then clapped his hands and addressed everyone in the area. "Due to unforeseen circumstances, it appears that not everyone managed to grab a device. We will hold another examination at a later date for those who came out empty-handed. The rest of you have your assignments! We'll be in this area for the next week if you wish to complete the trial."

***

"Well, this is a problem," Aer said as he and Alius pored over the textbook. "I thought this trial would be over by the end of the day. But it turned out to be a long-term examination."

"It's a bit different from what I expected, but what's the problem?" Alius asked.

"The problem is, we're going back to cleaning the Perch tomorrow," Aer answered. "When will we find the time for this?"

"Oh, right," Alius said. "We might be in for some sleepless nights."

Aer let his irritation show on his face. "Just one more problem to deal with. Couldn't you have held back a little? We could have delayed this trial and had more to work with if you decided not to grab anything."

"Things aren't that bad," Alius replied, trying to reassure him. "At the very least, we don't have a lot of competition here. Barely anyone from the Perch attended. And not everyone in the Charity Tree even knows how to read. They have to pass *some* people, and we're probably some of their best candidates."

Aer reluctantly nodded. That was true. Many of the fledglings' educations here were limited to what they had learned from the caretakers as infants. They had the option to learn more by attending public lectures that the caretakers held within the stone pillars of the island, but because of the hostility that many caretakers and Perch fledglings showed to those of the Charity Tree, most didn't. As a result, there were more people here who didn't know how to read than those who did.

Aer and Alius had learned as much as they did because Alius had frequently dragged Aer to those lectures while completely disregarding everyone's hostility. As the main reason the lectures were held in the stone pillars instead of the Perch was because the caretakers wanted to keep up appearances of being fair supervisors to all fledglings, they couldn't turn the brothers away without blatantly contradicting themselves.

"Anyway, knowing all this is quite useful," Alius continued, looking back at the textbook. "As Charity Tree fledglings, we don't see tools like these very often. But they'll be more common once we leave this island. At the very least, it's a good chance to learn more about the world outside. Just look at some of the stuff written in here."

Alius pointed to a picture of a long gray object that Aer couldn't name but was certain he had seen before.

"Apparently, it's a broadcasting device," Alius said. "By setting this up inside a building, people can communicate with others over a long distance by increasing and modulating the sound waves traveling through it. Sound waves, huh? Good thing Nira explained this subject recently. It would be even more helpful if we saw it in action."

"We did," Aer stated, recalling where he had seen the device. "The head caretaker used it in front of us a few days ago."

"Wait, he did?" Alius asked.

"Yeah, he used it to call Gail over when we first went to the Perch, remember?" Aer said.

"Oh, yeah. It's a shame the proctor didn't give us one to use."

"I think an entire pipe system would be harder to carry than these devices you grabbed without thinking." Aer looked at the dozen recorders Alius had brought home. "Seriously, what are we going to do with all these?"

"You never know. Might as well take whatever we can. The proctor said that these things allow people to leave messages for others. We can definitely find some use…" Alius trailed off.

"What is it?" Aer asked.

Alius seemed deep in thought. "Hey, Aer. You can control how sound travels now, right?"

"Yeah."

"And you can control the pitch of your voice too?"

"Yes. Why?"

"Could you try imitating Gail's voice for a second?"

Aer, curious as to what Alius was contemplating, emitted a noise while changing the pitch of his voice.

"Go lower, lower," Alius said. "Wait, that's too much. Go back."

"Care to explain?" Aer asked in a voice quite different from his own.

"Later. Just keep going… all right, stop there."

"This okay?"

"Not quite. You're supposed to be imitating Gail right now. You need to have a more stuck-up tone. Just imagine everybody else as garbage underneath your feet."

"How dare you talk to me in that manner!" Aer joked in Gail's voice. "Clearly, you Charity Tree fledglings need to be reminded of your place!"

A grin slowly crept across Alius's face.

"I think I might have figured out a way to get us out of our punishment," Alius said as he picked up a recorder. "Now, repeat what I say in that voice."

Chapter 9:
Tools, Schemes, and Spite

My son's behavior has changed recently. The caretakers tell me he has started questioning some of our conventional wisdom since the last time I saw him. They also say he disappears for long stretches of time without a proper explanation of where he's been. I am growing worried. I may have to examine him in secret once I have the time.

Aer's stomach sank when a caretaker showed up at their doorstep to drag him and Alius back to the Perch. So many things could go wrong with what they were about to do.

After Aer had finished following his brother's directions the night before, Alius had explained how they were going to free themselves from their punishment. Aer had noticed more than a few flaws in his plan, but Alius had fallen asleep before Aer could find the words to voice his objections. And now that a caretaker had arrived, Aer couldn't help but feel that he had missed his chance to dissuade Alius from carrying out his scheme. They certainly couldn't discuss it with other people present.

The issue was quickly put to the back of Aer's mind once they started cleaning, however. Gail clearly still carried a grudge based on the way he was treating them.

Sweat rolled down Aer's back as he and Alius frantically struggled to wipe the floor clean.

"Don't you dare stop," Gail threatened. "I don't care if you collapse. I want this done as quickly as possible."

Neither Aer nor Alius answered him. Or rather, they couldn't. Neither had the energy to spare. Unlike the previous days, Gail's voice held no glee as he ordered them around.

"I would have done better if I weren't stuck supervising you two," Gail muttered. "I shouldn't be wasting my time here."

From that, Aer could guess that the trials Gail had taken time off for had gone poorly. He seemed to be seriously considering what Alius had said to him the last time they met.

While the brothers got some small satisfaction over the fact that he was no longer laughing at their situation, it was overshadowed by the exhaustion produced by their much heavier workload. Any attempts at a reprieve had ended with Gail pushing them even harder.

Alius made several attempts to tell Gail off before Aer signaled for him to settle down. They both knew that no one would take their side. All Gail would have to do was say that they were slacking off, and the caretakers would agree with him. The best thing they could do was bear with it.

As Gail's orders became increasingly strenuous, however, Aer reconsidered their options and thought about making a run for it. But Alius shook his head when he spotted Aer eyeing the exit. The caretakers could just follow them back to their treehouse. Trying to hide wouldn't do them any good either. The caretakers had proved they were familiar with every hiding spot on the island back when they searched the Charity Tree. Furthermore, the brothers would have to come out to participate in any future trials.

In the end, both Aer and Alius silently came to the same conclusion. If they were going to get out of this mess, it would have to be with the caretakers' consent.

It was still bright outside when they finished cleaning their first floor for the day. A stark contrast compared to last time, where they couldn't even finish one by nightfall.

"Well, looks like we're done here. Let's go, Alius." Aer kept his tone casual as he tried to hurry away from Gail.

Gail immediately shot him down. "And where do you think you're going? We're going for five floors today. If I see you trying to leave again before we're done, I'll increase the number to seven. Also, don't think that just because we're going faster that you get to be sloppier. I still want everything spotless."

Aer's heart sank. *Five?* There was no way they could go on for that long.

"That's ridiculous!" Alius shouted, voicing Aer's thoughts. "It took everything we had to clean this floor this quickly! We would have to *pick up* the pace to finish five floors today!"

Gail gave them a nasty smirk. "Deal with it. If I have to suffer through this, I'll at least make sure you two suffer more."

***

Aer briefly wondered if his arms would fall out of their sockets after they finished cleaning two more floors. For the past few hours, he had blown gusts to push himself in the right direction, as he no longer physically had the energy to move. Alius, who could do no such thing, looked like he was on the verge of collapse. Gail couldn't have cared less, however, as he ignored their protests while ordering them to move to the next building.

Aer lifted Alius, who was even more exhausted than he was, and dragged him forward. Last night, his brother had been convinced that they would be free from their punishment, but Aer wasn't optimistic. They were too busy to attempt anything at that moment.

Gail stopped shouting orders at the brothers as soon as they entered their fourth floor, however, as the caretakers were having a disagreement with a visitor close by.

Gail shoved them back outside, clearly not wanting to alert the adults to their presence. The brothers, grateful for the small reprieve, leaned against the wall of the building as the adults' voices rang out.

"Head Huntress Islea," a caretaker called out, "there's no need for you to come this far down. You know we have room for you up at the top."

"It's fine," the woman responded in a rather distinct tone that Aer was certain he had heard somewhere before. "The building up top is far too luxurious for me. I'm used to sleeping in more sparse conditions."

The caretakers exchanged nervous whispers before continuing the conversation. "Yes, but we'd rather you didn't step into this place."

"Is my presence here a problem?"

"Not at all! It's just that someone of your status clearly deserves more than what we can offer here."

"As I've said, I'm used to living in unflattering conditions. Even this building might be too much for me," the woman said.

"Then let's discuss where you would like to stay at."

"I can figure that out for myself, thank you," the woman answered before she exited the building.

Upon seeing her face, Aer remembered where he had heard her voice before. She was the lecturer for the Hunter's Trial. She briefly looked him and his brother over before she walked away. Aer then heard discontented whispering among the caretakers the woman had left behind.

Gail snarled at the brothers once the disgruntled caretakers left the area. "And who gave you permission to laze around? Move your filthy backs off the wall and get back to work!"

The brothers groaned as their quick break ended. Or so they thought. It wasn't long before they ran into a much bigger commotion between the caretakers and another visitor.

"Please make your lodgings at the top of the Perch, Orator Mistral. It'll be easier for us to accommodate you there," one of the caretakers said, looking rather annoyed.

"While I appreciate the sentiment, I feel as if I would get a better picture of how the fledglings live if I stayed here," the visitor replied.

"Are you implying that we have something to hide about the fledglings here?" another caretaker asked, looking somewhat offended.

"Not at all," the visitor said dismissively. "Now, if I could get a few more caretakers to show me around, that would be lovely."

Gail, looking impatient, hurriedly shoved Aer and Alius to another part of the building, only to spot another visitor walking around by himself.

Frustrated, Gail continued to drag Aer and Alius around the Perch in search of a place to clean with no visitors. He clearly didn't want their downtrodden appearance staining the Perch's perfect image.

Eventually, Gail left the brothers by themselves as he walked away to talk to a group of fledglings.

"What's going on here?" Gail asked. "Why are there so many visitors here?"

"Don't ask me," one responded with a gruff voice. "Your father offered to house them here. The caretakers have all been rushing to make everything presentable."

"I know that. But why are they coming down to the lower buildings? They were supposed to stay at the top of the Perch."

"Looks like a lot of them were curious as to what the caretakers were doing down here," another fledgling joined in. "You think they'll stay in the Charity Tree next?"

"That would be a laugh," Gail scoffed.

"Speaking of which, why are they here?" one of them asked, pointing toward Aer and Alius, staring at their dirty clothes.

"They're here to help clean as punishment. I'm stuck making sure they don't mess things up," Gail answered.

"What are they being punished for?"

"These idiots sabotaged the Rain Provider's Trial then tried to attack me after I beat them anyway."

"Are you serious? Leave it to Charity Tree fledglings to screw up that badly. Think I can get them to do some things for me?"

"Sure, why not?" Gail shrugged. "Get some use out of them while they're here."

"Hey, you two! Get over here!"

Aer and Alius shared a look of exasperation before reluctantly stepping forward.

"I present to you Dumb and Dumber," Gail said. "Which one's which, I'll leave for you all to decide."

The other fledglings laughed. One of the taller fledglings shoved some hollow wooden containers into their hands.

"What's this?" Alius asked.

"Canteens. I want you to fill them with water and bring them back to us."

"And why would I do that?"

"Because I said so. You should be thanking me. Being our errand boys is probably the most meaningful thing you two will do in your entire lives."

Aer ignored him, trying not to focus too hard on his words. Reacting would only invite him to continue. Alius, however, shook in anger.

The older fledgling didn't fail to notice. "What, you have something to say? Then say it."

Aer gave Alius a warning glance, signaling him to not fall for the bait. Alius nodded and stayed silent.

But the older fledgling wasn't done. "What, can't you speak properly? You have some sort of brain damage? Guess that's to be expected. The reason you're staying there and not here *is* because you lot at the Charity Tree are all dysfunctional in some way."

That was Alius's breaking point.

"You must be so proud of yourselves," Alius spat. "Is it a requirement at the Perch to look down on everybody else?"

"We have a reason to," Gail sneered. "In case you didn't notice, we're the ones the caretakers chose to represent the Nesting Islands."

"Big words for someone whose entire existence is defined by how well their father sucked up to people better than him!" Alius taunted.

Gail's face twisted hatefully. He grabbed Alius's collar and yanked him forward. Alius responded in kind, pulling on Gail's clothes.

Aer glanced nervously between the two, looking for a way to deescalate the situation. He then saw Alius slip something into Gail's pocket and froze. This was the opportunity his brother had been searching for the entire day. Alius was going ahead with his plan.

Gail, thankfully, didn't seem to notice. He was too preoccupied with telling Alius off.

"Who gave you permission to lay your hands on me? Honestly, why do people like you still exist? I thought the Great Arbiter let all the worthless parts of humanity die off when he created Atravel."

The tension in the room broke as a caretaker barged onto the scene.

"What are you all doing?" he hollered. "If you have the time to stand around, then go and prepare more for the trials!"

Hearing that, the Perch fledglings looked away nervously and made a hasty retreat.

All except for Gail. "They've been assigned to clean the Perch," he said, pointing to Aer and Alius. "I need to supervise them."

"Well, get to it, then," the caretaker replied. "This place doesn't look any cleaner than before."

"That's not my fault," Gail said, loud enough for everyone to hear. "These guys stain wherever they go just by existing. Blame my father for setting them up to *clean*, of all things."

The fledglings still within earshot laughed before departing.

Alius suddenly started deliberately rummaging through his clothes, giving Aer a knowing look as he did so.

"What are you doing?" Aer asked, knowing full well what was happening.

"Just making sure I have everything. I thought I saw one of those fledglings picking the others' pockets earlier," Alius said rather loudly.

"Don't be ridiculous," Gail interrupted. "They're not you. The people here wouldn't be so unrefined as to steal from others."

"You sure about that?" Alius asked. "You really know exactly what everyone here would or wouldn't do? Then again, it doesn't matter to me if you get pickpocketed, so feel free to ignore me."

Gail frowned and quietly started checking his pockets before pulling out a small silver recorder.

"When did I get this?" Gail asked, puzzled.

"I don't know," Alius lied. "What is it?"

"Nothing I would expect a Charity Tree fledgling to know anything about," Gail said rudely before muttering to himself, "Someone must have left a message for me."

A hushed, raspy voice came out of the recorder as Gail blew into it. "Gail Desen, please come out to the Eastern Borders alone as soon as you get this message. As a proctor, I would like to discuss your results in the previous trial and what it'll mean for your future. Do not discuss this with other people."

Gail blinked in surprise before looking back at Aer and Alius.

"Just stay there for now!" he shouted. "Make sure none of the visitors see you!"

"So we're really going through with this?" Aer asked his brother once Gail left them alone.

Alius blinked. "Obviously. Why else would I set that up?"

"We can still stop here, you know," Aer said. "So many things could go wrong with your plan."

"But Gail didn't notice you were the one speaking in that recording." Alius grinned. "Things have gone perfectly so far. Now, quick, we have to get to the top of the Perch before he comes back. We're going to make him regret everything he's done these past few days."

"You do remember why we're here in the first place?" Aer asked. "If we get caught—"

"Then we'll just have to not get caught."

"And if we do?"

"So, you're okay with him treating us like this?" Alius snapped.

"No!" Aer snapped back. "That's why I don't want you to do anything. The sooner we're done with this and don't have to interact with the Perch, the better!"

"Yeah, that's why I've planned this out. Now, come on. I need you to come with me."

A moment of silence passed before Aer gave in.

"This better work," he said, fully aware that Alius would go by himself if he didn't tag along. Aer was sorely tempted to let him do so, but they would likely be punished as a pair if Alius got caught. And Aer had no confidence in his brother's ability to handle things subtly.

They hiked to the top of the Perch, pushing through the strain on their bodies as they snuck around any caretakers they heard coming along the way. Fortunately, most were too preoccupied with the visitors to pay the brothers any attention, so it was easy to stay out of sight so long as they remained vigilant.

The biggest problem came when they had to exit a building to enter the one above it. The Perch's buildings were all connected to one another by stone staircases, each brightly lit by an ascending row of lanterns. There was nowhere to hide on the steps, so they had to make sure no one was there before hurrying their way up.

Aer's anxiety spiked at those moments. The potential consequences of being discovered made his aversion to other people's gazes worse than usual. He also couldn't shake off the feeling that someone had been following them all this time. Whenever he stopped to observe his surroundings, however, he found no one.

Hearing footsteps approaching as they entered their next stone staircase, they both backed away and hid in a corner.

"As you can see, we spare no effort in teaching our future generations," someone declared in a high-pitched voice. "The rumors going around about our negligence are unfounded."

"Yes, I see. What about those from outside the Perch?" someone else asked.

"Ah, yes. They're there, too, I suppose," the person with the high-pitched voice answered. "Unfortunately, we do have to prioritize those who can make use of our tutelage. It would be wasted effort otherwise. Now, if you'll follow me, I'll take you to your rooms."

"Lousy caretaker," Alius muttered once the adults had gone. "As if you care one bit about what you're saying. You just want to look good in front of other people."

Aer quickly looked down and memorized the path they had come from as they ascended to a higher floor.

"Just making sure we can find our way back," he explained when Alius gave him a questioning stare. "You brought the right recorders, didn't you?"

"Yeah, don't worry." Alius nodded. "I double-checked them last night. Here. You'll need this one."

Once they reached the terrace at the top of the cliff, they looked around to confirm no bystanders lingered nearby. As soon as they were certain they were alone, Aer leapt to the top of Head Caretaker Desen's roof. Aer then gave Alius the signal, prompting him to knock on the door.

The head caretaker peered outside and scoffed once he saw who it was.

"What are you doing here?" he asked menacingly. "You're supposed to be with Gail, cleaning the lower floors."

"A caretaker told me to drop everything and give you this." Alius said, holding out a silver recorder.

The head caretaker reached for the recorder only for Alius to quickly step back before he could take it. Looking annoyed, the head caretaker came out of his home and reached for it again, only for Alius to take another few steps back.

"What are you doing?" the head caretaker growled.

"Sorry, involuntary reflex," Alius responded. "I get like this when people try to grab at me."

The head caretaker marched angrily toward Alius, who kept stepping back, and took the recorder from his hands. As Alius led the head caretaker away, Aer jumped down, softening and silencing his landing with the proper application of Sky Control. He then entered the head caretaker's home and hid in the corner of the room.

The recording of his caretaker imitation echoed from outside. "Head Caretaker Desen, I asked a fledgling who looked free to take this message to you. I don't have much time to explain, but the visitors are growing dissatisfied with our services. We require your presence at the bottom floor immediately."

"Where were you handed this?" Aer heard the head caretaker growl at Alius once the recording ended.

"On the bottom floor," Alius replied. Aer could tell that he was restraining himself from snidely saying, *Where else?* just from his tone.

"Lead me there," the head caretaker ordered.

Aer heard the head caretaker close and lock the door with a key before barking orders at Alius as they walked down the Perch's cliff.

Aer waited several minutes before unlocking the door and peeking outside, making sure that the head caretaker and Alius had left the vicinity. He then sighed in relief and searched the room. Unbelievably enough, everything so far had gone exactly as his brother had planned. Those recordings Aer had prepared last night by altering his voice with Sky Control had successfully fooled both Gail and the head caretaker. Now, just one remained.

Finding the gray tube that both he and Alius had studied the night before attached to the wall, Aer took a deep breath to calm his nerves before holding out the recorder Alius had given him to broadcast its contents to the rest of the Perch.

A speech rang out through the buildings. "Hello, everybody. This is Gail Desen. I am speaking to you right now to explain a few things about my recent actions."

Aer's heart thumped in his chest as he willed himself to not run out of the room. He couldn't leave until the recording had finished, but if a caretaker came to check out what was going on while he was still there…

"Recently, my father has placed some heavy expectations on me along with others of the Perch to excel in the coming trials. To meet my father's demands, I sabotaged the Charity Tree fledglings, trying to make them look even worse than they usually do so that we would look better in comparison. When things failed to go my way despite all this, I blamed the closest Charity Tree fledglings I could find and falsely accused them of sabotaging me, as such lowborn trash deserved. However, I believe that the Great Arbiter is now moving me to confess my faults to you all, admonishing me for using such underhanded tactics. So here I am. I ask the Great Arbiter to forgive me for my mistakes."

As soon as the message ended, Aer grabbed the recorder and rushed straight for the exit, making sure to take any evidence of his presence with him. Unfortunately, still fatigued from the work earlier, he stumbled and collapsed at the doorway.

Aer swore in frustration. That broadcast had doubtlessly stirred up everyone close by. It would be all over for him if he got caught exiting the head caretaker's home.

Forcing himself to his feet, Aer opened the door.

To his horror, someone was already waiting for him on the other side.

Chapter 10: Discovered

It is my opinion that every event is a result of the Great Arbiter's machinations. From every conversation we have, to every action we take, to the roles we fulfill throughout our lives, all was planned from the very beginning by the Great Arbiter, who sees the effect such details will have with perfect clarity. There are no blind spots in his absolute knowledge.

The person outside wasn't the head caretaker. They weren't someone who reported directly to him either. No, standing at the door was the visitor who had left the caretakers to examine the Perch by herself, the one they referred to as Head Huntress Islea.

The fact that she wasn't from the Perch did little to calm Aer down; anyone could tell just by looking at his tattered clothes that he wasn't supposed to be there.

"You there, boy," the woman called.

"Yes?" Aer replied warily.

"If you have enough free time to be wandering around, I would like you to guide me through this place. As a visitor, I'm quite unfamiliar with the area."

Aer blinked. She wasn't questioning why someone like him had just exited the head caretaker's home. "Ah, sure."

Aer made his way to her side, eager to distance himself from the scene as quickly as he could. Did she really not notice anything?

He stayed silent as they descended the Perch. Thankfully, the head huntress was taking paths that let them avoid being seen by others. Why that was, he hadn't quite figured out.

In the meantime, chaos echoed throughout the building below. It appeared as if his announcement had caused quite the uproar throughout the Perch, though he didn't get close enough to make out what they were saying. Aer patted himself down, confirming he hadn't left anything incriminating behind in the head caretaker's home.

He didn't dare let himself feel relieved, however. The head huntress had yet to reprimand or punish him, but she could easily report where he had been once the caretakers started asking questions. That she had been silent throughout the entire trip didn't help his sense of unease. Why did she ask him to be a guide if she didn't have questions about the place?

Not that he would have been able to answer any questions about the Perch, even if she did ask. If anything, she knew the place better than he did, as she was the one leading them down.

The head huntress then spoke, interrupting his thoughts. "How do you feel about the Perch?"

It took Aer a moment to realize that she had asked him something. While the sentence itself was undoubtedly phrased as a question, it sounded more like a statement.

He finally understood what was distinct about the way she spoke. Nira had gone over intonation with him and Alius when they were practicing for the Conductor's Trial. She'd explained how some sounds were emphasized through a change in pitch during both speech and music. The head huntress didn't use intonations in any of her words, making it difficult to understand what she was expressing even when her words were perfectly clear. Combine that with her face, which was as devoid of emotion as humanly possible, and Aer couldn't help but feel somewhat unsettled by her presence.

"What... do you mean?" Aer asked.

"As a member of the Charity Tree, how do you feel about the Perch? Do you hate them for the way they look down on you?"

"No, I don't have any bad feelings about them," Aer lied, still holding out hope that she hadn't figured out he was the one who'd made the announcement.

The head huntress turned to inspect his face. Aer struggled to keep his expression in check as the older woman evaluated him.

"Let me tell you a story," she said after a pause. "A pair of siblings lived on the Charity Tree. One day, someone from the Perch, the child of someone important, had a disagreement with them. Having lived completely different lifestyles, the siblings and the Perch fledgling were incompatible with one another."

Aer froze. How much did she know about him and Alius?

"Or so they thought. The children talked, and after seeing things from the siblings' point of view, the fledgling from the Perch came to change his mind about many things."

Aer stared at her. For a moment, he had been certain she was referring to their quarrel with Gail, but this didn't match up with what had happened. Was it just a coincidence?

"The parent of that Perch fledgling didn't like this. They pushed the Perch to enforce stricter rules on their child. In response, the Perch fledgling grew rebellious toward the parent."

Aer furrowed his brow as he tried to decipher the meaning behind her ill-enunciated words. The way she told the story was dull and monotone, and had he not been so concerned with what the older woman knew, he would have likely filtered it out as meaningless noise.

"In the meantime, friction occurred among the siblings as well. The older sibling, who loved the younger sibling with all their heart, was afraid they would get hurt, being so involved with those who had done nothing but look down on them their entire lives."

The head huntress paused. Aer couldn't be sure, since her face was so unreadable, but if he had to guess, she was deliberating about telling him something. "In the end, a fight broke out, and the Perch fledgling along with the younger sibling ended up cutting ties with their respective relatives. They never saw each other again."

Aer blinked. That wasn't how he expected the story to go.

"The parent was quite displeased. He blamed everyone on the Nesting Island for the 'negative influence' those Charity Tree fledglings had on his child. The older sibling, on the other hand, ended up resenting the parent and the Perch for ruining the siblings' lives."

"I see," Aer replied, unsure what she was trying to tell him with her story.

"Let me hear your thoughts. Who do you think was in the wrong? The siblings? The Perch fledgling? The parent? The Perch? Or something else entirely?"

"The parent and the Perch, I suppose," Aer answered honestly.

"How do you think they should have handled the situation?"

"The parent should have tried listening to their child, and the Perch…" Aer trailed off as he thought about it a bit more. "Maybe the Perch couldn't do much in that specific situation, but it's because they looked down on everyone else that the whole mess happened in the first place."

The head huntress stared at him impassively. "The expected answer from someone who grew up on the Charity Tree."

Aer mentally berated himself. He had forgotten about acting innocent while trying to figure out the older woman's intentions and had just given away his true feelings about the Perch.

"And what if that attitude didn't originate from the Perch?" the head huntress asked, her face remaining ambiguous.

"Where would it have come from, then?" Aer asked, watching his words and tone.

"Many of those with greater roles in our society believe that they have been given such responsibilities by the Great Arbiter," the head huntress replied, her voice and style of speech shifting ever so subtly. "I'm sure you noticed it while gathering information about the trials. Certain occupations are worth more than others. Certain *people* are worth more than others. When everything happens in accordance with the Great Arbiter's will, the logic that follows is that those without a higher purpose have less meaning in his eyes than those who do."

Aer could only stare in response. Was this leading somewhere?

"Is that what *you* believe?" he asked.

But the head huntress didn't answer him.

"Head Huntress Islea. How unexpected to see you down here," an unfamiliar voice echoed from above.

Aer turned to find a *floating* old man staring down at them.

The head huntress bowed deeply. "A rather eventful evening, wouldn't you say, Emissary Striaen?" the head huntress asked, no longer paying Aer any attention.

"Yes, quite," he replied as he landed gracefully. "The head caretaker and those under him seem to have lost their heads over an announcement that his son made. Might I ask what you are doing here?"

"I was having this child show me around," the head huntress answered, turning her head toward Aer. "It's been a long time since I was last on this island, after all."

The old man eyed Aer, looking specifically at his dirty, baggy clothes.

"Is that so? You seem to be associated with quite a number of people I wouldn't have expected you to be familiar with."

Aer might have just imagined it, but he thought he saw the head huntress's face twitch just a bit.

"Shall we walk down this building together?" the old man continued. "Quite some time has passed since we've last conversed about anything that wasn't related to business."

***

The sky had grown dark in the time it took for them to descend the Perch. Finding Alius standing outside, Aer hobbled toward him.

The old man blinked when he saw them side by side.

"Twins?" Aer heard him mutter.

But Aer didn't care about that. He needed to confirm some things with his brother right away.

Alius's face paled as Aer approached, the two stern-looking adults tailing him.

"What happened?" Alius whispered. Aer immediately silenced the surrounding air to make sure they weren't overheard. "Who are these guys? Did you get caught?"

"I'm not sure," Aer whispered back. Alius gave him a look of both worry and confusion. "I'll explain later. How did things go on your end?"

"I shook off the head caretaker onto a group of nearby caretakers." Alius's face broke into a light, self-satisfied smile. "Isn't it brilliant? As the head caretaker's son, Gail is the only one who should be able to enter his father's home and use that device. Plus, he was out to talk with some visitor who doesn't even exist, so he doesn't have an alibi to defend himself. Now the caretakers will have to let us go if they want to look fair in front of the visitors."

"Just one question." Aer sighed.

"What?"

"Even if we assume that the people behind me don't suspect us, the head caretaker will definitely question Gail about this."

"Right."

"So what's stopping them from going over what happened, realizing their stories don't match up, and figuring out that someone else was messing with them?"

Alius's face fell. "They don't have proof it was us."

"You say that like it matters. If Gail needed proof to blame us for things going wrong, we wouldn't be here in the first place. What's stopping them from accusing us anyway?"

Alius turned his gaze toward the visitors, then to the Perch, and then back to Aer. "You know, you really need to point things like this out earlier."

"Alius."

"Well, I'm sorry! I got caught up in the idea of getting Gail in trouble and didn't think that far ahead. For now, let's go back and pretend you've been cleaning this entire time. We'll figure things out from there."

The brothers headed inside to find a crowd of over fifty people, evenly split between the caretakers, fledglings, and visitors. The head caretaker and Gail could be heard arguing at the center of it all.

"I'd like you to explain this to me, Gail," the head caretaker said menacingly. "You know you're not allowed to use the intercom for your own purposes. Furthermore, to tell such *lies* to the Perch, especially when the visitors were present, I wonder what you could have been thinking?"

"It wasn't me!" Gail said frantically. "Why would I say something like that in the first place?"

"That was your voice, wasn't it?" one of the caretakers in the crowd asked. "Also, no one else could have possibly unlocked the head caretaker's front door."

"I'm being set up. I wasn't anywhere near the intercom when it happened."

"Where were you, then?" the head caretaker asked.

Gail hesitated for a moment before responding. "The Eastern Borders. I got called there by a visitor."

"Which visitor?"

"I don't know. They weren't there when I arrived."

"Awfully convenient story," one of the visitors commented as she approached.

The head caretaker gritted his teeth. "This matter is between me and my son, Orator Mistral. I ask that you not interfere."

"And what is all this?" a voice echoed through the room.

Aer turned around. The old man had walked through the doorway with the head huntress.

"Emissary Striaen!" The head caretaker bowed, as did every other adult in the building.

Both Aer and Alius blinked and looked closer at the old man, curious as to what kind of authority he had over everyone there.

Gail's eyes narrowed once he spotted Aer and Alius. "Out with it! You did this, didn't you?"

"I don't know what you're talking about," Alius answered, feigning ignorance.

"Then why weren't you two where I left you?"

"We had to go to the bathroom, okay?" Alius said defensively.

"Lies. You two can't be trusted. You have everything to gain by besmirching my reputation, making you the obvious culprits."

The head caretaker looked thoughtfully between them and nodded.

"Yes, that would make sense. One of them called me down earlier. The other could have been hiding somewhere to sneak into my room and use the intercom."

Aer swallowed nervously. He didn't like where the conversation was heading. All they needed to do to confirm their suspicions was ask where he had been during that time. As he didn't know his way around the building, he wouldn't be able to give a different location than where he had headed.

Gail appeared to have the same realization and smirked. "Tell me, where were you when I was absent?"

Aer paled. They had him.

What happened next, however, caught everyone by surprise.

"It's not him," the head huntress said.

The head caretaker looked confused. "Head Huntress Islea? I wondered where you were. The caretakers tell me you've been absent from their sight since noon."

The head huntress ignored him. "I found that boy wandering around the lower floors of the Perch. I asked him to show me around. He couldn't have been in your room because he was with me the entire time."

Aer stood in still silence. What was she saying? Why was she lying about where she had met him?

"Why?" the head caretaker asked. "He doesn't live here. Anyone else would have done a better job of guiding you around the Perch."

"Irrelevant. I felt the desire to explore other parts of this island, and for that, he was as good as any person here. After all, he seemed to be quite free."

"Where did you go?"

"We examined the river that leads down to the Spiral Forest. Isn't that right, boy?"

"Y-Yes," Aer lied, not questioning how she knew that landmark.

"B-But—" Gail stammered.

"Regardless, my point stands." The head huntress directed her gaze at the head caretaker. "This boy couldn't have done what you accused him of."

The visitor that had spoken first smiled. "Which means the only one who could have done this is your son," she declared. "Unless you doubt the validity of Head Huntress Islea's words?"

The head caretaker fell silent for a moment.

"I see." He stared at Gail.

Gail looked back with wide eyes, an expression of pure fear etched on his face.

Emissary Striaen then faced the other visitor. "I'm rather surprised, Orator Mistral. I wasn't aware you knew the head huntress."

The orator blinked before looking away from the expressionless woman.

"She once helped me out in a difficult stage in my life. Her name has stuck with me since then," she said before quickly changing the subject. "I'm a bit more curious as to why these fledglings were here when they don't live in the Perch."

"They were carrying out a punishment for a previous misdemeanor," the head caretaker answered. "They picked a fight with my son, you see—"

"He picked a fight with us!" Alius interrupted, ignoring the head caretaker's death glare. "He attacked us for 'cheating' in the Rain Provider's Trial. Which we didn't do."

"Oh?" Orator Mistral piped in. "Does your son have evidence of this? So far, he hasn't shown himself to be the most honest individual. And he seemed far too eager to shift blame for his wrongdoing to these two."

Gail spoke up. "You can't believe them! We've received packages of food that made us feel sick during the Rain Provider's Trial. Only those from the Charity Tree would gain from doing this."

"Interesting," Emissary Striaen mused. "Do the caretakers here not check for security?"

"Rest assured, we consider the safety of our fledglings our highest priority," Head Caretaker Desen answered.

"Then I don't see what the problem here is." Emissary Striaen sighed. "Unless you're suggesting these *fledglings* were able to hoodwink your best caretakers, in which case we have a much bigger problem to discuss."

The head caretaker paled. "No. Of course not."

"Then end this unreasonable punishment," Emissary Striaen ordered.

"Yes, of course," the head caretaker muttered as he walked toward Aer and Alius. "Please excuse us."

Aer didn't dare believe what he had just heard. How had everything worked out so perfectly?

"Hey, Aliu—" he started.

"Shh, not yet," Alius interrupted with a smile as wide as his face.

The head caretaker noticed their not-at-all repressed glee as he grabbed their shoulders and dragged them outside.

"Enough," he whispered, his face red with fury. "You two have been a complete hassle to deal with. Just get out and stay away."

"What about our punishment?" Alius asked, feigning innocence.

"Leave!" the head caretaker snapped. "I don't want to see you two here ever again!"

They needed no more encouragement as they ran away as quickly as their exhausted bodies would allow.

***

The brothers broke down in relieved laughter once they were certain they were out of the head caretaker's earshot.

"What just happened?" Aer asked, still in disbelief.

"We freed ourselves from cleaning the Perch," Alius smugly responded before collapsing onto the ground in exhaustion.

"Yes, but how?" Aer asked. "Why did the head huntress lie for us?"

"Who knows?" Alius shrugged. "Anyway, this is why you should listen to me more. Things work out when you do."

Aer rolled his eyes. "This was a fluke, and you know it. You definitely didn't predict a visitor covering for us, and I don't even want to think about what would have happened if she didn't."

"Okay, but still, it's good that we went ahead with my plan. If we did nothing, like *you* wanted, we'd still be stuck there."

"Say that again when things actually go according to your plan," Aer fired back, but his responses held a lot less venom now that the tension had lifted. "I saw you freaking out when the head caretaker started piecing everything together."

"Yeah, well…" Alius looked embarrassed as he changed the subject. "Anyway, did you see Gail's and the head caretaker's faces when the visitors disagreed with him?"

"Yeah, I'll be keeping that image in my head for a while." Aer laughed as he helped Alius back to his feet. "I'm just glad we don't have to come back. I was sick of dealing with everyone here."

"And now we can focus on what to do next," Alius stated. "Think we can somehow use what we learned about the Perch to our advantage?"

"Just make sure you don't do anything to bring us back here," Aer warned. "I'd hate to get caught up in *another* mess you made after all that trouble."

"I know. I know," Alius responded. "I'll do my best to hold back when dealing with the Perch. Just *hypothetically* speaking, if we were to do something like spread the word of tonight's incident around the island to slander Gail's reputation so no one takes his side the next time we have a fight—"

"No."

"But—"

"No."

The two continued to bicker like that throughout the night, leaving the Perch with their spirits much higher than when they'd entered.

Chapter 11: Path to One's Goals

The stories of our beginnings speak of an all-powerful being who saved us in our time of need. Humans all sinned without exception, but as we were made in his image, the Great Arbiter refused to abandon us completely. Instead, he took those who found favor in his eyes and gave them dominion over all the heavens and everything that resides within. Which is why every time we wield our Sky Authorities, we exercise a right that he has granted us. This blessing is meant to aid us in our efforts to maintain this domain.

As such, there can be nothing to question about our actions. Everything we do here is permitted by the Great Arbiter to preserve Atravel as it is.

Azel fixed his gaze on the person responsible for his troubles as he chased after them. He wouldn't let them ignore him any longer. Not until he had the answer he wanted.

"Head Huntress Islea," he called out. "Head Huntress Islea!"

The woman turned to face him. "Azel."

"You need to reconsider my appointment as a chef," Azel pleaded. He didn't know what he would do if she refused. While his cooking had improved recently, it was still only a matter of time before he lost his job. "I don't think I can survive in this line of work."

Even as Azel explained his predicament, the head huntress's face remained emotionless. Her lack of response enraged him. How dare she act like his issues weren't her problem?

"Take me back as your subordinate." Azel demanded. "Or… Or I'll go to the enforcers over this."

It was a hollow threat. The head huntress wasn't guilty of any crime by dismissing him from her service. All Azel was doing was antagonizing the person he needed a positive response from. And yet he was too outraged to care. If she refused, she wouldn't have any authority to punish him.

Silence fell between them.

"Very well, if you're that insistent about it," Head Huntress Islea eventually conceded.

Azel blinked, hardly believing his ears. Did his appeal finally get through to her?

"I can come back?" he asked. "I don't have to continue as a chef?"

"Everyone is busy preparing for the upcoming celebrations, so remain at your station until then," the head huntress answered. "Once the Grand Sabbath has ended, we can discuss your return to your previous duties."

***

Aer found it a challenge to get up the next morning. Every muscle in his body screamed at him to stop, no matter which way he moved.

"Why does everything hurt?" he groaned as he forced himself to his feet. Yesterday's soreness had grown even worse throughout the night.

"Oh, you can stand. How nice for you." The deadpan voice came from below.

Aer looked down to see Alius struggling to get off the ground. Amused as his brother put on a show of flopping across the floor, Aer waited a few moments before pulling him up.

"Stupid Gail," Alius grumbled, his legs trembling as he leaned into Aer for support. "Even when he's not here, he's still causing us problems."

"So what are we doing today?" Aer asked. "Doesn't look like we're in any state to move around that much."

"That's fine," Alius replied. "Let's just stay here and focus on the Mechanic's Trial. If Kiel or Nira want anything, they can come find us."

Picking up the textbook assigned for the Mechanic's Trial and seating themselves on the floor, they began studying the recorders in more detail. It wasn't until late in the morning when they were interrupted by a knock on their door.

Aer got up and opened it to find Nira looking up at him from her wheelchair.

"I didn't see you guys leaving for the Perch," Nira said with a questioning look. "Is it all right for you two to still be here?"

"Oh, we got the caretakers to end our punishment early," Aer explained.

"How did you guys manage that?" she asked incredulously.

Aer hesitated. He didn't feel comfortable revealing what had really happened the day before. If what he said somehow reached the head caretaker's ears…

Alius, seeing Aer freeze up, interrupted them. "Come in and close the door. I'll explain."

Aer gave his brother a worried look.

"I'm sure she can keep a secret," Alius whispered. "I doubt she would have offered to teach us anything in the first place if she was the type to snitch on us."

Aer held his reservations. He still wasn't sure why Nira was putting so much effort into helping them. While there had never been animosity between her and the brothers, they hadn't been especially close before the trials. Rather, her status as a former Perch fledgling had made navigating conversations with her difficult. Even now, there was an unspoken agreement to not delve too deeply into each other's personal matters.

Or maybe he was the only one who felt that way, as Alius didn't leave out a single detail of what they went through at the Perch.

"I can't believe you guys got away with that," Nira remarked, looking utterly stunned.

"We shouldn't have gotten away with it," Aer said. "I still can't believe some outsider bothered to cover for us."

Nira stared at them in amazement for a moment before resuming the conversation. "Think you guys can practice music with me, then? You two need as much experience as you can get before the Conductor's Trial."

"We were focusing on the Mechanic's Trial for now because its deadline is coming up soon," Alius said. "That said, we're not making any real progress. Remind me what the Conductor's Trial is about?"

"It's a musical performance," Nira replied. "We're going to perform in front of proctors well versed in compositions, theory, and execution."

"Are you sure you want *our* help for this?" Aer asked, recalling his disastrous attempts at music. It was a reasonable question from his perspective, but Nira appeared a bit upset.

"I told you before that I didn't want to face the Perch by myself," she replied testily.

"We can't play any instrument nearly as well as you can, though," Aer pointed out. "Also, wouldn't the Perch give you a harder time if we were there with you? Honestly, it feels like us getting involved would hurt your chances more than help."

"The problem is that a solo performance won't be particularly impressive in the proctors' eyes," Nira explained. "Back when I was still living at the Perch, the caretakers taught me that the value of a conductor is in how they can control and coordinate the various types of sound that reach the audience. The trial will likely test how we can make distinct sounds come together. For that, I need more people. Honestly, the three of us aren't enough, but I'll take what I can get for now."

"Why don't I ask Kiel to convince some of the fledglings here to help?" Alius suggested. "I'm sure he could get dozens of people to join."

Nira shook her head. "There's no way I could teach that many people new to music to be proficient in this short of a time. They probably wouldn't listen to someone who originally came from the Perch anyway."

"Are you sure?" Alius asked. "I thought the fledglings here were pretty understanding of your situation."

"They try their best to avoid setting me off so they don't get wrapped up in my issues." Nira's shoulders slumped. "That's not the same thing as caring about me or what I have to say. Guess that shouldn't come as a surprise. Whether it's the Perch or the Charity Tree, you'll find people turning a blind eye everywhere."

Hearing that, Alius stood, clearly set on helping her.

Aer, however, was less than eager. Fledglings from the Charity Tree didn't have many opportunities to learn music. Meaning those taking part in the Conductor's Trial were all going to be from the Perch. The last thing he wanted to do right after being released from his punishment was to stand out before them as an adversary.

Still, it was hard to turn down Nira after how much support he and Alius had received from her.

"Anyway," Nira said. "If I'm putting on a performance with complete novices, I'd much rather work with people willing to hear what I have to say."

"That makes sense, but our focus is all over the place right now," Aer said. "We still haven't figured out anything for the Mechanic's Trial, no thanks to being stuck cleaning the Perch."

He exchanged a look with his brother. "Unless you want to set this one aside so we can take our time with the Conductor's Trial?"

Alius frowned.

"I don't want to give up on the Mechanic's Trial. It's the one trial I feel like I can succeed in, seeing as it doesn't involve Sky Control. But I also want to help Nira in whatever way we can, considering how much she's gone out of her way for us."

Nira looked conflicted.

"What do you two have to do for this trial?"

"The proctor wanted us to study the things we took and explain what they do and how they do it. He also wanted us to think of an unconventional way of using the devices to explore the possibilities they offer," Alius explained while fiddling with a recorder. "I think we understand the recorders well enough, but for the second part..."

"Unconventional uses, huh?" Nira mused. "I feel like how you guys used these recorders to fool the Perch should count. I doubt anyone expected something that only leaves messages to be so useful in tricking others. Too bad you can't explain in detail without getting into serious trouble."

"Now I'm tempted to tell everyone just to see how the Perch would react to realizing how they were all duped." Alius snickered. "But yeah. Best for us they don't figure that out. Still, it's a waste. We have a solution, but we can't use it."

"If you're that set on the idea of tricking others, why don't we just fake a performance?" Aer half-heartedly proposed, fully expecting to be ignored. "We could finish both trials by using these recorders to prerecord performances for the Conductor's Trial, place them in Nira's instruments, and pretend to play as they go off."

Both Alius and Nira fell into stunned silence.

"Aer, you're a genius." Alius grinned.

Aer tried not to roll his eyes. "Alius, I was just throwing out whatever stupid thought entered my mind. I'm not actually suggesting we do this."

"Well, why not?" Alius asked. "That's brilliant, and it solves all our issues here! We'd make up for our lack of numbers and skill, while the proctors for the Mechanic's Trial might consider that an innovative use of these recorders!"

"There's no way the proctors for the Conductor's Trial would fall for such a thing," Aer objected. "You think they won't know something's up when the way we play doesn't match the sounds coming out?"

"Yeah, recognizing how sound travels through air and instruments is part of their job," Nira said. "We wouldn't be able to trick them that easily."

"See!" Aer winced as his muscles ached. "Even if we pulled it off, we'd still have to come clean to the Mechanic's Trial proctor if we wanted to use that to pass their test. And the proctors are working together. You really think he won't say anything about how we cheated on one of the other trials?"

Alius frowned. "I thought we had something here."

Nira remained silent for a few moments before nodding. "Everything Aer said is right, but…"

"But?" the brothers prompted.

"But we might get away with it if we explained it to them beforehand."

"What do you mean?" Alius asked eagerly.

"Instead of trying to trick them, we could just tell them we're planning to use recordings of my performances with other instruments to make up for the people we don't have," Nira explained. "Since I'm the one we're recording, they might not consider it cheating, and the proctors for your trial would still consider it a unique way of using these recorders."

"Would something like that really be allowed?" Aer asked.

"I don't think there's any rule against something like this, but they might decide that it goes against the spirit of the trial," Nira answered. "Since it is supposed to be a performance, not a recording. Still, if we do manage to convince them, we'll have more than enough people without asking anyone to join."

"Let's try it," Alius insisted. "What do we have to lose?"

"All right." Aer sighed. "The proctor for the Mechanic's Trial said he would be waiting near this area, so we should confirm it with him first. Nira, do you know where the person overlooking the Conductor's Trial is?"

"Yeah. I've been looking into this trial since it was announced, after all."

Alius patted Aer on the back before sitting back down on the floor. "Well then, good luck convincing them."

Aer's eyes narrowed. "You can't be serious."

"I'm still sore," Alius said. "This was originally your idea, and you're in better condition than I am, so go out for me."

"I'm not exactly jumping with energy right now either," Aer argued. "Besides, you're the one who wants to go through with it the most, so shouldn't you go?"

"I'm in a *wheelchair*, and I still want to go outside to check this out." Nira said, looking exasperated. "Could you two stop complaining and just come with me?"

Neither brother could find it in himself to refuse after hearing that argument. Soon enough, all three were trudging along to the site of the Mechanic's Trial.

***

Nira waited at a distance as Aer and Alius explained all they had learned about the recorders to the proctor of the Mechanic's Trial. The proctor nodded in approval before asking whether they had discovered a unique way of using the devices.

"Fascinating! What a novel idea!" the proctor exclaimed as Alius gave him their answer. "Quite efficient, too, using this trial to overcome another one."

"You're fine with it, then?" Alius asked, giving Aer a grin.

"Oh yes." The proctor nodded. "Though I would like to see a demonstration before making my final evaluation. You plan to use the recorders as part of your performance in the Conductor's Trial?"

"Yes."

"Let me see your forms for this trial," the proctor said. "Alius and Aer, I see. Would you two happen to know your last names?"

"No, we don't," Alius admitted.

"Of course. Please excuse me," the proctor apologized. "I look forward to seeing your performance!"

The brothers, having received an answer, made their way back to Nira.

"See, Aer! The proctor thought it was a great idea!" Alius said. "You should have a bit more faith that things will work out instead of getting all pessimistic."

"And you should hold back your expectations. We still need to clear it up with whoever's running the Conductor's Trial," Aer pointed out.

"Well, let's get their approval, then," Alius said, looking livelier than he had in the morning.

Despite his confidence, however, the people involved with the Conductor's Trial seemed much less thrilled with their plan.

The examiner overseeing the trial, a bespectacled woman with a sharp gaze, gave them an odd look before shaking her head. "Rejected."

"Told you," Aer said.

"Guess that's to be expected." Nira sighed.

The proctor of the Conductor's Trial frowned. "Was that all you wanted to talk to me about?"

"Wait, wait, wait!" Alius exclaimed. "The Conductor's Trial is supposed to judge how well we can make distinct sounds come together, right?"

"Correct. Which is why I'm forbidding this. How is playing a recording supposed to measure your musical sense in any way?"

"You still need to blow air into these things to make them work, right? What if we measured the timing on separate recordings to make it all come together as one song and used Sky Control to adjust the volume for each recording? Wouldn't that be making distinct sounds come together?"

The proctor hesitated. "I suppose that's one way of looking at it."

"It has to be!" Alius desperately insisted.

"Even though that takes away seeing your personal skill with an instrument?" the proctor questioned.

"I'll still play something," Alius said. "My brother here will be responsible for the recordings. Managing the recorders along with controlling how the sound travels with Sky Control could be considered playing an instrument by itself, don't you think?"

The proctor looked conflicted. "Very well. I'll decide whether or not to accept that reasoning after seeing your performance in person."

***

"I still can't believe you managed to talk her into reconsidering," Nira said as they headed back into the Spiral Forest.

"The proctor didn't seem to know what to do. I doubt anyone's ever tried something like this before," Alius said. "So I pressed the point before she could think it over."

Nira looked impressed. "Persistence really seems to work out for you."

"Sometimes," Aer interrupted. "Other times, it just gets us in more trouble."

Alius ignored him. "You just have to learn how to push through the looks and criticisms. If you're too conscious of what other people think, you'll end up like Aer."

"What's that supposed to mean?" Aer asked indignantly.

"All right, now we can focus on both trials at the same time," Alius declared, pretending he hadn't heard anything. "That should take care of all our issues."

"Actually, there's one more thing." Aer turned to Nira. "Do you know how to speak with birds?"

"Why do you ask?" Nira asked.

"It's just that the Falconry Trial's also coming up soon, and I don't have the faintest idea of how to go about it."

"Oh, right." Nira leaned back in her chair. "I forgot I asked you to join me in that one too. If you want more details, I think there are some places that talk a bit more about the subject. We can go there right now. We've just made a ton of progress on what to do for the Conductor's Trial, and I'm the one who urged us to participate in both these trials, anyway. That fine with you, Aer?"

Aer nodded, feeling a little guilty for his reluctance to help her earlier.

The brothers treaded cautiously as Nira led them toward an ornate building near the Perch's cliff. Neither Aer nor Alius relished the idea of meeting the fledglings in this area again so soon but found the ones they encountered here much more respectful, or at the very least, much less verbal about their contempt.

The three of them stepped, or in Nira's case, wheeled, into the main room of the building. As they entered, the brothers' attention was immediately drawn to a colored glass window depicting a giant figure standing over forests, mountains, plains, and bodies of water. His arms were raised over his head, while his hands were bound in chains.

No. Not bound, Aer corrected himself, recognizing it as a depiction of the Great Arbiter. *He's holding the chains up.*

"Hey, Nira. What is this place?" Aer whispered.

"You wanted to learn more about Sky Authority for the Falconry Trial, right?" Nira asked. "This place has people who talk a lot about the authority the Great Arbiter has over the skies. The people here have a harder time turning others down because they want to keep up appearances, too, so I thought maybe you could ask one of the caretakers to fill you in for more details."

They seated themselves in an empty row of chairs, which the room had no shortage of. In front of the colored glass window, an old man preached to a gathering of about fifty people.

Wait. We saw that old man yesterday, Aer realized. *He's the one who everyone in the Perch was especially polite to.*

He then took a closer look at the audience. More than just fledglings were in attendance. Caretakers, proctors, and visitors from other islands all listened attentively to him.

"I'm sure you've all heard of the legends of Atravel's origins," the old man said. "Of how the Great Arbiter rescued us in our time of need. How he gave our ancestors, his chosen ones, authority over the sky and everything in it. I would like you all to reflect on this point a bit more. Why were we of all people chosen?"

"Because we refused to take part in the world's conflicts," a visitor answered. "We desired peace, unlike everyone else. The Great Arbiter found that pleasing and saved us."

"Correct. These skies are our haven from the treacherous world outside. We must ensure it stays that way. And so let us continue to do our part in maintaining the peace. Let those who have his blessing continue to thrive in this haven he has prepared for us! May his enemies continue to be cast away from us and this sanctuary!"

Signaling that the sermon had ended, one of the visitors stood and spoke. "Thank you for taking your precious time to enlighten us, Emissary Striaen."

"You are welcome. Recently, there have been some heated debates over how Atravel is structured. Usually, things like this settle down on their own, but these arguments have been growing in ferocity since the beginning of this Sky Cycle. As an emissary, I believe it my duty to guide everyone through these trying times."

"*Emissary?*" Aer heard Nira's voice crack, her eyes wide with shock.

"What's wrong?" Alius asked.

"An emissary is the most important position you can hold in all of Atravel, said to be the human representatives of the Great Arbiter himself," Nira explained. "What's one doing here?"

Aer had no time to prepare himself for what happened next. By the time he was aware that Alius had left his seat, his brother was already halfway between them and the old man.

Alarmed, Aer moved to drag him back, but it was too late. Alius had already caught the attention of everyone in the room.

"I want to ask you something," Alius said to the old man.

"Good children should be seen, not heard," one of the caretakers rebuked, prompting them to leave without explicitly saying so in front of the emissary.

The old man stared at Alius and Aer, his gray irises flitting between the twins.

"Ah, yes. I believe we met at the Perch. You should properly introduce yourselves before requesting something. What are your names?"

"I'm Alius. And this is my brother, Aer," Alius answered.

The emissary closed his eyes and took a deep breath.

"Fine names," he said after a moment of silence. "And what can I do for you, my fellow children of the Great Arbiter?"

"We came here to study more about Sky Authority," Alius explained. "The Falconry Trial is coming up soon, and—"

"Ah, say no more. Avian communication is simply an extension of the right over the skies that the Great Arbiter has granted us. If you seek to excel in the Falconry Trial, see the birds not as animals but as part of the sky that you control. After that, assert your commands by using Sky Control on them as you would the air."

Aer took a moment to process that. He imagined a bird in front of him and molded the air that it occupied in his mind.

Seeming to realize what Aer was doing, the emissary gave an approving nod. "Very good. Now, a crucial thing to keep in mind is the difference between instinctive and conscious commands. Instinctive commands are, as the term implies, forms of Sky Control made without active thought. The controller instead 'feels' the surrounding air as an extension of themselves, enabling quick and intuitive use. Thinking or voicing specific instructions to what you are controlling, however, can magnify the strength and precision of your Sky Control. Which is why, if you're aiming for the best possible results, you should make your commands as mindful as the situation allows."

Aer blinked. He hadn't thought to check for such a thing, but it made perfect sense.

"Beyond that, there's the matter of your Sky Authority itself," Emissary Striaen continued. "I'm sure you're aware that it is a blessing granted by the Great Arbiter. Meaning that you will feel most in tune with it when living in accordance with his wishes. How consistent do you believe your recent actions to be with the precepts he laid out for us to follow?"

Aer looked away from the old man's piercing gaze, unable to say anything in response. They were always taught to avoid conflict and to remain untethered to worldly grudges and ambitions. While the emissary hadn't made any specific criticisms about him or Alius, their plans to confront and upstage the Perch suddenly felt like something to be ashamed of.

The emissary gave a knowing smile. "Sometimes, those around you can make the path forward unclear. If you seek to better your understanding of Sky Authority, feel free to talk to me again."

The caretakers nearby looked flabbergasted.

"But, sir! Surely, you have better things to do than to entertain some children!"

"They are no less the chosen of the Great Arbiter than I," Emissary Striaen declared as he faced those in protest. "If they seek higher understanding, I have no right to refuse them."

The emissary then looked back at the brothers. "Aside from that, what trials do you plan to participate in?"

"The Conductor's Trial. Also, the Mechanic's Trial," Alius answered.

The old man nodded. "I see. I wish you luck."

A sense of unease swept over Aer as he spotted Nira signaling them to withdraw. The emissary had taken their behavior in stride, and yet Aer couldn't help but feel that his words had been a warning of some kind. To not let himself be swayed by others and their desires for him, lest he be dragged into their battles and risk the same fate met by those the Great Arbiter condemned. Maybe he and Alius needed to take a step back and rethink their actions.

"You two keep surprising me today," Nira remarked as they exited the building. "I thought that you guys would just get the general idea of how Sky Authority related to the Falconry Trial after listening to a sermon or two. I didn't think you would go up to an *emissary* of all people and get him to teach you himself."

"It is pretty unbelievable," Aer admitted, uncertain of how to feel about the turn of events. It wasn't the first time Alius had blindsided him as of late. His brother had become far too reckless ever since they'd learned about the trials and the Ascension Ceremony. "Honestly, Alius. What's gotten into you?"

"I saw a chance, and I took it," Alius said, brushing him off. "Anyway, Nira, when should we start preparing for the Conductor's Trial?"

Aer frowned at how Alius had avoided his question. Things had turned out fine this time, but Alius had practically been asking for trouble by marching up to one of the most important people in Atravel in front of the caretakers. Those very same caretakers were doing everything they could to look presentable in front of the visitors and pretend those from the Charity Tree didn't exist. The brothers easily could have been given another punishment if things had gone differently.

Feeling ever more wary, Aer made a mental note to keep a closer eye on his brother. *Someone* had to keep them away from trouble, and it most certainly wouldn't be Alius.

Chapter 12: Recognition

I have taken some time off my duties to keep an eye on my son. While observing him, I have noticed that he has an easier time getting along with other people than I do—a useful trait to possess. But as a result, he is also much more easily influenced by his peers. The people he has talked to have put some strange ideas in his head. I grow more worried for him with each passing day. And yet is it not a father's duty to support his child in his endeavors?

"I've actually been composing a song for this trial," Nira explained the following morning. "I was thinking we would have to gather more people to play it, but not anymore. I can proficiently play all the instruments this song needs. We just have to record my performances."

"So you're going to play it all by yourself?" Aer asked.

"That can't be right," Alius said. "I told the proctor that we would all be doing something during the trial, even if Aer's main job is just to activate the recorders at the right time."

"And we are. Just leave *most* of the performances to me," Nira asserted, handing Alius a flute and a sheet of paper. When Alius looked at her questioningly, Nira explained, "It's your part for our performance. It'll tell you what notes to play and when to hit them. You focus on learning how to execute that properly while Aer can start fine-tuning his control over sound by making sure that our noises don't interact with each other. Any objections?"

The brothers shook their heads. Best to leave the job of conducting their performances to the actual musician.

"Good. Now, hand me those recorders so I can record myself playing."

Following Nira's instructions, the brothers practiced their part for the Conductor's Trial. Some curious fledglings had popped in to listen to the noises they were making, but none stepped forward to say anything to them. Based on their general reception, however, Aer could tell that they had a long way to go.

Once Nira had finished recording herself, the three sat down to listen to her performances.

Unfortunately, Nira seemed dissatisfied with the results, as she shook her head in distaste while listening.

"I can do better than this," she complained. "Let me try these parts again."

"I didn't hear anything wrong," Alius objected.

Aer nodded in agreement.

"Well, I did," Nira curtly replied. "Just keep practicing your parts."

Soon after, Nira put the recorders together again, only to find more nitpicks that the brothers could not understand.

It wasn't until the end of the day that Nira seemed halfway satisfied, giving a slow nod after listening to the recordings one last time.

"This is turning out decently. Let's try putting it all together," Nira said, pulling out an instrument noticeably different from those she had been playing up until then. "Alius, start playing the song I gave you as soon as I start. Aer, I want you to play the recordings in the order I arranged them when I give the signal. We'll both use Sky Control to make sure that the sounds harmonize and reach the right distance."

Aer nodded. While he was still laughably bad with all instruments, the timing of when to go through the recordings was simple to execute. And he had grown much better at controlling noise since their last practice session.

Nevertheless, their performance clearly wasn't up to Nira's standards.

"Alius, your sense of rhythm was off," she criticized the moment they finished. "You finished two whole beats before I did. You need to learn how to match your tempo with mine. Also, you were a bit flat throughout the whole thing." She then turned to face Aer. "Aer, you fell apart in the middle of the performance. Try mixing the sounds more naturally. You're focusing too much on the individual parts. You need to let them blend."

The brothers gave each other a look. Nira was much more animated than they had ever seen her, which would be fine if her demands weren't rising to match her enthusiasm.

"You're really getting into this, huh?" Alius asked.

Nira, who had been nothing but moody and critical up until that point, let out a small laugh. "Yeah. This is the first time I've been able to focus on something I'm good at since I got kicked out of the Perch, so I don't want to do this halfheartedly. Now, let's try again."

They continued playing until an annoyed caretaker marched up to their platform and yelled at them, telling them it was far too late in the night to be making so much noise, at which Nira reluctantly put away her instruments.

"Can I keep these until the trial?" Nira asked Alius, holding the recorders. "I want to listen to these a bit more to get a clearer picture of the whole song. Also, I need to show the proctor that I was the one who played these parts."

Alius nodded.

***

"No, no, no!" Nira snapped the next day after an admittedly lackluster performance. "I need you guys to focus. Alius, you're blowing too hard. Aer is supposed to make your part reach the audience, so you don't have to focus *that* much on volume. Speaking of which, Aer, why are you holding back on how far the noise travels?"

"I didn't want another caretaker yelling at us about how we're making too much noise," Aer answered defensively.

"It's still early in the day, and we have a solid reason for making the noise," Alius said. "Go wild."

"No, Alius. Control is important too. Being too loud can be worse than being too quiet," Nira rebuked. She then sighed. "Just match my volume, Aer. Alius, you're not in a position to instruct others. Worry more about yourself. We're doing this again. *Focus.*"

Alius looked somewhat annoyed. "Okay, okay. Forget I said anything. Just relax, Nira. We're doing the best we can."

Aer quietly nodded, feeling a little overwhelmed by Nira's passion. He sensed that things were about to take a turn for the worse.

Their next few attempts at the song proved him right.

How did we get to this point? Aer wondered as Alius and Nira started screaming at one another. Both had lost their tempers as the brothers continued to make mistakes in their performances.

"I only gave you a simple accompaniment piece!" Nira criticized. "Why are you having so much trouble with this?"

"All right, I get it!" Alius snapped in frustration. "You don't need to tell me how terrible I am. I already know!"

"Then do this properly!" Nira snapped back. "Don't say you have it down when you don't. You're doing worse than when you started!"

Alius stepped forward to meet Nira's glare. "For someone who's just started playing, I think I'm doing fantastic, thank you!"

"Hey, guys? I think you both need to calm down," Aer meekly interjected. Not that he wanted to, but the judgmental looks from the fledglings listening in were growing more painful by the second. He had muted Alius and Nira's argument from those passing by, but their angry, flushed faces, along with their aggressive movements, were still on full display. And when he had tried muting them from each other, Nira had just undone his use of Sky Control to continue speaking normally. The only thing he could do at this point was mediate between them.

"Alius?" Aer asked.

"What?" Alius shouted, not taking his eyes off Nira.

"You don't need to be in her face like that. Back off." When Alius didn't budge, Aer turned to Nira. "Nira? I think Alius is slipping more *because* you're yelling at him."

Alius and Nira continued glaring at each other.

Eventually, Nira looked away and sighed.

"Let's take a break, then," she said, wheeling herself away from them.

Once tempers had cooled enough for both sides to talk civilly to one another, the three of them continued from where they had left off.

"Sorry," Nira said. "I should have explained things more calmly. I got too caught up in wanting things to go perfectly."

"You really want to do well in this trial, huh?" Alius asked.

Nira leaned into her wheelchair. "Yeah, the other trials were just afterthoughts for me. This was something I was great at when I was back in the Perch. Better than most of the fledglings there. I wanted to show those who wrote me off that just because I'm not in the Perch anymore doesn't mean that part of me vanished."

"Of course not," Alius said. "The reason I wanted to rally others was because I wanted to prove there's more to people than what the caretakers decided."

Nira nodded. "You know, I was afraid for a while that what they were saying was true—that there wasn't any worth left to me anymore, that the Perch and my parents cast me aside for a reason, that there was something wrong with me to be sent here."

The implications of that last sentence didn't escape Aer's notice. "Meaning you thought there was something wrong with the rest of us?"

Nira was hesitant in her reply. "The general attitude at the Perch is that the Charity Tree is filled with people everyone would be better off without. Since my parents shared the same view, I never really questioned the idea. Of course, I don't believe a word they say anymore. Not after they left me here, despite how hard I tried to make them proud."

"Is that why you're so invested in this?" Alius asked. "So you can get your parents to admit they made a mistake abandoning you?"

"Pretty much," Nira admitted. "Looking back, I think the biggest reason I agreed to help you was because you were willing to apologize to me, an ex-Perch fledgling. Seeing you do what my parents couldn't, despite being someone from the Charity Tree, helped me realize their views of other people never mattered."

After a moment of silence, Alius picked up the flute and started practicing again. Aer, relieved at how smoothly things ended, tried harder to avoid making mistakes that could stir up another argument between the two.

The three spent the next few days like this. The fledglings passing by listened quietly, occasionally dropping a comment or two before walking away.

Based on their reactions compared to before, Aer was certain they had noticeably improved. He just wasn't sure how their performance compared to those from the Perch.

***

The night before the trial, the three of them played their song one last time, putting together everything they had learned during their practices.

Nira closed her eyes and fell silent once they were done, leaving Aer and Alius to fidget nervously as she evaluated their performance.

"This is as good as you'll get with that instrument, given the time we have," she said to Alius after what felt like an eternity. "I wouldn't say that you're great, but you're at least playing the same song I am. The proctor can't say what you're doing isn't music." She then turned to Aer. "Aer, your control over how sound travels through the air is perfect. Just don't panic, and you'll be fine."

Aer and Alius sighed in relief. That was the first time Nira sounded satisfied with their performance.

Once they headed back home, both brothers lay on the ground, trying to imagine the movements they would have to make in the trial the next day.

"We can do this," Alius said. "We just need to repeat what we did tonight."

"The only problem left is whether the proctor will accept this as a proper performance or not," Aer said.

"Even if she doesn't, if the visitors watching are impressed, we'll still have accomplished what I originally aimed for," Alius said. "Although for Nira's sake, I hope the proctor approves."

The following morning, Nira led them toward a stone pillar close to the edge of the island. Inside was a dimly lit auditorium.

"Here we are," Nira whispered.

"Someone should really do a better job of differentiating the stone pillars," Alius complained. "I don't know how they expect us to tell one apart from another."

"Most of the people participating in this trial have probably come here enough times to commit it to memory," Aer replied. "Anyway, look at the fledglings lined up over there. I'm guessing that's where we're supposed to wait."

Alius nodded and pushed Nira's wheelchair toward the back of the line leading to the end of the hall. There, the proctor for this trial stood on top of a wooden stage, facing the visitors and caretakers who were presumably there to listen to the day's performances.

Aer gauged their competition. Based on the appearances of those before them, it was clear that all the other fledglings who would be performing were from the Perch. He, Alius, and Nira stood out like stains on clean clothing.

"We will now begin the Conductor's Trial," the proctor announced once everyone had gathered. "Those standing behind me will start us off."

The fledglings on the stage took that as a cue to draw their instruments.

Aer broke out in a sweat. He could tell how experienced these people were by the mere coordination of their movements. His feeling of hopelessness only grew when they started playing.

Once the recital ended, polite clapping emerged from the crowd. The people next in line then stepped forward and played their pieces with similar levels of skill.

As the trial continued, Aer grew increasingly grateful that most of their performances had been done by Nira. He even briefly entertained the idea of quieting Alius's portion to make his lack of experience less noticeable. What was worse was that the crowd looked somewhat bored with the excellent performances before them. How would they view his and Alius's haphazard preparations? Would they be laughed off the stage?

Suffice to say, he didn't feel very confident once it was finally time for them to step forward.

The proctor eyed them for a moment before sighing.

"Ah yes. You three," she said wearily. "Go ahead and start."

Aer's heart beat faster as the audience's gazes focused on him. This was different from the Rain Provider's Trial, where all he'd had to do was run. Any mistake he made would drag down the other two. The more he thought about that, the harder it became to remember what he had learned in the past few days.

Aer took a deep breath. The best way to calm down in a situation like this was to pretend that the crowd didn't exist. He had gotten through life as a Charity Tree fledgling by turning away from everything he found unpleasant—the fledglings from the Perch, the world outside his Nesting Island, his potentially bleak future. He had freed himself from his fear of such things by refusing to look at them. Which was why he needed to do the same here.

Aer's pulse slowed. Regaining some composure, he checked on how the other two were doing, trying his hardest to avoid looking at the crowd.

Alius was clearly shaken but was steeling himself to keep going. Nira, in contrast, seemed completely composed. It was plain to see that this wasn't her first time performing in front of a crowd.

Hushed whispers passed through the crowd when Nira organized several recorders in front of Aer. Ignoring the audience and keeping his eyes focused solely on his task, Aer let the first recorder play once Nira gave the signal.

A somber tune echoed throughout the auditorium. Aer reinforced its pathway through the air while waiting for the right point in the song to start the next recording.

Once he had done this for all the recordings, Aer focused on his surroundings, paying attention to the sounds that Alius, Nira, and the recorders made. He paid close attention to Alius in particular, preparing to mute any mistakes his brother might make.

Despite Aer's fears, Alius was doing much better than he thought possible. Instead of being close to having a nervous breakdown like Aer, Alius was taking the intense pressure of the crowd as a challenge to perform better.

Relieved, Aer then focused on making the echoes of their song snake throughout the audience without overwhelming them with noise. Thinking about everything he had learned about sound, Aer methodically replicated what he had practiced the past few days, mimicking Nira's Sky Control and shaping the noises throughout the air as skillfully as he could.

The crowd broke into whispers once the song finished. Eventually, an audience member stepped forward to talk with the proctor.

"What was that? Why were they using recorders for this trial?" he asked.

"They came to me with this idea," the proctor answered. "They wanted to use these recordings to fill in for the people they didn't have."

"This is an obvious violation of the rules of this trial," another person objected. "It needs to be their work, not anyone else's."

"It *is* their work," the proctor replied. "These recordings were all done by that girl over there. It was a fine performance too. Regardless, I don't think I'll accept them as potential conductors. With so many of the performances being done by one person, it's hard to tell how well they would have coordinated with a larger group."

Nira's face fell. Alius turned to the proctor, likely to protest, only to be stopped by a shout from the audience.

"Wait, please!"

Aer and Alius both blinked. The interruption had come from the Mechanic's Trial proctor, who was making his way toward the stage.

"Mechanic Kasir," the conductor hissed, staring down at the portly man in disdain. "To what do I owe this pleasure?"

The mechanic panted as he came to a halt. "Aer, Alius. Consider yourselves approved for my trial. If you want a future as a mechanic, I'll show you where to start."

He then turned toward the conductor, speaking loudly enough for everyone to hear. "They used ingenuity to make up for their shortcomings. I urge you to reconsider your evaluation."

"That's all well and fine for your little Mechanic's Trial, but the Conductor's Trial is a music recital," someone from the crowd said snobbishly. "This performance of theirs does nothing to show what kind of music they're capable of creating in the future."

"Wouldn't it be possible for them to record different kinds of music using these devices?" the portly man countered.

"As if that would be a substitute for true music," the person replied.

"Well, why not? You people are always like this! Placing misplaced value on some vague, unquantifiable element over actual results! They, using tools anyone could handle, matched the performances that the other fledglings only achieved with a lifetime of focused tutoring, a privilege they had access to from birth! I would think—"

"That's enough," the Conductor's Trial proctor interjected. "As the proctor for this trial, I have the final say on how their performance is to be judged."

Claps from above suddenly echoed down the hall. Everyone looked up to see an old man with a mane of graying hair floating to the front of the stage. A hush fell upon the crowd once people recognized who they were looking at.

The Conductor's Trial proctor looked mortified. "What might you be doing here, Emissary Striaen?" she asked timidly.

"I was just in the mood for some music. Imagine my surprise when I saw this," the old man answered.

"I apologize for this poor showing," the proctor replied frantically. "These children urged me to give them a chance. I didn't mean to—"

Emissary Striaen gave a slight smile. "It's fine. On the contrary, I think they did quite well. These children overcame their weakness of having little support through sheer resourcefulness. Furthermore, they displayed skilled Sky Control in their performance. They should be praised for their innovation and talent."

The proctor looked relieved.

"Is that so?" She then bowed her head. "If an emissary is saying as much, then I'll reconsider my opinion. I'll at least recognize that you three performed well. Good work."

Aer said nothing, seeing that as the best they could hope for.

Alius apparently disagreed, instead choosing to speak up. "If you're doubting Nira's ability to work with a larger group, let me just say that Aer and I knew nothing about music before this trial. The fact that she can coordinate with us and make up for our shortcomings is, quite frankly, a miracle. You guys should be lining up to recruit her."

The proctor stared at him for a moment before nodding. "Understood. I'll keep that in mind."

With everyone having had their say, Aer, Alius, and Nira were then dismissed from the trial to allow the conductors to discuss the day's performances uninterrupted.

Alius pumped his fist into the air as soon as they exited the building.

"That went better than I expected!" he exclaimed. "There's no way they can ignore us now."

"Calm down," Aer said as he wheeled Nira out the door. "I doubt any of the conductors watching will be interested in us two in the end. The proctor knows Nira did most of the work."

"Maybe," Nira said. "But you guys were just aiming to make a name for yourselves, right? I don't think anyone who watched will forget us that easily, especially when an emissary approved of our performance."

"Exactly!" Alius grinned. "This is great. We've finally managed to grab everyone's attention. I don't think the visitors were even paying that much attention to the Perch fledglings after us."

"Is this the type of attention we want, though?" Aer asked. "A lot of the audience seemed conflicted about how to judge us."

Alius patted Aer's back. "Aer, you need to stop worrying about the little things. We just need to leave a positive impression on them now that we're on their minds."

Aer didn't argue. He couldn't deny how well things had gone for them today. So much so that he had to reevaluate his opinions about the trials. He had thought of them as nothing more than a chore to go through, but now…

Feeling a bit more motivated, Aer listened to his brother as he started making new plans, humoring some of Alius's more far-fetched ideas while ignoring the wriggling doubts in his mind, at least for now.

CHAPTER 13:
AUTHORITY AND OBEDIENCE

I have discovered some rather unsettling things while trying to better understand my son's recent behavior. He has been ignoring my advice to stay away from the Charity Tree. What's worse, he seems to have gotten attached to the siblings he once argued with, taking the time to converse with them whenever he is free.

I cannot allow this to continue. But what action should I take at this moment? I feel it unwise to confront him about this directly.

For now, I will observe him while regularly imparting some wisdom into his life. Perhaps my words will resonate with him in time.

Predictably, Aer found his good humor wearing out quickly the next morning as Alius thrust new trial participation forms upon him, telling him what kind of preparations they would have to make.

"Let's finish the ones we've already signed up for before throwing ourselves at more," Aer said. "We still need to do the Falconry Trial, remember?"

"Yeah, yeah." Alius waved him off. "At least *look* at our options before complaining."

Aer grimaced as he went over the forms. More than a week's worth of trials still remained. "Now that I think about it, we've already finished our required three trials, haven't we? Can't we just relax after the Falconry Trial?"

Alius shook his head. "What, are you kidding? We can't stop here, not when the visitors finally know our names. We need to keep impressing them so everyone sees that this isn't a fluke."

Aer sighed. "Fine. Let's talk it over while we get something to eat. We're running low on food and water again."

The brothers carried their usual pots and bags as they went out to resupply. Alius took the participation forms with him, reading over them along the way.

"So what do you think about this one?" he asked, waving a form in front of Aer's face.

"The Enforcer's Trial." Aer quickly shook his head. "Wasn't that about subduing other fledglings in combat? No way. Sounds terrifying."

"You've gotten a lot better with your Sky Control recently, though," Alius said. "You've learned a lot from practicing with Nira."

"Not enough to be sure that I can overpower someone from the Perch with it. And I'd rather avoid getting into a sanctioned fight with them after all that's happened. Who knows what they might try to get away with doing to me?"

Alius sighed. "All right, some other trial, then."

Once they reached the familiar river near the base of the Charity Tree, the brothers set down the jars to fill them with water.

"Feels weird, doing something so routine after everything that's happened," Alius remarked. "It's calming in a sense."

"Speak for yourself," Aer replied testily. "Last time we were here, you ditched me to bargain with Kiel about getting everyone to try harder in the trials. Now I have to be on the lookout for any sudden decisions you might make."

"Oh, that's right," Alius said, ignoring Aer's jab. "We haven't seen Kiel since the day we got out of our punishment. I should talk to him about our plans."

Alius then ran up to Kiel's home, leaving an irked Aer to gather water by himself.

"Hey, Kiel." Alius knocked on the door. "About the next trial—"

The door swung open violently.

"Why didn't you two tell me about the Conductor's Trial?" Kiel demanded. "If I knew there was a way to complete a trial without Sky Control, I would have gotten everyone I could to join you!"

Both Aer and Alius froze. Kiel looked downright furious.

Alius recovered first.

"That's exactly why," he answered hesitantly. "Nira told us not to. Said she couldn't teach that many people at once."

"If I had known such a big shot would attend that trial, I would have joined you three, regardless of what she wanted," Kiel muttered with a dark expression. "Seriously, an *emissary*? What an unbelievable opportunity to get connected to Atravel's higher authorities."

"How did you even learn about that?" Alius asked, looking somewhat abashed.

"News spreads quickly when someone like an emissary is involved," Kiel answered. "Anyway, it's great that things went well for you. More fledglings have been coming to me since then, asking about you two and talking about what trials they want to participate in. But I thought we were working together on this. Kind of feels like you went behind my back to hog all the glory."

"Sorry," Alius said. "I didn't expect that trial to be as big as it was."

"Next time, keep me updated about whatever you're planning," Kiel said curtly before closing the door on them.

The brothers left the river and climbed back up the Charity Tree once they finished their business. With Kiel's words fresh on his mind, however, Aer suddenly felt a lot more conscious of the fledglings they passed. He had been vaguely aware of it on the way down, but it was clear that many of them were holding hushed conversations just out of the brothers' earshot. The way they hurried away once he or Alius got too close only confirmed Aer's suspicions.

Curious as to what they were saying, Aer let the wind carry their voices to his ears, trying to catch some of their conversations.

"Hey, it's those two. Heard they got the attention of an emissary recently."

"Why didn't they include us?"

"Isn't it obvious? They wouldn't stand out as much if they were grouped with the rest of us."

"I hear they've been going back and forth to the Perch. Think they're trying to join?"

"Speaking of which, they've been hanging around that wheelchair girl from the Perch a lot recently."

Aer scowled. Word of their success had evidently become quite the popular topic. But rather than congratulatory words, they were instead being given looks of envy.

Aer's annoyance only grew as he and Alius continued to scale the Charity Tree. He wasn't used to being scrutinized within the Spiral Forest. Everywhere else, sure, but people tended to mind their own business here. Had he been a bit bolder, he might have told off those gossiping. He had run himself ragged ever since the trials were announced. Now he couldn't relax even around his own home?

"Alius, I'm heading back," Aer announced suddenly.

His brother blinked in surprise. "We still haven't gathered any fruit."

"I just don't feel like doing it right now." Aer sighed. "I'll carry home the water we drew, so could you handle gathering food by yourself?"

Alius gave him an odd look before heading out on his own.

***

Once Aer and Alius had finished putting away their supplies, a hand popped out from the window of Nira's treehouse and waved in their general direction. They stared at the hand in confusion, only for Nira to wheel herself to the entrance of her home and impatiently gesture for them to come inside.

"What's going on?" Alius asked once they stepped into her home.

"I'd rather not go outside right now," Nira replied.

Aer noted her expression. She looked as annoyed as Aer felt.

"You too?" Aer asked.

"From that, I'm guessing you're going through the same thing right now?" Nira asked.

Aer nodded before discussing everything he had noticed about their neighbors. Alius, oblivious to the end, stared at him in bewilderment.

"You guys got off easy," Nira scoffed once Aer had finished.

"What do you mean?" Alius asked.

"You two weren't ever part of the Perch, so most people will leave it at gossip and speculation," Nira explained. "Meanwhile, the people I came across are all convinced that I intentionally excluded everyone else to keep them below me, just like any other Perch fledgling. Honestly, I can't believe how stupid and petty some people are."

"Let's hold our heads high and focus on what we're going to do from now on," Alius said, looking uncomfortable at Nira's less-than-charitable descriptions of their neighbors. "Right now, we need to go over what to do in the Falconry Trial. The emissary said to just see the birds as part of the sky and control them as such, but I can't do any Sky Control in the first place. Nira, you have any experience with what they're talking about?"

"Sorry. I'm as clueless as you guys for that trial," Nira admitted. "The only time I've seen animals around here was when people from other islands brought them over for display. Communicating with birds was never part of the Perch's curriculum."

"The lecturer for the Hunter's Trial did say that they kept wild animals caged on other islands," Alius said thoughtfully.

Aer nodded. "The head huntress said it was a hunter's job to keep the populations of different species stable. Guess they don't want kids like us messing that up."

Nira frowned. "It doesn't look like we can get in any practice for this trial. The only thing we can do at this point is get better at Sky Control until the day comes."

To Aer's surprise, Alius grinned. "That's perfect. This means none of our competition has prior training in this either. There won't be any huge gaps in knowledge or experience to overcome. It'll be an even playing ground."

***

Once the day of the Falconry Trial arrived, the trio made their way toward a field placed near the center of the island. Kiel, who had been pressing Alius to keep him updated, joined them along with a group of Charity Tree fledglings.

Unsurprisingly, they were once again outnumbered by the Perch fledglings at the trial site. They, along with the caretakers and the visitors, also seemed less surprised to see those from the Charity Tree. Instead, Aer saw recognition in their eyes, with some of the visitors pointing out Aer and Alius specifically.

"Those two are…"

"Aren't they the ones who made everyone argue on their behalf during the Conductor's Trial?"

"Even before that, I heard they created quite the commotion in the Rain Provider's Trial."

"I remember seeing them in the Perch. They were accused of something by the head caretaker only to be cleared of all suspicion by the head huntress."

"A friend of mine told me that they went up to Emissary Striaen and demanded that he answer their questions."

"Oh, those two! I wonder how they'll do in this trial."

Aer didn't need to look at his brother's face to know he was smiling. He could just *feel* how ecstatic Alius was over them being recognized.

In contrast, Kiel frowned, clearly upset at how little attention he was gathering in comparison.

The proctor's voice soon drowned out every other voice in the area. "All fledglings, eyes this way!"

Everyone faced the proctor, who cleared her throat in response. In front of her were steel cages holding birds of various species.

"For this trial, each of you will be handed a cage," she explained. "Your first job will be to try and soothe the bird. If you can get past that point, your next goal will be to communicate with them. If you can accomplish even that, come to me. I will give simple tasks for your bird to follow, such as flying around a certain area and collecting things off the floor. Depending on how far you get, we may give you an endorsement as a falconer once you leave this island. You are forbidden from talking to or receiving help from others during this trial."

The proctor then passed the cages among the fledglings. Aer was handed a bird with black plumes.

"Now, once you are ready, you may begin."

Aer peered into the cage, uncertain of what to do. He wasn't the only one. Many of the fledglings were as perplexed as he was, doing nothing but staring blankly at their cages.

Aer tried speaking to it like he would any other person. "Can you hear me?"

The bird gave no response. It didn't understand him and made no attempt to.

Aer couldn't understand it either. The bird didn't have human expressions or body language that could give Aer a clue about what it was thinking. The only thing Aer could tell from its frantic twitching was how uneasy it felt from being so close to him.

"How are we supposed to get them to do anything if we can't even communicate with each other?" Alius grumbled next to him.

Aer tried to remember what the emissary had taught him about this subject.

Avian communication is simply an extension of the right over the skies that the Great Arbiter has given us. If you seek to excel in the Falconry Trial, see the birds not as animals but as part of the sky that you control.

Curious, Aer tried steadying the bird's agitated movements as if easing a gust of wind.

Success. The bird was slowing down, to the point where it appeared drowsy.

Aer then considered his next move. If he could control its physical movements, could he also control its will?

Following that line of thought, Aer reached out to its mind, trying to perceive its emotions the same way he would detect motions through the air. After a few moments of struggling, he found success once again. The signals Aer received from its consciousness weren't clearly defined, feeling more instinctual than a coherent chain of reasoning, but that was enough.

Can you do as I say? Aer thought to it.

The bird froze. It seemed to have gotten the message, though whether it would obey him was another question entirely. Thinking that this might be enough, Aer walked up to the proctor to show his results.

"Well done." The proctor nodded after inspecting the bird's response to Aer's attempts at communication. "Now, see if you can control where it flies. I want you to make it circle around this area." The proctor then opened the cage.

Aer ordered the black-plumed bird to fly, which it promptly ignored. Annoyed, Aer forced its body forward, trying to communicate his intentions with the movements he made it perform. This was clearly a mistake, as it rebelled against Aer's grip, trying to fly in the opposite direction he led it toward.

Aer frowned. The bird clearly didn't like him much.

Getting an idea, Aer released his hold on the animal, letting it fly on its own. He then prompted a change in its movements subtle enough that it didn't notice his intent. From there, he slowly increased his control to see how much Sky Control he could use without it noticing. Soon enough, he had it flying the way he wanted it to. He couldn't get it to make any sudden movements, but he could choose the general direction it flew in by making it believe that every move it made was its own.

The proctor let out a noise of admiration.

"Now, try to get it to pick up that twig over there."

Aer frowned. Getting the bird to stop flying and pick up something wouldn't exactly be subtle.

Seeing Aer's hesitation, the proctor nodded. "I guess that was a bit too much to expect. Don't worry, you still did very well."

Seeing that his evaluation was coming to an end and deciding there was no harm in trying, Aer used sheer force to override the bird's control over its body. The bird once again resisted him, meeting his power with its own. But the strength it mustered wasn't anything Aer couldn't handle. After a few moments of struggling, the bird gave up control over its body and picked up the twig.

"Impressive!" the proctor exclaimed. "Most fledglings don't get this far in their first attempt! Let me see your form."

Aer handed his form to the proctor, releasing his control over the bird as he did so. Immediately, the bird dropped the twig it was holding and started pecking at Aer.

"*Go back into your cage,*" the proctor commanded the animal before chuckling.

"Just for future reference, it's much better for the long-term relationship between you and your bird if you don't force it," she advised. "But for the purposes of this trial, you did spectacularly."

Some nearby adults broke into whispers as he stepped away from the proctor.

"That was surprising. Mental communication on his first attempt?"

"Yes. It's abnormal for any fledgling to perform that well in the Falconry Trial."

"He's one of the twins, isn't he?"

"Yes. They've been doing quite well for Charity Tree fledglings, haven't they?"

"I've heard from Soleil that those from the Perch feel threatened by the Charity Tree fledglings. Guess I now know why. Why weren't they in the Perch to begin with?"

Feeling uncomfortable over being discussed, Aer quickly excused himself and quietly waited for the trial to end, ignoring the bewildered looks that some of the other fledglings gave him. Once the proctor had called for everyone to stop, Alius joined him.

"How did you do?" Alius asked.

"Good, I think," Aer answered. "How about you?"

"Couldn't even do the first part," Alius said. "I wasn't the only one struggling, though. I think most of the fledglings here did rather poorly, even those from the Perch. No one looked like they were ready for this trial."

Aer could tell from one look at the crowd that Alius was right. Most of the fledglings looked dissatisfied. Only a handful were being praised by the adults.

Nira wheeled herself to where they stood.

"Guess my dream of getting birds to do things for me won't come true anytime soon," she grumbled.

"Even if you could get them to listen, I doubt they're strong enough to do any heavy work," Aer replied.

"Still." Nira sighed. "Getting them to fetch things I can't reach would have been nice."

Alius looked around the area.

"Did things go well for you, Kiel?" he asked once he spotted the figure towering over everyone else.

Kiel shook his head. "No luck. But it's not a total loss. I think I'll stay here for a while. A lot of people from outside the Nesting Island gathered for this trial. What better chance to get acquainted?"

***

Aer's stomach growled upon returning home. A mouthwatering aroma had filled his nostrils as soon as he and Alius had stepped through their doorway.

"Do you smell something?" he asked.

"Aer, look over there."

He turned to where Alius was pointing. There, in the corner of their room, sat a decorated package.

Alius was the first to act, running to the box and unwrapping its contents.

"I think this is supposed to be meat," he said as he peered inside.

Aer blinked. Meat was a luxury food generally only available at the Perch. "Meat? Why is something like that here?"

"I think someone sent it to us as a gift. I don't recognize what kind of animal it is, though. Looks like it might have been a type of bird, judging from the shape. Think it's one we had to talk to in the trial?"

"I seriously doubt it," Aer said. "Does it say who sent it?"

"No, but who cares? Let's dig in! I heard that you're supposed to warm meat by holding it over a fire. Think we can start one right now?"

"Of course not!" Aer shouted. "In case you haven't noticed, *everything* around us is wood. We're prohibited from making fires for a reason!"

"Oh, right," Alius said sheepishly. "I think we're fine, though. This meat looks like it's already been cooked."

"Already been cooked?" Aer questioned. An unfortunate possibility then occurred to him. "Alius, wait."

"What?" Alius asked. "I'm starving."

"I know. So am I. But something's weird here. Who would go to the trouble of sending something like this to us?"

"Does it matter?"

"Yes, it matters! How do we know someone didn't poison it or something?"

"Oh, come on," Alius said. "Who would do something like that?"

"Hmm, I wonder," Aer deadpanned. "Have we made any enemies recently? Maybe upset some prideful fledglings and caretakers? No way, couldn't be."

Alius fell silent, realizing what Aer was getting at.

"Speaking of the Perch," Aer continued. "Gail thought we did something to their food during the Rain Provider's Trial. You think they might be trying to get revenge the same way?"

Alius's face fell. "Yeah. I see your point. We probably shouldn't eat this."

Alius grudgingly resealed the package and set it back on the floor. Even so, the uneaten meat continued to tantalize them throughout the night.

Chapter 14: Impatience

My son and I had an argument today. He discovered my presence on his way to the Charity Tree and demanded to know why I was trailing him. As the secret was out, I saw no point in withholding my thoughts any longer and asked him to explain all his actions up until now. He replied by telling me that I understood nothing outside my ivory tower.

In my anger, I told him he was little more than an unruly child and that if he wished to challenge the wisdom our nation had gained through countless generations, he would need to prove himself as someone worth paying attention to.

He then made a wager with me, telling me to properly listen to his opinions and reconsider my views if he did well in his upcoming trials. While I was under no obligation to accept, I agreed. I do not feel the need to oppose him in this matter if it will motivate him to prepare for his future.

Soleil calmed herself as she sat among the representatives of the other islands once more. Since their last meeting, she had memorized all their names and faces and had visualized herself speaking to them as she would any other person. She knew that if she wanted to persuade anybody, she would have to carry herself with the confidence befitting a higher authority.

A familiar voice invaded her ears, irritating her with its self-importance. "That concludes my report for the Caretaker's Trial."

"Thank you for your hard work, Head Caretaker Desen," a visitor replied. "Now then, I would like to ask about some of the more unusual animals Head Huntress Islea intends to bring to this island. I assume they are for your trial?"

"Most of them," Head Huntress Islea said. "The largest beast, however, is something we're preparing to butcher for the Grand Sabbath banquet."

"Ah, I see. I haven't seen such a ferocious specimen before. I hope the meat it provides is appetizing enough to compensate for the troubles it has given us so far."

"But of course. Emissary Striaen himself has descended here, after all. No expense will be spared. If possible, I'd like to place it under the caretakers' care."

"Understood," Head Caretaker Desen said. "We'll take it into our custody. In the meantime, is everyone finding their stay in the Perch pleasant?"

"It's been pleasant enough," Emissary Striaen idly replied. "However, I'd like to pay a visit to the Charity Tree here. A few of the fledglings there have caught my eye."

The head caretaker looked displeased as many of the visitors nodded.

"Ah, yes. The Charity Tree, of course," he muttered bitterly.

One of the visitors gave an awkward cough. Everyone there knew by now that the Perch fledglings from this island were noticeably underperforming compared to their peers. In contrast, the Charity Tree fledglings were doing far better than what people had believed them capable of. Many had begun wondering if the caretakers had indeed made a mistake somewhere in their recruitment for the Perch, with claims of nepotism becoming popular gossip among the visitors. Not the best situation to be placed in, especially when one of the most important people in Atravel had personally come down to observe.

Soleil smiled. All according to plan. The Perch performing abysmally had gone as well as she could have hoped. The Charity Tree fledglings on this island doing as well as they had wasn't something she had foreseen, but that only served to reinforce her points. Perhaps the Great Arbiter was on her side after all.

Soon, she assured herself as she stood to speak. *Soon.*

***

Aer held back the urge to smack his brother aside as Alius shook him awake. They had *just* finished the Falconry Trial the day before. Couldn't Alius at least let him sleep in peace?

"What is it now?" Aer groaned. "Can't it wait?"

"Not the time! Look outside!" Alius exclaimed, ushering him from their treehouse.

Aer groggily made his way outside and immediately broke into a cold sweat. People he had never seen before were occupying the platforms of the Charity Tree. From their attire, it was clear they weren't caretakers of any kind.

"These are visitors from the other islands, aren't they?" Alius asked. "Aren't they supposed to be at the Perch? What are they doing here?"

"I don't know," Aer replied. "Maybe they're having a trial here and scouting the place?"

"No, nothing of the sort," someone above them replied. "I apologize for this inconvenience, but they're all likely here because of me."

They looked up to see Emissary Striaen floating over their house.

"Good morning, Alius, Aer," the older man said kindly. "It's good to see you two again. I've taken some interest in your recent actions and wanted to learn more about you personally. Do you mind if we talk?"

"Not particularly," Alius answered, ignoring the looks the nearby caretakers and fledglings were giving them.

"Then let's go for a walk." The old man quietly floated down next to them and walked ahead.

The brothers followed as he walked across the bridge to the next platform, only to freeze when they heard someone else tailing them. They all stopped and turned to look at their pursuer. It was a bespectacled man with a long beard who looked to be nearing middle age. The emissary then gave a resigned smile and signaled for him to draw closer.

"Allow me to introduce you. This man's name is In Resin. He happens to be my personal doctor."

"Hello," Alius said nervously.

"It's nice to finally meet you two," the older man replied quietly. "Your names have become quite a popular topic in the past few days."

Emissary Striaen shook his head. "Honestly, Doctor Resin. Do I look so frail to you?"

"You can never be too careful," the man replied. "It'd be disastrous for the rest of Atravel if you were to come to harm."

"He's been checking up on me more frequently as of late," the old man explained to the brothers. "I suppose I've reached an age where I appear as if I could collapse at any moment! Speaking of which, are you two injured in any way? You're both moving a bit sluggishly."

"No, we're just a bit tired," Alius answered. "We came back from a trial late last night and woke up early to this."

"Ah, I apologize. Still, I'm curious. How do the caretakers apply treatment for the sick around here?"

Aer would have rolled his eyes if not for the man in front of him. The most any caretaker had done for a sick fledgling here was to toss them a fruit and tell them to not get close to other people. Calling that "treatment" would be a bit generous.

The old man shook his head in distaste, almost as if he had read Aer's mind. "I believe it wise to have a professional opinion. Let him inspect you two for a second."

Emissary Striaen then snapped his fingers, at which the doctor rushed to examine them.

Aer stiffened as the bearded man circled them, feeling rather self-conscious as he eyed their tattered clothes and messy hair.

"Rather thin, the two of you," Doctor Resin noted. "Your complexions are rather pale too. I've noticed that's a common trait around these parts. What do you two usually eat?"

"Whatever we can gather from the forest," Alius said.

"Just that?" the doctor asked.

Alius nodded.

"An imbalanced diet," the doctor muttered. "Do the caretakers here not push for you to get proper nutrition?"

"Don't even get me started," Alius grumbled. "I can't remember the last time we've eaten something other than Charity Tree food."

Emissary Striaen raised an eyebrow. "That's strange. What happened to the meat I sent you last night?"

Aer and Alius exchanged glances.

"Wait, that was you?" Alius asked.

"Oh, yes. I was gifted quite a bit of meat recently," Emissary Striaen answered. "There was enough for me to spare, so I thought to share some."

"Oh… um, thank you," Aer said awkwardly, trying to avoid Alius's criticizing gaze.

"So, what happened?" the old man asked.

"We… kind of ignored it," Aer answered.

"Why?"

"Aer was afraid that it was a trap from the Perch," Alius said with a huff. "They thought we sabotaged them in the Rain Provider's Trial by tampering with their food, so he was sure that it was their idea of revenge."

Emissary Striaen blinked. "I see. I never considered that possibility. I should have sent a message. But is the relationship between you two and those of the Perch that abysmal?"

"You don't know the half of it," Alius scoffed.

"Explain it to me thoroughly, then," the emissary replied. "I'm here because of growing unrest over how the Nesting Islands are handled. One person went as far as to organize all those dissatisfied into a coalition against the caretakers. Some of them even want a complete revolution of Atravel's long-held traditions. What's more, I may have inadvertently given this movement some legitimacy by addressing the involved parties and personally showing up down here to settle the dispute. The situation has devolved into a fiasco, and I'm trying to identify the root cause."

Alius's face brightened. While certain topics that the older man mentioned had gone over their heads, the brothers understood that many people outside weren't happy with the caretakers. This was an unprecedented chance to drag their reputations through the mud.

But do we really need to stir up more trouble with them? Aer wondered.

"Well, it looks like someone out there knows what they're talking about," Alius said. "I think we'd be better off without the caretakers completely."

Emissary Striaen sighed. "What compels you to say such a thing? How have the caretakers here been raising you exactly?"

"They don't do much, really."

"Have you spoken up about this to them?"

"They wouldn't listen anyway. If anything, I'm sure the ones in charge are happy things are this way."

Aer, sensing that others were listening in, signaled his brother to keep his voice down. He was, of course, ignored.

"Why do you believe this?" Emissary Striaen asked.

"They don't like us," Alius boldly declared. "I'm sure they'd be glad if we all died of starvation."

"You believe their actions are driven by malice rather than negligence? What makes you so certain they feel that way?"

"Easy. They don't want us to succeed. They all believe that Sky Authority is something the Great Arbiter gave them, so when we can't use Sky Control, it justifies their belief that it's our fault we're here and that they're not doing anything wrong by treating us this way. It contradicts everything they say if we do well, which is why they have their special lessons that they don't like us participating in."

The older man blinked before muttering something that Aer didn't catch.

"What did you say?" Alius asked.

"No, it's nothing. This conversation just brought back some memories, that's all," Emissary Striaen replied. "Is this what inspired you two to compete against the Perch?"

"Yes," Alius answered.

The old man then focused his gaze on Aer. "I now properly understand your brother's views on this matter, but how do you feel about this?"

"It's all a pain to deal with," Aer said. "It's so much easier to just avoid thinking about them."

Emissary Striaen nodded. "Proper attitude to take. While I won't deny that some people could do their jobs better, I think it's a bit much to say that all the caretakers are going out of their way to put you down."

Alius looked annoyed. "So what? You don't believe us?"

Aer elbowed his brother. Was he trying to get them in trouble?

Fortunately, the old man seemed to take Alius's confrontational attitude in stride. "I never said that. Situations like these are quite common outside the Nesting Islands as well, even if many try to pretend otherwise. But without a concrete comparison between you and the Perch, the rest of the visitors can't definitively accuse the head caretaker of unfair treatment."

Alius's expression turned thoughtful. "I have a few questions of my own, then. What trial are the visitors most interested in?"

"That's difficult to answer," the older man responded. "Different people value different things. If you're looking to participate in the trial with the biggest impact, then I would advise you two to look out for the Hunter's Trial. It's the last trial before the Grand Sabbath, you see. It would be your best chance to leave a good lasting impression on the visitors."

"Thank you for the advice," Alius said.

Guess that's one more trial we'll be taking later, Aer mused.

They stood for a few moments in silence. Doctor Resin then whispered something into Emissary Striaen's ear, eliciting a sigh from the old man.

"Is that all?" the emissary asked. "Our discussion here was quite illuminating, but unfortunately, my station forbids me from lingering for much longer."

Alius, who looked like he was still thinking of things to ask, reluctantly nodded.

"Well then, take proper care of yourselves until we next meet," Emissary Striaen said before walking away with Doctor Resin, leaving the brothers by themselves.

The moment he was out of sight, Aer and Alius were swarmed by caretakers who had been eavesdropping but had not dared to interrupt the emissary. There were questions here and there, but most of it was criticism over the way Alius had spoken of them.

Aer, noticing most of their ire was focused on Alius, found an opening to disentangle himself from the chaos and left Alius alone to deal with the backlash. Once he made his way home, he shut himself in and helped himself to the meat he now knew was safe to eat. When he had finished his half, he lay down, trying to catch up on the sleep he had missed.

***

After some time had passed, Aer woke to Alius slamming open their door.

"Welcome back," Aer greeted him as he drowsily sat back up.

"You just *ditched* me back there," Alius replied.

Aer yawned. "I didn't see a point in staying. It's *you* they're mad at, and it's not like they would be less angry just because I was there with you."

Perhaps it was out of a desire to vent his frustrations over how hard Alius had been pushing him lately, but Aer felt some twisted satisfaction as Alius fumed.

"Next time, don't say things that will obviously get us in trouble," Aer continued goading him. "Seriously, what did you expect, saying all that in a place where everyone could hear?"

Before Alius could tell him off, someone else loudly cleared their throat. They both turned to see Kiel standing in their doorway.

"I've been wanting to speak to you two," Kiel said.

Alius gave a frustrated sigh. "If this is about the attention we got from the emissary without involving you, I'd like to point out that we didn't *plan* any of tha—"

"No, no, I figured that out by myself," Kiel replied dismissively. "This is about something else."

"What is it?" Alius asked.

"You know about the Enforcer's Trial, right?"

Alius nodded.

"Okay, good. There aren't many trials left to sign up for. The fledglings who procrastinated and haven't done their required three yet all came up to me, looking for a trial where they won't embarrass themselves. I want you two to help them out there."

"What do you want us to do, exactly?" Alius asked.

"Just give them a hand in the exam. You guys already got the recognition you wanted, right? Give others their chance to shine."

"Sure," Alius promptly agreed.

Aer gave his brother an incredulous look.

"All right, then." Kiel nodded. "See you there."

He then closed the door and left.

"I thought we agreed we weren't going for that one," Aer said in a panic.

"I did, but I changed my mind." Alius gave a vindictive smile. "Anyway, it's the best way for us to directly compare ourselves to the Perch fledglings. You heard what the emissary said, right? If we can beat them outright in front of everyone, we'll give the visitors a lot more to criticize about the caretakers."

"And if we don't?" Aer asked.

Alius shrugged. "Just make sure we do."

Aer's eyes widened as Alius picked out the form for the Enforcer's Trial. He quickly grabbed it out of Alius's hands before moving out of his reach.

"Aer, what are you doing?" Alius asked.

"Just wait! You're telling me to go fight people from the Perch?"

"What's the problem with that? We've been doing well so far."

"That's because we've been avoiding facing them directly this entire time. You know that a lot of the Perch fledglings hold a grudge against us. Something like this would be a perfect chance for them to hurt us and pass it off as an accident."

Alius's voice hardened. "Aer, come on. Would you stop shaking in fear at literally everything I bring up? What's your problem?"

Something in Aer snapped.

"Easy for you to say!" he yelled. "You've been dragging us around, needlessly placing us at risk wherever we go. I'm the one who has to do all the work for your stupid plans!"

Before Alius could say anything back, Aer stormed out of the house.

Wandering outside the Spiral Forest, Aer looked at the form in his hand and resisted the urge to tear it apart. He closed his eyes as he leaned against a nearby stone pillar, taking a deep breath to manage his irritation. He remained in that position for a while, stirring only when a woman's voice reached his ears.

"Yes, I understand, Mother. But don't you think you're going a bit too far with this?"

Aer got ready to leave before realizing he had heard this voice somewhere before. Feeling drawn to it for some reason, he looked around for the source.

He eventually spotted two women arguing with one another. One of them looked slightly older than him. The other, presumably her mother, looked like one of the visitors he had spotted back at the Perch.

"You're just like everyone else," the older one stated. "Don't try to stop me. If anything, you should be standing by my side for this."

"B-But that's—"

The younger woman abruptly stopped and turned around.

"W-Who's there?" she stuttered.

Aer froze. Both women were staring at him now.

"Y-You're a fledgling from the Charity Tree, aren't you?" the younger woman asked. "What are you doing here?"

"I was just walking around," Aer responded, stepping away from them. "Sorry if I interrupted anything."

"W-Wait, don't leave!" the younger woman stammered. She then looked nervously at the older woman. "S-Seriously, don't worry about it. We shouldn't have been arguing here anyway."

The older woman stared back for a moment before walking away. "Ciel, we'll continue this talk later."

Aer blinked in recognition upon hearing her name.

Ah. I remember now. She was the one who first announced the trials, Aer thought, realizing why her voice sounded so familiar. Her breathtaking recital of Atravel's origins that day was still fresh in his mind.

Ciel breathed a sigh of relief once the older woman left the vicinity.

"Sorry about that. My mother was pressuring me to do something I'm not too sure about. You gave me some time to think things over. Between her and the caretakers, I feel like I've been drowning in nothing but expectations recently."

"Was it the caretakers who pushed you on stage when the trials and Ascension Ceremony were announced?" Aer asked. Normally, he would have left by then, but something in Ciel's voice urged him to continue the conversation.

"O-Oh, were you there?" Ciel looked nervous. "Yes, they did. Did I give a decent performance? I felt like the fledglings in the audience didn't think much of me."

"I wouldn't worry about that. You told that story like you were born to do so."

Ciel looked relieved. "Glad to hear it. Apparently, public speaking is a talent that runs in my family. Unfortunately, my nerves get in the way most of the time."

"Yeah, I get how that feels," Aer said. "I felt like throwing up when I had to step in front of everyone for the Conductor's Trial."

"I-Is that right? What's your name?"

"Aer."

"Wait, you're Aer?" Ciel asked.

When Aer blinked in surprise, she quickly shrank back. "Y-You and your brother have been making quite a name for yourselves. Where's Alius?"

"Not here right now." Aer's mood darkened as he was reminded of why he came there in the first place.

Ciel appeared to have picked up on this, as her face paled. "W-Wait. Did I say something wrong?"

"No."

"R-Right." Ciel took a breath. "I-I'm sorry if I'm being nosy, but I have to ask. Why are you two going so far?"

"Why do you want to know?" Aer asked sourly. "If it's because you think we're pushing our luck and gathering too much attention, then I already figured that out for myself."

"N-No, it's just that I'm feeling a little lost. Honestly, I'm rather envious. I wish I could have that much conviction in something, so I was hoping you could tell me more."

Aer sighed. It was tactless of him to take out his anger against Alius on other people. "It's more because of my brother than me," Aer said, calming himself. "He didn't like the fact that we're considered worthless by the Perch and wanted to prove them wrong to the world. Unfortunately for him, he doesn't have any talent in Sky Control, so he's using me to achieve glory for the two of us instead."

"Does this have anything to do with why you're so annoyed right now?" Ciel asked.

"Yeah," Aer grumbled. "He just keeps pushing and doesn't know when to stop. But he was always like that. I have to keep an eye out so he doesn't dig himself in too deep of a hole. I'm just tired of it."

"So why do you keep going along with him?"

Aer gave her a questioning look. "What do you mean?"

"You two have participated in several trials by now. If it really annoys you that much, why don't you just say no?"

Aer blinked. While he could have easily said that his brother was just too forceful to refuse, what had happened today showed that if he truly wanted to, Aer could have walked out at any time. "I…"

"The truth is that what he wants is what you want, too, isn't it?" Ciel continued. "It's just that you won't let yourself hope in anything because you're afraid that you'll be disappointed, like you always have been. Which is why you try to not care about anything. You've been running away this whole time."

Aer found himself at a loss for words. Ciel, who had been talking in a timid stutter just a moment earlier, was scrutinizing him with alarming intensity.

"You know, it sounds like your brother's been fighting for you this whole time. He's been trying his hardest to make sure you both have a future. And I think you know that. Actions speak louder than words, you know. Despite all your complaints toward your brother, you've followed through on everything he wanted to do. I seriously doubt you would go so far if you truly believed it was pointless. The fact that you can talk about him like this is telling."

Aer stuttered as he struggled to find his voice. "W-What's with you?" he snapped. "What do you even know about us to lecture me like this?"

Ciel flinched, looking as if Aer had slapped her awake. "I-I apologize. It's just that… I had a younger brother who acted the same way. He always said nobody would care about your problems more than yourself and that if you didn't care enough to do anything to fix them, then you couldn't expect anyone else to either."

"I hope the two never meet," Aer grumbled. "I have a feeling that Alius would get even more annoying if he knew there were other people like him."

"I don't think you have to worry about that." Ciel looked away dejectedly. "I said that I *had* a brother just like yours."

"Wait, what? What happened to him?" Aer immediately regretted asking upon seeing Ciel's expression. "Sorry, forget I said anything. I didn't mean to pry—"

"D-Don't worry about it," Ciel replied hurriedly. "Anyway, I've started thinking more about the people in my life and the impact they had on me and the people they knew. I've come to realize a lot of things that I wish I understood earlier. What you were saying reminded me of myself from back then, so I ended up using you as a proxy. Sorry."

The two fell silent. Before Aer could decide how to walk away without seeming rude, however, Ciel asked him a question.

"Do you know how you two ended up this way?"

Aer leaned back on the stone pillar as he reflected. "We've been like this for a long time. Alius and I have been on the Charity Tree since birth, and the caretakers who were stuck raising us ignored us whenever they could. So we learned to rely on each other and no one else. The only time anyone noticed we existed was when I first discovered Sky Control. I got a bit carried away with the attention I was receiving and showed off a lot. I overdid it and ended up embarrassing some of the fledglings from the Perch. They got angry and got into a lot of arguments with me. In the end, I just avoided them by staying home. But Alius didn't like that. He went out and argued with them. I had to drag him back when he started getting into fights with everyone. What we're doing now is just an extension of what we've always done."

"So what do *you* want to do?" Ciel asked.

"I don't know," Aer admitted. "Sometimes, I can't help but think it would be better for the rest of the world if I weren't here. The Perch and the caretakers certainly don't want us here, and I don't feel like putting up the energy to go against them."

"But your brother disagrees?"

"Alius and I don't always see eye to eye. He's never cared about the opinions of others over his own. Sometimes, I think he'd be better off by himself if he didn't need my Sky Control. Which makes me wonder why he wasn't the gifted one. I don't even know what to do with it."

"The Great Arbiter decides who is gifted and who is not," Ciel said.

"If this is all because of the Great Arbiter, then I'd like to ask what he thinks he's doing."

"There might be a reason for it," Ciel replied. "If your brother could do everything by himself, he might not rely on you at all. Likewise, I don't think you could really live without him either."

Aer tried to imagine a life without Alius. Without him, Aer likely would have moved to the top of the Charity Tree and not gone out much at all. He might have avoided interacting with other people entirely and would have been completely forgotten by everyone else.

Ciel smiled knowingly. "I think you should make up with your brother soon."

"Right," Aer replied. "Sorry I wasted your time."

"No, I'm glad we had this talk," Ciel said. "It makes me more certain of what to do next."

With their conversation finished, the two headed their separate ways.

Aer felt oddly vulnerable as he hiked back up the Charity Tree. What had just happened? Why did he just go along with Ciel's questioning? She might have had a point, sure, and he might have put his thoughts and feelings in order thanks to their conversation, but for him to reveal that much of himself to a stranger didn't feel natural for him. It was as if something had compelled him to do so.

Now that Aer had the time to think, he considered backing away from his brother a little while longer. But he found himself forgetting all that once he peered into their treehouse and saw a dejected Alius sitting on the floor.

Aer quietly entered the room. An awkward silence settled between the two until Alius found the courage to speak.

"Sorry, I got a bit heated," Alius muttered.

"No, I shouldn't have walked off like that," Aer replied.

"I shouldn't have pressured you into this trial. After thinking about it for a while, I get why you wouldn't be happy to get in a fight with the Perch," Alius said. "It's just that we've been doing so well lately that I forgot to consider how you would feel about it."

"That, and you've been worried about what would happen if we didn't do anything," Aer said. "Which is why you've been pushing so hard to make things easier on us."

"Yeah. I'll admit it. I've been worried about myself this entire time. I don't know anything about life beyond the Charity Tree. I'm also not gifted with a high Sky Authority like you, and everyone seems to care so much about it. What'll happen to me once we're forced to leave this island? Can I even survive by myself?"

"Come on," Aer said. "It's not like I would just leave you to fend for yourself."

"Yeah, but if I can't pull my weight—"

"If you aren't there to push me forward, I doubt I would work up the nerve to do anything," Aer interrupted. "We'll stick together, like we always have. We need to cover each other's blind spots, after all."

"Thanks," Alius muttered.

Another awkward silence ensued.

"So, what's next?" Aer asked, trying to hide his embarrassment. "We need to think about what trial to go for to best impress the visitors, right?"

"I promised Kiel we'd help him out in the Enforcer's Trial," Alius answered. "But if you're not okay with it, then—"

Aer took a deep breath as he tried to muster a courage he didn't have. "Fine, I'll give it a try. Just don't expect too much."

Chapter 15: Hidden Struggles

I must give my son his due credit; he has been working diligently since our quarrel. He has paid close attention to my recent lectures and has revised some of his views, acknowledging the validity of many of my points. As a reward, I have taken some time to listen to his ramblings.

In the end, this gamble between us has become completely pointless, as I have already lent an ear to his opinions before he has proven himself. He's noticed this as well, as he has changed the initial conditions of our wager, asking me instead to grant him one of his wishes if he excels in the trials. He refused to disclose what the wish was, telling me he would only do so once he accomplished his goal. As proud of him as I am, I told him that if it was within my ability to do so, I would grant it. Perhaps I am too lenient with him as a father.

Gail took a deep breath as he stopped in front of his father's room. The reason for his summons likely wasn't a pleasant one.

"Enter," the person inside commanded.

Gail stepped in. His father was holding some familiar sheets of paper.

"You called for me, Father?" Gail asked politely, now knowing full well what this was about.

"In my hand are the proctors' evaluations of our most recent trials. Tell me, Gail," his father said as he thrust a sheet of paper into Gail's face. *"Why are there fledglings from the Charity Tree placing above you?"*

Gail flinched. The Forewarner's Trial should have been simple for Gail to do well in, as all it required was a sensitivity to the wind. Yet *that girl* had outperformed him.

"You know Nira Ducol wasn't originally from the Charity Tree," Gail argued. "Plus, she's always been great at music. That experience with handling sound must have given her a sensitivity to the air—"

The older man interrupted him. "Enough. You're giving me excuses like I should care. I do not. Nira Ducol is no longer being taught by the caretakers. Furthermore, the visitors are not privy to the pasts of every fledgling living on this island. As far as they are concerned, you, my son, who have been taught by the best caretakers on this island, lost out to someone with no special education whatsoever."

Gail fell silent, unable to argue.

His father sighed. "Gail, take a seat."

He silently obeyed, keeping his posture straight as he did so.

"You need to understand that this is a crucial point in your life. Your future depends on how well you do here, and with the current political climate, mine does as well. It's too late to simply accept these fledglings into the Perch now. Doing so would be openly admitting that we caretakers didn't examine them properly the first time."

"Yes, Father."

"I'm sure I've told you how a particular orator has stirred people outside into a frenzy. They're calling into question the entire system of the Nesting Islands and the caretakers. It's at this time we need to shut up any naysayers with uncontestable results. So why are you and the rest of the Perch underperforming? The visitors were all eager to tell me how this iteration of the Perch has had the worst trial performances in living memory."

"I told you we've been sabotaged," Gail complained.

"I had the caretakers look into that. No traces of poison have been found. And I'm to understand that you were in perfect condition for the Forewarner's Trial?"

"Yes, Father," Gail grudgingly admitted.

"And yet you still lost to that girl in something so simple. How disappointing. Then there was that incident with the intercom—"

"You know that wasn't me! Those twins from the Charity Tree set me up with those recorders!"

"Yes." His father sighed. "I know. But it baffles me to see how you let yourself get tricked like that."

So did you, Gail silently fumed. That incident was still a sore point between the two of them. But Gail wasn't willing to voice his complaints. Considering how mercilessly his father had beaten him after it had happened, it was better to stay quiet whenever the subject arose and pray that his father moved on quickly.

He didn't want to end up like Kiel, after all.

The head caretaker crossed his arms. "Gail, do you understand how much time and effort I poured into your education?"

"Yes, Father."

"Then why do you keep disappointing me?"

Gail took a sharp, pained breath as his father grabbed the closest thing he could find and struck him with it. A tense silence settled between them.

"No more excuses. Try harder next time."

"Yes, Father."

***

Gail cursed under his breath as he exited the room and went back down to his living quarters. Of course his father had called him up for that. Why had he expected anything else? That was how it *always* was.

When his father had first discovered how gifted he was with Sky Control, he had instructed the caretakers to give Gail the best possible education in every subject they had experience teaching. As a result, Gail became a top student in almost every discipline.

Even so, he couldn't be the best at *everything*, which never failed to enrage his father. If there was so much as a hint that Gail might not measure up to another fledgling in any given field, his father tore into him mercilessly, telling him to do better or to give up on the subject entirely.

Of course, whenever Gail *had* tried to quit, his father became even more displeased, telling him he had just wasted his father's efforts and tutelage for nothing, leaving Gail with no choice but to continue.

As a result, one subject Gail had dreaded most growing up was music. A certain girl had consistently made him look like an amateur whenever they were compared.

She was someone like him; her parents were caretakers who had placed a lot of pressure on her to do well and had taught her strictly. Still, Gail was certain he was above her in most areas. But her constant dominance in music remained a sore spot for his father, who punished Gail severely for his inability to keep up. And as his father was their superior, the caretakers around Gail often looked the other way whenever unexplained bruises appeared on his body.

That continued until one night, when Gail walked in on Nira practicing her music on top of one of the Perch's buildings, out of everyone else's earshot. Seeing nobody else around, Gail pushed her off with a well-placed gust.

It was a decision made on a whim. Maybe he wanted her to stay away from practicing music for a while; maybe he was just venting his frustrations at what he saw as the root cause of his suffering. Whatever it was, the result was a lot more drastic than he had expected. Nira lost all feeling in her legs due to the fall and became unable to walk properly.

Because of all the setbacks that incident caused for her, Nira became unable to keep up in most of her subjects and eventually had to drop out of the Perch. Her parents privately relocated her to the Charity Tree to hide their shame.

No one, not even Nira, had discovered that it was Gail who had pushed her off. They had all assumed that it was just an accident. Gail felt a bit of guilt over it, but that was nothing compared to the sense of relief knowing his father wouldn't ever compare him to her again.

Or so he thought. Today proved otherwise. What was worse, Nira seemed to have recently been tutoring the twins in Sky Control.

Gail grimaced. Right, the twins. If his father was furious at him for losing to other Perch fledglings like Nira, then he was downright apoplectic over Gail being outperformed by fledglings who weren't even part of the Perch and had no formal education.

One of the twins, Aer, had shown him up in a display of Sky Control in front of everyone back when they were children. The punishment his father gave Gail as a result was worse than anything he had experienced before.

Since then, Gail had made things miserable enough for Aer to think twice before showing off, doing his best to destroy Aer's confidence. He didn't need more rivals for his father to compare him to.

Despite Gail's efforts to keep Aer in line, however, his brother, Alius, had dragged him out again and again. Gail had made sure to discredit them in front of everyone whenever they insisted on sticking their noses where they didn't belong. Lies, provocations, anything to keep them out of the caretakers' favor. And yet Alius kept coming back with his brother at his side.

Gail's face contorted with rage whenever he thought of Alius. He hated that mouthy, oblivious brat. He didn't know how lucky he had it, not having any expectations placed on him. Neither of the twins could possibly understand the pressure Gail endured. And yet he continued to act without any prudence while being utterly convinced that he was in the right.

Gail forced himself to calm down as a nearby group of fledglings spotted him. It wouldn't do for them to see him worked up. Any sign that things weren't going perfectly well for him would be taken full advantage of. He couldn't show a hint of weakness if he wanted to stay on top.

"Hey, Gail. Have you signed yourself up for the Enforcer's Trial?" a rather stocky fledgling asked as Gail approached.

"No, I haven't, Iad," Gail replied.

Almost everyone here was from the Blessed and was, therefore, a potential rival, but that was exactly why he needed to memorize their faces and outwardly get along with them so he could stay updated on what they were doing. Plus, many were eager to toady to him, willing to stay subordinate to his authority knowing he was the head caretaker's son. He would gladly take advantage of that.

"That's a surprise," Iad said. "It's a trial where you can directly pit the strength of your Sky Control against others. I thought you'd jump at the chance, considering how competitive you are."

"I've been busy." It was true. Gail had been practicing for a lot of different trials. He didn't need to add more on a whim.

"Well, that's too bad. The Perch's reputation has been taking a hit recently. Some of us were thinking that we should be a bit more selective. Find our weakest members, put them all in one group, and make it look like they were dragging the rest of us down in the previous trials. Then we can cut them out of our lives and send them to the Charity Tree. But if you really don't want to be a part of it, that's fine."

Gail straightened and paid closer attention to everyone in the group. "Tell me more."

***

Aer took a deep breath to mentally prepare himself for the day's trial. He and Alius seemed to be the first ones there.

They were at the site of the Enforcer's Trial, near a prominent stone pillar at the edge of the forest. They had gotten there very early in the morning, as both were too anxious to sleep.

Naturally, that meant they were wet from head to toe due to the morning rain.

Kiel eventually joined them, bringing a multitude of other fledglings with him.

"Good, you guys are already here," Kiel said. "I was worried you bailed on us when I didn't see you at your house."

Alius nodded. Aer shrank back, grateful that his brother said nothing about how he had initially refused to participate.

He didn't get much time to relax, however, as fledglings from the Perch soon arrived.

Aer quickly surveyed the people he would be competing with and groaned once he spotted a familiar face. "Gail."

Alius's gaze hardened. "Perfect. This is our chance to pay him back for the Rain Provider's Trial."

"Don't get into a fight with him this time, regardless of what happens," Aer admonished. "I don't want a repeat of what happened back then."

"I know, I know. I'll just have to settle for showing him up in front of the visitors."

***

Gail listened carefully to the people beside him, on the alert for any sign of betrayal.

He had agreed with Iad's proposition to frame the weakest fledglings as the reason for the Perch's recent failures. As every fledgling from the Perch was supposed to be under the caretakers' guidance, this would undoubtedly create more problems for his father, but he wasn't too concerned about that. So long as Gail himself performed well and his involvement remained a secret, his father's anger wouldn't be directed at him.

Assuming everything went as planned, he could wash his hands of the Perch's recent failings. The only problem was whether he could trust the group to keep their word. He recognized most of them and knew that many in the group saw him as an enormous obstacle in their own bid for recognition and success. It wouldn't be surprising if some secretly planned to embarrass him in front of the visitors. It would be their best chance to rid themselves of a powerful rival.

Once they arrived at the trial site, however, Gail felt a sense of unease. The Charity Tree fledglings, much to his confusion, completely outnumbered those from the Perch.

Why are so many of them here? he wondered as hundreds dressed in shabby clothing glared at him and his peers. As far as he knew, being an enforcer wasn't a particularly favored occupation within the Charity Tree. He grimaced when he saw the twins lining up. *Them again?*

He shifted his focus to the visitors who were coming to observe the trial. His father was there too, busy directing the caretakers to lead the visitors to the right location.

While his father was distracted with the visitors, Gail signaled for everyone who was in on the plan to gather for a discussion. Soon enough, the group he had talked to that day, consisting of roughly a fifth of the Perch fledglings there, huddled together just far enough from everyone else to not be overheard.

"Who do we target for this?" asked a girl whose name escaped Gail.

"Anyone who isn't here listening is fair game," Iad answered.

"Anyone?" someone behind Gail asked.

"If they get caught underperforming, then that's their own fault," a short fledgling said scornfully.

Gail made a mental note to keep an eye on the fledgling who just spoke. His name was Rial, and he was one of the more gifted and ambitious fledglings in the Perch. Out of everyone there, he likely had the most to gain by betraying Gail.

"There's one more thing," Gail added.

"What is it?" Iad asked.

"The Charity Tree fledglings. The biggest threat from them should be a fledgling named Aer."

"Ah, right. Heard of him." Rial nodded. "He's one of the twins who's been getting a lot of attention recently, right? The one who's supposed to be good at Sky Control despite living in the Charity Tree? While the other is the loudmouth who's been going up to visitors he has no business talking to. Where are they now?"

"They're the ones in wet clothes, standing next to the giant."

"I see them. Did they get themselves wet to draw attention?"

"Probably," Gail scoffed. "How stupid."

"No kidding," Rial agreed. "Which one is which? I can't tell the difference."

"They look identical, so it's probably easier to memorize what they're wearing. I'm certain Aer's the one wearing that oversized cloak and leggings while Alius is the one talking to the giant right now."

"You sure?"

"That's how they usually dress."

"All right, then. We'll have to make sure Aer doesn't do well in this trial so Alius can't use his performance as an excuse to talk to the more important visitors."

***

Aer shuddered as eyes suddenly bored into him. He would never be okay with the feeling of being observed. But before he could locate the source, a group of men marched between the fledglings. One blew a whistle, demanding everyone's attention.

"Listen up," the man in the center said in a firm voice. "I will be serving as the proctor for this trial."

The participating fledglings settled down immediately. The proctor carried a steel baton, and he looked like the type of person who knew how to use it.

"This trial will be split into two parts," the man started. "First, we will hand half of you armbands with numbers emblazoned on them. If you receive an armband, your job will be to track those who don't and capture them before they can leave their designated area."

He then inspected the fledglings in attendance, evaluating their physiques. "So long as you do no permanent damage to the people involved, you can use whatever means to detain the others, be it Sky Control, physically pinning them to the ground, or anything else. Proctors scattered throughout the area will declare a fledgling captured when they have been properly subdued."

Aer frowned, bothered by how loose the rules sounded. What would qualify as "permanent damage" to the proctors?

"If you have not been handed an armband, your job will be to reach certain landmarks without being detained. Like the opposing side, you can use any method you can think of to make this happen."

The proctor then pointed to something pinned to the nearby stone pillar. "We have marked these landmarks with signs to let you know they are safe zones. These landmarks will grant you immunity from being subdued by those with armbands for a limited time once you make physical contact with them. The proctors standing at these landmarks will let you know when the time is up. The longer you last and the more distance you can cover before you're eliminated, the less points will be deducted from your overall evaluation. If you can leave the designated area entirely, all the better for you. This is to ensure none of you willingly surrender to your pursuer, expecting they will do the same for you when it is your turn to detain them."

Aer and Alius exchanged glances. That ruled out one idea they'd considered. Best to stay on the same side, then.

"To those wearing armbands, the more fledglings you personally subdue, the higher your score will be. The proctors will keep track of how many you capture using your armband's number. You will also be penalized collectively on how many fledglings you let leave the designated area. Once we're finished, we will begin the second section, where you will switch roles. Those who were given armbands will then hand them over to those without. Any questions?"

When no one answered, the proctor nodded.

"Now then, we will begin assigning you to your roles. Register your names with the proctors as I do so."

As the proctors walked around handing armbands to the participants, it quickly became clear to Aer and Alius that they were assigning roles based on where each fledgling stood. The brothers adjusted their positions accordingly to make sure they would end up on the same team. Some of the other fledglings also caught on and began subtly shifting places.

Kiel stepped closer to them and searched the crowd. He then signaled some of the other Charity Tree fledglings to rearrange their positions, causing the proctor walking by to hand them all armbands, placing them within the same group.

Once the proctors had finished assigning roles, they led Aer, Alius, and the others with armbands away from those without. The one giving orders then amplified his voice to address everyone in the vicinity.

"One last thing. Only the fledgling who first subdues another will get credit for the capture. You can choose to act either independently or with the other fledglings knowing that. Similarly, those without armbands can choose to either help or sabotage a fellow runaway based on whatever they think will let them last longer. Now then, begin!"

***

Aer chased down the fledgling in front of him, only to sense gusts of wind from five different locations intended to knock him away. He jumped back, giving yet another target enough time to reach a nearby landmark.

"Aer, over here!" Alius shouted from a distance.

Aer quickly made his way to Alius, who was still accompanied by Kiel and those under his command.

"What is it?"

"We need to talk," Kiel said. "You haven't caught a single fledgling since we started."

"I've noticed," Aer muttered. "The guys from the Perch are doing everything they can to make sure I can't reach them. Even those who are supposed to be in our group are sabotaging me."

"They've been completely ignoring me, though," Alius said. "Looks like they're all focusing their attention on you specifically. The fact that you did so well in the previous trials is working against us right now."

Alius looked thoughtfully at Aer. "How do you think they're telling us apart? We look identical."

Aer gave him an odd look. "The same way everyone else does? From our—" He stopped, catching on to what Alius was thinking.

"Let's get out of everyone's sight first," he whispered.

Alius nodded before turning around.

"Kiel, could you guys buy us some time and distract everyone nearby?"

***

Gail deftly evaded the fledgling in front of him as he reached for the nearest landmark.

How slow, he thought as the proctor nearby declared him safe.

He was in excellent form today. As a runaway, he had effortlessly avoided everyone's attempt to pin him down, allowing him to save his strength as he kept track of those who were working the hardest. Once it was time for them to switch roles, he planned to rush those who had exhausted themselves using full force.

As others with armbands gathered around the area, Gail left the landmark he was leaning on and jogged to a safer location. He had little time to prepare himself when someone who was supposed to be an ally aimed at his feet, trying to trip him.

"What are you doing?" Gail yelled as he caught his balance and avoided falling headfirst to the ground. "I don't have an armband, same as you!"

"What of it?" the fledgling replied. "The proctor said that we could do anything as long as we don't leave lasting damage."

Gail inspected the fledgling who had tried to trip him. He was from the Perch, but he wasn't one Gail had teamed up with to frame the weaker fledglings.

"Look, we're both from the Perch," he said in a deceptively calming voice. "We should work together. Let's both just focus on doing better than the Charity Tree."

"I don't believe you," the fledgling replied. "You just want me to get caught early to make yourself look better in comparison. That's what you guys all decided on, right?"

Gail stiffened. He wasn't supposed to know that. Who had told him?

Gail ran away from the distrustful fledgling only to be targeted with a strong gust of wind from another Perch fledgling.

Gail swore as he parried the blow with his own. That person didn't have an armband either. What was even happening?

Gail asked those he had teamed up with to get a clearer picture of what had happened. Apparently, Rial had blabbed and framed Gail as the main perpetrator. Judging from his actions, he likely didn't consider those from the Charity Tree a genuine threat. Instead, he saw knocking down Gail as the more important objective.

The rest of the Perch had effectively split into factions upon hearing the news. Those who had become paranoid over being considered sacrificial were actively sabotaging each other.

Gail briefly considered seeking out Rial and sabotaging him in retaliation before stopping himself. He could always get revenge on Rial later. It would be better to let him go for now than to use precious trial time to satisfy a petty vendetta.

He was shaken out of his thoughts when another fledgling charged at him in all the chaos.

It was Aer.

So he's here, Gail thought as he jumped away. Easily evading Aer's attempts to grab him, Gail put some distance between them with a casual jog.

That was too easy, Gail thought only to be flabbergasted when Alius emerged from nowhere and fired a burst of air at him too quickly to defend against.

"What?"

Gail, blown off his feet, lost his balance as he tumbled onto the ground. Kiel, who must have been seeking this opportunity from a distance, sprinted over and pinned Gail down while he was still disoriented.

"Well, well, fancy seeing you here, Gail." His older brother smirked. "How's Dad doing?"

Gail was at a loss for words. What was going on here? He couldn't sense a presence through the air at all. Did *Alius* manage to silence himself? When did he become so proficient with Sky Control?

"Captured," a proctor nearby declared. "Wait here until the first half of this trial is over."

Gail lay there in shock, trying to process what had happened.

Comprehension dawned on him as he observed the brothers. It wasn't that Alius was suddenly displaying skills he'd never had. Rather, the twins had swapped clothes, pretending to be the other. Knowing that those from the Perch were keeping an eye out for Aer, Alius had set himself up as a decoy, chasing their targets straight into his brother, who lay in wait to strike them down.

***

Aer took a deep breath as he aimed for his next target. Everything was going smoothly. The Perch fledglings had been wary of him specifically, which was why they had all been blindsided when he and Alius switched clothes. The fact that everyone from the Perch had turned on each other made things even easier, as they all refused to spill the secret in hopes that others performed as badly as they had.

Fulfilling the deal Alius had made with Kiel, Aer left most of those he knocked down to be captured by the other Charity Tree fledglings in the vicinity, only subduing them himself when no one else was near.

Kiel grinned at them as he wrestled down Gail.

"Keep up the good work!" he shouted as Aer and Alius continued forward.

Things were looking up. At the rate they were going, they were certain to outdo the Perch fledglings in this trial. There was so much infighting and sabotage among the Perch, while those from the Charity Tree had a considerable advantage in both unity and numbers, thanks to Kiel's involvement. Some of the Charity Tree fledglings without armbands were even making sure that they got caught only by others from the Charity Tree, preventing the Perch fledglings from getting any points off them.

After some time had passed, the proctor blew his whistle. "Time's up! Take a moment to catch your breath. Whatever roles you had just now will be swapped once we resume."

Aer fell to the ground, panting. Alius soon joined him. They had lost track of how many fledglings they had eliminated in that half of the trial, though both were sure the majority were from the Perch.

Kiel patted them both on the back, prompting Alius to turn around.

"Well, Kiel? This enough to satisfy you?"

"Yeah," Kiel replied. "Almost everyone on our side with an armband got at least one fledgling. A good number of them were from the Perch too. Almost everyone from the Charity Tree who participated in this trial is in my debt now. And Gail… well, let's just say I'm *quite* happy with the results."

***

Gail looked at his father, who stared back at him with a malicious gaze. The message was clear. Unless he turned things around in the second half of the trial, he would be facing a very harsh punishment once he got home.

Gail felt like screaming. Everything was going wrong. Whose fault was this? Whose fault was it that he had been put in this situation? Rial? Kiel? No, it was those brothers, who used a cheap trick to get him captured far earlier than he should have been.

No, he shouldn't have been captured at all. They would pay for this. If he could just get them out of everyone's view…

The head proctor blew his whistle.

"That's enough rest," he announced. "We will soon begin the second half of this trial. If you have an armband, hand it to someone who does not and wait. Those who receive an armband, confirm your numbers and your names with the proctors. We'll start once everyone's ready."

***

Several fledglings rushed the brothers as soon as the proctor blew the whistle. Aer blew back the person running toward Alius then grabbed his brother before dragging him to the nearest landmark.

The proctor there declared them safe. This brought little comfort to Aer, as many of the Perch fledglings in the area began circling the brothers, waiting for the timer to run out.

Fortunately, Kiel saw that moment as an opportunity to lead the fledglings under his command to run. When those surrounding Aer and Alius realized how many people were getting away, they gave chase.

Aer watched their backs as they left. None seemed to be on the same page. They were still sabotaging each other more than aiming for their targets.

Taking advantage of the opportunity, the brothers followed Kiel's group at a distance, distracting those chasing him and splitting their focus even further.

Aer took a deep breath as Alius grinned at him. The way things were going, they could probably get by just fine.

Then it happened. Gail, entering the scene ahead, blew the fledglings without armbands off their feet with a single gust of wind. He then dropped his full weight onto Kiel, who struggled relentlessly against his younger brother's grip.

"Don't drag me down with you, you failure!" Gail spat as he slammed Kiel's head onto the ground, causing a nearby proctor to declare him subdued.

Gail's eyes turned toward Aer and Alius.

"There you two are," he said in a murderous tone.

Aer stared in terror as Gail charged at them in full force. Alius, however, ran straight, trying to meet Gail's charge head-on. Gail responded by grabbing Alius and throwing him to the ground before pressing his foot to Alius's face.

Aer frantically scanned his surroundings as a proctor near them declared the flailing Alius captured. Seeing a tree marked as a landmark up ahead, Aer leapt into action, hoping to reach it before Gail could get him.

Aer briefly felt the tree connect with his right hand before Gail crashed into his stomach, violently wrenching him away.

"Stop!" the trial proctor yelled, pulling Gail away from Aer. "You cannot attack another fledgling once they make contact with a landmark."

"Come on. He didn't touch the tree!" Gail shouted at the referee.

"He did. Now, step away."

Gail reluctantly stepped back, but he did not leave. Instead, he paced in front of the tree, making his next target clear.

Aer's eyes shifted nervously as he looked for an opening to escape Gail. But he found none. The proctor next to him then notified him that he wouldn't be able to stay at this landmark much longer.

Seeing no other option, Aer circled around the tree, keeping his hand on it as he did so. Once the tree was between him and Gail, he let go and raced toward the next landmark.

Not even a second later, Gail was in pursuit.

Aer sprinted as quickly as he could. Gail, however, was faster. His movements had a frenzied desperation Aer had never seen before. Was Gail always so ferocious? He didn't remember Gail moving in such a *bestial* manner back in the Rain Provider's Trial.

As soon as that thought entered Aer's mind, Gail roared as if to unnerve Aer in the same manner as back then. Aer saw it coming that time, however, and silenced the air around his ears. He then produced a strong headwind to blow Gail back.

But Gail was not easily deterred. He resisted with his own gusts of wind and tackled Aer. Aer twisted to get out of his grip before Gail could pin him down, only to have Gail slam his fist into Aer's face and close his hands around Aer's throat.

Choking, Aer signaled for Gail to stop, trying to surrender, but Gail kept going. Aer tried calling for help, but no proctors came to stop their scuffle. Gail had led him to a blind spot.

I'm going to die here, Aer thought in silent panic. He couldn't breathe, and his vision was darkening. *Gail is going to kill me.*

"Enough! *Get your hands off him!*" he heard a voice thunder.

The pressure on Aer's throat vanished as someone descended from up above.

Aer coughed. When he looked up, Emissary Striaen stood over him and Gail.

Why is he here? Aer thought in a daze.

"Explain yourself," Emissary Striaen asked a stunned Gail.

"He was still resisting after I subdued him," Gail said. "There weren't any proctors around, so I assumed he was trying to throw me off and pretend I never got him."

"I want to hear the truth. I know that is not what happened because I was observing you two the entire time."

"Y-You were?" Gail stammered.

"Yes, and I would like to know why you were aiming to kill a fellow fledgling," Emissary Striaen stated in a menacing voice.

"I wouldn't have killed him!" Gail shouted defensively.

By now, the surrounding proctors had noticed the commotion and were gathering around the area.

"Emissary Striaen, what are you doing here?" one of the proctors asked.

"Halt the trial," Emissary Striaen ordered.

The proctors exchanged glances with one another. One of them nodded and ran toward the head proctor. Soon enough, the visitors and the caretakers had gathered around their location.

The head caretaker was there too.

"Emissary Striaen. What is going on he—" Head Caretaker Desen started.

"How abhorrent," the emissary interrupted him. "To think that your son would be capable of such violence."

"I'm sorry?"

"This is your son, yes?" Emissary Striaen gestured toward Gail.

The head caretaker nodded.

"I was observing this trial from above. Imagine my surprise when I saw your son choking this young man to death."

The head caretaker fell silent.

Aer massaged his throat as he listened to their exchange.

Alius found him and rushed over.

"Aer, are you all right?" Alius asked with a worried look.

"Give me a moment," Aer managed to cough out as the adults' conversation continued.

"The Enforcer's Trial is an examination, and only that," the emissary continued. "Surely, lethal force is not permissible."

A proctor nodded. "Correct. We explicitly forbade lethal force before the trial started. Gail Desen's results today will be considered invalid. Now, I ask that all visitors and caretakers as well as the affected parties step away from the premises. The proctors will go back to our positions as we resume the trial."

***

News of the conflict spread like wildfire among the caretakers and fledglings alike. By the end of the trial, everyone there had learned of what had happened between Gail and Aer.

Gail looked around helplessly as the other Perch fledglings started bad-mouthing him in front of everyone else.

"I always knew Gail wasn't the best person," Rial said loudly. "He went way too far in this trial, trying to seriously injure another fledgling, even if they were from the Charity Tree."

Iad, who was clearly looking to sever all association with Gail, nodded. "Right? And to come up with the idea of framing other fledglings from the Perch as liabilities. Who does that?"

Gail said nothing. He couldn't. Whatever defense he could muster would ring hollow. When an emissary spoke out against someone, there was little they could do to refute it. Doing so would be seen by others as going against the Great Arbiter himself.

What was most terrifying was that he wasn't the only subject of their gossip. His father was suffering similar slander from the visitors.

"The emissary didn't seem very happy with the head caretaker, did he?"

193

"Serves him right. The head caretaker assumes the main responsibility for raising the fledglings here. When his own son goes out and does something like this…"

"This is practically a scandal. Orator Mistral will have a field day with everything that's happened here."

His father, hanging his head in furious silence through it all, locked eyes with Gail. His menacing expression told Gail all he needed to know about what was in store for him once they were alone.

CHAPTER 16:
ENDS AND BEGINNINGS

My son has introduced me to the siblings he's been going out to see. They are a pair of sisters. The younger sister is a girl you could find anywhere. The older sister, however, unnerves me. Something about the way she presents herself is odd.

My son then revealed his wish; he wanted my blessing on his union to the younger sister. I refused. I told him to not get too attached to them, warning him it was unlikely they would see each other again after the Ascension Ceremony. Of course, when he pressed me to explain myself, I remained silent, as those details should not be disclosed to him just yet.

Soleil happily waited for the representatives of the other islands to pay attention to her. The situation was just too good to be true. The head caretaker's son had made her job *so* easy.

She wasted no time directly addressing the head caretaker once it was finally time for her to speak. They all knew why they were there. There was no point in dragging it out.

"Looks like another disappointing performance from the Perch, Head Caretaker Desen," she mocked. "Their average performance in the Enforcer's Trial was even lower than those from the Charity Tree. Honestly, after such an abysmal performance, I have to wonder what it is you even teach down here."

The head caretaker had no retort. Soleil almost pitied him, seeing him in such a sorry state. Almost.

"Incidentally, wasn't it you who called the Charity Tree fledglings disgraceful savages for attacking your son?" she continued mercilessly.

"How would you describe your son, then? He ended up nearly killing said fledgling in cold blood. Unprovoked too."

"Accidents happen in the Enforcer's Trial," Head Caretaker Desen said weakly. "I'm certain my son had no intention of murder."

"Are you implying that the emissary is lying about what happened?" Soleil countered. "He was quite clear on what he saw."

"N-No. Of course not," the miserable-looking man stammered, glancing toward Emissary Striaen, who stared him down in displeasure.

"Then I'll get straight to the point," Soleil said. "One Sky Cycle prior, my son failed to pass his Ascension Ceremony. I do not believe it was due to an innate lack of ability. Rather, I believe the nepotism displayed by you and your caretakers prevented him from learning the skills to pass it. I have ample reason to believe this. We have all seen that the fledglings you refused admission to the Perch are more than competitive with the ones you chose despite their lack of tutoring. Which is why I am calling for a complete restructuring of how we manage the Nesting Islands. What do you think, Emissary Striaen?"

"I have taken your words into proper consideration," the emissary answered. "I will discuss your views and what I have seen here with the other emissaries, but do not expect a massive reform anytime soon."

Soleil frowned. She wanted a more affirmative response. "Surely, you can't end this with just that?"

Emissary Striaen shook his head. "I alone lack the power to change a tradition that has endured throughout the ages. Emissary I may be, but it is up to the will of the Great Arbiter to make any final decisions on Atravel's customs."

Soleil would have sworn loudly then and there had she not been standing in front of an emissary.

This still isn't enough? she screamed in her head. *How far do things have to escalate for you all to realize that something is wrong with the way things are run down here?*

"I understand," she managed to get out before sitting back down. "How disappointing."

***

Aer grimaced as he ran his fingers down his face and neck. The bruises that Gail had left there the day before had yet to fade. He then caught Alius staring at him and quickly lowered his hands. His brother had been uncharacteristically quiet since Aer got injured, likely blaming himself for pushing Aer to participate in the Enforcer's Trial.

"We just have the Hunter's Trial left, right?" Aer asked, trying to get Alius back to normal. As much as Aer complained about Alius's usual attitude, seeing him act this way was deeply unsettling.

"No, let's just end it here," Alius answered. "I think we've done enough."

Aer blinked. "You sure? Normally, you would—"

"I'm sure."

When Aer gazed at his brother in concern, Alius started explaining himself.

"It's fine. We've accomplished everything we set out to do. I kept my side of the deal with Kiel, and we've completely humiliated the Perch and its caretakers. Every visitor knows our names at this point. There's nothing more to be gained by participating in another trial. Let's just leave it at that and focus on recovering."

The brothers went outside to get rid of the waste that had piled up in their home as well as to stock up on food and water. A few of the fledglings passing by gave them a curt nod before walking away. Aer gave them a short nod back. Most of their neighbors had eased up on them since the Enforcer's Trial. As many of the participants had directly benefitted from their actions, the complaints going around about him and Alius had died down.

Once they reached the nearest river, Aer knelt to scoop water into one of their jars. He then paused. The water's surface reflected an unreadable expression on Alius's face.

"What's wrong?" Aer asked.

"I was just thinking this might be the last time we gather supplies like this," Alius answered. "The trials are about to end, and we'll be able to leave this place for good once we're done."

Aer nodded and continued drawing water in silence.

"Hey, Aer?" Alius asked after another pause.

"What is it?"

"What kind of places do you think exist outside this island?"

Aer gave his brother an odd look. "Why ask me? I've been here with you my entire life. I wouldn't know any more about that than you would."

"We'll soon be free of this Nesting Island," Alius continued, as if not hearing him. "We'll be able to go around Atravel as we please."

"Right." Aer nodded. Where was Alius going with this?

"That got me thinking, what do we do after that?"

"Did you have something in mind?"

"I was thinking maybe I'd like to find the rest of our family, find out why we were left on the Charity Tree."

Aer blinked in surprise. He hadn't expected that. The idea of contacting the rest of their family had never even occurred to him.

"You know that they probably abandoned us, right?" Aer asked. "No one ever visited us while we were growing up, which tells me they don't care about us all that much, regardless of whether they had a choice to leave us here or not. I don't see why we should go to the trouble of looking for such people and getting them involved in our lives."

"That's… probably true," Alius reluctantly agreed. "But still, aren't you at least a bit curious?"

"Maybe a little," Aer admitted. "What's got you thinking about this, anyway?"

Alius's voice lowered into a whisper. "When you nearly died in the last trial, I began wondering who I would have left if you were gone."

Aer fell into a surprised silence. He hadn't expected that answer either.

"If you're that worried, you shouldn't have pushed me to participate in the Enforcer's Trial in the first place," he joked, feeling a little uncomfortable with the direction their conversation had taken.

"I didn't think things would go that far!" Alius said defensively. "You think I wanted Gail to choke you out?"

"Yeah, yeah. I know," Aer replied, dismissively waving away Alius's concern, much to his clear irritation. "Anyway, it's nothing you have to worry about. I'm fine now, aren't I?"

"Well, that's true," Alius said in a huff. "If you're well enough to be *this* annoying, then I guess I was worrying for nothing."

Aer shook his head. "I can't believe you have the gall to tell me that. *You*, of all people. How many times have you ignored my worries whenever I brought them up?"

"What are you talking about?" Alius looked completely serious. "I don't remember anything like that ever happening."

Aer stared at his brother in utter disbelief. Then a smile broke out on Alius's face, and the two burst into laughter.

As if laughing with them, the trees nearby began to shake. Confused, the two stopped laughing and faced the source of the disturbance.

"What is that thing?" Alius asked.

Aer had no answer. He was just as confused as Alius.

It was an animal that neither of them was familiar with, a magnificent creature cloaked in gray fur with two horns protruding from its head. One that, despite being on all fours, was more than twice as tall as the brothers were and nearly five times as wide.

Aer had the feeling that the beast wasn't friendly. It then lowered its horned head and charged, removing any ambiguity over its intentions.

Aer quickly grabbed Alius and blew heavy gusts downward to propel them onto the nearest platform. Not even a second later, the beast had trampled where they had been standing, crashing into the roots of the Charity Tree.

The platform they stood on trembled. Both fledglings and caretakers alike began gathering at their location to find out what was going on.

Aer and Alius carefully examined the animal below. The beast had hooves, making it incapable of using the ladders that one would normally use to reach the platform. The only other way up was to find a tree with a low enough incline to walk on, but those tended to be much farther from the center of the Spiral Forest. So long as they stayed off the ground, they should be safe.

The brothers sighed in relief as the beast slowly backed away, only for it to charge and leap to where they were. The surrounding onlookers ran away in panic as the beast found its footing on the platform.

Aer grabbed Alius and leapt once more.

"What's going on?" Alius shouted. "What's that thing doing here?"

"I don't know!" Aer exclaimed. There wasn't supposed to be wildlife on this island. The only time they had ever seen an animal was when they were brought in from the outside, like in the Falconry Trial. Neither of them had ever seen one as large or as feral as this one.

Now properly on the structures built around the Charity Tree, the beast rampaged as it ran across the necessary bridges to reach the brothers, shoving aside any fledglings and caretakers it passed along the way.

"Can't any of them stop it?" Aer asked frantically, dismayed at how easily the beast overpowered the people in front of it.

"The caretakers here definitely can't!" Alius replied as they landed on the ground. "Let's get help from the visitors. An enforcer or a hunter has to be better suited for this than the caretakers. Let's get off the Charity Tree and run for help!"

Aer nodded. Unfortunately, they had no time to look for a safe path off the Charity Tree's platforms, as the beast rapidly gained on them.

"Oh, come on! Why is it so focused on us?" Alius complained before he dislodged himself from Aer's grip. "Split up!"

The two ran in opposite directions. The beast paused for a second before chasing down Alius, recognizing him as the slower target.

Aer cursed. It was clear from their respective speeds that Alius would be overtaken and trampled. Wasn't there anything he could do to stop the thing?

Aer then recalled the Falconry Trial. The beast wasn't a flying creature, but he didn't have the leeway to worry about that right now. Maybe the fact that it had been raised in Atravel was enough to make it a resident of the sky.

"*Settle down!*" Aer screamed, trying to recreate the sensation of controlling a living creature as he did the air.

Much to the brothers' surprise, the beast stopped. Before either of them could sigh in relief, however, the beast spun and ran straight toward Aer.

Aer frantically called for the beast to halt. He had certainly gotten the creature's attention, but it refused to obey him. If anything, it grew more hostile with every word he spoke.

Realizing the beast wasn't going to stop, Aer fled the vicinity. He had enough time to see Alius asking for help before they lost sight of one another.

***

Aer ran for what felt like hours, crossing one bridge after another. The fledglings and caretakers on the way had all leapt to the side in terror when they saw what was chasing him, not even trying to slow it down.

The beast was faster than he was, but its ability to stop and turn was considerably lower due to its weight. Running up the bridges that spiraled around the Charity Tree had impeded the animal's movements enough for Aer to stay just out of its reach.

Eventually, the topmost platform of the Charity Tree entered his view. The bridges connecting it to the other platforms converged into one midway. There was nowhere left to run after that.

As soon as he reached that final platform, Aer took a deep breath as he looked back and confirmed that the beast was still chasing him, only a few strides behind.

Just before it could run him over, Aer jumped as high as he could and used his baggy clothes and Sky Control to slow his fall as much as possible. Upon seeing this, the beast struggled to stop its charge and teetered toward the edge, leaning on the railings to prevent itself from falling.

The railings, however, were too small to support the beast. They were meant to stop *humans* from falling; the beast easily outmatched any person Aer had seen in both size and weight. It was, at best, a foothold for the animal.

Aer, recognizing his chance, willed all the wind that his Sky Authority would allow him to muster to push the beast forward. The beast, unable to properly balance itself, toppled over the railing, flailing to the best of its ability as it went over the platform's edge and fell to the ground below.

Aer's legs collapsed as soon as he landed on the ground. He was still alive. One misstep, one wrong judgment would have been all it took for the beast's horns to skewer him, but he had survived. He didn't know whether to be relieved or terrified at how close he had come to dying.

Eventually, Aer stumbled down the Charity Tree to see what had become of the animal. Seeing people gathered around the site of the crash, he looked down at the epicenter. There, the broken body of the beast lay still, never to move again. Confirming that it was dead, Aer surveyed the crowd, looking for Alius, and found him standing on the outskirts.

Alius looked relieved once he noticed Aer staring at him. He ran up to Aer and explained what had happened on his end.

While Aer had been running away from the beast, Alius had gone to the Perch to seek help. A few caretakers who had regained their composure enough to think of reporting what had happened to the head caretaker had accompanied him to verify his story.

Upon hearing their reports, the head caretaker had come out discretely with a select group of caretakers, not wanting to alert the visitors to what had happened. Unfortunately for him, a few visitors had still caught wind of the incident and spread the word.

In the end, the news had reached Emissary Striaen, who had flown there as quickly as possible, leaving the head caretaker struggling to explain what had happened.

Aer examined the center of the crowd more closely. There, he saw several familiar figures arguing beside the beast's corpse.

"Head Huntress Islea, I believe this creature was under your care," Emissary Striaen said from the middle of the crowd. "Wasn't this the animal you were about to butcher for the upcoming banquet?"

"The very same, but I recall leaving this creature in the caretakers' hands," Head Huntress Islea responded with a completely neutral expression. "It was their responsibility to ensure the animal stayed within its confines until the Grand Sabbath. How did it escape custody?"

The caretakers from the Perch exchanged nervous looks.

Eventually, one of them spoke up. "I admit we were unaware of its absence until just now. But that shouldn't have been a problem. The creature was confined deep beneath the Perch. It shouldn't have been able to find its way outside, much less do it unnoticed. Not unless someone with thorough knowledge of the location had led it out."

Another person entered the conversation. "As questionable as I find the actions of the caretakers here at times, I don't believe them to be so incompetent that they could misplace such an animal. Of course, things would be a lot easier to understand if this wasn't an accident."

"What are you implying, Orator Mistral?" Emissary Striaen asked, addressing the woman who had spoken up.

The woman smiled in response. "Doesn't it seem odd to you that this beast found its way here from the Perch without alerting anyone? I believe the head caretaker suffered quite a humiliation due to the fledglings residing here recently. I find it hard to believe that the two events are unrelated."

The visitors then started whispering frantically among themselves. Aer let the wind carry their voices to him, trying to overhear what they said.

"Did the head caretaker try to take revenge on the fledglings who caused his disgrace by inciting the creature to attack them?" one visitor asked another.

"I think Orator Mistral might be right. Do we really want to leave our children in the hands of such a man?"

The emissary's eyes narrowed. "Head Caretaker Desen?"

The head caretaker paled. "I had nothing to do with this! I don't know why the beast suddenly went on a rampage."

"But this creature was under your jurisdiction, yes? I recall you taking it in during one of our previous meetings."

"That… is true. But—"

"At the very least, this is gross negligence on your part," Emissary Striaen continued. "You could face criminal charges for that alone."

"There's no need to go that far, is there?" the head caretaker shouted in desperation. "Even if there had been an accident, it would only have involved those from the Charity Tree!"

Head Caretaker Desen flinched as the emissary gave him a scornful glare.

"Enough. Regardless of what might have happened, it's clear to me that Orator Mistral's concerns about this island's caretakers were well founded. I assure you that you will not keep your position after this."

Head Caretaker Desen hung his head in silence. Despite everything that had happened between them, Aer couldn't help but feel a bit of pity for the man.

Contrary to everyone else's expectations, Orator Mistral frowned.

"Is that all?" she asked Emissary Striaen.

"Yes," Emissary Striaen answered before facing the Charity Tree caretakers. "More importantly, were there any fatalities?"

"None," one responded. "A few are injured, but thankfully, none were gored by the beast's horns."

"Praise be to the Great Arbiter. How was the creature stopped?"

"One of the fledglings took care of it. He led the beast toward the top of the tree by calling out to it with his Sky Authority then pushed it off the edge."

"Oh? And which child managed this?"

"His name is Aer, I believe."

"Ah, him again?" Emissary Striaen looked rather pleased. "Where is he now?"

Aer froze. All eyes were now on him and his brother. The emissary signaled for them to draw near.

"Congratulations are in order," Emissary Striaen said, facing Aer. "Your brother deserves his share of praise as well. I heard he was the one who led the effort to contact the Perch about this incident."

Aer stayed silent, slightly surprised that the emissary could flawlessly tell them apart on just their third meeting.

What he said next, however, was a much bigger surprise for those present. "I expect great things from you in the times to come. Once the Ascension Ceremony has passed, come to me. I will personally ensure your future."

CHAPTER 17:
THE ASCENSION CEREMONY

I cannot deny that my faith in our way of life wavers from time to time. At such moments, I question whether the Great Arbiter truly meant for us to spend our days like this, detaching ourselves from the world to avoid being caught in the same follies that once plagued humankind.

Of course, the failings of those foolish enough to put such doubts to the test serve as a reminder that we are indeed justified in our actions. We must be.

"I let you out of my sight for a week only to learn that an emissary has taken you in." Nira shook her head. "Seriously, what kind of sorcery have you two been using behind everyone's backs? I want in on it."

"Things just worked out for us," Alius replied. "Sometimes, you just have to keep pushing to get results, even when things look bleak."

Nira gave Alius a meaningful look before nodding. "Thanks for the advice. I'll keep it in mind."

Alius blinked. "It kind of freaks me out when you agree with me so easily. I'm used to Aer shutting me down whenever I bring up something like this."

Aer opened his mouth to retort before thinking better of it. It *was* true that they wouldn't be in such a good situation had Alius not pushed him as far as he had. Not that he would ever say such a thing out loud.

A small smile appeared on Nira's face. "You know, Alius, the best way to convince someone of something is often to lead by example. I've lent a hand until now, hoping you and Aer would show up the Perch a bit, but I never imagined you two could get this far. Clearly, something's working out for you here."

Alius grinned.

Aer decided to change the subject before his brother got too pleased with himself.

"Anyway, what have you been doing for the past few days?" he asked Nira.

"I was practicing for my own trials," Nira replied.

"So you finished your required three?"

Nira nodded. "Got that done when I participated in the Forewarner's Trial. I did better than I expected on that one too. And I just finished wheeling myself back home after the Carrier's Trial when you two decided to come for a visit."

"You could have told us you were participating in those," Alius complained.

"You guys looked busy. Didn't want to interrupt. Anyway, what are you two planning on doing from here on out? You accomplished everything you were aiming for. The caretakers from the Perch most definitely regret not taking you two in now. You made them look completely incompetent in front of everyone they wanted to impress."

"Yeah," Alius scoffed. "Some of them even tried to get us to join the Perch these past few days to try and save face."

Nira paused. "You didn't consider accepting, did you?"

Aer, sensing some sudden tension, shrank back a bit. Fortunately, Alius's next words defused the situation.

"As if," he answered. "It's way too shameless for them to make the offer this late. There's not even a benefit for us at this point, seeing as we're all about to leave the island."

Nira visibly relaxed. "That's good. I don't think that place suits you, anyway."

"What, did you really think we'd say yes?" Alius laughed before handing Nira a bagful of fruit. "Anyway, a gift for you."

"What's this for?" Nira asked.

"It's our way of thanking you for all your help."

Nira stared at the bag before breaking into a smile. "What will you two do once you leave this island?"

"I'll make sure Aer takes up Emissary Striaen's offer," Alius said, exchanging looks with Aer. "After that… we'll figure things out as we see more of Atravel."

The brothers talked with Nira a little longer before parting ways, knowing that this might be the last time they interacted as neighbors.

"You know, I might actually miss living here once we leave," Alius commented as they walked down the Charity Tree. "I know it's not all that glamourous, but it's where we grew up. It's hard not to feel a little attached."

Aer silently disagreed. He would be fine never setting foot on the island again. None of his memories associated with the place were positive ones.

Time had passed quickly since Aer had stopped the wild animal's rampage. As the brothers grew increasingly aware of how little time they had left before the Ascension Ceremony, they felt the need to wrap up any remaining business.

It had been Alius's idea to contact the people they were indebted to one last time. For once, Aer found himself in complete agreement with his brother. He didn't want anything to tie them down in the future. If they still owed someone something, he wanted to clear things up with them right away.

For that reason, he let Alius lead the way. The sooner they were done, the better.

***

"So, Kiel. Are you still busy with your trials?" Alius probed the tall fledgling once they reached his front door.

"Honestly, there's no point in keeping that up at this point," Kiel answered. "I've finished my required three, and the visitors aren't paying attention to them anymore."

That was true. The interest in the trials had become secondary to the head caretaker's reputation, which had been trashed beyond repair. Gossiping about his comeuppance had become a popular pastime in the Charity Tree and Perch alike. All of his subordinates were actively dissociating themselves from him since the emissary's condemnation.

"So you're done with the trials?"

"More or less. Now, I just need to make sure I'm not forgotten by anyone I'm currently associated with. That, of course, includes you two."

Kiel then looked Aer in the eye. "I don't suppose I could ask you to put in a good word for me with the emissary who picked you up?"

Aer internally groaned; this was exactly what he wanted to avoid—being tied down to expectations from other people. Aer didn't even know why Emissary Striaen had taken such an interest in him. He certainly didn't feel confident enough to talk up someone else in front of the man, especially when he still didn't fully trust Kiel himself.

"I don't know if I have enough of the emissary's favor to promise anything," Aer replied.

Kiel looked disappointed. "Maybe not at first, but can't you work your way into it?"

When he received nothing but silence from Aer as an answer, Kiel's face soured.

"Easy, Kiel," Alius said, trying to placate him. "He's not saying no, just that he isn't sure he can do it."

"If he asks about the people who've helped me along the way, I'll mention you," Aer offered as an appeasement.

Kiel paused.

"Fine," he let out eventually. "Well, see you guys later, then. That is, if you two still care to keep in touch with someone like me once we get out of this place."

Still sensing some animosity from Kiel, the brothers promptly excused themselves.

"He didn't have to add that last bit," Alius grumbled once they left.

"I kind of saw it coming," Aer replied. "He does like being connected, and there's no better connection than an emissary. He couldn't let the chance pass him by, even if he had to guilt-trip me into doing it."

"Still, he didn't have to be so aggressive about it," Alius said. "We already made sure the fledglings loyal to him performed better in the trials than they otherwise would have. What more does he want?"

Stepping away from Kiel's home, Aer and Alius took in the scenery as they walked through the Spiral Forest for what might be the last time.

"Where do you think we'll stay once we leave?" Alius asked. "Do they have a place for us fledglings from the Charity Tree? Or will we have to find that by ourselves?"

"They'll tell us once we get off the island, I imagine," Aer replied. "For now, I don't want to worry about it."

"So laid-back, as always," Alius murmured. "Sometimes, I wonder whether you would get *anything* done if I weren't around."

***

The days that followed were as uneventful as Aer could have hoped for. When their last day on the island finally arrived, several caretakers accompanied by an enforcer showed up on their doorstep in the morning.

"It's time," one of them announced. "Come with us, please."

The two stepped outside and followed their directions to descend the Charity Tree. As a caretaker wheeled Nira down not too far from them, Aer turned around and watched the caretakers stop by every treehouse to direct the fledglings off the platforms. Like the last time the fledglings had been dragged out, the caretakers were extremely thorough in checking every nook and cranny, searching places Aer had never once thought to hide in.

Oh, so that's it, Aer realized. *They know all the hiding spots because they've done this every Sky Cycle, to make sure no stragglers stay behind on the Nesting Island during the Ascension Ceremony.*

A caretaker jotted Aer's and Alius's names onto a sheet of paper once they joined the growing crowd of people at the base of the Charity Tree. Aer couldn't help but be impressed at how thorough the usually indifferent caretakers were in making sure that every fledgling was present.

Once the caretakers finished, they were all escorted to the Eastern Borders, where the Perch fledglings soon joined their numbers. They then waited as the caretakers began confirming every fledgling's attendance.

Just like the day they were first introduced to the visitors, the brothers stood in front of the steel gates fencing them from the edge of the island. And just like then, the sheer number of people gathered at this site was overwhelming.

Aer flinched when he spotted Gail among the crowd. Upon noticing a horrific bruise on the side of the fledgling's face, however, Aer found himself unable to stop gaping until Gail noticed his gaze and glared back. Aer quickly looked away and focused his attention on the steel gates. Whatever had happened to Gail wasn't his business.

They stood in silence until one of the caretakers gestured to his colleagues. Several nodded and moved to open the gates.

Curious as to what would happen next, the fledglings stared as the gates opened. Behind the gates were numerous metal poles firmly embedded in the ground. Attached to every single pole were steel chains that stretched out toward the higher parts of the sky. Some of these chains held aloft stacks of giant metal carriages, likely meant to be used as transportation.

Aer and Alius looked up, their eyes searching for the other end of the chains, but the clouds surrounding the island stopped them from seeing where they led.

The caretakers then signaled for them to wait. Soon, the ground beneath them rumbled, and the incline of the chains attached to some of the carriages lowered until they slanted downward.

Once everything had settled, one of the caretakers in the front turned around.

"Is this everyone?" he asked.

"Yes, all three thousand nine hundred fifty-seven fledglings of this Nesting Island have been accounted for," another caretaker answered.

"Good. Let's get this over with, then."

The caretakers then started organizing the fledglings into groups. Once they had finished, some of the caretakers accompanied each group into separate carriages, while others leapt up the poles and undid locks attached to the tops of the carriages, one by one, causing them to slide down the chains off the island.

And just like that, the brothers took their first venture away from the land they had called home their entire lives.

***

Aer laughed as Alius looked around excitedly at their new environment. He wasn't the only one either. Many fledglings appeared entranced by the surrounding sea of blue and white outside the carriage.

Excitement wasn't the only reaction, however. Several fledglings who clearly had a fear of heights were doing everything they could to not look outside. Nira, who was in the same carriage as them, looked outright nauseous. If Aer had shared their phobia, he would have likely reacted similarly. He could see no ground beneath them.

As they passed over a row of chains running perpendicular to the one they were currently on, Aer turned to the side, curious as to where those chains led. He spotted a floating landmass in the distance, on top of which was what appeared to be an array of buildings, some cliffsides, and a tree.

That gave Aer pause. That tree would have to be quite massive for him to make out its shape from so far away. Was he staring at another Charity Tree?

He then faced the other side of the chains, only to find another landmass with the same mix of white bark and autumn leaves on its surface.

Do all the islands have their own Charity Tree? Aer wondered.

Until then, Aer hadn't really considered the world outside his Nesting Island. But seeing the island that had been his world until that point being one of many put into perspective how small his existence was in the greater scope of things. The sheer number of people he had encountered during the day was overwhelming enough. The realization that every island had something similar taking place on its surface filled Aer with a sense of utter insignificance.

***

It was practically evening when their destination finally came into view. Their carriage was taking them to an island much larger than the Nesting Islands surrounding it. From where he stood, Aer could see other rows of chains, carrying carriages just like theirs, attached to all sides of the island. Based on how these chains had been on an incline until that morning, the island must have been at a much higher elevation at the start and lowered itself to allow transport.

Now that the end of their ride was in sight, the caretakers gradually increased the air resistance around the carriage to slow its descent until it came to a gentle stop within the island's borders. The caretakers then gave instructions, leading the fledglings toward a camping ground. Once they had finished setting up camp, they were handed some food and told to rest until the next day.

Aer and Alius ate and waited with the other fledglings as various types of people flooded into the area. As the number of adolescents waiting there continued to grow, the brothers understood that some of these people had to be fledglings from other Nesting Islands.

Aer, who had no desire to converse with anyone, ignored them and lay down on a sleeping mat provided for the fledglings en masse. Alius, despite looking somewhat intrigued by the newcomers, soon joined him, presumably wanting to be rested for tomorrow.

***

The brothers woke the next morning to see that the number of people surrounding them had grown tenfold overnight. They weren't all fledglings and caretakers either. Many were adults who, based on their clothing, weren't from the Nesting Islands. Most were accompanied by at least one infant.

This must be when and where newborns are assigned to their Nesting Island, Aer realized as a caretaker jotted something every time an adult passed them holding an infant in their arms. *Do they replace us as soon as we leave?*

Separate from that crowd was another group of adults, likely there on business of some kind. Aer recognized several as the trial proctors. Most notably, he saw Emissary Striaen standing in a place of honor among them.

The old man eventually noticed his gaze and smiled kindly. Once he had finished his business with the people surrounding him, the emissary walked over to the brothers. The people between them looked surprised but nevertheless parted to let him pass.

"Good evening, you two," Emissary Striaen greeted. "Had a pleasant trip?"

"A-Ah, yes," Aer stuttered, still unsure how to address him. He looked to Alius for help.

"Have you been here since we last met?" Alius asked without missing a beat.

"Why, yes. Ever since the trials ended, I've been here observing the caretakers as they made the final preparations for the Ascension Ceremony."

"Do you do this often?" Alius asked. "I get the feeling that most people think it's a waste of your time to be so involved with what happens down here."

Aer gaped. What was Alius doing? Why was he being so frank with the emissary?

Emissary Striaen blinked at Alius's bluntness. Thankfully, his next words weren't ones of rebuke. "Under normal circumstances, I would not. But this occasion is special, for various reasons."

"And why is that?"

"All in due time. I'll discuss things in detail once the Ascension Ceremony has passed."

"Sir," a bespectacled man Aer quickly recognized as the emissary's personal doctor interrupted them.

"Ah, of course." Emissary Striaen frowned. "If you two don't mind, I must discuss something with Doctor Resin privately. Do excuse me."

"Alius, wasn't that a bit much?" Aer whispered once the emissary left. "I don't think we're supposed to talk to him that way."

Indeed, the feeling of being isolated by the people watching had grown stronger. The nearby fledglings, both familiar and unknown, were gaping at the brothers, while heated whispers passed between many of the adults.

"I was testing how far I could go with him," Alius whispered back. "I would have apologized if he got mad."

"And why would you do such a thing?" Aer asked in exasperation.

Alius stared closely at Aer's face. "It just occurred to me why someone like him might be paying us so much attention. Aer, do you think—"

"All fledglings here for the Ascension Ceremony, please follow me!" an adult shouted, cutting off Alius's question.

The caretakers took that as their cue to start barking orders. Before Alius could properly explain himself, the caretakers surrounding the brothers hurried them away to their next destination.

Aer, sensing some tension in the caretakers' behavior, stayed silent throughout the journey. The sheer number of people marching would have drowned out any noise he could make anyway.

They were led to a stone field located at the very center of the island. There, a giant fissure stretched across the ground as far as they could see.

The adult who had led them there, a man dressed in stylish clothing, began whispering with the head caretakers of the other Nesting Islands once they reached the site. Meanwhile, the adults who had followed kept a close eye on every fledgling in attendance.

Aer frowned. A disproportionate number of enforcers were present. Was it necessary for so many of them to monitor the fledglings this closely?

After some time, the sharply dressed man faced the fledglings, his discussion with the head caretakers having come to an end.

"Now that we have confirmed everyone's presence, we will commence the Ascension Ceremony!" the man shouted. "Before we start, however, you fledglings need to hear one last message. Traditionally, one of the head caretakers would deliver this final speech. But the head caretaker originally assigned this task has recently proven unfit for the role. Instead, an emissary has generously offered to speak in his place. A rare honor. Naturally, we would be foolish to ignore such an opportunity. Emissary Striaen, would you please do us the honors?"

The man stepped aside as Emissary Striaen addressed everyone present.

"I welcome you all to these hallowed grounds," the old man's voice echoed throughout the area, amplified with the same form of Sky Control Aer had used during the Conductor's Trial. "I advise those present to take in the scenery, as we stand on a historical landmark at this very moment. According to legend, this stone field was where our ancestors stood ages ago, when the Great Arbiter acted to save his chosen ones and raised the earth to the sky. It is for that reason we refer to this island as the Isle of Judgment. It is the place of our very origin."

Hearing that, the fledglings looked around, some peering down the split at the center before timidly backing away. At the bottom of the chasm was nothing but clouds, with no footholds to be found.

"It's not something one can notice unless they view Atravel from the outside, but this nation is constantly in movement through the power of its inhabitants," the emissary continued. "We consider this a proper display of the glory of the Great Arbiter's blessing. Only at the end of every Sky Cycle does Atravel truly rest and stay stationary over the section of the outside world where we first rose into the sky. Only here, on this landmark, over the site of our creation, do we dare hold the Ascension Ceremony."

The emissary took a long, hard look at the fledglings present. "The question that follows is why? Why go to all this trouble? I believe it is finally time you all understood the purpose of this ritual. I'm certain many of you have wondered why we kept the details a secret."

Aer didn't need to look to his side to know that the emissary had captured Alius's complete and undivided attention. He had been the most inquisitive about this subject when it was first announced, after all.

In truth, it had bothered Aer too. What was it that was so important to keep a secret until this exact moment?

The brothers paid careful attention as the old man continued.

"First, we should discuss how the Great Arbiter chose to save us over the rest of humanity. I'm sure you've all heard the stories of how a war on an unprecedented scale ravaged the earth and how the Great Arbiter chose those who sought to flee the war and blessed them with the authority over the heavens so they could live in peace." Emissary Striaen paused. "And yet not all those who live in Atravel are equally blessed by the Great Arbiter. It is something frequently seen in the Nesting Islands. There exist many fledglings who do not strongly possess the gift the Great Arbiter has granted us. Why is this?"

The emissary examined the audience before answering his own question. "Our ancestors have long since discovered a strong correlation between the way one lives their life and the strength of their Sky Authority. The more attached one is to the world, the more willing they are to stand and fight for their benefit, the weaker their Sky Authorities are. It's only natural. This way of thinking is incompatible with the way the Great Arbiter wishes us to live. It strays from the path he set out for us. And as a result, they are bound to the earth, as the Great Arbiter is not with them."

Grief clouded the old man's face. Aer was filled with a sudden sense of foreboding as the adults moved to surround the fledglings present.

"The error of the rest of the world was that they were unable to free themselves from their ways of thinking and view things from a more detached viewpoint," Emissary Striaen preached. "It led to their ultimate demise as they continued to fight to the bitter end for what they viewed as important. To prevent Atravel from degrading into such a state, to protect ourselves from violence emerging within our numbers, to ensure we remain in the Great Arbiter's favor until the end of time, we must purge these elements from our nation. We hold this ritual here for that purpose, to rid ourselves of those unworthy of the sky's sanctuary."

Both brothers' faces paled. What was the old man saying?

Emissary Striaen turned around and raised his hands. Following his movements, the clouds at the bottom of the chasm rose to ground level. He then stepped onto the clouds and walked on them as if they were solid matter.

"The goal of the Ascension Ceremony is simple. All of you must step forward and walk across these clouds. Once a fledgling manages to do so, they have been judged fit to traverse Atravel and live among us."

"And if they can't?" a fledgling asked.

"Then they fall through the clouds to the world below, being judged unworthy of life up here by the Great Arbiter," the emissary replied sadly.

A deathly silence filled the air before panic set in among the fledglings.

"What are you talking about?" one fledgling screamed hysterically. "Are you people insane?"

Aer grabbed Alius's arm and backed away quietly, looking for an escape. A couple of enforcers near them responded immediately, holding them both against the ground along with the other fledglings who'd had the same idea.

The brothers stared at each other in dread. They had imagined a lot of different scenarios for the Ascension Ceremony, but something like this was…

The scene around them had descended into pandemonium as many of the fledglings tried to run. The enforcers surrounding them, however, clearly had a lot of experience with this, as all dissenters were easily overpowered and suppressed.

Once the chaos had settled, the enforcers holding the brothers down lifted them and moved them toward different locations, forcibly separating the two.

Aer, frozen in fear, could only watch as Alius grew farther from him, struggling against his captor with all his might.

The enforcer holding Aer dragged him toward the chasm, in front of which everyone had gathered in rows. Some of the fledglings had not resisted. Whether they were sure of their ability to pass the Ascension Ceremony or had just given up, Aer couldn't tell.

Aer watched as the row closest to the crevice advanced. The enforcers held the fledglings over the clouds for some time before letting go.

The fledglings who survived either laughed or cried in relief. The screams of those who didn't quickly faded as they plunged to the world below.

The enforcers then pulled the survivors from the crevice as the next row stepped forward. In that row, Aer spotted an indignant Gail shoving aside the enforcer restraining him. Instead of running away, however, Gail marched forward with confidence, more defiant than afraid.

Meeting Gail's expectations, the clouds did not give way, even as he made a show of jumping up and down. The enforcer that Gail had shoved aside nodded as he gestured for Gail to step away from the chasm.

One row over, Aer saw Nira being wheeled forward by an enforcer. Said enforcer, however, stepped aside when a caretaker tapped his shoulder.

The caretaker and Nira then stared at each other in silence with an indescribable gaze. Aer, despite being panicked, realized upon seeing their similar faces that the caretaker must be Nira's mother. The caretaker then lifted Nira off the wheelchair and gently set her on the cloud.

Nira didn't fall. Her mother then lifted her back to the chair and left her without a single word.

A couple of rows later, Aer saw two enforcers struggling to hold up Kiel's large frame. Once they released him, Kiel screamed as he fell through the clouds, clawing at something to grab on to.

Dread took hold of Aer as the rows of people between him and the crevice diminished. How was he supposed to walk on clouds in the first place? He hadn't been taught a single thing about it! He didn't even know it was a form of Sky Control until now!

Finally, his turn. The enforcer holding onto him lifted him up and held him over the crevice. As he felt some humidity at the soles of his feet, Aer's heart beat faster.

Please don't let me fall, Aer begged the clouds with all his might.

Feeling a sudden change in the sensation at his feet, Aer took an uneasy step forward.

Noticing that the brunt of Aer's weight had shifted to the cloud, the enforcer behind him slowly released his grip.

It was an *incredibly* strange sensation. The clouds didn't *feel* solid. Rather, it felt more as if they were exerting a force to oppose Aer's weight. Regardless, Aer's breathing calmed as he shakily moved across the cloud. The danger had passed.

But that sense of relief lasted only a second. Now that his safety was secured, his mind was set on one person and one person alone.

Alius, Aer thought as he frantically looked around. *Where is he?*

Ignoring the protests of the enforcers behind him, he immediately ran to search for his brother. Aer examined every inch of the crevice, blocking out the screams of the falling fledglings as he sprinted forward.

Had someone already thrown Alius down without him noticing?

No. Surely, Aer would have spotted him, known somehow that he was safe.

"Aer!" A familiar voice shook him out of his thoughts.

Aer turned around. Behind him, Alius flailed frantically as the enforcer who had taken him away now held him over the crevice. His touch, however, failed to have any effect on the clouds beneath him, regardless of how much Alius strained himself.

Alius looked to Aer for help as the enforcer behind him shook his head and released him.

The last look on his brother's face was that of terror and despair as he fell through the clouds and vanished from Aer's sight.

Chapter 18: Torn in Half

My son has gone missing. The caretakers have reported to me that a couple of fledglings from the Charity Tree have gone missing as well. I suspect that information about the Ascension Ceremony has somehow been leaked to them. The caretakers are on high alert, searching the island carefully for any escapees. And yet we have still not managed to find them. Where could they have gone?

Aer's mind simply refused to comprehend what his eyes saw.

What had just happened? Why wasn't Alius in front of him? Where did he go?

In a daze, he made his way to where his brother had hovered just a moment prior. Before he could look down the man-sized hole at his feet, however, the clouds beneath him moved quickly to seal the opening.

Aer's legs collapsed, leaving his rear end to collide with the cloud. The cruel and hateful sea of white remained steadfast to his safety, despite so mercilessly discarding his brother to the world below.

The events that followed went by in a blur. Aer didn't remember leaving the cloud-filled chasm, and yet the next time he bothered to spare some attention to his surroundings, he was back on land. When it finally occurred to him that time was still passing, that the world around him was still moving, the Ascension Ceremony had already ended, and the surviving fledglings had been brought before the emissary and the sharply dressed man.

"So these are the results," Emissary Striaen stated, looking over the noticeably diminished crowd. "Those who have made it past the Ascension Ceremony, I welcome you to Atravel. We will hold a feast later to celebrate the rise of a new generation. Let us thank the Great Arbiter for—"

The following words failed to register in Aer's head. He was only aware that the speech had ended when the well-dressed man gave them their next instructions.

"You may now run to your families or do whatever it is you wish to do. Those who have no official guardian, please follow the caretakers so they may discuss your future."

Upon hearing those words, Aer wandered off on his own. Maybe he would find Alius somewhere else on the island, having climbed back up somehow.

He stopped when several adults blocked his way, some telling him he should follow them to discuss his future, others claiming to have come by to congratulate him. All were being unusually deferential, but he cared nothing for that. Alius had been the one who dealt with social interactions, and Aer was in no mood to figure it out for himself.

Aer turned away from them and marched off in a different direction, not wanting to hear another word.

Regardless of where he went, however, people paid close attention to him, and as if purposely ignoring his wishes, their whispers forced their way into his ears.

"Where is that child going? The emissary was looking for him."

"I don't know. But don't you think this is all rather unusual? The emissary showing so much favoritism for a single fledgling, one from a Charity Tree at that. Do you think—"

"Let's not discuss that here."

"Why not? I'm sure everyone's thinking it. It's why they're all looking to cozy up to him. It would explain a lot about the results of the trials that took place."

"Nevertheless, spreading rumors about the emissary could get you in trouble, especially while he's still around."

Aer made a show of blocking his ears. What were they even talking about? Their voices were irritating. Couldn't they just shut up? Didn't they have anything better to do with their lives than gossip endlessly about things that had nothing to do with them?

Unable to take it anymore, Aer sprinted away. He needed to be anywhere but there.

He then heard someone call out to him. "Wait."

Aer ignored it.

"I said, *wait*," the person continued, a bit more forcibly that time.

Instinctively feeling like he had to obey the command, Aer stopped and turned around.

Behind him, Emissary Striaen scrutinized him with an intensity that Aer had never seen from the old man before.

"You're alone." Emissary Striaen sighed. "How unfortunate. But I suspected this would be the result once I got to know you two bet—"

"What's beneath those clouds?" Aer screamed. At that moment, it didn't matter to Aer that the person before him likely had the authority to end his existence. More than anything, he *needed* answers.

The emissary looked taken aback, but his expression quickly shifted to one of gentle understanding as he met Aer's accusatory glare.

"I don't know," he answered simply.

"Then where do those who fail the Ascension Ceremony go?"

"I don't know."

"Where's Alius?"

"Only the Great Arbiter would know the answer to that question."

"Right, the Great Arbiter!" Aer shouted, noticing the desperation in his own voice. "He's the one who determines the results of the Ascension Ceremony, right? You're supposed to be his representative! Maybe he'll bring Alius back if you pray to him for it!"

Emissary Striaen gave him a look of pity. "Aer, he's gone."

Aer staggered back. The old man might as well have hit him.

"*Why?*" Aer asked, not quite sure of what he was asking. Perhaps he was demanding to know why Alius wasn't with him anymore or why such a cruel ritual like the Ascension Ceremony existed in the first place. Did he want to know why the supposedly merciful Great Arbiter would allow such a thing? Or was he going even further and questioning everything the adults had told him?

Maybe he wasn't really asking anything at all and was simply raging at everything around him.

"We have… many things to discuss when this is over," Emissary Striaen said carefully, appearing to have picked up on the questions Aer couldn't verbalize. "For now, please head to the banquet."

Aer fell silent, unable to muster the will to disobey. Instead, he listlessly headed in the direction the old man pointed him toward.

Emissary Striaen walked next to him. "I want you to know that I do understand how you feel. It's a shame about your brother, truly. Nevertheless, I'm overjoyed that at least you survived."

Aer didn't respond. Instead, he silently noted the emissary's care for his well-being as one more thing he couldn't understand.

***

Emissary Striaen observed the boy's pitiful figure while taking in the wealth of information he had just received. As expected, Aer did not trust him. Talking to him earlier in the morning had confirmed his initial evaluation of the youth. A posture that betrayed a lack of confidence, eyes that shifted to gather as much information as he could to protect himself, and an obvious knack for avoiding troublesome situations. Getting such a person to open up voluntarily would ordinarily be quite difficult. But the conversation they just had told the emissary all he needed to know about the child's mentality. The proper way to guide him had become clear.

Only one loose end remained for him to deal with. With any luck, it would all be over soon.

He walked to the banquet site with Aer at his side, taking care not to unduly upset the youth. There, the other visitors stood by, greeting him the way society dictated. He didn't fail to notice just how many of them were eyeing the boy walking beside him.

He paid special attention to the lone individual standing off in the distance. Her presence was unexpected. Or perhaps it wasn't.

"Head Huntress Islea." Emissary Striaen walked away from the others to address the stoic-faced woman. "Can I take your presence as confirmation that the banquet is ready?"

"Unfortunately, no," she replied, her voice as emotionless as ever. "While I believe myself to be quite adept at hunting prey, my skill in the culinary arts is rather lacking. Instead, I had someone else take my place in overseeing the cooks preparing the meat."

"Ah yes, I took it upon myself to learn of the details beforehand," Emissary Striaen said. "Out of everyone you know, you believe Azel to be the most suitable person to handle this task?"

"Yes," she answered after a pause.

"I see."

A silence settled between them before Doctor Resin made his way over.

"Emissary Striaen, I believe it's time."

"Yes, of course," the emissary replied before turning to face Aer. He would have to make sure the boy was safe in his absence.

"Go and join your peers," he instructed, gesturing toward where the other fledglings had gathered.

Silence. The boy gave no indication he had heard. Emissary Striaen then drew closer and looked him in the eyes.

"*Go and join your peers,*" he repeated. "*I forbid you from taking any actions that might lead you to harm.*"

***

Aer walked down to where the other fledglings were. Most were sitting on seats placed next to polished stone tables, accompanied by a caretaker or supervising adult. A few fledglings were made to sit on the ground, seemingly ostracized by the others. Notably, Gail was among them, silently bearing the looks of contempt directed his way. Standing beside him was his father, who, judging by his murderous expression, was also there against his will.

Aer went to the nearest stone table and sat, paying no attention to everyone else's questioning stares.

There, he waited, ignoring the attempts at conversation the adults beside him made. He didn't recognize this place. They should still be on the same island, but the scenery before him was completely different from the one burned into his mind.

Aer sat still as food that he had never seen before started to pile on the table, *cooked* meals that exuded mouthwatering odors. But he couldn't care less. Nothing would have drawn a reaction out of him at that point.

A few fledglings made a grab for their food before the caretakers standing by rebuked them, telling them to wait until the banquet officially started.

Aer just watched blankly, his mind detached from his surroundings. It was inconceivable that people could still care about the taste of food after everything that had happened.

***

Once he had concluded his business with Doctor Resin, Emissary Striaen made his way toward the table elevated for him and him alone. He observed his surroundings. Everyone currently residing on the Isle of Judgment had been gathered at this location so he could conclude the day's events ceremoniously. Piles of food and drinks decorated the lines of tables in front of him. Yet not a single bite had been taken. As expected, none had dared to start eating before he did. As he was the guest of honor, they were all waiting for him to begin the feast.

Good. All was as it should be. As soon as the banquet had been set up properly, he stood, ready to address those listening. He had considered his words carefully, mindful of the influence they held coming from a representative of the Great Arbiter.

"I'd like to thank the Great Arbiter for the presence of every individual here," he started, making sure to first bring his existence to the forefront of everyone's minds. "To all the children before me, you stand here today alive, meaning the Great Arbiter has found you exemplifying the sky's ideals. After today, you are no longer fledglings but full-fledged citizens of Atravel. As you step forward into this new stage in your lives, take the time to consider what's truly valuable to you."

***

Aer listlessly looked up as the emissary addressed him with the rest of the fledglings. What the old man said had barely even registered. Instead, their conversation from earlier was repeating in Aer's head.

You're alone. How unfortunate.

Aer, he's gone.

The terrifying reality of it all was finally sinking in.

Alone. Alone. *Alone.* He was alone. Alius was no longer there for him to trust and rely on. He was alone in a world that couldn't care less about him as a person, one that would happily take advantage of him and any weakness he dared to show.

How had this even happened? It was just this morning that the brothers had been cautiously hopeful about their futures. And now, the path ahead couldn't look bleaker.

Alius, for all his impulsiveness, had been the only one to understand Aer's fears and faults. He was Aer's companion from birth and had covered for his failings as a person, taking the initiative and acting when Aer couldn't.

Aer recalled Alius worrying over how weak his Sky Authority was and wondering whether he would be all right by himself once they left the Nesting Island. Aer had reassured him they would stick together. But he had said that for his own benefit as much as his brother's. Aer had needed Alius as much as Alius had needed him. Despite how much Aer grumbled over his brother's actions at times, he knew Alius had done everything with him in mind. He was the one person whose intentions Aer didn't have to doubt.

And now, he was gone.

Tears trickled down his face as what he had lost became clearer to him. What was even left for him at this point? Emissary Striaen's mentorship? The old man had been nothing but a stranger up until then. Aer didn't know why the emissary had taken such an interest in him, but he certainly didn't trust him as a person.

Then, among those he *was* familiar with, who could he possibly rely on?

Certainly not anyone from the Perch. Not only did they likely hold a grudge against him for humiliating them, but even if they were on friendly terms, they were the type of people who would backstab him without hesitation if it benefited them in some way. What had happened to Gail the moment public opinion had turned against him and his father was clear proof of that.

Then, what about those from the Charity Tree? Most were nameless faces that had been envious of his success in the trials. Kiel? He had died in the Ascension Ceremony as well, not that the opportunistic fledgling had seen him as anything other than a means to gain prestige. Nira? The only reason they interacted was because of Alius's meddling. They both lacked the disposition to initiate contact without him around.

Why did this have to happen right after they had left the Nesting Islands? He, who had no ability to reach out to others for help, would have to face this new, unknown world by himself. Alius had disappeared, and with his disappearance, the existence that the brothers had been until now was torn in half. Just like how a bird couldn't fly with only one wing no matter how hard it tried, Aer couldn't see how he could manage by himself.

Something grabbed and twisted Aer's heart. What was he going to do? Why was he still alive? It would have been easier on him if he had died with Alius in the Ascension Ceremony than to be here right now. The recent acclaim they had obtained, the emissary's favor, a path for a successful future—none of it mattered. He would trade it all away in a heartbeat for Alius to be standing beside him.

A choked sob entered Aer's ears. It took a moment to realize it wasn't his. He was not the only one crying—many of the people sitting around him also seemed to have lost someone they knew. Some of the adults looked sympathetic, others apathetic, while the rest straight-up gazed at those crying with disdain for daring to be so unsightly.

****

Emissary Striaen watched the crowd in front of him with what he hoped was a compassionate gaze as many broke down.

"I understand that some of you have suffered a loss that may feel overwhelming, but I assure you that the pain will pass. Just remember that even when you are uncertain of what is to come, whatever has and will transpire is due to the Great Arbiter's will. Everything will turn out the way he benevolently intended in the end. Remember this, even during your darkest times."

****

Sitting several seats away from Emissary Striaen, Soleil felt her anger flare as she listened to the old man's tone-deaf speech. The pain of losing her son to the Ascension Ceremony had not faded at all since it had happened. Rather, it had become her drive, pushing her forward when she felt she could no longer go on. It had spurred her to make passionate speeches all over Atravel to gain allies for her cause. It had brought her to challenge Head Caretaker Desen directly, the man who oversaw the Nesting Island that had raised her son. His gross negligence toward the fledglings who weren't connected to someone higher than him had given her son no chance to learn the skills necessary to pass the Ascension Ceremony.

But he had defended himself by saying that the discrepancy of the results between those he chose to give special attention to and those he didn't justified his actions. That the Great Arbiter had blessed more of those under his care with superior control of the sky was a sure sign that he had chosen wisely. An excuse impossible to disprove, as no one had any way of knowing how things might have gone if he had made sure everyone was taught equally.

To use his own line of thought against him, she had sabotaged the fledglings Desen favored and had persuaded some of the proctors who agreed with her to lower their evaluations of the Perch fledglings while raising those of the Charity Tree. Then she stood back as the visitors, many of whom it took significant effort to convince to come down here, observed the results.

Even if it had been underhanded, she'd hoped to show the higher authorities how horribly broken the system of the Nesting Islands was and just how much it encouraged those in control to favor those who were well connected. It was all to persuade them that the Ascension Ceremony was not a test of virtue but a classification of one's birth.

In the end, nothing had changed. Yes, it was gratifying to see the person responsible for her son's death disgraced in front of everyone, but it had been dismissed as an unpleasant incident, not a reflection of the system's problems on a larger scale. The Ascension Ceremony had gone on like nothing had happened. There was no sign that any sort of revolution was on the way despite all her actions.

What was the point of doing all this? she wondered.

***

"Let us now look to the future untethered by the profane matters of the world as the Great Arbiter intended. Praise be to him!"

Emissary Striaen sat back down, covering his mouth as he finished his speech. Polite claps from the caretakers and visitors soon followed.

Good. Now all that was left to do was to try the food before him.

"To Atravel's future," he declared, raising his chalice in a toast.

***

Many stared in anticipation as Emissary Striaen brought the cup to his lips then took a bite of the food, seeing that as the signal to begin the feast. All thoughts on the matter were quickly set aside, however, when the old man suddenly and unceremoniously collapsed onto the table.

Chapter 19: Changing Plans

We have finally located my son. He was found underground with the two missing Charity Tree fledglings. Somehow, he had managed to smuggle some construction tools and dig a tunnel underneath one of the stone pillars without anyone noticing. The caretakers are currently remodeling the tunnel for their own use.

As I feared, the other missing fledglings happened to be the sisters he got so attached to. They are all now being detained on the Isle of Judgment until we can decide what to do with them.

Silence filled the air as many stood in shock.

Eventually, one of the people sitting next to the emissary worked up the nerve to speak.

"Sir?" he asked with trepidation.

There was no response.

At that moment, Doctor Resin sprinted toward the table, shooing aside the concerned onlooker. After examining Emissary Striaen for a split second, he carried the old man's body away from the scene.

Uncertain of what to do, everyone waited until Doctor Resin reappeared.

"Emissary Striaen has passed away," he announced.

***

Chaos erupted once more. Only this time, the adults were the ones panicking.

"How did this happen?" a caretaker asked frantically.

"I'm not entirely certain, but I suspect he was poisoned," Doctor Resin answered.

"How?"

When Doctor Resin gave a pointed look at the food in front of them, many backed away from the banquet table in alarm.

"Who would do such a thing?" a visitor asked.

"I don't know," he said simply.

"Then whose responsibility would it have been to detect this?"

"That would fall to those involved in the feast's preparation, as well as the caretakers and the enforcers," another visitor informed them.

Some of the named parties froze in terror.

A brawny man who many recognized as the head enforcer rose to protest. "Please wait! We don't even know if the emissary was actually poisoned. It's too early to draw such a conclusion."

"The higher authorities will have our heads if they find out that an emissary died under our care!" one of the caretakers wailed.

"Maybe not," another caretaker tried to reason. "If we can pass it off as due to natural causes—"

"No one's going to believe that!" a third caretaker shouted. "Everyone saw what happened. The timing is too suspicious. We need to figure out right now who's to blame here."

"Everyone, please calm yourselves," Head Huntress Islea chimed in, looking perfectly stoic. "There is a simple solution to all this."

Everyone turned to face her. "Which is?"

"As it so happens, a young hunter named Azel handled preparations for the late emissary's last meal. I believe it prudent to assign all blame to him."

"So you're certain it was the food?" the head enforcer asked.

"Not quite, but do you wish to risk the possibility that it wasn't?" the head huntress replied, drawing closer to the head enforcer. "If it's discovered instead that there was some other reason you and your enforcers overlooked—"

The head enforcer paled. "Are you sure about this? Isn't this hunter your subordinate? Wouldn't that mean—"

"No. As it so happens, Emissary Striaen placed Azel under his employ before the trials began, releasing him from my command," the head huntress replied unflinchingly. "Furthermore, we don't even know if this poisoning was intentional or not. It's entirely possible that this was an accident brought on by his inexperience."

"Was it not you who presented the animal for this banquet?" the head enforcer continued, pressing his line of questioning. "If what you're saying is true, then wouldn't it fall to you to instruct him on how to prepare it correctly?"

"I assure you nothing about the beast itself is toxic. My hunters and I have partaken of its meat before the banquet without coming out any worse for wear. Which must mean that the cause lies within how the beast was seasoned. Many can vouch that I had nothing to do with its cooking process, as I judged my own culinary skills to be lacking."

"But—"

"It would also be far easier to explain how you, as the head enforcer, missed a food seasoning error over an assassination attempt, would it not?"

The head enforcer fell silent.

"That is true," he said slowly. "Yes, what you say must be what happened."

***

Aer stayed silent with his fellow fledglings, who he guessed felt much the same as he did, scared of the recent chain of events. They were still sitting at the banquet table, completely ignored by the adults arguing back and forth over who was responsible for the emissary's death. None had dared to touch the food after the doctor's announcement.

For a moment, Aer wanted to partake of the feast anyway. It would be a relief to him if he could just leave his pain and worries behind. What better way to go than to enjoy some delicious food that he had never seen before? The way Emissary Striaen had gone seemed so quick and painless too. But in the end, he couldn't go through with it. Whether it was self-preservation, a fear of death and what lay beyond, or something else entirely, Aer could not bring himself to take a bite.

He envied how easy it had been for Emissary Striaen, who had been blissfully unaware that he was going to die, even in his final moments. Honestly, what was with that stupid old man, promising explanations and guidance only to die without following through? It wasn't fair.

What was going to happen now? Who did he have left to turn to after all this? Would he somehow be blamed for the old man's death?

They had been seen together right before the banquet. Would people consider that suspicious?

Another layer of weariness attached itself to Aer's soul as that line of thought hit him. Too much had happened today, the majority of which he would rather shut himself away from. As the night continued and the fledglings sitting next to him began to nod off, he prayed to the Great Arbiter that the day's events would turn out to be nothing more than a nightmare. Even if it wasn't possible, he wanted to believe that what he was experiencing now was but a figment of his twisted imagination.

***

That night, Aer dreamed.

He was drifting in the air, surrounded by the sky's familiar blue hue. Feeling some discomfort, he tried moving, only to notice chains wrapped around his body like strands on a cocoon. Dissatisfied, he struggled against the oppressive grip of his bindings. At that moment, the chains holding him snapped. His body then lurched downward while his surroundings gradually grew darker. He then realized in a panic that he hadn't been floating; the chains had been holding him in the air. Without them, he had no means of stopping himself from falling.

Terror gripped his heart as he plummeted out of the sky. Other people's screams filled his ears as he fell, drowning out his own. Worst of all was his sheer helplessness. He had no control over the situation—no way to slow his acceleration, to change his direction, nothing.

The sensation of falling came to a sudden halt as an excruciating pain erupted from his skull. Darkness clouded his vision as he lay there, unable to move.

There, he waited. Even in that state, he could somehow feel the presence of someone approaching. A figure whose form he was unable to make out. But even without a clear view, he instinctively understood that this being standing over him was in some way different from anything he had seen before, that something about them was completely alien to what he had previously defined as common sense, that their very existence defied what was natural for the world.

***

Aer woke to a tap on his shoulder. He looked up to see Doctor Resin peering down at him.

"Come with me."

When Aer failed to respond, the man drew closer.

"Emissary Striaen wanted you out of harm's way. You will be taken to a safe place until we can sort this out."

Aer rubbed the sleep from his eyes as he stood and observed his surroundings. The color of the lights peering through the holes of Atravel's outer clouds told him it was early in the morning. Most of the fledglings next to him were sound asleep, looking blissfully unaware of what he'd experienced.

Aer shivered. He didn't remember his dreams often, and when he did, the details were never very clear. But that dream had been different. The pain and the images had been so vivid.

The dream had meant something. He was sure of it. What he wasn't sure of was whether he wanted to know what it was trying to tell him.

The doctor led Aer to a building located on the outskirts of the island. As soon as they entered, most of the visitors and caretakers who had been arguing the night before turned to stare at them.

"Doctor Resin, you're finally here," one of the caretakers greeted them. "This child is—"

Doctor Resin interrupted him. "You called me here because you wanted me to give an account of what happened yesterday, yes?"

The caretaker nodded. "Yes, you're right. Are you ready to give your testimony?"

Aer stood back quietly as the adults arranged their seats into circular rows. Once they were finished, they sat as the head enforcer made his way to the center to address them.

"We are here today to identify the root cause of Emissary Striaen's death," the burly man announced. "Doctor Resin has identified the most likely reasons as either a lethal combination of substances used in the preparation for the feast or a contamination of the food through unchecked bacteria. He is currently uncertain if this is transmissible in any way, so he has taken the time to seal off the emissary's corpse while continuously disinfecting himself. As per his instructions, all food presented at the banquet has been properly disposed of."

Doctor Resin nodded, to which the head enforcer continued.

"The primary suspect is a young hunter named Azel. According to the testimony of several different people associated with the incident, he was responsible for preparing the feast's primary meat dish."

The head enforcer then dragged a human-sized cage holding a young man to the center of the building. Aer questioned why they even had such a thing in reserve. A chilling possibility then occurred to him. Perhaps its intended purpose was to detain fledglings who had discovered the details of the Ascension Ceremony ahead of time.

"Hunter Azel, you have been charged with the crime of negligent homicide of the late Emissary Striaen. What do you have to say in your defense?"

The hunter named Azel frantically shook his head.

"Head Huntress Islea is to blame for all this!" he screamed. "She's the one who assigned me the job, even though I have no experience preparing meat of any kind!"

To this, the stoic-faced woman who Aer had become familiar with rose from her seat.

"I have no recollection of that," she declared, her voice as emotionless as ever. "What happened was that you, desiring a change in occupation, begged me and the late emissary for a chance to prove yourself as a chef."

"What?" Azel replied incredulously. "That isn't what happened!"

"I advise you all to ignore his excuses," Head Huntress Islea continued. "He's attempting to deflect blame by making up stories. My hunters can confirm he's tried something similar in the past."

"Yeah!" one of the hunters behind her exclaimed. "He tried weaseling out of responsibility for a hunting accident by framing other people!"

"Tell the truth!" another hunter shouted.

"I am!" Azel shouted back. "I want a proper trial on the Isle of Criminal Investigations!"

The head enforcer shook his head. "Unfortunately, you'll have to settle for us for now. Everyone here has elected to not let news of this incident spread to the other islands until we have a proper explanation for what happened."

Azel's eyes narrowed. "Don't give me that nonsense! You mean until you can think up a proper story to feed them that frees everyone here except me from being implicated, right?"

"Your accusations are unfounded," the head enforcer replied.

Aer couldn't help but be relieved that no one seemed to consider him a suspect. Based on what he was witnessing, he doubted he could have mustered a proper defense for himself. The people surrounding the hunter named Azel had all clearly decided his guilt before they'd started the interrogation. They were asking him leading questions and dismissing his attempts at a rebuttal at every turn.

Ultimately, Aer was certain there was no chance of changing their minds. The only thing that seemed to be up for debate was what degree of responsibility other individuals held in the incident. Most of those in the room had agreed that someone named Soleil Mistral held some indirect blame by leading the emissary down to this island. Some questioned Head Huntress Islea, but the inquiries died down once she declared that Azel was no longer under her jurisdiction by the emissary's orders, which she had no authority to overturn. The hunters under her command verified this as well, all confirming that Emissary Striaen had taken Azel off her hands at an earlier date.

Once it had all ended, Doctor Resin led Aer down a section of the building away from the others until they reached a door. Inside was a white-walled room with a bed and clean clothes on one side and a desk on the other, on top of which was a sizable meal that had been specifically prepared for him.

"This is where you will stay until further notice," Doctor Resin stated. "I apologize for how small and sparse this room is, but you'll have to bear with it for now."

Aer tried not to laugh. He had shared a treehouse smaller than this with another person all his life. Any amusement he felt was immediately squashed as his brother returned to the forefront of his mind, bringing back all of yesterday's pain along with him.

As soon as Doctor Resin exited the room, Aer helped himself to the food. He hadn't realized how famished he was until its scent entered his nostrils.

Once he had finished his meal, however, he was left alone with his thoughts.

Blinking away the tears pooling at the corners of his eyes as images of yesterday's events reinforced themselves into his memory, Aer tried to go to sleep, doing his best to avoid thinking about his brother for as long as he could.

***

The following day went by rather similarly. Having questioned the main culprit, the visitors and the caretakers moved on to pressing every individual involved in the creation of the feast for all possible details. Aer, trying his hardest to distract himself from Alius's absence, listened in once more to get a feel for the people speaking.

The head enforcer clearly wanted to end the investigation as quickly as possible, having made up his mind on what had happened. In contrast, Doctor Resin was asking every possible question, deliberating over every new piece of information he learned.

Many people questioned were terrified at the idea of being involved with an emissary's death. In particular, the proctor for the Mechanic's Trial looked like he was on the verge of a nervous breakdown despite having had nothing to do with the feast's preparation.

The biggest enigma was Head Huntress Islea. Like all the other times he had seen her, Aer couldn't tell what was going on in her head. He had never felt such apathy from another human before. It wasn't natural, especially considering she was more closely implicated with this case than most.

On the other hand, Orator Mistral, who Aer now recognized as Ciel's mother, was easy to read. She looked completely lost on what to do as everyone interrogated her. It didn't seem possible that she could have brought Emissary Striaen there knowing what would happen to him.

Trying to make sense of it all was headache inducing, but it gave Aer something to do until the end of the day. Once the meeting ended, however, thoughts of his brother returned, and the only place he could look for refuge from the pain was in slumber. He retreated to his room and lay on the bed, praying to the Great Arbiter that he could forget his brother, at least within his dreams.

***

Soleil weighed her options for the future—how much further she wanted to push this cause for her son, how much further she *could* push it. The atmosphere around the visitors had changed significantly since Emissary Striaen's death. As things were, how the Nesting Islands operated was probably the last thing on their minds.

Even if she brought their attention back to the topic somehow, merely being associated with the death of an emissary would be enough to scare away many of the supporters she had gained. She had come as far as she had by appealing to their consciences and frustrations, but that wouldn't be enough to absolve her of all doubts in this situation. An emissary simply had too much importance in the public's mind to be brushed aside, and there was clear evidence and testimony confirming she had brought Emissary Striaen down here.

Maybe it would be better for her to give up. Even before the emissary's passing, it seemed unlikely that she would bring about significant change to the Nesting Islands. The sooner she could disentangle herself from the mess, the better.

Soleil then noticed a familiar figure standing in her way and felt hope rekindle in her chest. Maybe *they* had a way forward.

***

"Good morning, everyone." The head enforcer's voice boomed in Aer's ears the next morning as he addressed every visitor and caretaker there for the day's meeting. "It's now the third day after the incident. I'm sure many of you have noticed that Atravel has resumed sailing the skies once more. Surely, those from above have begun questioning why the visitors, especially Emissary Striaen, haven't returned to their posts."

"And yet none have come down for an answer," Head Huntress Islea noted. "I see no need for worry. It won't be long before we have a detailed explanation for them."

"Before we start our discussion, I feel the need to mention that not everybody related to the incident is present today," Doctor Resin pointed out. "Is this all right?"

The head enforcer looked around. "You're right. Where is Orator Mistral?"

Aer blinked, noticing the older woman's absence for the first time.

"Did she flee?" someone in the crowd asked.

"Do you think she might have had a hand in the poisoning?" Doctor Resin asked. "She was the one who brought the emissary here."

"We all agreed this was an accident, yes?" the head enforcer asked nervously.

"Just pointing out a possibility." Doctor Resin sighed. "At any rate, having someone related to the incident go missing is troubling."

"You're right. I'll assign some enforcers to search for her."

True to his word, the head enforcer ordered his subordinates to conduct a sweeping search of the island. It wasn't long before Orator Mistral was found and brought before them all.

"Where have you been?" the head enforcer demanded.

"I received a letter from Emissary Venar." Orator Mistral looked tense. "I felt confirming the contents of this letter took priority over a matter that has already more or less been decided."

Her statement was met with cries of alarm. Aer didn't know who Emissary Venar was, but those familiar with the name were visibly terrified.

"Emissary Venar?" Doctor Resin asked incredulously. "Did you tell him about what was going on here?"

Orator Mistral shook her head. "No. He already knew."

"How did news of what happened here reach Emissary Venar so quickly?" Doctor Resin asked.

"He's an emissary," Head Huntress Islea replied. "Perhaps the Great Arbiter gave him a revelation."

"And he didn't contact anyone else?" Doctor Resin questioned. "How strange."

"Because I'm an orator, he left it to me to deliver his message to everyone here," Orator Mistral stated.

"What did he say?" the head enforcer asked.

At this, the orator's voice dropped to a murmur. "First, he expects me to take responsibility for bringing Emissary Striaen down here."

"As you should!" a caretaker cried.

"What else did he say?" Head Huntress Islea asked.

"Aside from the caretakers, fledglings, hunters, and the parties directly involved in this incident, such as Doctor Resin and me, everyone is to return to their respective positions until everything is sorted out."

Aer sensed the tension ease among those listening. Many present seemed to consider that statement good news, as the assembly of visitors broke into excited whispers.

"If he's asking for our return without keeping a record on us, then we're not being held accountable for this. Let's leave while we can."

"But I still want to know more about what happened here."

"We'll hear about it later. I don't want to be anywhere near this incident as they're investigating."

"Why did Emissary Venar ask the hunters to stay behind?"

"Isn't it obvious? The higher-ups want a profile of Azel, the primary suspect, from the people who worked with him."

"I want to clarify something before we act on your message," Doctor Resin said as he approached Orator Mistral. "Are you certain this letter was from Emissary Venar?"

"What are you implying?" the woman replied.

"It just seems odd that he contacted only you about this incident. May I see the letter?"

Orator Mistral nodded and handed him a sheet of paper.

Doctor Resin frowned as he read it. "I don't know Emissary Venar's handwriting well enough to tell whether this is a forgery or not."

"What purpose could she possibly have to forge such a thing?" Head Huntress Islea asked. "Furthermore, if this is a lie, why would Orator Mistral cast blame on herself for bringing Emissary Striaen down here?"

Aer listened as Doctor Resin tried and failed to voice a suitable answer. In the end, everyone's desire to leave and disassociate themselves from Emissary Striaen's death simply drowned out his doubts.

***

Over the next few days, the news spread across the entire island. As expected, the visitors who received permission to leave wasted no time in vacating the premises.

Aer watched listlessly as a sea of clouds gathered at the island's borders to carry away the last of the visitors. Soon enough, the only people remaining would be him, the other fledglings, the caretakers who had accompanied them to the island, the hunters, and a few notable names he had become familiar with during his time there.

The past week had not been pleasant to him emotionally. The emptiness caused by Alius's absence continued to gnaw at him without mercy. And with the mystery of Emissary Striaen's death no longer fresh in his mind, nothing kept him distracted from the guilt and fear threatening to overwhelm his being.

To keep his mind clear of unwanted thoughts, Aer had gone back to see what had become of the other fledglings, most of whom had been staying within the camping grounds ever since the night of the feast. Many seemed to have formed their own opinions on what was happening, the most popular theory among them being that Head Caretaker Desen had poisoned the emissary.

Aer gave that idea some consideration. It made sense. The head caretaker had reason to want revenge. The emissary had humiliated him by stripping him of his position in front of everyone. It wasn't unthinkable that he had gotten one of his caretakers to contaminate the feast.

But without Alius by his side, Aer was unable to work up the nerve to discuss the topic with anyone. All he could do was listen quietly until it was time for him to leave.

So instead, he had taken to messing around with the clouds that surrounded the island. Having watched them provide transportation for the visitors, Aer couldn't help but wonder how they functioned. Doctor Resin had, of course, forbade him from getting on one and leaving the island, but he had been allowed to try moving them as much as he pleased, provided he did it at a distance.

Aer didn't know how to feel about the clouds. On one hand, he couldn't help but associate them with Alius's death. At the same time, they were the only thing distracting him from his pain. They held a surreal beauty, swirling around the island and carrying people to the landmasses above.

As the clouds carried the last of the visitors from sight, Aer wearily made his way back toward the building he was staying in. The adults there didn't question his presence anymore, though he wondered how long this would be the case. Uncertain of what was to become of him and having nowhere else to go, Aer couldn't help but dread the moment when they would ask him to leave.

He then noticed other fledglings nearby. No, everyone left on the island was now in the building. Confused, Aer used his Sky Control to let the air around him carry their conversations to his ears, trying to understand why they were there.

He relaxed when he learned Orator Mistral had gathered everyone to wait for Emissary Venar to question them. Feeling less out of place, Aer prepared to release his Sky Control.

Then it happened. Aer sensed the shock waves of what felt like several explosions of air in the distance. He looked back in alarm before trying to call out to someone, but his voice failed to come out, silenced by his thoughts. To mention the explosion, he would have to explain how he had been using the air to eavesdrop. Even if he managed to push through that, he wasn't sure how to put what he had just felt into words.

He stood in silence as everyone else carried on with their business. This was another painful reminder to him just how much he had relied on Alius to take the initiative for them. Aer had consistently shied away from anything that seemed bothersome. Alius had always been the one to drive them into action.

The sound of metal shifting on a large scale reached Aer's ears. This time, it wasn't just him who heard it. It was audible to all those around him.

Before anyone could ask what was happening, violent tremors shook the very ground they stood on. Aer's heart skipped a beat as the earth beneath him distanced itself from his feet. The sensation felt terribly familiar.

He then registered that he was falling, just like in the nightmare he'd had on the night after the Ascension Ceremony. But this was no dream. He, everyone around him, and the island they inhabited were all very much in free fall.

Chapter 20: Falling Heavens

A complication has arisen. The younger of the two sisters has been discovered to be pregnant. The only male known to have contact with her during this past Sky Cycle would be my son.

I have never been so conflicted on what to do as I am now. If this girl truly is carrying my son's child, then I cannot send her to the Ascension Ceremony as woefully underprepared as she is. At the same time, I cannot ignore my responsibilities to the Great Arbiter and Atravel.

Aer panicked as the ground grew farther from him. The feeling of helplessness as he fell, the fear that enveloped every corner of his mind as he realized he was about to die—it was all reminiscent of that nightmare.

His surroundings weren't helping either. The screams from the people around him as they realized what was happening only reinforced the similarities between his nightmare and reality.

A voice reverberated throughout the building. Using Sky Control to speak over the crowd's cries, the head huntress began passing instructions to everybody there.

"Everyone, please calm down," she said, sounding completely unfazed by this turn of events. "We need to act prudently if we are to survive."

Despite the sheer dread he was experiencing, Aer had to briefly marvel at the older woman's composure.

Does this person even feel emotions? he wondered.

The head huntress then addressed those listening to her. "First, we need to slow the descent of the island until all of us are touching the floor. We'll die if we collide with the ground below at full speed. Imitate what I do."

"R-Right!" one of the hunters replied.

As many of the adults began collectively wielding their Sky Authorities, Aer felt the pressure of the air below the island heighten dramatically, pushing back against its weight. He, along with some of the more skilled fledglings who were able to instinctively sense what the adults were doing, desperately imitated them to the best of their ability.

His teeth began chattering as a noticeable chill pervaded the building. More importantly, however, the distance between his body and the land beneath him was slowly shrinking.

Aer reached out with his hands as he gently touched the ground. Things still felt off. His body was too light, and the sensation of falling had not entirely left him, but he had calmed down enough to stop screaming in fear.

Once everyone had landed, Head Huntress Islea gave more orders.

"The island is still falling too quickly. Slow the acceleration more."

"We're trying! There's just not enough of us left to hold up this much weight!"

That was the reality of the situation. The Isle of Judgment had not stopped falling. They had only slowed it down enough for gravity's hold on them to outpace the falling speed of the island.

More people joined the effort to stop their descent, asking for directions on what to do. Try as they might, however, the weight was just too much for the people present. None of them were carriers specially trained for this sort of thing. The skill and manpower needed to halt the island's descent simply weren't there.

Aer sensed through the air that the island beneath him was steadily approaching a much larger mass. He closed his eyes, preparing for the harsh impact. He then felt the ground beneath him jerk upward for a few moments before coming to a complete halt.

Everyone breathed a collective sigh of relief. Miraculously enough, not one of them had been injured during the collision.

"Everyone outside," the head huntress ordered.

Not needing to be told twice, everyone exited the building.

The first thing Aer noticed once he stepped outside was the enormous formations of stone and ice jutting out from the sides of the island. What lay beneath them was unclear, as a sea of clouds veiled the landscape below.

"What is this?" an adult asked. "And why is it so cold right now?"

"What a disaster," another joined in, observing their surroundings with great interest. "Which island did we crash into?"

"There are no Atraveli islands below or even level with this one aside from the Nesting Islands," Head Huntress Islea stated. "Judging from what I can see and sense, we've landed between neighboring mountain cliffs. Most likely, we're not within Atravel's borders anymore."

The head huntress's declaration was met with shock and despair.

"You mean we're standing on the surface right now? The same surface we've fled since Atravel's creation?"

"Great Arbiter have mercy. We've left the sky's protection. We're all going to die."

"What do we do now?"

Doctor Resin then clapped his hands, grabbing everyone's attention.

"For now, we should make sure of where we are," he calmly stated. "After that, we can decide on a course of action."

"Agreed." Head Huntress Islea nodded. "I'll have some of my subordinates gather information about our current location."

***

Aer waited with the other fledglings as some of the hunters went out to the edges of the island. When they returned, a grim expression had settled on every single one of their faces.

"Your evaluation was correct, Head Huntress," one of the hunters reported. "We most certainly are not in Atravel right now."

"Do you have any idea how this might have happened?" Doctor Resin inquired.

"I don't know whether it happened before or during our fall through the sky, but the chains keeping this island attached to the rest of Atravel have all come apart," the hunter answered.

"*Every* single one of them?" a caretaker asked incredulously.

"Yes." The hunter nodded. "Of all the islands that make up Atravel, this island, detached from the others, is the only one down here."

"Meaning we can't get help from the residents of the other islands," the head huntress said for everyone to hear.

The panic that erupted among the listeners made Aer want to flee the scene. He could sense that they were looking for someone to take responsibility for their fear and frustrations.

"Don't we have anything to fall back on in case of a situation like this?" Orator Mistral asked.

"Yes. The contraptions placed around the islands were made for this very purpose," Head Huntress Islea answered. "To keep us afloat until we can fix the situation. But they've clearly failed at their function if we're all the way down here."

"Useless pieces of junk!" one of the caretakers cursed. "Why do we even keep the mechanics around?"

"It might not be their fault," a hunter piped in. "Said devices seem to have been compromised."

"Compromised, you say?" Doctor Resin asked.

"Yes. Every single one of them was deactivated, one way or another."

A heavy silence filled the air as the implications of that statement sank in. Those around Aer exchanged accusatory gazes before one of the caretakers lunged at Orator Mistral. When the people between them pulled the man back, he laughed maniacally.

"Do you people honestly believe all this happened simultaneously by sheer coincidence?" he spat. "This had to be premeditated! You're behind this, aren't you? You've been protesting against the Nesting Islands this whole time!"

"What? No!" Orator Mistral shouted back. "Why would I do such a thing? If I were behind it, I certainly wouldn't strand myself here with you all!"

"Calm yourself," Doctor Resin told the offending caretaker. "Let's not make any judgments until we fully understand what happened."

"Yes, we can argue over who's to blame for all this later," Head Huntress Islea agreed. "The first thing we should focus on is our next course of action."

Those maintaining their composure seemed to agree as they began discussing their options.

"Can't we just raise this island back to its proper location?" one of the hunters asked the head huntress.

"We were barely able to soften our landing. I doubt we have the Sky Authority necessary to carry this island anywhere," Head Huntress Islea replied.

"If only Emissary Striaen were still with us. He'd have no problem lifting us back up," a caretaker muttered.

"What about the rest of Atravel?" someone else asked. "Can we expect any help from them?"

"Yeah," another joined in. "Wasn't Emissary Venar supposed to show up here to talk with the suspects of Emissary Striaen's poisoning? Surely, he'll notice the island's absence."

"Well, he's not here now. Otherwise we wouldn't have fallen in the first place," the head huntress pointed out. "And Atravel has been moving at full speed for the past few days. By the time anyone notices we're missing, it might be too late for them to find us."

"So we might be stranded? Can anyone here fly? Maybe we can send someone up to deliver an emergency message."

When nobody gave an affirmative, Doctor Resin stepped in.

"None of us can fly, and the surrounding clouds won't last all the way to Atravel. I think the only thing we can do for now is wait for our fellow citizens of the sky to come down and save us."

"I disagree. We have no guarantee that anyone will come to save us at all," Head Huntress Islea argued. "I suggest instead that we descend the mountain cliffs and live off the land."

Aer stared at her in shock. He wasn't the only one either—others were looking at her as if she had uttered something blasphemous.

"Are you mad? Do you know what horrors might await us down here?"

"That type of thinking is why I doubt we will be rescued. Even if others are aware of our predicament, they may abstain from joining us out of fear of our current location."

"But—"

"And because of that, we must take the initiative to find new sources of food and water if we wish to survive. We may not have the strength and supplies needed to find them if we decide too late."

Doctor Resin shook his head. "I see your point, but if we are to be rescued, it would be best for us to stay put so they can find us. Furthermore, we have plenty of resources for now. Surely, it would be best to deliberate until it becomes certain that we've been abandoned?"

"And how long would we wait?" the head huntress countered. "We have no information about the layout of this land. None of us have any idea how long we would have to travel before finding a way to sustain ourselves. With that in mind, moving immediately would give us the best chance of survival."

Doctor Resin looked distressed. "We also have no idea if it's even possible to sustain ourselves in this world. Don't you remember the stories of Atravel's creation? Of how the rest of humanity destroyed themselves here? Our best chance of survival is to stay put and hope that Atravel sends enough people down for us to lift the island back into its proper place."

Aer listened to the two argue. Doctor Resin had proposed the much more comforting plan: Stay there, do nothing, and wait for Atravel to find them. Aer could tell that almost everyone wanted to go with his suggestion, but it didn't answer the doubts that the head huntress had placed in their minds. *What if they weren't rescued?*

Meanwhile, Head Huntress Islea's argument was unappealing at first glance. Agreeing with it would mean giving up hope of being rescued entirely. At the same time, it assumed that the world below was hospitable enough to sustain them. Furthermore, with her emotionless voice, her rhetoric wasn't persuasive at all. But her argument held an undeniable thread of logic.

Most seemed to side with Doctor Resin, but some seemed torn in their decision. Based on their whispers, at least a handful of the hunters and caretakers were seriously considering Head Huntress Islea's proposal.

"The head huntress has a good point. I know I would do everything I could to stay away from the surface if I were still back in Atravel."

"If not for her quick response in this situation, we'd all be dead. But can we really survive down there?"

"The hunters are specially trained to hunt down wildlife and to tell what's edible and what's toxic to our bodies. We also know that wildlife exists outside of Atravel, as they enter our borders every so often."

"What about other humans, though? If our legends are true, then there was a very good reason we fled to the sky way back then."

"If our legends are true, then they would have killed each other off long ago, right?"

In the end, the consensus was to wait for help for the time being. Some, however, expressed a willingness to change their minds should their situation grow more desperate with no help in sight.

***

With the chill of the air seeping through his clothing, Aer joined the rest of the crowd as they headed inside the building, which had been empty except for one person.

Hunter Azel, still trapped within his cage in the corner of the hall, had not been able to step outside. Everyone who passed by ignored him, presumably preoccupied with the more pressing matter at hand.

Upon seeing his lonesome figure, Aer paused for a moment and empathized with how lost he must have been, hearing others discuss matters he wasn't privy to and mentioning parts of a conversation he hadn't been a part of. Aer had felt the same way over how the adults around him had behaved recently. Why wouldn't anyone explain anything to him? What did they know that he didn't?

"Hey, kid," the young man whispered.

Aer looked around, wondering who he was speaking to.

"You. I'm talking to you." Azel looked straight at him.

Aer froze, unsure if he should answer.

"You mute or something?" the older boy asked in frustration as Aer stayed silent.

Feeling pressured to respond quickly, Aer faced the hunter. "What is it?"

Azel paused and examined their surroundings before continuing, presumably to make sure no one was listening in on them. "Tell me what happened out there."

"Why me?"

"Does it look like I have any other choice?" Azel asked. "You still look like you're unsure of how to deal with me, unlike everyone else, who've already made up their minds."

Seeing no reason to refuse, Aer explained the situation outside. By the time he had finished, Azel looked utterly dumbstruck.

"Wow." He shook his head. "Things are even more of a mess than I thought. Think you can do something for me?"

"What?"

"Get me out of this cage."

Aer immediately took a few steps back.

"Wait!"

"Ask someone else," Aer replied. "I don't want to get involved with you more than I have to. It's been one thing after another ever since I left home. I don't need to go looking for more trouble."

"One thing after another?" Azel repeated. He took another look at Aer before giving him a knowing nod. "Oh, I get it now. You lost someone to the Ascension Ceremony, didn't you?"

Aer paused. "What makes you think that?"

"You look rather young. Also, your eyes have the same look a lot of fledglings have when they go through the Ascension Ceremony."

Aer fell silent. That only seemed to urge Azel to push further.

"I bet a whole bunch of things don't make sense to you right now. I'll also bet the caretakers around you all gave you the same nonsense about the results being the will of the Great Arbiter. Do me this one favor, and I'll answer any question you have, as someone who went through the same thing not so long ago and figured it out by myself."

Aer gave Azel a wide-eyed stare. The smart thing to do would be to walk away, but his legs wouldn't let him leave. The thought of finally getting someone to answer the questions that had been raging in his mind over the past week was just too alluring.

He then realized he was thinking in the way Azel wanted him to and grew suspicious of the older boy.

"You're pretty good at talking to get your way, aren't you?" Aer asked. "How do I know you really have any answers and won't just run as soon as you're free?"

Azel blinked before putting up a smile. "You'll just have to believe in me."

Aer hesitated. He didn't trust the hunter at all, but...

"How would I free you exactly?"

What more did he have to lose? There was no point in worrying about his own well-being now that Alius was gone. Things couldn't possibly get worse than they already were.

"You would need to grab the key for this cage." Azel pointed toward a lock at the cage's center. "Now's probably the best time for you to act. The others are too preoccupied with what's happening to pay too much attention to me."

"Where would I find this key?"

"Check the head enforcer's room," Azel stated. "I saw him heading toward the far-right hallway whenever he was done for the day. It should be empty now, seeing as the head enforcer was one of the first people to leave the island when Emissary Venar gave his orders."

***

Aer examined the hallway. Not many people were there, but it wasn't completely empty. The fact that fledglings were now a common sight in the building was convenient. If anyone asked him why he was there, he could just claim to be lost.

Aer silently walked through the hallway and used his Sky Control to sense if there were people breathing in each of the rooms he passed, marking every empty room in his mind. He then walked back and waited for people to leave. Once he was sure he wasn't being watched, Aer reentered the hallway and peered inside each empty room, one by one.

Fortunately, the rooms that had been vacated the past few days had been left unlocked, making it rather easy for him to enter and lock the doors while searching every corner.

Unfortunately, he couldn't find anything, as everyone had already gathered their personal belongings before leaving the island.

The head enforcer couldn't have taken the key with him, could he? Aer considered before shaking his head. He doubted the head enforcer would take the key to some other island while Azel was still here. The more likely scenario would be that he'd handed the key to someone else. That itself was a problem, though. Aer would have to widen his search and enter the rooms of people still on this island if that was the case.

While he was mulling that over, another problem quickly presented itself. He found that he couldn't open the next door, though it was a door to a room that he had previously marked empty, and he still couldn't sense breathing on the other side.

249

A dreadful thought entered his mind. *What if someone's behind this door, but they're silencing the air around them to catch people like me lurking around?*

Aer quickly backed away from the door. If the key was behind it, he would have to give it up as a lost cause.

Thankfully, that wasn't the case. After entering a few more rooms, Aer spotted a rusty key matching the colors of Azel's cage at the top of a desk. Pocketing it, Aer left the hallway and headed back toward his room.

***

Aer waited until nightfall, when everyone had cleared out of the main hall, before running toward Azel, silencing his footsteps with Sky Control as he did.

"You've got it?" Azel whispered excitedly. "Great! Hand it over."

Aer grabbed the key but didn't hand it to him. Instead, he held it just out of reach.

Azel's eyes narrowed. "What do you think you're doing?"

"Answer my questions first, then I'll hand you the key," Aer stated. He still didn't trust the older boy.

"Free me first."

"You're not exactly in a position to bargain here. I'll put this key back where I found it if you don't give me answers."

Azel gave him a hard glare before sighing. "Fine. Ask me anything you want to know about the Ascension Ceremony."

"Why does it even exist?" Aer started.

"I'm sure there's more to it than this, but the way I see it, the main reason is more pragmatic than pious."

"What do you mean?"

"Atravel has limited resources. We can't make big moves to get anything from the world outside our clouds, so eliminating the dead weight is the nation's way of regulating its population."

Aer blinked. That possibility had never even crossed his mind.

"Vegetation and animals don't normally thrive in the sky," Azel continued. "Furthermore, oxygen is a limited resource, being so high up. People who can't use Sky Control to continuously moderate the atmosphere and change the air around them to supply their own oxygen are considered a drain. The times in history when Atravel had more people than breathable air were the few occasions where we were in danger of not staying up in the sky. We had to dip closer to the earth to resupply."

"So to make sure that doesn't happen, they test whether or not we can walk on clouds?" Aer asked incredulously.

"If you can cloudtread, then you should be able to change the air around you enough to justify your existence. If you can't, then it's probably not worth the effort to keep you around. You'd be surprised at how accurate of an indicator it is."

"Cloudtread?" Aer repeated.

"The common term used to describe standing on clouds," Azel explained. "Moving on, the entire reason for the Nesting Islands is to make sure they don't miss anyone with this testing. It's required by law to bring any newborns down here at the end of every Sky Cycle."

Aer needed a moment to take everything in. What would Alius say about all this?

"How has this system lasted so long?" Aer asked. "Has no one found out about the Ascension Ceremony ahead of time?"

"Oh, there have been leaks before," Azel answered. "It's just that even if you found out, what are you going to do? You can't leave the Nesting Islands without cloudtreading, in which case you should have no reason to avoid the Ascension Ceremony. The only thing you can do is hide, which some *have* done in the past. I wouldn't recommend it, though. The punishments when you get caught are rather harsh. Although, if you're sure you're going to fail, I guess you have nothing to lose."

"But if you could stay hidden—"

"You *will* get caught, sooner or later. The caretakers and the enforcers are completely used to sniffing out stragglers and have knowledge of all the Nesting Islands' hiding spots. It's just much less of a hassle for them if you go willingly without knowing anything, which is why they try so hard to keep everything a secret."

Aer shuddered. The caretakers *were* unusually competent in searching the Spiral Forest when all the fledglings had to be present for a gathering. If he and Alius had learned more about the Ascension Ceremony ahead of time…

"So, when they talk about how passing the Ascension Ceremony means that the way you live lines up with the way the Great Arbite—"

"Ah, yes. The judgment of the Great Arbiter," Azel scoffed. "How convenient it is for the people preaching his values. Coincidentally, these same people are the ones speaking for him, yes?"

"What are you implying?"

"It's all a sham. As if there's some higher being watching over us. They'll say whatever is convenient."

"Nothing proves beyond any doubt that there isn't one either," Aer pointed out. "And the fact that we do have powers relating to the sky that we can't explain naturally has to mean something."

"Well, if there is such a being, these guys don't speak for him. The whole spiel about the Great Arbiter giving his blessings is just something the higher-ups tell everyone so that they feel better about killing their own people to survive."

"How has no one revolted yet?" Aer questioned.

"That's another reason I think the Ascension Ceremony exists. It's a convenient way to weed out possible dissenters. It's a well-known fact that those with the best Sky Authorities tend to avoid conflict and are the most detached from the world. Those more likely to commit themselves into changing the status quo are gotten rid of before they can influence others to do the same."

Aer's eyes widened. "That… can't be right."

"That's just how things are." Azel shrugged. "Haven't you ever wondered why the islands we live on are chained together? It's so people can't go off on their own and develop viewpoints that might bring them into conflict with Atravel down the line. Our shared environment, history, and teachings justify the laws we made for ourselves and mold our current thoughts and opinions. Take those away, and people will eventually break off into factions, some with interests hostile to our way of living. Which is why those in charge are so desperate to keep everything as is, to maintain our peaceful seclusion."

Aer went into brief contemplation. Was that what would happen?

He then looked down to see Azel holding out his hand.

"I've told you everything I know about the Ascension Ceremony," the young hunter insisted. "Now, hand over that key."

Doubt crawled into Aer's mind. Was it really okay to free someone convicted of a crime like this?

"What will you do once you're out?" he asked, trying to reassure himself that whatever happened as a result was none of his business.

"Me? I'm heading out on my own. Based on what I heard from the people passing by, everyone's looking for someone to blame. Considering how I ended up here, I'll probably be one of the top suspects. Even if we are rescued, my life in Atravel is over. Whether it was on purpose or not, people still believe I'm responsible for the death of an emissary. There's no future left for me there. I might as well take my chances on the world outside."

"*Did* you kill him?"

"Do I look like I have a death wish?" Azel replied, annoyed. "No, I didn't. What would I gain from doing that? Now, hurry up and let me out of here already."

Hoping he wouldn't regret it later, Aer tossed him the key.

Azel grinned.

"Thanks," he said as he unlocked the door. "Take care of yourself."

Chapter 21: Desperation

A decision has been reached. I have convinced the relevant authorities to be lenient with the young escapees. We will hold a private Ascension Ceremony just for them. Furthermore, this date of judgment for the girl and my son will be delayed until after their child is born. If the Great Arbiter determines they are to remain in Atravel after all this, there will be no additional punishment for their actions.

Aer stood in silence as he tried to process everything he had just learned. It took him a few moments to realize how bad it would be if people spotted him next to the empty cage. He hurried back to his room, careful not to be heard.

Unfortunately, he wasn't the only one wandering around the building at that time. Much to his horror, a familiar figure was roaming the hallway connected to his room.

"Boy, what are you doing here?" Head Huntress Islea asked.

Aer's eyes darted around the hallway as he searched for an excuse. The situation felt eerily familiar. Was it a coincidence?

"Re-Restroom," he mumbled.

"Is that right?" The older woman eyed him from head to toe, her face betraying no emotion as always.

Aer shuddered as the head huntress scrutinized him and their surroundings. He still couldn't tell what was going on in her head. Eventually, the head huntress looked away from him and headed straight toward the area he had just left.

Aer paled. It wouldn't take a huge leap of logic to link him with the empty cage still in the center room of the building. Unable to think of anything else to do, he headed inside his room and plopped onto his bed

"

before the head huntress could reappear, fear tormenting his mind as it went over the possibilities of what would happen next.

***

Aer peeked out of his door once morning arrived, trying his best to ignore his exhaustion. Sleep had thoroughly evaded him throughout the night, his mind too preoccupied with everything he had learned and the consequences he might have to face as a result.

Seeing that no one was searching for him, Aer took a few cautious steps outside. When no one made a commotion, he slowly made his way back to the center room of the building, where people crowded around the empty cage in the corner. Not liking where this was heading, Aer listened as the adults surrounding the cage discussed Azel's disappearance.

"How did he free himself?" one asked.

"The people charged with watching over him should have paid more attention," another commented.

"They were probably too preoccupied with our current situation," a third person added.

Before Aer could step away and go back to his room, a few more adults joined the scene, Head Huntress Islea and Doctor Resin among them. Aer froze then blended in with the crowd, trying his best to remain inconspicuous.

"Who was supposed to be responsible for him after the enforcers left?" Doctor Resin questioned. "The hunters?"

"Does it matter?" one of the hunters asked. "Where can he even go now that we're stuck down here?"

"That's right. He must be somewhere in the building. There's no way anyone could descend these mountains without the necessary supplies."

"Who's to say he doesn't have those things?" the head huntress asked.

Upon hearing that, some of the caretakers ran to check. They soon came back looking both angry and anxious. "We can confirm that some of our reserve food and clothing have gone missing. He's likely taken some tools as well."

Their report was met with more worry. Aer shrank deeper into the crowd. Would he be blamed for Azel's actions?

"How much did he take?"

"Enough to sustain one person for a long time, at the very least," one of the caretakers answered.

"He likely had a helper," Head Huntress Islea stated. "The key to his cage is missing."

"Who?"

"I'm not sure," she replied, much to Aer's relief. Her next words, however, filled him with dread. "I do have a suspect, however."

"You do?"

"Yes. I ran into a boy late last night." She then turned to face Aer immediately, as if she had known he was there the whole time. "And there he is now. How kind of you to join us."

Aer averted his gaze. He had held out the faintest hope that she would cover for his actions as she did back in the Perch. Instead, he had the feeling that she had deliberately waited until that moment to announce her suspicions in front of everyone. The crowd's eyes were fixed on him.

"Incidentally, weren't you with the emissary before the banquet?" the head huntress asked.

Doctor Resin looked alarmed. "You're not implying—"

"I am. It's strange how he was the last nonobligatory contact the late emissary had before he died."

"Weren't you the one insisting this whole affair was an accident?" Doctor Resin argued.

"The situation has changed," the head huntress stated simply. "Along with associating with the late emissary before the feast, I saw him conversing with Azel yesterday. Later, I saw him wandering around a hallway he shouldn't have been in. Of course I would suspect that he had a hand in the emissary's death and made a move to free his co-conspirator last night."

Aer cursed his own carelessness. She had been watching, and he never noticed. Now he was getting blamed for something much bigger because of it.

"Wait just a moment!" Doctor Resin persisted. "This boy never left the Nesting Island before this incident. How would he have colluded with Hunter Azel beforehand? Furthermore, Emissary Striaen approached the boy of his own accord. People here can attest that it was the emissary who was looking for Aer rather than the other way around."

Much to Aer's relief, a few of the adults nodded at Doctor Resin's words.

"Be that as it may, this boy is still our only suspect," the head huntress argued. "I suggest we lock him away until we figure out what to do with him."

"It's too early to decide to imprison him," Doctor Resin said. "We have nothing but speculation and hearsay from you tying him into any wrongdoing in the first place."

Aer opened his mouth to speak, only to find that the air around him had been silenced by someone.

"Very well. I'll drop the accusations for now," Head Huntress Islea conceded. "We have more important matters to discuss, after all."

"Such as?"

"Our future actions," Head Huntress Islea answered. "A day has passed, and there is still no sign of Atravel taking any actions to rescue us. Furthermore, we've just confirmed that Hunter Azel made off with quite a bit of food and clothing, cutting down our supplies even further. It's time for us to act."

"It's still too early to give up hope of being rescued," Doctor Resin stated.

"And when will it be too late?" Head Huntress Islea asked. "Are you content to sit here until we can no longer sustain ourselves and starve to death?"

"It needs to be a collective decision. Neither you nor I can make that choice alone."

Aer gauged the audience's reaction. While a few more people seemed to agree with the head huntress than yesterday, the majority still sided with Doctor Resin.

The head huntress bowed her head. "Understood. Just know that the longer it takes for us to decide, the more unlikely it is that we'll survive out there. We need enough supplies to descend these mountains and find another way of sustaining ourselves. The natural resources of this island will not be renewable under these weather conditions."

Following that ominous declaration, the discussion soon came to an end.

Afterward, Doctor Resin dragged Aer back into his room.

"Stay put for now," he ordered. "If someone questions you about what happened, say nothing. Don't do anything you're not supposed to."

Aer nodded silently. Doctor Resin looked quite frustrated. It probably wouldn't do him any favors to admit that he *had* been the one to free Azel, much less have that information spread to the public.

***

The next few days were painful. Confined to his room with no new disastrous events to distract him, Aer's mind naturally drifted back to his missing brother. Desperate to avoid being alone with his thoughts once more, Aer used his Sky Control to sense those passing by and listen in on their conversations.

Based on what he heard, the hunters had searched everywhere for Azel, from the main building all the way to the very edges of the island, all the while gathering any natural resource they came across. Most, however, had concluded that it was unlikely Azel was still on the Isle of Judgment.

Aer felt both relieved and guilty upon hearing that news. Azel being gone meant that Head Huntress Islea couldn't interrogate him and confirm it was Aer who had set him free. On the other hand, the grumblings of the people sharing this news were difficult to ignore.

"What a waste of food," Aer overheard a woman mutter. "There's no way you could survive down there."

"What if you can?" a man replied. "In that case, wouldn't we be the ones wasting resources by just waiting here?"

"Quiet," the woman snapped. "The rest of Atravel has to have noticed that we're missing by now."

"Sure, but will they do anything about it?"

The only response was a gloomy silence.

Those two weren't the only ones who felt that way. As supplies continued to dwindle, the feeling of abandonment pervaded the building. Many had grown pessimistic over the idea that Atravel would come back for them. More and more people were voicing their agreement with the head huntress. Some had even begun exploring the mountain cliffs holding the island in place, mapping out the terrain and giving an estimate of how long it would take to descend.

As night darkened his surroundings once more, Aer released his Sky Control, accepting that he likely wouldn't be able to listen in on any more conversations for the day. Trying to shut off his mind and go to sleep, Aer rolled fitfully on his bed for a while before a knock on his door forced him to his feet. He unlocked and opened it to see a woman nervously trying to make herself look less conspicuous in the middle of the hallway.

"H-Hello, Aer," she stammered.

It took Aer a moment to recognize her as Ciel, the speaker who had first announced the trials back on the Nesting Island. He had, quite frankly, forgotten she existed. "What are you doing here?"

"I'm helping my mother out of the hole she's dug herself into," she answered. "Can you help me?"

"What are you talking about?"

"I can't explain here. I need you to follow me."

Aer pulled away from her, remembering Doctor Resin's orders. He had to avoid getting involved. But before he could close the door on her, she drew closer.

"Wait, p-please hear me out," she pleaded.

He hesitated, which only served to embolden Ciel.

"I-I just need you to talk to my mother," she whispered. "You don't have to do anything beyond that. I think it'll benefit everyone involved if we discuss everything that's happened recently."

"And we can't do this during the day?" Aer hissed.

Ciel shook her head, which gave Aer pause. What did they know that couldn't be discussed openly?

"Doctor Resin is already furious with me. If he finds me sneaking off to have a conversation with your mother—"

"Ah, you don't need to worry about that. My mother's distracting both him and the head huntress right now. She told them she plans to make a speech tomorrow about whether we should stay up here or not, and both are doing everything they can to convince her to their side."

"All this so I can have a conversation with her in private?"

Ciel nodded, causing Aer to fall silent.

She then added one last remark. "I think what she hears from you might be the deciding factor in what she says tomorrow, more than anything they say."

Aer blinked. Now he was *really* curious.

"Where to?" he asked after a moment of deliberation.

Aer threw on some warm clothes and followed Ciel, who led him toward the opposite end of the island by circling around its borders. There, they waited until Orator Mistral joined them.

Aer stared at her. The older woman looked as restless and defeated as he felt.

"You are Aer, yes?" she asked once they stood in front of one another.

Aer nodded and responded with a question of his own. "Why did you have me come all the way out here?"

"I don't want the wrong people to overhear this conversation," Orator Mistral answered. "Now, I need you to confirm a few things for me. Did you have anything to do with Head Huntress Islea and the hunters before the Ascension Ceremony?"

Aer opened his mouth to deny it before pausing.

"I met the head huntress on the Perch once before," he admitted, remembering how she had caught him sneaking out of Head Caretaker Desen's room. "She wanted me to guide her around, even though I was from the Charity Tree."

Orator Mistral stared at him. "Yes, I think I remember seeing her defend you and your brother from Head Caretaker Desen and his son. What did you two talk about before that?"

"We talked about the Perch and how unfair it was. I don't really remember the details."

Orator Mistral fell silent.

"Just to be sure, you were the one who killed the beast back on that Nesting Island?"

Aer nodded.

"Were you the first fledgling it encountered?"

"Me… and my brother, yeah," Aer replied.

Orator Mistral's eyes narrowed. "Was that a coincidence, or were you being targeted even back then?" she muttered to herself before she asked him another question. "And Emissary Striaen took an unusual interest in you around this time, yes?"

"Even before that, I think," Aer said, remembering the meat Emissary Striaen had sent them right after the Falconry Trial. "He went to the Charity Tree to meet with us before that had ever happened."

Orator Mistral grimaced. It appeared as if he had confirmed something unpleasant for her. At the same time, however, some hope shone in her eyes.

"Mother, what's wrong?" Ciel asked.

"We might need to find another place for him to stay after this," Orator Mistral answered.

Aer looked between the mother and daughter in confusion. "Sorry, but what are you two talking about?"

"If you are who I think you are, then it's not safe for you to go back to that building," Orator Mistral replied.

Aer backed away in worry. "Doctor Resin told me to stay in my room."

"You'll have to disobey him, then," Orator Mistral said simply.

Aer shook his head. "Look, I'm in enough trouble already. Doctor Resin is *not* happy right now. I'm pretty sure he knows that I was the one who got Azel out of his cage. I can't just ignore him when he's the only one who's making sure I'm still doing all right."

Orator Mistral raised an eyebrow. "So you *were* the one who freed Hunter Azel? Tell me the details."

Aer berated himself. That was such a stupid way of letting that slip. He needed to stop talking.

Faced with Aer's silence, Orator Mistral sighed. "Fine. I was planning on revealing everything when I came here. I'll just have to come clean first."

Ciel gave her a look. "Mother, are you su—"

"I was the one who gathered people from all across Atravel down here," Orator Mistral continued, causing her daughter to go silent. "I turned public perception against the caretakers and worked with Head Huntress Islea to sabotage the Perch during the trials. The Perch underperformed because of our actions."

Aer blinked, wondering if he had heard her correctly.

"There," Orator Mistral stated. "Now I can't reveal anything about you without you exposing my secrets. So let's be completely honest with each other."

"Why would you—" Aer began.

"To slander the caretakers," Orator Mistral interrupted him. "You fledglings aren't the only ones affected by the Ascension Ceremony. I lost my son in the previous one, which might not have happened if they didn't show blatant favoritism toward those they preferred while completely ignoring those they didn't."

Aer had nothing to say. Having experienced both the caretakers' scorn and the loss of a loved one firsthand, he found himself unable to condemn her actions.

"I was distraught over his death, but I planned to accept it and move on," Orator Mistral continued. "What else could I do? This was supposed to be the Great Arbiter's decision. My son was gone, and nothing would bring him back."

She then took a deep breath. "It was then that Head Huntress Islea wrote to me, telling me to not let his death go to waste. She told me I could be doing so much more than what I was. We then met to talk about what she meant."

Aer stared at her incredulously. That emotionless woman who acted on pure pragmatism had really reached out to her in such a way?

"I'm not sure how much of it is fact, but she opened my eyes about why some parts of Atravel work the way they do," Orator Mistral stated. "Our leaders say we travel through the skies to display the Great Arbiter's power, but that always seemed dubious to me. Islea gave a much more believable reason for why Atravel is constantly in motion. We're fleeing the unknown. According to our legends, our origins began when we fled from the rest of the world. We don't know if humanity still exists down here, but if they do, the best way to avoid discovery would be to keep moving. It's the same reason we cover the sky around us in clouds, to hide our presence."

Orator Mistral paused. "But for us to maintain this charade, we first need to be able to sustain ourselves. Do you know why the Ascension Ceremony exists?"

"Azel said something about it," Aer openly admitted. He saw no point in hiding it, not when she seemed to know everything. "He said it was a way to weed out those who don't fall in line while keeping those who can change the atmosphere into breathable air."

"He probably picked that up from Islea." Orator Mistral nodded. "From what I know, she's been subtly spreading that idea. It wouldn't be surprising for a subordinate of hers to have heard about it."

She sighed. "Anyway, it infuriated me that what she was saying might be true. If it is, then the Ascension Ceremony isn't something mandated by a divine being. It would instead be a matter of not having enough air to go around, air that we had less of simply because the caretakers wanted to focus on those who offered the most personal gain over teaching everyone properly."

Bitterness crept into her voice. "So much of what she told me made perfect sense. She offered to help me change the Nesting Islands for the better. I agreed, and we've been working together ever since."

"So why bring me out here?" Aer questioned. "It sounds like you thoroughly planned everything out, so why risk me revealing it to everyone now?"

Orator Mistral paused. "Recently, I've had doubts. All these accidents happened simultaneously, and Islea was prepared for every one of them, almost as if she expected them to happen. I understand that she's good at keeping a cool head under pressure, but a few facts line up just a little too well for me to believe that it's all a coincidence. And now that she's insistent on imprisoning you, I felt like I couldn't stand by any longer."

"Why does it matter whether she wants to detain me?" Aer asked. "I *was* the one who let Azel go."

"That does lower my suspicions of her a bit," the orator agreed. "But I can't ignore the possibility that she has an ulterior motive, knowing who you might be."

"Who exactly do you think I am?" Aer asked.

Orator Mistral gave him a long, hard look before answering. "I suspect you're a relative of some sort to Emissary Striaen. I can think of no other reason that would have made that detached old man take such a strong interest in you."

Aer fell silent. That would explain a lot of things, but...

"Though there are a few things that don't quite add up," she said, voicing his thoughts. "There's the fact that you were raised at the Charity Tree. The caretakers surely would have placed a direct relative of an emissary in the Perch."

Orator Mistral closed her eyes. "I'm also *fairly* certain that the only family that man had was his son, who died during his Ascension Ceremony," she said, her face pensive in recollection. "Do you know anything about your family?"

Aer shook his head. "I don't know any of my relatives aside from my twin brother. We were raised together on the Charity Tree as far back as I can remember. I think I told your daughter as much."

Ciel nodded, which seemed to put Orator Mistral even deeper in thought.

"You told me earlier that who I am would make it unsafe for me to return to my room," Aer said, keeping the conversation going. "Why would being related to Emissary Striaen put me in danger?"

"Because you could be targeted for that exact reason," Orator Mistral answered. "I... think Head Huntress Islea might have intentionally set up the poison that took Emissary Striaen's life."

"What?" Aer shouted in alarm. "Why?"

Orator Mistral signaled him to lower his voice. "I'm beginning to suspect that she deliberately stranded us down here. And if that's true, then she wouldn't want anyone with a powerful enough Sky Authority to remain here. They could lift this island back to where it was."

"What does that have to do with me?" Aer whispered.

"You may not know this, but Emissary Striaen's family line has a history of producing those with unrivaled Sky Authorities," Ciel informed him.

"If you are a relative of his, you might be the only one who can lift this island back to Atravel." Orator Mistral pulled her coat tighter. "That's probably why Doctor Resin is trying so hard to keep you safe."

"Then shouldn't I be staying with him?" Aer asked.

"Doctor Resin won't have the ability to protect you for long," Orator Mistral said. "This is a genuine warning. I don't want your life on my conscience. I've got enough to feel guilty about."

Aer stared at her with suspicion. "And why would you feel guilty? What exactly did you do to help her?"

At that, Orator Mistral's gaze fell to the ground, her eyes refusing to meet Aer's.

"I've made up my mind," she declared after a moment of silence. "I'll reveal everything about what I've been doing to Doctor Resin. Maybe he can piece together exactly what's going on with that information."

Ciel's eyes widened. "Are you sure that's okay?"

"Ciel, stay with him until I get back." Orator Mistral then turned to face Aer. "If you ever succeed Emissary Striaen, I want you to remember how painful things are for the people down here."

Aer said nothing, dissatisfied by the turn of events. He still had unanswered questions. Why was she just ending the conversation now?

Orator Mistral, seemingly oblivious to Aer's annoyance, headed back toward the island's main building. She hadn't taken more than a few steps, however, before an all-too-familiar voice called out to her.

"I see. So you decided to betray me in the end."

The three of them turned to the source. A figure obscured by a snow-white cloak undid her hood as she drew near, revealing the face of Head Huntress Islea.

Aer stepped back. How long had she been there?

Orator Mistral stared at Head Huntress Islea in fear and disbelief. Rage and scorn had transformed the stoic woman's ordinarily blank features into something incredibly terrifying.

Before they could react, the head huntress ran into Orator Mistral, causing her to gasp in pain as she stared down at her chest in shock. A large knife was protruding from her chest, piercing her heart.

"None of this would have needed to happen if you just kept your mouth shut and did as you were told," the head huntress spat venomously.

Ciel stood frozen in horror. "Mo-Moth—" she stammered.

Aer wasn't faring any better. It was the first time he'd seen the head huntress openly display emotions. The intensity of her bloodlust was enough to make him want to vomit.

With the last of her strength, Orator Mistral turned her head to face them.

"*Run,*" she mouthed before slumping to the ground.

Chapter 22: Hunted Down

The girl has given birth to twins. And despite my initial misgivings, I have begun praying earnestly to the Great Arbiter for her survival after seeing how happy she makes my son. Given enough time, I'm certain she could be educated to be a proper citizen of Atravel.

How uncharacteristic of me. It appears as if my son's arguments have affected me more than I initially suspected. Perhaps I need to reevaluate my beliefs about the less fortunate. There may be another purpose as to why they have been placed under such circumstances.

That final action was enough to shake both Aer and Ciel out of their trance. They sprinted off in different directions, trying to put as much distance as possible between them and Head Huntress Islea.

The head huntress hesitated for a split second before chasing down Ciel. Before Aer could exit her line of sight, however, she fired several blasts of air with enough shearing force to split a person in two in his general direction.

Sensing the attack, Aer met the slashes of wind with heavy gales of his own. The resulting impact echoed through his entire body as it violently threw him off the ground. Managing to catch his balance midair, he deftly landed on his feet, continuing his sprint with no change in pace.

Having escaped the scene of the murder, Aer dove straight into the nearby forest for cover, gasping for air as he slowed. How had Head Huntress Islea known they were there? Had she been following them from the beginning without them noticing?

He then realized what a stupid question that was. The woman was a huntress, someone whose job it was to track animals and hunt them down. Hadn't she specifically mentioned during her lecture that a hunter would need to know how to conceal their presence? He had been too careless, taking it as a given that he would be able to stay hidden and sense any who approached.

Realizing his footsteps could still be traced, Aer leapt onto a nearby tree and climbed as high as his limbs would carry him. He then jumped from tree to tree, silencing his breathing and keeping his senses up, meeting any changes in the surrounding air with intense scrutiny.

Head Huntress Islea, as far as he could tell, had not followed him. She appeared to have identified Ciel, the older and more influential of the two, as the bigger threat.

That was probably the correct choice, Aer realized. If Ciel could reach the main building and inform the people what the head huntress had done to her mother and what she planned to do to her, they should be safe. Even if the head huntress could do something about Orator Mistral's body, her absence would still be noticed by the other adults. That, along with the information Ciel had on her involvement with the trials, would be enough to, at the very least, lock the head huntress away until they could confirm the truth.

If Ciel didn't make it, however, it would be Aer's word against the head huntress's. And she had already cast suspicion on him for freeing Azel and being involved with Emissary Striaen's poisoning. Nothing would stop her from framing him for both Orator Mistral's and Ciel's deaths.

The thought filled him with dread. Would Ciel be okay? Would she reach the building before the head huntress got to her? If she didn't, what options were left to him?

If he could reach the building himself and alert the people inside while the head huntress was still dealing with Ciel, he might be able to convince them of his innocence. However, if Ciel died and he failed to get to the building before the head huntress, public opinion would turn on him rather quickly. Should that happen, it would be better for him to avoid contact with others entirely. He would have to follow in Azel's footsteps and steal food and supplies, taking his chances with the outside world. Either way, he would need to return to the building at some point. The sooner the better, as others wouldn't be on the lookout for him until Head Huntress Islea relayed her distorted version of the events.

As he reached the end of the forest, Aer leapt off the tree he was on and blew a gale that carried him across, landing on the ground as gingerly as he could. Best for him to continue with wind-assisted jumps over running to keep his tracks as spaced out as possible.

It would be difficult to track him from his faint and sparse prints with the sky as dark as it was. Now that he had left the cover of the trees, however, the danger of being spotted increased considerably. He still didn't see Head Huntress Islea, but he knew better than to trust that as a fact.

The silhouette of the main building was faint but visible. Trying to remain aware of his surroundings, Aer tuned his senses to the air that lay ahead. Something was approaching him from above—at an angle he couldn't hide from.

Aer tensed for a moment before realizing what he was detecting couldn't be the head huntress. For one thing, the air displacements were too small to belong to another human. For another, there were too many movements for it all to be made by a single person. Lastly, Head Huntress Islea couldn't fly.

Or at least, he hoped that was the case. Evading her would become outright impossible if she could.

Much to his relief, what entered the scene wasn't the head huntress but a flock of birds with dark patterns covering the backs of their heads. They looked like they had seen better days, as their frazzled appearance was clear to Aer even at a distance.

The lot of them flew rather erratically, zigzagging around one another only to come to a complete stop once they noticed him. They stared at him for a moment before turning around and flying back in the opposite direction.

And with that unusual action, Aer's sense of relief immediately gave way to confusion and unease.

Wait, why are there birds here? Aer questioned. The island, like the Nesting Islands, had been cleared of natural wildlife. So where could they have come from? Did animals from the outside world choose to nest up here? When the weather was *this* cold?

A terrifying possibility occurred to Aer. As far as he was aware, the only animals that were supposed to be on the island were what the hunters had brought to butcher for the banquet. It was also possible to use Sky Control to communicate with animals of the sky. Putting those facts together…

As if confirming his fears, the figure of another human entered his view not long after. The cutting winds aimed at him by said figure were enough to tell him who it was.

Terrified, Aer turned and sprinted in the opposite direction with all his might, avoiding Head Huntress Islea's attacks by a hair's breadth.

Aer raced back to the forest, desperately trying to lose the head huntress within the cover of the trees. As she followed, Aer blew at the ground to scatter the fallen leaves, dirt, and snow into the air.

Undeterred, Head Huntress Islea willed a gust to clear everything in front of her before firing a wide slash of wind, aiming to cut down the surrounding trees and decapitate Aer at the same time. Sensing the attack, Aer ducked. He then blew at the chopped trees behind him, tipping them to fall toward the head huntress, who leapt to the side.

Using the fallen trees to obstruct her pursuit, Aer circled around in the opposite direction.

His pulse quickened as he exited the forest. His movements were faster than he remembered them being. The meals he had been eating the past several days were giving him more physical energy than he'd ever had in his life prior to coming to this island.

But that wasn't enough. The head huntress was still closing the distance between them. He might be able to defend himself against her blows in a contest of Sky Control, but it would all be over once she got into melee range. He stood no chance in a physical entanglement with someone armed and trained to hunt down beasts.

Aer hated how the island's main building was even farther away than before. It would be impossible for him to reach it before the head huntress got to him just by running straight ahead. The times he had gone up against Gail during the Enforcer's Trial and the wild beast back at the Charity Tree made it clear that he couldn't just run and hope to outpace those more physically able than him. Instead, he had to proactively take measures to impede their movements. Which was why he was at a loss as the head huntress exited the forest into the open field behind him. There was nothing left for him to use as a distraction or cover.

Aer took a deep breath to calm his nerves. He couldn't freeze up in fear. Unlike in the Enforcer's Trial, there would be no Emissary Striaen to save him if he got caught. He needed to think of something.

He nearly lost his footing as the ground before him began to divide. They were fast approaching the crevice at the center of the island, the site of the Ascension Ceremony. An idea then started forming in Aer's mind. Unlike back then, this crevice was empty of clouds, now just a gaping abyss. If he could push her off like he had with the beast…

He moved to the left, running parallel to the crevice on the opposite end of the main building. After covering some distance, he looked back and confirmed that the head huntress had followed him to the same side. He ran straight ahead until the chasm was just wide enough for him to cross before leaping over it with a wind-assisted jump, careful to block the incoming attacks from the head huntress midair.

Aer stumbled and rolled onto the snow-filled dirt once he reached the other side. As soon as he sensed that Head Huntress Islea was about to make the same jump, he stood and turned to face her. Once the head huntress leapt and reached the center of the chasm, Aer created a strong headwind, blowing her back.

A look of surprise flashed across the head huntress's face as her momentum slowed. When she realized she wouldn't reach the other side, she increased the strength of her tailwind, trying to overpower Aer's attempt to drop her into the abyss.

They struggled for several moments, testing the strength of their Sky Authorities against the other's. In the end, much to Aer's surprise, Head Huntress Islea conceded and blew herself in the opposite direction. Using the gales created by both her and Aer, she managed to land back on the side she had jumped from.

Aer paled. That wasn't what was supposed to happen. He had put too much strength into their contest and inadvertently gave her the opportunity to recover. He tried to pull her back in, but she had rooted herself firmly to the ground and could defend herself properly by meeting his gales with her own.

The head huntress then unleashed all different kinds of Sky Control to attack and unbalance Aer, many of which Aer had never encountered before. There were her typical air slashes, yes, but there were also bursts of compressed air, spirals of wind that tried to pull him into the crevice as they drew near, attempts at changing the air around him so he couldn't breathe, and so on.

The distance between them, however, gave Aer enough time to feel how each use of Sky Control was created and find a counter to every one of her attacks. The bursts of compressed air could be dealt with by expanding them as soon as they were created. The spirals of wind could be blown off course, and any changes in the air could be halted with the same trick he used for silencing, by keeping the air around him in stasis. Nothing she could do was beyond what he could deal with.

Apparently realizing that herself, the head huntress paused to observe him and their surroundings. Aer, keeping his eyes focused on her, used the moment to catch his breath and gather his thoughts.

They were at a stalemate. If the head huntress made any move to jump to where he was, Aer could just blow her back. But if he left the area to go for the main building, nothing would stop her from crossing the crevice and catching up with him.

What worried him most was the fact that the head huntress had been aiming for him alone. What had happened with Ciel? Did the head huntress already get to her? If so, then why didn't she head toward the building immediately and frame him for Ciel's and her mother's deaths? Did she feel like she had the leeway to eliminate all witnesses and avoid any suspicion?

***

The stalemate continued throughout the night. Head Huntress Islea had tried circling around Aer's range a few times, only to get blown back when she tried crossing the gap between them. To be at a distance where Aer couldn't reach her would require her to leave his line of sight entirely. So his best option would be to stay until the head huntress gave him a reason to move.

As time passed, however, Aer began doubting his judgment. He had to force himself awake more than a few times as fatigue started to overtake him. A lapse in focus would be fatal, but he found it difficult to keep this up. He hadn't slept at all during the night and had instead spent it pushing both his body and mind to their absolute limits. The cold weather didn't help either.

In contrast, Aer couldn't detect any exhaustion from the head huntress. Whether it was because she was more accustomed to this than he was or because she was better at hiding her weakness, he couldn't tell. He could honestly believe either.

Aer began wondering what would happen if they just stayed like that. Would others eventually notice their disappearance and search for them? If they did, who would they choose to help?

Aer's heart skipped a beat. If a search party was sent out, the most likely people to be chosen would be the hunters, who were all under Head Huntress Islea's control. Was that why she was content to wait? Because she knew it would eventually end in her favor?

Getting desperate, Aer went on the offensive and fired air slashes at the head huntress, trying his best to recreate the shearing force she produced. If he could injure her badly enough to stop her from following him, he could break the stalemate to his advantage. Unfortunately, his attempts were easily repelled. Defense was far easier than offense at that distance, especially with the mutual ability to sense the other's actions.

Aer stopped, knowing that whatever he tried would be pointless, just as it had been the other way around. He could only pray that something or someone would save him.

***

Once dawn arrived, extremely heavy winds descended upon their location. Soon, a full-blown snowstorm covered the area, obscuring their vision.

Aer shivered as he tried to still the air around him. The gales were too powerful and sudden to be natural. They would also push him away from the crevice if he wasn't careful.

Strangely enough, Aer could see this was true for Head Huntress Islea as well. The winds blew in opposite directions at the center of the crevice, pushing the two away from one another.

Aer blinked as he came to a sudden realization. The winds were acting as a strong headwind for the head huntress. She wouldn't be able to jump the crevice, with or without his input.

Taking full advantage of the opportunity, Aer dashed toward the main building, letting the wind carry him forward.

Once he left the area, Aer looked back, aware that he wouldn't be able to sense any human-sized movements due to the turbulent winds. The head huntress had not followed him.

He breathed a sigh of relief. He had gotten away purely through a stroke of luck.

His destination now visible ahead, Aer hurried along the trail that led to the main building's entrance. He just needed to reach someone, anyone who would listen to him.

Something shot out from under the snow and grabbed his ankles. Falling face-first to the ground, Aer turned his head to look at his legs, which were both painfully entangled in rows of steel chains.

It was a trap set by Head Huntress Islea.

Aer struggled with the chains, trying to pull them apart and free himself. When they didn't budge, he tried cutting them with slashes of air to no effect.

Seeing nothing else he could do, Aer amplified his voice and called for help, praying that someone from the building would hear him and come out to see what was going on.

But no one came.

In the direction opposite to the building, however, a figure emerged—one that Aer recognized as the head huntress. Aer could only watch in terror as she drew closer, closing the distance he had worked so hard to gain.

"Predictable," she said once they were face-to-face. "I knew you wanted to reach this building, so you would have to pass by this area eventually. I had this trap set up before I began chasing you."

Aer gave in to his fear, rapidly firing a frenzy of air slashes at her. The head huntress sidestepped most of them and efficiently deflected the ones she couldn't dodge. She then yanked at the chains, causing them to pull at Aer's feet and force him back to the ground.

"Again, predictable," she scoffed as she took out her knife. "A hunted beast is most likely to lash out when it's cornered. I won't be caught off guard by such a thing."

"W-Why?" Aer managed to get out.

"I suppose you *would* want me to explain why I'm doing this," Head Huntress Islea stated as her face morphed into one of fury. "Honestly, all of you are so frustrating. From that pathetic old man dying before his time to Resin picking apart everything I do and say to Soleil not keeping her mouth shut and forcing me to eliminate her and her daughter to you learning things you weren't supposed to. Why does every single one of you insist on making things as difficult as possible for me?"

Aer could only stare in shock. The woman he had always considered emotionless was displaying her hate and anger quite expressively. It almost felt exaggerated. Despite the situation, he couldn't help but be engrossed by the sheer contrast with what he was used to.

"Well, I suppose we would have ended up here regardless of what happened, seeing as I never intended to let you live." The head huntress brandished her knife. "For all the caution you have around other people, you're still quite naïve, boy. Did you really think that the key to Azel's cage would be left unattended? The head enforcer handed it to me before he left. You're just lucky Resin intervened."

Aer, understanding that he had been set up, couldn't help but think that it might have been pointless for Doctor Resin to interfere if this was how it would end.

"Why can't anything go the way I planned?" Head Huntress Islea ranted. "I already had to compromise over and over and over and over… Do you know how much time and effort it took me to set everything up? Convincing Soleil to create enough of an outrage to bring everyone important down to the Isle of Judgment, getting that mechanic to tell me how to break down the chains along with every emergency device meant to keep this island afloat, I had to handle it by myself because no one else would dare to lead the masses dissatisfied with those in power in any sort of organized revolt."

The head huntress then leaned closer. "Why am I even telling you this? You know absolutely nothing. It's only because that foolish old man went and died before I could release everything I've been holding back. Curse your own bad luck for being the next best thing to take my anger out on."

So this is how I die, Aer thought as he stopped struggling. There was nothing he could do to resist at this point. All that was left was for him to accept his death.

Aer felt strangely calm once he realized he was out of options. Maybe dying wouldn't be so bad. Maybe he would be able to see his brother again.

Or perhaps not. Who knew what happened after death? Either way, it was pointless to dwell on the matter. He would find out soon enough.

Aer absentmindedly gazed at the sky, noticing for the first time how it looked from the outside. It looked a lot prettier from down there, with more colors in the scenery to contrast with the clouds. And the clouds themselves were… *darkening?*

Aer blinked as the knife at his throat suddenly flew out of Head Huntress Islea's hands. Immediately after, the woman was blown away from his person.

"You're still resisting?" the head huntress growled in frustration as she steadied herself on her feet.

Lightning struck between him and the head huntress, startling Aer and causing her to jump back in alarm. Before the crack of thunder could reach him, however, the air around him stilled unnaturally, dampening the noise.

A familiar voice then reached their ears. "So, you were the ringleader behind everything after all."

Both Aer and the head huntress turned their heads to the source. Above them hovered Emissary Striaen, looking as healthy as his age allowed.

CHAPTER 23:
A LONG-HELD DECEPTION

The Ascension Ceremony has ended. The girl, the younger sister, the mother of his children, was found unworthy. My son passed, as expected, but dove after her in a despair-induced delusion. And now, both have fallen.

The elder sister, the only one to survive, cursed me to my face for this outcome. I could not muster the will to punish her for her insolence. My beloved son has died. I would like to die too.

"But you died," the head huntress said simply.

"Before the banquet, I requested Doctor Resin to fake a diagnosis," Emissary Striaen replied, taking out some sort of mouth guard. "I never ingested the food or drink set in front of me."

Head Huntress Islea glared at him. "So that *was* staged. I thought it was strange how you collapsed immediately. That poison was designed to kill over time. I thought that perhaps I miscalculated, that I might have mistaken my dosages, or that your old age made you more susceptible. I couldn't confirm anything due to how stringent Resin was with sealing off your body. When did you discover my plan?"

"When indeed? I suppose I had an inkling on the day you dropped that confused young hunter at my feet."

"Azel?" the head huntress asked. "But he knew nothing."

"Yes, and that was the problem. He possessed neither skill nor experience with what you had assigned him. Judging from his account, you didn't hold a particularly positive opinion of his abilities either. Odd thing to present to an emissary. Ordinarily, you would offer the best of the best."

The emissary then floated down and fired a burst of air between Aer's ankles, utterly shattering the chains that bound him. Aer wasted no time unraveling them before making his way behind Emissary Striaen, putting the old man between him and the head huntress.

"I could dismiss that alone as a spiteful gesture from you," Emissary Striaen continued. "But when a crowd marched to my home and my home alone in an outrage over the Nesting Islands, I began to suspect something more sinister was at play. I went along with the crowd's wishes to see how my grandchildren were doing, since they were about to come of age."

The old man looked back at Aer. "It took me longer than expected to find them. For quite some time, I was searching in the wrong place. I thought the caretakers would at least have the decency to place them in the Perch, but it looks like those who took them here wanted to deny their origins entirely. Disappointing, but I suppose I shouldn't be surprised, considering the circumstances of their birth."

As worn out as he was, Aer's mind was racing with questions upon hearing those words. So he and Alius were the emissary's grandchildren? What did he mean by the circumstances of their birth? If he knew of their existence, then why didn't he place them in the Perch himself?

The emissary turned back to Head Huntress Islea. "But because I was looking in the wrong place, I caught wind of the strange rumors surrounding the Perch. Several fledglings there reported feeling ill during the Rain Provider's Trial. Many claimed that they had been poisoned. When I went to investigate, I found you skulking around the premises. Furthermore, I learned on the very same day that you and Orator Mistral were acquainted."

Aer recalled when he and Emissary Striaen had first met. Come to think of it, that was also when he first saw Orator Mistral.

"Considering you were once a Charity Tree fledgling, I was initially uncertain whether I should dismiss your actions as those of a petty vendetta," Emissary Striaen remarked, scrutinizing the head huntress. "But once the beast under your control went on a rampage around the Charity Tree and nearly killed some of the fledglings there, I stopped giving you the benefit of the doubt."

"And that was when you decided I was a threat?"

"Yes," the emissary said. "When I learned that Azel was in your place preparing the feast, I guessed your intentions and consulted with Doctor Resin beforehand. I then went through the motions of being poisoned to prevent anyone from consuming the food and had Doctor Resin carry me from the scene. There, I was free to watch what would unfold in my absence."

"And what would you have done if nothing had happened?" the head huntress asked.

"Then I would have returned no worse for wear, deeming it the will of the Great Arbiter that I stay in the world of the living. Now, it's time for you to answer *my* questions."

Head Huntress Islea got into a combat stance, looking at him spitefully. "Do you honestly expect me to comply?"

Emissary Striaen sighed. "Not voluntarily, no. *Kneel.*"

The head huntress's eyes widened as her body spasmed. Aer could only stare as an invisible force brought her to her knees.

"Wh-What is this?" she managed to get out, struggling.

"The power the Great Arbiter granted us over the creatures of the sky isn't restricted to mere animals," Emissary Striaen explained. "It applies to *all* inhabitants native to the heavens, even other human beings. The greater your Sky Authority, the more absolute your commands are to those listening."

Both Aer and the head huntress stared at him in shock.

"What?" the head huntress exclaimed.

"Strange," Emissary Striaen said. "I thought you were aware of this. After all, you've used this very power for your own goals."

"What are you talking ab…?" The head huntress fell silent.

"That's right," Emissary Striaen said, as if reading her mind. "Orator Mistral was quite proficient in a subtle form of this Sky Control. It's why she was so unusually captivating to those unaware. Naturally, I recognized its use and guarded myself against it, which is why it never influenced me."

Horror appeared on Head Huntress Islea's face as the emissary continued.

"While I admit I am not quite as experienced in the subtler, more persuasive aspects of the art, the might of my Sky Authority far exceeds that of the late orator's. I have no need for subtlety in this instance. You have no choice but to obey my commands due to the sheer disparity of power between us. Now, *answer my questions*. Was this revenge for what happened to your sister?"

Head Huntress Islea gritted her teeth as she struggled to resist.

"Yes," she eventually gasped.

"What would you have done if I had chosen to stay away from the Nesting Islands?"

"I knew you wouldn't. Your grandchildren were about to come of age, after all. And despite everything you say about remaining detached from the rest of the world, I knew you were desperate for some form of companionship. You couldn't possibly ignore your last chance to avoid dying alone."

The emissary looked rather disturbed at her answer. Despite all his power and authority, the old man seemed like any other person to Aer at that moment. Vulnerable. Mortal.

"So you predicted my thoughts and actions. How peculiar. I don't recall us ever being close enough for you to manage such a thing."

When the head huntress remained silent, Emissary Striaen asked another question. "That young hunter, Azel. I presume he was meant to be your scapegoat?"

"Yes," Head Huntress Islea answered. "He was quite convenient for that role. He had previously made enemies with the rest of my hunters by falsely accusing them of killing the birds I sent you. He also had no real value to the rest of Atravel, so no one would go to the trouble of vouching for him."

"And you imposed his presence on me to establish him as a chef to the public so he would take the fall for your poisoning attempt?"

"Yes. Otherwise, suspicion would have fallen on me as the one who supplied the animal for the banquet."

"Then I will need to grant him a pardon," Emissary Striaen noted. "That is, if he's still present on this island. Moving on, were you the one who sabotaged the Perch?"

"I made them ingest substances that slowed them down, yes."

Emissary Striaen shot the head huntress a look halfway between disgust and disbelief. "You used your poison on children?"

"Not the same poison I used at the banquet, no," she answered. "The ones I used back then only have minor effects, like nausea, difficulty breathing, and mild paralysis."

"Why?"

"As a test," Head Huntress Islea said, still visibly straining against the emissary's commands. "Those substances aren't lethal like the one I used in the Ascension Ceremony, but they all contained a different component of that very poison. I needed to know if any of them were detectable through inspection before I made my move. Fortunately, none of the caretakers nor visitors could find anything, not even after trying the food themselves, as these substances lose their potency and decompose within a short time frame. Soleil, or as you prefer to call her, Orator Mistral, convinced the visitors that those privileged brats were faking the symptoms to cover up their failures in the Rain Provider's Trial."

Aer's mind flashed back to the accusations Gail had made against him and Alius.

"I see," Emissary Striaen said. "Your occupation does give you the best position to procure knowledge of such uniquely untraceable poisons. But what would you have done if you were caught in the act?"

"I had Soleil create a commotion and distract the caretakers after the first time so I wouldn't be," Head Huntress Islea answered. "She happily obliged, thinking it was all for the sake of humiliating the Perch. Still, there was a time when I worried that the caretakers might have reached the same suspicions you did. They even questioned where I was when I disappeared. I could hardly tell them I was skulking around their stores, contaminating their food."

Her eyes then turned toward Aer. "Fortunately, your grandson happened to be at the Perch at the time, wandering in places he shouldn't have been. I used his situation to give myself an alibi."

Aer avoided her gaze. So that was why she had covered for him when they first met.

"Yes, I remember that incident," Emissary Striaen reminisced. "That was when I first saw my grandchildren side by side."

"Now that I think about it, you knew even back then, didn't you?" Head Huntress Islea asked.

"I had my suspicions, but nothing conclusive," Emissary Striaen answered.

Head Huntress Islea glared at him. "If you suspected me all the way back then, why didn't you stop me earlier? You could have used this form of Sky Control to order me to confess like you are now. It would have been far simpler for you to demand answers from me and stop my plans before they went into motion."

"The thought entered my mind, yes," Emissary Striaen acknowledged. "But I wanted a more… perfect victory. Due to Orator Mistral's prior actions, Atravel's citizens have grown more distrustful of their higher authorities. If I made you confess in front of everyone without due cause, the late orator could have simply spun that as me abusing my authority, forcing you to lie to unjustly remove you from your position. Such an outcome would only serve to further divide the nation, escalating future conflicts."

The head huntress looked unconvinced, spurring Emissary Striaen to continue explaining himself.

"Furthermore, I wasn't certain whether you truly were behind everything until now," he stated. "If I forced you to confess and it turned out you were under someone else's command and weren't even aware of the ringleader's identity, you might have spoken out about your questioning and alerted those responsible to conceal themselves more thoroughly."

"You could have just silenced me," Head Huntress Islea said, as if it was the most obvious thing in the world.

The old man shook his head. "Unfortunately, it's not that simple. Unlike your subordinate, Azel, you can't be removed from the public eye without good cause. And this form of Sky Control has limitations, as I'm sure you're aware. Like with the birds under our authority, I need to maintain my focus on you and continuously enforce my control of all that the sky entails over your will, lest the command be broken. As a result, I can't make a single order last over an extended period when I need to rest or keep my focus elsewhere."

Aer, remembering how he had to continually force his will over his bird's to make it obey during the Falconry Trial, saw the potential complications in keeping the head huntress quiet over a long period.

"So instead, I faked my death to embolden the guilty parties while allowing myself to observe in secrecy until I had decisive evidence of your wrongdoing," Emissary Striaen explained. "I also instructed Doctor

Resin to act on my behalf and keep Aer safe while interrogating those who might be involved."

"So that's why Resin was being so difficult recently," Head Huntress Islea said. "He kept an annoyingly close eye on me this entire time, limiting what I could do without giving myself away. I thought he was a much quieter person than what he's demonstrated these past few days."

"You misjudged him," Emissary Striaen replied. "While he may not be the most gregarious person, he's always been rather outspoken. Quite diligent in his work, too, I might add. Though I will admit that he was little more than my mouthpiece this time. I had many questions about our situation down here and ordered him to voice them in my stead."

The old man then examined his surroundings, scanning the mountain cliffs they were stuck between. "Even so, I never once imagined that you would take things *this* far. If I had, I might have taken more drastic actions."

"If anything, I didn't take things nearly as far as I wanted," Head Huntress Islea muttered. "I originally wanted to bring all the Nesting Islands down to the surface, completely shattering Atravel's system of dealing with children as well as robbing them of an entire generation. But the sheer scope of that plan made it unfeasible. I had to settle for your death and one island."

Aer pulled his clothes tighter, uncertain if the chill he felt was from the cold or the head huntress. What ideas had she considered before reaching that conclusion?

Emissary Striaen looked as shocked as Aer felt. "Unbelievable. You wanted to bring *every* child to the surface?"

"Yes," Head Huntress Islea answered unflinchingly. "The unknown would be better than letting the alternative continue, where many would have no choice but to meet death through the Ascension Ceremony."

Emissary Striaen gazed at her with a complicated expression. "Back to my questions, then. You intentionally made that beast under your control rampage, correct?"

"Yes," Head Huntress Islea admitted. "I used my Sky Authority to make it go berserk. I was so thorough in provoking it that all attempts made to communicate would cause it to instantly turn hostile toward the person trying. I couldn't have anyone just forcing it to calm down."

"For what *possible* purpose?" the old man inquired.

"To satisfy Soleil. Her plan was to build up the Charity Tree fledglings then make it look like the head caretaker intentionally killed them out of spite. She wanted to use that incident to make everyone take a better look at the system of the Nesting Islands and the Ascension Ceremony. But she needed me to do the dirty work, so I did. If I hadn't done so, she might have grown suspicious of my intentions and spilled our secrets earlier."

Aer's eyes turned to the head huntress's knife on the ground, still stained with traces of Orator Mistral's blood. That would explain the older woman's guilt.

"So you two had differing goals," Emissary Striaen noted. "I wondered why she would ally herself with you. Who else was complicit in your plan? I want a list of names and motives as well as an explanation of how they assisted you."

The head huntress visibly struggled against this command. It was all for naught, however, as she eventually complied.

"I convinced Soleil to persuade Forewarner Aviense, a sympathizer to her cause, to look the other way whenever I made suspicious movements," she admitted. "Mechanic Kasir felt underappreciated for his efforts and wanted to show everyone how reliant they were on the mechanics' contributions. He taught me how to disable the contingency devices made to keep the island afloat. He also made a few adjustments to the chains holding the island in place before he left and told me how to undo their hold. I also promised promotions for the hunters under me who would side with my arguments while we were trapped down here. I don't recall their names, but most agreed. There was also…"

Against her will, the head huntress continued to recite the names of everyone involved. Aer recognized a few of the names as those belonging to the visitors who came to observe the trials.

Once she finished, Emissary Striaen shook his head.

"I can't believe how many people you dragged into your little scheme." He sighed. "No, that term doesn't properly convey the weight of your sins. You led what was effectively an insurrection against the higher powers of Atravel. You should have known that there is no future where you walk out of this alive."

"I was prepared for that from the beginning," Head Huntress Islea spat scornfully. "My life became meaningless to me a long time ago. My continued existence would at least have had some purpose if I succeeded here."

Her gaze fell to the ground. "You faking your poisoning was where it all went wrong. It wasn't supposed to happen that quickly. Your 'death' stopped everyone who was supposed to be poisoned from eating."

"Everyone?" Emissary Striaen inquired. "Who else were you targeting?"

"All those responsible for perpetuating this system," Head Huntress Islea answered. "Along with those in positions of power. And for practical reasons, all the carriers as well as anyone who could fly."

"Why would you…?" Emissary Striaen's face changed into one of realization. "Ah, I understand now. It would have been problematic if the remaining people on the island flew back to Atravel and called for help. And if too many strong Sky Authorities remained, they simply could have lifted the fallen island back into place. You chose your targets carefully to make certain that those remaining could only slow our descent enough to survive."

"Exactly," the head huntress replied. "I worked around the setback of them surviving by convincing Soleil to lie and say that another emissary called them back to their positions."

Aer blinked. It hadn't occurred to him before, but the island had been vacated right before it fell to the surface. The timing couldn't have been more perfect.

Emissary Striaen looked down at her with eyes full of judgment. "You certainly made excellent use of the late orator, didn't you? Did you not feel a shred of shame in taking advantage of her as much as you did?"

"We had a mutually beneficial relationship," Head Huntress Islea declared unabashedly. "She used her charisma to bring the right people down here while I handled the dirty work. Our goals were never the same, though. I doubt she would have approved of my actual plan, even if I tried justifying it to her."

"She never questioned your true intentions?"

"I think she suspected that I was using her once this island came crashing down," the head huntress admitted. "She was certainly a lot less cooperative after that. She even planned to reveal what we've been doing."

"That's why you killed her. You sought to silence her."

"Yes."

Emissary Striaen took a deep breath. "You were always unnaturally good at hiding your thoughts. I was never at ease around you for that reason. From all the way back to when my son first introduced me to you and your sister, I couldn't read you like I could everyone else."

A bitter smile twisted the head huntress's lips at that statement. "I know how to avoid showing my feelings, at least in front of others. I did it all the time growing up in the Charity Tree. It always scared my sister when I displayed my feelings about the circumstances we grew up in, so I learned to hide them perfectly."

Aer took a step back. The pure bloodlust the head huntress emitted was enough that even a newborn child would be able to tell how dangerous she was.

And yet, now that he'd had the time to calm down and take a closer look, he couldn't help but feel that there was something forced about her outrage.

"I needed this mask," she continued. "If I didn't have it, I couldn't hide how much I despised you. But it stopped me from being persuasive to other people. That's why I needed Soleil. I needed her to bring as many people as she could down to the Nesting Islands."

The head huntress then gave a derisive laugh. "Soleil thought, with some extreme methods, she could reform Atravel into a better society. But I know better. Atravel doesn't hold the Ascension Ceremony just to get rid of the deadweight. They hold it to get rid of anyone who's headstrong enough to stand their ground and challenge things directly. Which is why a large-scale change was never possible. Those who survive the Ascension Ceremony just don't care enough. They'd rather run from their problems than face them. Our very existence up there proves that; the very principles Atravel is founded upon prove that. Detach yourself from the world around you? Free yourself from earthly matters? It's all just an excuse to run away and avoid getting hurt."

Confronted with words that denied his entire worldview, Aer closed his eyes. He didn't know what to believe anymore. If the head huntress was right, then why were they up in the sky to begin with, granted a power encouraging such teachings?

"It is your failure to understand the reasoning behind those principles that brought you to where you are now," Emissary Striaen admonished. "You were so caught up in your sister's death that you manipulated a grieving mother into inciting a rebellion. You aimed to murder children who had nothing to do with your feud. All because you couldn't let it go."

"Be quiet!" the head huntress screamed. "The only reason you get to say things like that is because you have the luxury to do so. What gives you the right to lecture me from up high? Did you think I would just forget how you willingly let my sister die? The only thing giving me purpose from day to day?"

"You were not the only one who lost someone precious that day," Emissary Striaen argued. "I lost my son——"

"I don't care!" Head Huntress Islea shouted over him. "You chose to let him go when you accepted the results of that Ascension Ceremony. But I was robbed of my life's meaning! Just like everything else, you, along with the rest of Atravel, took it away."

The two stared at one another, hatred becoming apparent on both sides.

"There is no point in continuing this argument," Emissary Striaen declared. "It is clear we will never see eye to eye. One last line of questioning, then. Why did you choose to endanger Aer and Alius?"

"I did what I had to."

"Is that so?" Emissary Striaen asked skeptically. "I doubt it would have been difficult for you to spare them if you truly wanted to. Back when you sent the beast to attack the Charity Tree, you could have simply led them somewhere else before you put your plans into motion."

The head huntress offered no rebuttal. Emissary Striaen seemed to have struck the truth.

"But that's not all," Emissary Striaen continued. "You specifically targeted Aer after this island fell. Why?"

"Because I knew you cared for him," the head huntress admitted. "I wanted to make sure nothing that could bring you solace remained in this world, just as it had been for me."

"And for that, you were willing to sacrifice the twins born to your younger sister? Surely, if you loved her that much, you would have spared them for her sake. Or did you honestly believe she would approve of your actions?"

Aer's eyes widened. The sister that the head huntress had been speaking of was his mother. That meant she, along with his father, the emissary's son, were…

"She's already dead!" Head Huntress Islea screamed. "What she would have wanted doesn't matter anymore!"

"And yet you still wanted to kill Aer after you believed me to be dead just to spite my memory?" Emissary Striaen asked. "Be honest with yourself. Your 'love' for your sister wasn't what drove you this entire time."

For the first time, something other than hatred showed on Head Huntress Islea's face. A mixture of fear and self-loathing defined the woman's features as she looked up at the old man staring down at her.

"This wasn't how it was supposed to go," she muttered. "I wanted to tell you all this while you were slowly and painfully dying from the poison I set up. I was supposed to be standing over your feeble body, watching the despair in your eyes as I went into detail about how I planned to destroy everything you spent your life upholding while escaping retribution by fleeing to the world you taught everyone to avoid."

A twisted smile then forced itself onto the head huntress's lips. "But in the end, I'll have to satisfy myself with this. Even if I failed to kill you, I still set things in the right direction. Now everyone in Atravel will know that it's possible to live down here."

Emissary Striaen scoffed. "Spare me. You didn't do this for some noble cause. You couldn't care less about the people you claim to be fighting for. That's why you had no compunctions over murdering the innocent. It's also why you didn't hesitate to lure Aer in to kill him just to spite my memory, even though it's the last thing your sister would have wanted. Your assertions are a pathetic attempt to justify your actions."

He drew closer to the head huntress until they were face-to-face. Aer sensed the winds around them growing more turbulent with each step the old man took.

"It's over," he told her. "I now know exactly what methods you used. I'm confident that if I searched the places you've been with everything you revealed in mind, I would find a trail of evidence proving your guilt. Later, I can question the people you admitted to being complicit in your crimes about their involvement. Your most useful ally is dead, killed by your own hands. My grandson is a witness to the entire event. I imagine the people here will be very receptive to what I have to say once I restore this island to its proper place and rescue them from their predicament."

"Even so, everyone will know that a world outside of Atravel exists," Head Huntress Islea replied. "They'll learn from those here that it's not hostile enough to kill them right away. Let's see how long you can keep running from what you fear, how long you can keep Atravel separate from the rest of the world now that they've figured that out. At the very least, I'll drag you into eternal torment and despair with me."

"You'll be going alone," Emissary Striaen replied, his voice just a whisper. He backed away from the head huntress, pulling Aer along with him as he stilled the air around them once more.

Islea gave one last defiant and scornful laugh as relentless flashes of lightning came down upon her. The sight of her laughing and screaming as she was continuously struck remained in Aer's eyes long after her lifeless body had slumped to the ground.

Chapter 24: Chains of the Sky

I can no longer bear to look at the world around me. Everything reminds me of the son I have lost. To free myself of this pain, I have cut off all my emotional attachments to him and had everything associated with him removed from my presence.

I have heard that the caretakers responsible for watching over my son have taken his children and discretely placed them within the same Nesting Island where their parents had been hiding, though standard policy dictates that the caretakers wait until the upcoming Ascension Ceremony before formally registering them as citizens of Atravel and placing them within a vacated Nesting Island. All to avoid the humiliation of this incident becoming public and having their names disgraced.

I could have fought this, but if I had, the custody and care of those children would go to me. And I cannot bring myself to look after them when they are a living reminder of his existence. Even if I could, there is the possibility that I may grow attached to them, only to lose them as well.

No, I have made up my mind. I must remain unaffected by them. I will give myself time to recover and announce their heritage only if they survive their Ascension Ceremony. Until that time comes, I will keep this journal as a reminder of my failings.

Aer repressed the urge to vomit as he stared at what remained of the head huntress.

"A rather gruesome sight," Emissary Striaen stated calmly. "I advise you to avert your eyes."

Aer said nothing. Even if he looked away, the image of Head Huntress Islea's charred corpse wouldn't fade from his mind anytime soon.

Possibly interpreting Aer's silence in a different way than intended, the old man turned to face him directly, meeting Aer's gray eyes with his own. "Forgive me for not interfering sooner. The truth is, I was resting throughout the night and was unaware that your life was in peril until just now. Doctor Resin interrupted my slumber to alert me that you and the head huntress had gone missing. As soon as I learned of your disappearance, I extended my senses throughout the island to search for your whereabouts until I found you two in conflict at the crevice."

Aer still couldn't find it in him to respond as Emissary Striaen gave an account of his actions, desperate to convince Aer of something.

"The winds that helped you get away were of my doing," Emissary Striaen continued. "I knew I needed to separate you two as quickly as possible. When you stopped moving toward the building and called for help, however, I came out in person to learn what had happened. It was quite a shock to see you caught in that trap."

When Aer still failed to say anything, Emissary Striaen sighed and drew closer, pressuring him to respond.

"I can't exactly approve of how reckless your actions have been in my absence, but I can't deny how they directly led to the head huntress's confession, so I'll overlook them for now. There is no need to fear punishment from me."

Aer, not knowing how he should reply nor having the energy to figure it out, instead blurted the first thing that came to mind. "I'm tired."

That was the simple truth of the matter. He was drained: physically, mentally, and emotionally.

"Ah," Emissary Striaen said in realization. "Of course. How thoughtless of me. Let us head inside."

Leaving the chill of the snow behind as they headed into the building, Aer was greeted with a peculiar sight. The people inside were scrambling in a panic—some busy arming themselves with weapons, others trying to hide. Either way, none stood idle.

As soon as he and Emissary Striaen entered the chaotic scene, attacks launched toward them from all sides. Fortunately, the old man was quick to react and blew away the attacks with ease. One of the attackers, noticing who they were, called for everyone to stop.

"Emissary Striaen, you're alive?" he asked.

"Quite," Emissary Striaen answered. "Though that might have no longer been the case had I been a touch slower. What is going on?"

"Then… we're saved!" another cheered. "You should easily be able to carry this island and the rest of us back to Atravel!"

"Yes, no need to worry," Emissary Striaen assured them. "I'll have everything back in its proper place. But first, an explanation."

"I don't understand," a person commented as they came out of their hiding spot. "How are you here?"

Emissary Striaen sighed. "All in due time."

"You're right," agreed the person who had called for everyone to stop. "We need to deal with the more pressing issues first. Like our immediate safety."

"Explain," Emissary Striaen ordered.

"We heard explosions mixed in with the screams of a woman outside. The hunters have also informed us that their leader has gone missing. We believe that those from the surface must have noticed our presence and are here to hunt us down."

"Explosions? Ah…"

Aer looked back outside. They must be referring to the lightning storm that Emissary Striaen had conjured.

"Rest assured—we are *not* being invaded," Emissary Striaen said. "Those noises were of my own making. It was all to protect this child here."

Aer gave Emissary Striaen a weary glare as everyone turned to face him.

"You again?" a man asked.

Aer was too exhausted to worry about the gazes he was attracting. They could think whatever they wanted about him. He couldn't care less about their opinions.

"Him again, you say?" Emissary Striaen asked.

"Yes, his actions have been rather suspicious during your absence," the man repeated. "He's been too quiet since this island's descent to the surface. Head Huntress Islea also saw him wandering around the night Hunter Azel escaped his prison. Some of us were wondering whether he might have had a hand in your poisoning."

"Of course not," Emissary Striaen said. "Why would a child who had never even left his Nesting Island be involved in such a conspiracy? What possible motive could he have?"

"I wouldn't put it past him. From what I hear, he was a Charity Tree fledgling back on his island. Both his character and origins are questionable."

The air around Emissary Striaen grew dangerous.

"I'll thank you to not treat my only remaining family like a criminal," he said in a whisper.

That made the accuser pause.

"So he is indeed your relative, then?" the man asked apprehensively.

"That is correct," the emissary confirmed. "As my late son's child, his full name would be Aer Striaen."

The man immediately bowed his head. "Then you have my most sincere apologies. There's clearly been a misunderstanding."

The others stood back as Aer and the emissary left for one of the hallways. As the name *Aer Striaen* registered in his mind, Aer looked back and noticed the fear in everyone's eyes.

***

Aer flinched at how forcefully Doctor Resin inspected him. The man was clearly not in a good mood.

"How is he?" Emissary Striaen asked.

"Nothing too serious," Doctor Resin gave his diagnosis, unsympathetic to Aer's protests. "His injuries are quite trivial and limited to his legs, which is where I assume he got caught by the trap you mentioned. There might be some bruising there, but nothing that won't heal in a week or two. There's also some mild frostnip here and there, but again, that should go away on its own. All in all, he's remarkably unharmed considering the danger he so foolishly threw himself into."

"Be more lenient with him," Emissary Striaen admonished.

"With all due respect, sir, I'm finding that very difficult," Doctor Resin replied. "I instructed him to stay put, to stay quiet, and to not do anything he wasn't supposed to. And now I find that he almost got himself killed because he blatantly disregarded everything I said."

Aer had nothing to say in his defense. Between freeing Azel and sneaking out to meet Orator Mistral, he had certainly caused Doctor Resin no shortage of trouble.

"Even so, his actions are why we know for certain that Head Huntress Islea was the mastermind behind this whole incident," Emissary Striaen said.

Doctor Resin took a deep breath and looked up at the old man. "Sir, what made you confront her directly? I thought your plan was to wait for her to give incriminating information because you wanted to be certain that she wasn't under someone else's orders."

"She admitted enough for me to be certain that wasn't the case," Emissary Striaen answered. "She even claimed that no one besides her would dare lead an organized revolt against Atravel's management."

"She said all that willingly?" Doctor Resin asked, incredulous.

"Enforcing your Sky Authority on others can be done through both direct command and subtle suggestion," Emissary Striaen replied. "While it's true that I have less experience in the subtler aspects, I'm perfectly capable of using both forms."

"What might you mean?" Doctor Resin asked.

"She had caught Aer in a trap and was preparing to kill him," Emissary Striaen explained. "Without her noticing, I prompted her to reveal what she knew before she made a move against him. So long as she believed she was simply boasting to someone who was going to die regardless, she had no reason to resist my Sky Authority."

"So you fooled her into giving herself away while you stayed hidden," Doctor Resin noted.

"Yes," Emissary Striaen confirmed. "Once she admitted to being the instigator, I felt that trickery was no longer necessary."

Doctor Resin nodded. "Just to be clear, the poison was her doing?"

"Yes."

Doctor Resin grimaced. "What a disgusting way of doing things. The symptoms remind me of—"

Emissary Striaen's face darkened. "I'm aware. If the head huntress was aiming to be as offensive to me as possible, she certainly succeeded."

Aer, not understanding what they were talking about, felt his focus drifting. Seeming to notice, Emissary Striaen dismissed Doctor Resin and led Aer to his room.

"I'm sorry you had to experience all this, but it's over now," the old man said gently. "I assure you that I won't administer punishment for your rash behavior, so you have nothing to worry about. Get some rest."

As soon as Emissary Striaen left the room, Aer collapsed onto his bed. Finally alone, he let sleep quickly overtake his consciousness.

***

Aer dreamed once more. He was meandering around in the middle of an empty snow-white plain, only coming to a stop once he stood face-to-face with a mirror image of himself.

No. Not a mirror image of himself. The person standing before him was someone he would never see again.

The familiar form of Alius Striaen glared at him resentfully. Thoughts vocalized in his brother's voice echoed inside Aer's head.

"Why is it always you? We look the same, share the same blood, and started at the exact same place, so why is there such a difference in where we ended up?"

Before Aer could answer, the shape of his brother's body changed. It grew taller until it towered over him. The face then morphed into Kiel's, who looked down at him with disdain.

"Must be nice to be born connected to the right people. While we all die horribly, you get to live in the lap of luxury thanks to your grandfather."

Kiel's figure then shrank, transforming into one of a woman's.

The emotional yet articulate voice of Orator Mistral pierced Aer's thoughts.

"I wish I had never spoken to you. I would still be alive if we hadn't discussed my secrets."

Orator Mistral's face then remolded itself. It turned into the face of her daughter, who, for the first time, didn't stutter when addressing Aer as an individual.

"You let me die. You used me as a diversion so you could escape with your own miserable life."

The person before Aer changed once more.

"There's no justice in this world." The hate-filled eyes of Head Huntress Islea stared at him with murderous intent. *"You and that old fool should suffer as I have. You don't deserve to live."*

***

Aer woke with a heavy heart. Uncertain of the time, he opened the door to his room and looked outside. Judging by the lighting of the hallway, evening was already upon them.

Aer stepped outside and walked down the hall. He came across a group of Perch caretakers, who all lowered their heads when they saw him.

"Master Striaen," they said, addressing him as respectfully as they could. "Do you need something from us?"

Aer, unaccustomed to being treated that way, could only stutter. "I-I was just looking around—"

"For Emissary Striaen, perhaps? Unfortunately, he is currently quite busy. Maybe it would be better for you to converse with your peers."

"Maybe it would," Aer repeated.

"In that case, you can find those who recently graduated from being fledglings in that direction." One of them pointed toward another hallway.

"Right. I'll do that," Aer said, eager to get away from them.

"Of course."

Once he reached the new hallway, Aer glanced at his surroundings. Youths who looked as lost as he felt were scattered throughout the area.

Aer had completely forgotten about them the past few days. He walked around until he spotted a familiar face in Gail. Upon noticing Aer's gaze, the normally proud and spiteful boy shrank away in fear. Not long after, he passed Nira, who briefly bowed her head before wheeling away.

The other fledglings were slightly less reserved in greeting him, but they were all so *sickeningly* polite. Judging by their reactions, news of his heritage had already reached everyone. Every single one, even those who had looked at him with contempt back on the Nesting Island. None dared to assume social superiority or even parity when they addressed him.

It was only because Aer was *his* grandson. Nothing about Aer himself could ever merit enough admiration to command such respect.

He couldn't take it anymore. He left for the building's main hall, where a crowd of adults had gathered in discussion. His grandfather stood at the center of it all.

"Now that we've finished questioning all those on this island who the head huntress named as her accomplices, I'd like to verify the fates of everyone involved in this incident," Emissary Striaen announced. "We will need to give an account for every single person once we rejoin Atravel, so I want to be thorough. Has Hunter Azel been found?"

"No," one of the hunters answered. "As far as we're concerned, he's already left the island's general vicinity. What should we do?"

"What are the chances that he might find a human settlement and divulge information about Atravel?"

"Very small. Even if other human settlements exist, these mountain peaks show no signs of life. Furthermore, Azel was far from the most accomplished hunter. The most likely outcome is that he'll meet his death on the surface."

Emissary Striaen nodded. "Leaving him behind would be the best decision, then. In the unlikely event he survives to tell the tale, we'll have erased all traces of our existence here. Quite the unfortunate young man. What of Orator Mistral?"

"Dead," the hunter replied. "Her body was found at the opposite end of this island. Blood loss from a stab to the heart was the most likely cause of death."

"As expected. And her daughter?"

"Also dead. Her body was found torn in two near the center of the island, likely due to an offensive use of Sky Control."

"Pity," Emissary Striaen said simply.

Aer's heart sank upon hearing how Ciel had died. Why had he survived when she and her mother had not? They had essentially died because of him. It would have been better if he had never met them.

What bothered him more, however, was how unaffected his grandfather seemed about everything. Aer couldn't understand how he could act so nonchalant about their deaths when he so easily could have prevented them.

"The events that transpired are quite unfortunate, but there's much to be learned from them," Emissary Striaen continued. "As those who receive the Great Arbiter's grace, we must not concern ourselves with the matters of this earthly realm."

Aer blinked. Was that it? Was that his secret? Was the old man just so detached from the rest of the world that other people's deaths didn't matter to him?

Maybe that was the best course of action. If Aer hadn't gotten himself emotionally invested, things might have been a lot easier. He might not have been in such pain over losing his brother.

Head Huntress Islea's words of scorn echoed in his head.

Detach yourself from the world around you? Free yourself from earthly matters? It's all just an excuse to run away and avoid getting hurt.

Aer paused. Was this why his grandfather hadn't come for him and Alius earlier? Did he just view them as earthly attachments to avoid getting emotionally invested in?

His grandfather's next statement only reinforced his thoughts. "Let us remember how Atravel came to be. The rest of the world was steeped in endless conflict, and the Great Arbiter chose to save those who had no desire to take part. Just like how Atravel is a haven from the outside world, our bodies and minds must remain free from the conflicts around us."

Aer finally understood why he felt so unsettled. His grandfather's actions were a mirror of his own. Avoiding everything to not get hurt and letting things go wrong through his inaction, things he might have otherwise changed for the better. He couldn't be hurt if he had no expectations to begin with. Aer's actions back on the Nesting Island had been no different. It was Alius who'd had to pick up the slack in the areas where Aer was so sorely lacking.

That Atravel was a mass of chains confining them within the free sky couldn't be more fitting. They had fled from the rest of the world, seeking freedom from its cruelty. Due to their fears of getting involved with it, however, they had ironically trapped themselves in a place where they couldn't interact and connect with anyone. And to uphold that way of life, their methods had gone on mostly unchallenged. In fact, the people in power supported and maintained the system that had killed Alius, his grandfather being one of them.

And with that revelation, Aer rejected the idea of turning out like his grandfather, rejected everything that the man stood for, rejected the society that had created him.

But what was he supposed to do? He was trapped in Atravel, leaving him no other choice but to follow in his grandfather's footsteps. Nothing could prevent that from happening.

No. He could still do something. The island hadn't departed for the skies just yet.

***

Aer left the main hall and searched for where the supplies were stored. A caretaker noticed him loitering and asked him what he was doing, to which Aer responded with a question.

"Do you know where the food storage is?"

"At the end of that hall," the caretaker replied. "May I ask why you are searching for such a thing?"

"I just want to get something to eat. If someone comes looking for me, could you tell them that I'm in my room and that I don't want to talk to others right now?"

Not waiting for an answer, Aer covered his face with the hood of his cloak and headed toward where the caretaker had pointed him.

Aer made sure the storage room was vacant before sneaking in. Up to that point, it had been the hunters' duty to guard the supplies. However, every hunter had doubtlessly been interrogated by his grandfather about their involvement with Head Huntress Islea. Now that an emissary could take them back to Atravel, nobody seemed to care enough about the supplies to assign new guards to keep them safe.

After taking as much as he could sneak into his clothing, Aer returned to his room and stuffed everything he might need inside a bag he made by tying clothing together. Once the bag was secure, he headed back outside.

Realizing that he wouldn't be able to go through the main entrance without his grandfather spotting him, Aer searched for a back door in the hallway. He knew the layout of the building rather well by then, having prowled around it for the past week. Managing to avoid prying eyes, he snuck out of the building one last time.

A familiar chill enveloped Aer as he stepped outside. Not wanting to come across any hunters potentially still inspecting the island, he steered clear of the crevice, along with any locations that he or the head huntress had been through.

Once he had reached the island's edge, Aer took one final look back, making sure no one had followed him.

He took a deep breath. Did he really want to go through with this? He would be leaving behind a life of luxury and safety for the complete unknown if he continued.

No, he couldn't accept such comfort. Even if the surface was as hostile as everyone described, dying down there would be more fitting for him than living in the sky unpunished. He didn't deserve what was being offered to him, not when people better than him had died for so much less.

He needed to make a decision. He wouldn't have another chance once the island rejoined Atravel.

Making up his mind, Aer jumped off the edge of the cliff.

Chapter 25: Parting Shot

Now that I have reflected on my actions, I can see where I have erred. I had forgotten the lessons that had been instilled in me since my youth. The nature of those who live in Atravel is a lack of attachment to all earthly things. I allowed myself to get too attached to my son. If I had not, I would not have turned a blind eye to his actions.

That must be why I am being punished now. Like those in the past who fought for their earthly desires and were abandoned by the Great Arbiter, I am feeling the pain of despair, knowing that everything I held dear has been ripped away from me. I should have exerted more effort to remain disconnected from the world around me. Only then would I have found the peace that the Great Arbiter offers to those in his grace.

Emissary Striaen stepped outside to face the sky. He had finished confirming the statuses of all those on the island that had fallen to the surface and had properly dealt with those among them related to the incident. It was time to leave.

As everyone watched with hopeful gazes, he exerted his power over the heavens and willed the air surrounding the Isle of Judgment to lift the landmass to the skies. Soon enough, the island hovered over the mountains, rising higher with every passing second.

Many behind him cheered. They were finally departing the cursed surface.

Keeping Atravel's standard pathway through the skies in mind, the emissary propelled the island forward as he increased the oxygen levels and stabilized the air pressure surrounding it. He also redirected all incoming air resistance as the island raced through the sky.

It was a tedious procedure but a necessary one. They were far from Atravel's controlled climate and needed to move at high speeds if they hoped to catch up. Most of those who were left on the island lacked the skills to ensure the proper safety measures, which left him to resolve such issues alone.

***

As they approached the familiar skies of Atravel, Emissary Striaen sent out several bursts of wind in coded patterns, signaling their identities to the observing forewarners. It would be *problematic* if the rest of the nation recognized them as a foreign force to repel and avoid.

After waiting for what felt like an eternity, he sensed a reply granting them permission to enter. Exhaling in relief, he parted the clouds before him as he brought the Isle of Judgment to its rightful place.

As soon as the landmass was properly secured, people from all around Atravel approached the island in droves, presumably to bombard them with questions. The emissary carefully prepared his account of the events that had happened under his watch, knowing it would take quite a bit of time and effort to work through the administrative complications that would inevitably come.

"It appears I'll remain busy for the foreseeable future," he commented. "Doctor Resin, as you were acting in my place for most of the incident, they will likely need your testimony as well. Come with me."

"What about Aer?" Doctor Resin asked. "Should I go and get him?"

One of the caretakers spoke. "I don't think that's a good idea. The young master told me he doesn't want to talk to anyone right now."

"Understandable," Emissary Striaen said, dismissing Doctor Resin's suggestion with a wave. "Leave him be. I doubt they will care to listen to a child's statements anyhow. I will collect him once it is time for everyone to vacate the island."

Having given his instructions, the emissary went to address the people awaiting his explanations.

As expected, Atravel's higher authorities were relentless in their questioning. The Isle of Judgment's descent to the surface had gained notoriety as one of the greatest incidents in Atravel's recent history. Not only had one of their more famous national sites gone missing, but they had also risked foreign powers discovering their existence. Not even someone with Emissary Striaen's position and influence could hope to keep everything that had happened under wraps.

Once everyone had finished testifying, enforcers were sent to the nearby islands to apprehend those named as the late head huntress's accomplices. Meanwhile, those investigating the case had been sent to Head Huntress Islea's island of residence to scour her home for more information.

Others were assigned to accompany Emissary Striaen in inspecting the late huntress's room on the Isle of Judgment. A little searching revealed a container crudely shoved within her drawers. Inside, several vials containing mixtures of unidentified substances were found stored together.

"Could these be the remnants of the poison she used?" one of the inspectors asked.

"If they are, then she did a rather sloppy job of concealing them compared to how well prepared she was for everything else," another commented. "I suspect she expected all those on this island who were qualified to investigate her would die before she made her getaway. When they didn't, she had to improvise a hiding spot."

Doctor Resin, who had come with them, looked over the vials.

"According to Emissary Striaen's account, these substances lose their effectiveness over time," he stated while examining the evidence. "She could have plausibly denied their effects even if they were found, so concealing them likely wasn't her top priority."

"Still, how did the enforcers assigned here not find this?"

Some of the enforcers looked away sheepishly.

"They didn't bother searching too hard because they already had a culprit in mind," Doctor Resin answered, ignoring their embarrassment. "Even when I tried to convince everyone to be more inquisitive, they were set on establishing what happened during the feast as an accident because they didn't want to take responsibility for missing an attempt at mass murder."

"Why didn't you search her room yourself, then?" one of the enforcers asked, his voice laced with accusation.

"Because I have some sense of self-preservation," Doctor Resin replied with scorn. "If I made my opposition to the head huntress that obvious, I might have been eliminated just like the late orator."

"You could have let us in on your suspicions in private," another enforcer countered.

"And what if you people happened to be collaborating with the head huntress?" Doctor Resin asked.

"As if we would aid a criminal!" the first enforcer protested.

Doctor Resin shook his head. "You people proved during the incident with Hunter Azel that you could be persuaded to look the other way when it's convenient. I would have to be a fool to trust you under those conditions."

Emissary Striaen interrupted them. "That's enough. I want these analyzed and, if possible, recreated. If these truly are the poisons used at the feast, then they should suffice as irrefutable evidence of her guilt along with the testimonies of those involved."

Those quarreling glared at one another before complying.

"Yes, sir."

Once their search of Head Huntress Islea's room had ended, the emissary and those accompanying him reconvened at the building's main hall. There, they waited until those who had been sent to the other islands brought in those complicit in the conspiracy as well as all articles potentially related to the case.

Upon hearing Emissary Striaen's account of what had happened and seeing the evidence piled before them, most of those apprehended confessed their involvement rather quickly but denied having knowledge of the head huntress's true intentions.

"I can't believe how much she prepared for this behind our backs," a caretaker commented, looking surprised at the number of people involved.

"Well prepared in some regards, ill prepared in others," Doctor Resin criticized. "Despite all the people she micromanaged, she miscalculated how many would be necessary for the island to safely land on the surface below. If Emissary Striaen hadn't intervened at the last moment…"

Emissary Striaen stayed silent as he examined everything the investigators had gathered as potential evidence—books, detailed notes, dissected corpses of animals presumably used as test subjects for the poison, and more. All demanded further analysis, but one thing drew his attention over everything else. A powerful wave of nostalgia struck him as soon as he caught sight of it.

His eyes widened once he realized why that was. "This is…"

"Sir?" Doctor Resin asked. "What is it?"

Emissary Striaen ignored him as he took a book from the pile of evidence. It had an unassuming cover, one that most people wouldn't have given a second thought. But he understood its significance just from a glance.

"Where did you find this?" he asked, trembling.

"A room hidden underneath the floor of the late head huntress's home, sir," one of the inspectors answered. "We found the room's very existence suspicious, so its contents were brought here for inspection."

"I see." Emissary Striaen's voice quieted to a whisper. "I thought I had lost this long ago. When did she find the opportunity to steal it from me?"

He opened and skimmed the book. Sure enough, the words inside were written in his handwriting.

As I reflect on how fleeting life is, I feel the need to write my thoughts to both aid future generations and leave a record of my existence. May those reading this find wisdom in what I transcribe here…

As expected, the contents of the book were the daily musings of his life, neatly organized into passages. For some reason, the head huntress had marked some of the sections, differentiating them from the others.

It has been twelve days since my wife's passing. Much to my regret, I find that the only person remaining who I feel any genuine sense of connection with is my son, my only child. As I look at him now, he reminds me considerably of my younger self. I am proud of him, so very proud. I just pray he does not beat his father to the grave as his mother did.

I have taken some time off my duties to keep an eye on my son. While observing him, I have noticed that he has an easier time getting along with other people than I do—a useful trait to possess. But as a result, he is also much more easily influenced by his peers. The people he has talked to have put some strange ideas in his head. I grow more worried for him with each passing day. And yet is it not a father's duty to support his child in his endeavors?

I must give my son his due credit; he has been working diligently since our quarrel. He has paid close attention to my recent lectures and has revised some of his views, acknowledging the validity of many of my points. As a reward, I have taken some time to listen to his ramblings.

In the end, this gamble between us has become completely pointless, as I have already lent an ear to his opinions before he has proven himself. He's noticed this as well, as he has changed the initial conditions of our wager, asking me instead to grant him one of his wishes if he excels in the trials. He refused to disclose what the wish was, telling me he would only do so once he accomplished his goal. As proud of him as I am, I told him that if it was within my ability to do so, I would grant it. Perhaps I am too lenient with him as a father.

The purpose of the markings became clearer with each entry. Every single excerpt contained his personal thoughts about his son. Through them, it would be a simple matter to understand what his priority at the time had been.

He continued reading, reliving the days his son had still been with him. Tears pooled in his eyes once he reached the last passage he had written. Memories of that time grieved him even now.

I can no longer bear to look at the world around me. Everything reminds me of the son I have lost. To free myself of this pain, I have cut off all my emotional attachments to him and had everything associated with him removed from my presence.

I have heard that the caretakers responsible for watching over my son have taken his children and discretely placed them within the same Nesting Island where their parents had been hiding, though standard policy dictates that the caretakers wait until the upcoming Ascension Ceremony before formally registering them as citizens of Atravel and placing them within a vacated Nesting Island. All to avoid the humiliation of this incident becoming public and having their names disgraced.

I could have fought this, but if I had, the custody and care of those children would go to me. And I cannot bring myself to look after them when they are a living reminder of his existence. Even if I could, there is the possibility that I may grow attached to them, only to lose them as well.

No, I have made up my mind. I must remain unaffected by them. I will give myself time to recover and announce their heritage only if they survive their Ascension Ceremony. Until that time comes, I will keep this journal as a reminder of my failings.

"Something had been bothering me about the head huntress's confession," he murmured, much to the confusion of the people around him. "How could she understand my thoughts and motivations so perfectly? But it all makes sense now. Of course she would be able to predict my actions with this."

He absentmindedly turned to the next page despite knowing that there was nothing more he had written in this book. Once he flipped the page over, however, he found something he didn't recognize, written in penmanship that was not his own. Curious, he read it to himself.

I despise you. You're nothing more than a pretentious coward who ran from your problems. And yet you still dare to look down on those you've wronged to preserve your fragile ego. Just stay in your own little world; it'll make it all the more cathartic when I drag you out and bring you to ruin.

Emissary Striaen shut the book in distaste before pocketing it. Had she left that passage for him in the event her plans failed? Or perhaps she had written it to motivate herself to carry out her actions. In either case, he could feel her disdain directed at him.

He scorned her in his mind, knowing that his thoughts would never reach her. *You failed. Your attempt to ruin me has led to your death. And for what? All you've accomplished in the end was to waste my time. A minor inconvenience, that's all your life was worth.*

Once the investigation had concluded, Emissary Striaen excused himself from the premises. No doubt the other emissaries would want to discuss future arrangements necessitated by the incident. It was time for him to leave the island. He just needed to take his grandson with him.

He knocked on Aer's door.

"Aer."

No response.

"It's time for us to leave."

Something was wrong. He couldn't sense any form of breathing within the room.

Filled with inexplicable dread, Emissary Striaen opened the door.

The room was empty. His grandson was gone.

Emissary Striaen took a deep breath. There had to be a simple and reasonable explanation for Aer's absence.

So why did he feel so uneasy?

He turned around and headed back to the main hall. There, he began questioning the people who might know of Aer's whereabouts.

"Do you know where my grandchild is?" he asked the caretaker who had relayed Aer's desire for solitude.

"He told me he was going to get some food," the caretaker answered. "I never saw him after that."

"When was this?"

"Before we left the surface, I think."

That did nothing to alleviate his fears. The better part of the day had passed since then. Why hadn't Aer returned to his room?

Emissary Striaen left the main hall to comb through every corner of the building. Once he was certain that Aer was not inside, he disclosed his grandson's absence to those best equipped to find him, expanding his search to the entire island.

Not again, he prayed.

***

"The hunters found faint footprints leading to the northern edge of the island," Doctor Resin reported. "The trail stops there, so most likely—"

"Leave me," Emissary Striaen ordered quietly.

"But—"

"I said *leave me.*"

Doctor Resin reluctantly obeyed, leaving Emissary Striaen alone in his room. The weary old man pulled out a chair and sat, contemplating

Aer's disappearance. At first, he wanted to believe that he had overreacted, that the budding panic had been a by-product of his experiences with his son and nothing more. Once those searching for his grandson had reported that food, clothing, and other basic supplies had gone missing, however, it became harder to deny what had occurred.

He must have jumped off the island before we left the surface. Emissary Striaen sank farther into his chair. *But why?*

Regardless of the reason, the result was set in stone. It was too late to go back and look for his grandson. He had broken enough protocols with how he had handled the situation with Head Huntress Islea. Leaving Atravel by himself and risking further exposure for personal interests would be tantamount to treason.

So what was left for him now? He had come down to the Nesting Islands to see if his grandchildren would be able to join him. Upon seeing Aer's prowess with Sky Control, he had dared to allow himself to hope in the boy. He had made sure not to repeat the same mistake he had made with his son and had prevented Aer from jumping after his brother by immediately closing any openings in the clouds during the Ascension Ceremony and having his subordinates carry him out of there as quickly as possible.

But in the end, it had changed nothing. What had he done wrong? What else could he have done?

Perhaps there was a more fundamental mistake in his actions. Perhaps he needed to reevaluate his core motivations.

Rummaging through his clothes, he took out his recently recovered journal and opened it. He reread his experiences, trying to view his actions with a more objective eye.

His hands trembled once he reached the last page. The final note written by Head Huntress Islea was still there, taunting his very existence.

Something in him broke at that moment. Almost as if possessed to do so, he grabbed the nearest pen he could find and began writing in the old book.

I told myself that I would take care of the twins only if they passed their Ascension Ceremony. I have once again failed in doing so. I should have put them out of my mind entirely. Everything that has transpired must be my punishment from the Great Arbiter for forgetting basic doctrine. Do not tie yourself down to anything. I should not have given myself hope in my son's children. By investing so much of myself in them, I have shackled my very being with these earthly chains. If I had truly followed our teachings to the letter, these events would not have wounded me so grievously. With this new understanding, I have truly become one with the sky.

Chapter 26: The World Unseen

I know you. The events that led you to where you are now, the actions you will take, and the future you will carve out for yourself and those you encounter—all are as I have declared them to be, long before you held your first breath. Now, go. It is time for you to fulfill the purpose for which you came into this world.

Azel squinted, trying to identify his whereabouts. The Isle of Judgment was no longer visible, obscured by the veil of clouds above. The path below showed no clear markers either.

The descent down the mountain was proving more difficult than he could have imagined. He couldn't tell which direction was safe to traverse with no knowledge of the landscape. As things were, he would run out of supplies before reaching the bottom.

He had underestimated the surface. He had seen it as an escape from Atravel's authorities, but the harsh conditions made it little more than a drawn-out execution.

A string of curses escaped his lips, aimed at those he saw as responsible for his plight. It wasn't as if he could just turn around and head back to Atravel when he was still being framed for Emissary Striaen's murder. He either found a way to sustain himself on the surface or died miserably. Those were the only options left to him.

For the sake of survival, nothing was off-limits anymore. He would hunt whatever he could find, use everyone he came across, and eliminate anything that could pose a threat to him. Those who wanted to object could direct their complaints to the people who drove him down to the surface.

The world had wronged him enough; he refused to let it claim his life too.

***

Aer shivered as he tried to navigate down the mountaintop. Snow. Ice. Clouds as far as he could see. His surroundings were blanketed in white no matter which way he looked.

What did he expect to find? He knew nothing about the surface world. He wouldn't be any less lost even if he reached the bottom of the mountain.

Was this how he would meet his end? Wandering aimlessly through a cold and barren landscape? Maybe that was for the best. It was what he deserved, after all.

Aer paused. Maybe his senses were off, but he could have sworn he heard a voice in the air. He followed the source of the disturbance, stopping only when his eyes made out a figure in the distance. Despite his misgivings, Aer ran and called out to them. Maybe they would know of a way down.

Upon closer inspection, the figure turned out to be a male perhaps a couple Sky Cycles older than he was. He was dressed in garments Aer had never seen in Atravel.

The stranger spoke first. "*Eiro tarus sin aosli?*"

Aer was at a loss for how to respond. Not a single word that had been uttered was one he was familiar with. The thought that he might not be able to communicate with those outside of Atravel had not occurred to him.

"I don't understand what you're saying."

The young man before him furrowed his brow. "*Esthria Major? Ni, deo...*"

He then cleared his throat.

"*Sen dau ereus ebe?*" (*Can you understand me?*)

Aer blinked, confused. The meaning of what the stranger was saying had become clear, but the words he had physically heard did not match what was being communicated.

"Yes, though I don't know how to make you realize that."

"Don't worry. I understand what you're saying." The young man looked quite pleased with himself.

It took a moment for Aer to realize that the stranger was still speaking in an unfamiliar speech. What he was communicating had become quite clear in Aer's mind, to the point that it was overwriting the sounds Aer's brain was registering.

"How are you doing that?" he asked.

"You mean the Unified Language? Legends say that the All-Knowing One from ages past left behind the ability to express all forms of speech before he died. Anybody who delves deep enough into Illudia Obscerai's branches of knowledge pertaining to wordcraft should be able to do the same."

"All-knowing One?" Aer repeated. "Illudia Obscerai?"

"So you've never heard these terms before," the stranger said. "You're definitely not a keeper of the light or darkness, then. Your clothes don't look familiar either. Where are you from? How did you get here?"

Aer looked over his shoulder. The Isle of Judgment had already left for the sky.

"From up there." Aer pointed back at the mountaintops. "An island was just up ahead, but it's gone now."

The stranger looked completely lost. "An island? Here?"

"Was here."

"Is this some sort of unique cultural idiom? Islands don't exactly vanish into thin air."

"Unique cultural idiom?" Aer shook his head. He would be there all day if he wanted an explanation for everything that he didn't understand. "The island hasn't vanished. It's just been carried back into the sky."

The stranger stood in silence for a moment.

"A flying island," he murmured. "So the Mirage Sky Civilization actually exists?"

"Mirage…?"

"Of course you wouldn't refer to yourselves as that. What do you call your lands? The place where you came from?"

"Atravel."

The stranger quickly pulled notes out of his bag and scribbled something down. It then occurred to Aer that disclosing this information to someone he knew nothing about might not have been the brightest idea.

What does it matter to me now? Aer reasoned with himself. *I have nothing to do with Atravel anymore.*

Despite that, Aer couldn't help but be on guard. "Why are you here?" he asked, trying to get a read on the stranger's motives.

"Something caused these mountains to tremble, and I happened to be the first one to make the trek here to discover why," the stranger answered. "I'm very glad I did. What's your name?"

"Aer," he said quietly. There shouldn't have been anything dangerous about merely giving out his name, but he remained wary all the same.

The stranger smiled. "It's nice to meet you, Aer. My name's Ephes. You and I have a *lot* to discuss."

"Ephes," Aer repeated, trying to memorize the name. "What will you do now?"

"Well, I originally came to observe what happened, but it looks like I'm a little late for that. Still, discovering you means that this was far from a meaningless trip. More importantly, what do *you* plan to do now? Where are you headed?"

"I… don't know," Aer admitted. "I was just going down the mountain."

"From this angle? Bad idea. I wouldn't recommend it. Going straight down this path leads directly to Death's Canyon. I suggest this direction instead."

A trail of light then lit to their left, showing them a way down with a relatively even slope.

Aer could only stare. How did he do that?

"Glad I kept track of my way up here." Ephes smiled at Aer's bewilderment. "We'll have to pass by the Valley of the Beasts on our way to the nearest hidden outpost, but that's far preferable to Death's Canyon. There's no way you'll survive once you set foot on *those* lands. Come on, follow me."

Aer hesitated before nodding. Their brief conversation was enough to convince him that he was out of his depth. He still didn't know anything about Ephes, but it would probably be better for him to stick with someone who knew their way around the surface than to wander aimlessly. If what the strange man had said was true, then Aer had been walking straight toward a death trap.

Before he ran after Ephes, however, Aer looked back at the mountain peaks one last time, Atravel at the forefront of his thoughts.

Had he really made the right choice in leaving it all behind? What would Alius have done?

Not this, Aer thought truthfully. Their last truly meaningful conversation had been about Alius's desire to reconnect with any existing family members. He wouldn't have chosen to cut them out of his life like Aer had.

Pain stung Aer's heart as that memory of Alius flooded his mind. It seemed inconceivable that they had been preparing for the trials and trying to find their place within Atravel only a few weeks earlier. Those were now the memories of a different life, one that he would never get back.

Aer took a moment to compose himself. It was too late for regrets. He had made his decision. The only path left for him was forward.

With that thought firmly embedded in his mind, Aer faced his new, unknown world.